PENGUIN BOOKS

# Girl Unknown

Karen Perry lives in Ireland. *Girl Unknown* is her third novel and follows *The Boy That Never Was*, which was selected for the Simon Mayo Radio 2 Book Club, and *Only We Know*, both of which were *Sunday Times* bestsellers.

*By the same author*

The Boy That Never Was
Only We Know

# Girl Unknown

KAREN PERRY

PENGUIN BOOKS

PENGUIN BOOKS

UK | USA | Canada | Ireland | Australia
India | New Zealand | South Africa

Penguin Books is part of the Penguin Random House group of companies
whose addresses can be found at global.penguinrandomhouse.com.

First published 2016
002



Set in 13.75/16.25 pt Garamond MT Std
Typeset by Jouve (UK), Milton Keynes
Printed in Great Britain by Clays Ltd, St Ives plc

A CIP catalogue record for this book is available from the British Library

PAPERBACK ISBN: 978–1–405–92030–8
OM PAPERBACK ISBN: 978–1–405–92032–2

www.greenpenguin.co.uk

Penguin Random House is committed to a sustainable future for our business, our readers and our planet. This book is made from Forest Stewardship Council® certified paper.

# Prologue

The water is cold but there is a promise of heat in the air as the dawn begins to break. It will not be long before sunlight reaches the garden. Insects buzz and rustle in the undergrowth, the scent of lavender drifts from pots on the terrace. Drips roll from the edge of the diving board, making lazy plopping sounds as they meet the rocking surface of the pool.

A seagull landing on the wall casts a beady eye downward into the water, scouting for food, or maybe just curious. The drips from the diving board slow.

The bird surveys the garden – the squat silent house beyond, shadows on the terrace. It raises a wing and with its yellow beak jabs at its feathers, rearranging them. It straightens up, folds back its wing and looks down again.

Something in the water rolls – or rather someone. The watchful seagull blinks. The water darkens. A face tilted, a figure submerged. The mouth is open but there is no shining thread of bubbles, no silvery breath escaping.

The only sound – the drip-drip of blood hitting the slick surface of the pool before moving slowly through the blue-green water, mingling until it disappears.

# PART ONE

# 1. David

I should, I suppose, go back to the beginning, to the first time we met. The first time she spoke to me, to be precise, for I had seen her before – spotted her among the first-year faces staring out at me from the lecture theatre. It was hard not to notice her, with that hair. A great glow of it, radiantly blonde in long loose curls, like a soft release of breath. In the dimness of Theatre L, it caught the light and reflected it back, golden and iridescent. I noticed the hair and the bright round face beneath and thought: *New penny*. Then my mind turned back to my slides and I moved on.

There is an energy on campus during the first weeks of the new semester that is like nothing else. The air is charged with the frisson of possibility. A cheerful vigour takes hold, giving a new life and sheen to every faded surface, every jaded room. Even the most hardened staff veterans have a spring in their step during the first month, and there is an infectious sense of hopefulness. Once the madness of Freshers' Week has worn off, and the pace of lectures and tutorials has been set, an industriousness falls over the campus, like a flurry of autumn leaves. It zips through the corridors and stairwells, hurries across the wide open spaces where the students gather to talk and drink coffee. I felt it too – the beat of possibility, the urge to get a head start on the year. After seventeen years at the university, I was still not immune to the buoyant lift of first-term energy.

It was a couple of weeks into the semester when she approached me. I had just given my Thursday morning lecture on Modern Irish History and the students were filing out, a buzz of conversation rising as they climbed the steps to the exit. I was closing my laptop and putting away my notes, silently calculating whether I had enough time to nip to the common room for a coffee, when I felt someone's presence and looked up. She was standing across from me, holding her folder against her chest, her face half hidden behind the long golden strands of her hair.

'Dr Connolly,' she said, and immediately I caught the hint of a Belfast accent.

'Yes?'

'I was wondering if I could talk to you.'

I slid the laptop into my bag, fixed the strap over my shoulder, and noticed a kind of wariness hovering behind the big round eyes. She was fair-skinned, and had a scrubbed-clean look about her; many female students come to class in layers of make-up, a miasma of chemical smells surrounding them. This girl was different: a freshness and simplicity about her appearance set her apart, and made her appear terribly young.

'Of course,' I said briskly. 'I have a meeting in a few minutes, but you can walk with me, if you like.'

'Oh. No, that's okay.'

Disappointment, a faltering expression that piqued my interest.

'Perhaps some other time,' she said.

'My office hours are on Fridays between three and five. You're welcome to drop in. If that doesn't suit, you can always email to arrange an appointment.'

'Thank you,' she said politely. 'I'll do that.'

We walked together up the steps to the exit, not speaking, an awkwardness between us.

'Well, goodbye then,' I said, checking my watch and ducking into the drift of students heading towards the stairs.

By the time I reached my meeting, I had forgotten her. Funny, recalling it now. Such a momentous thing, our first meeting. Since then, I've come to look at that moment as the point at which my life split – like a page folded over and creased down the middle so that everything fell into before or after.

My office is on the third floor of the Arts building. It's covered with book-filled shelves and framed prints: the 1916 Proclamation, prints of two William Orpen sketches from the trenches in the First World War, a framed and faded photograph of my grandfather with others from the Royal Dragoon Guards, and finally a cartoon from the *New Yorker* featuring two academics squabbling, the last a gift from my wife. There's also a family photograph of the four of us hiking to the Hell Fire Club in the Dublin Mountains, which I had taken with my phone the previous summer: Holly's hair is wind-tossed, Robbie is grinning and Caroline's eyes watering – we look happy, individually and as a family, my arms circling us all in a messy embrace; the city and suburbs, this campus and office are a distant blur in the background.

The closest thing I can see of that outside world and the most appealing feature of the office is the window that takes up the entire southern wall and looks out on to the courtyard at the heart of the building. A small copse of birch trees grows there, and throughout the year I like to observe the changing colours of the leaves and watch the passage of the seasons.

I've spent my entire adult life – apart from three years working for my PhD at Queens – on this campus. I've loved every minute of it and consider myself lucky to be here, gradually moving up the ranks from Adjunct to Associate Professor, and I love the interaction with students at lecture and seminar level. I love the enquiring minds I meet – the irascible and sometimes irreverent arrogance of a student's interrogations of the past. I'll admit I was ambitious, and I've had to work hard. It's not like things came easy for me – not as they have for others who seem to have a natural flair for reading the past. My work was painstaking, but it brought its pleasures.

Even so, she arrived at a special moment of opportunity in my career. My old teacher and the head of our department, Professor Alan Longley, was due for retirement in two years' time. He had hinted strongly, on more than one occasion, that his position could be mine if I played my cards right, so to speak. Of course, Head of Department would mean more work, but I was ready for the extra responsibility and willing to accept the challenge. Such was my life: the happy construction of work I had built around me – until last autumn, that is.

Back then, during those weeks in September, as the light changed and the air took on the first chill, I knew next to nothing about her. Not even her name. I don't think I thought about her again until that Friday afternoon when

I held my student hours. The first of them began trickling in shortly after three – a second-year wanting to discuss his essay, a final-year already nervous about the prospects of graduation, another considering a master's. One by one they came, and I found I began to search for *her* among them, each time expecting to see her bright face appearing around my door.

In my office, there were two small armchairs and a low coffee-table I'd brought from home where I conducted my meetings with students. I don't like the power imbalance when I sit and stare at them from behind the desk. I kept the door open throughout these meetings, with both male and female students alike. You see, years ago, when I was a junior lecturer, a colleague was badly stung by an accusation from a female undergraduate who claimed he had molested her in his office. I remember at the time being shocked: he was such a weedy guy, with an unattractive habit of sniffing continuously while concentrating on a point.

Strange though it may sound, I couldn't imagine him having any sexual desires. Most academics are normal people, leading their lives in the manner of any professional person. Some, however, are cloistered, ill-equipped to cope beyond the protective confines of the university. That was Bill – a hard-working historian, but naïve, it has to be said. Not an unkind man, and quite gentle, really, the accusation hit him like a rocket. Overnight, he became a wild-eyed loon, determined to proclaim his innocence, often at the most inopportune moments – in school meetings, in the staff room over coffee, once at an open day. The claims were investigated by the disciplinary board and deemed to be unfounded. Bill was exonerated. The student graduated and left. Bill continued with his work, but a change had come over him. He no longer came for coffee with the rest of us, and avoided all social interaction with students. It was no surprise when, a year later, he announced he had taken up a post at a university abroad. I've no idea where he is now, though I think of him from time to time, whenever some other scandal erupts on campus, or when I feel the weight of a female student's gaze a little too heavily upon me.

Something about the way she had looked at me that day, the way her voice had faltered, made me think of Bill. I was curious, but wary too. The doe-eyed ones, who seem young and innocent, they are the ones you have to be careful with. Not the savvy girls with their Ugg boots and fake tans – they can hold their own, and have little interest in pursuing a man like me. I'm forty-four, the father of two children. I eat well and I exercise regularly. Most days I cycle to work; three times a week I swim. I try to take care of myself, you could say. Now, I'm not the best-looking man in the world, but I'm not the worst. I'm just shy of six foot with dark hair, brown eyes and sallow skin. My dad said we had Spanish blood in our veins: 'From the sailors on the Armada, shipwrecked off the West of Ireland all those years ago.' I don't know if that's true or not. But after what happened to Bill, I have to presume it's not beyond the realm of possibility that an impressionable young student might develop a crush. But at that stage I'd been married for seventeen years, and I was aware of how costly a stupid mistake could be. Besides, I had too much to lose.

I suppose that was what flickered across my mind the first time we spoke. Her reluctance to walk and talk with me – as if the weight of whatever she wanted to discuss required privacy, silence, the full focus of my attention.

That Friday, I fully expected her to come to my office. She didn't. I have to admit I was disappointed. There was no explanation – not that I needed or expected one. Neither was there an email seeking an appointment. The following week, I saw her again in my lectures, her eyes fixed on the notebook in front of her, but when the hour was up, she filed out of the theatre with the other students.

The matter went clean out of my head, and I'm sure I would have forgotten about it completely in time. I was busier than ever, juggling my lectures and research along with various other work commitments, not to mention all the administration I had to do. I would also be talking to various media outlets about the 1916 centenary celebrations in the coming months. Caroline had started a new job. Between us we shared the school drop-offs as well as the kids' after-school activities. Life was full. I was busier than ever. I was happy. I know that now.

Then one afternoon, in October, returning to my office from a school meeting, I found her sitting on the floor next to my door. Knees drawn up, hands clutching her ankles. As soon as she saw me, she got to her feet, and pulled at her clothing.

'Can I help you?' I asked, my hand searching in my pocket for the key.

'Sorry. I should have made an appointment.'

'You're here now.' I opened the door. 'Come in.'

I went to my desk, placed my bag on it. The room was chilly. I walked to the radiator and ran my fingers along its top. The girl went to close the door.

'No, you can leave it open,' I said.

She gave me a slightly startled glance, as if she wished she'd never come.

'Let's sit, and you can tell me what's on your mind.'

I took one of the armchairs, but she just stood, fiddling with the zip on her sweater. She was small and thin, bony wrists emerging from her cuffs, which had been picked at and unravelled. Nervous fingers constantly moving.

'What's your name?'

'Zoë,' she said quietly. 'Zoë Barry.'

'Well, Zoë. How can I help you?' I asked, tidying a bunch of journals at my desk.

Her hands became still, and in a voice that came out as clear as a bell, she said: 'I think you might be my father.'

# 2. David

Students come through my door every day of the working week. Some have ordinary questions, course-related queries. Others are in trouble. They want my help. They may not even know what's wrong. And then again, others *are* trouble. Over the years, I've had my fair share of problem cases. They have ranged from benign to complex. But none was like this. None spelled trouble so clearly and lucidly, or announced the problem with such candid, if sheepish, clarity.

'I don't understand,' I said.

'Can I close the door?'

'No, I don't think that's a good idea.' I gestured for her to sit down in the chair opposite.

'I know it's probably a shock,' she said, taking a seat and putting her bag down by her feet .

'A shock?' I said. More of an intrusion, or a preposterous allegation, than anything else. I inspected my itinerary for the day. It was full: one meeting chased by another. The module review committee was going to be particularly taxing. I also needed to get to the library to talk to Laurence about the oral histories he was sourcing for me from the British Library.

'Well, yes . . . I've come in here out of the blue and revealed to you that I am your daughter.'

'Sorry, I'm still struggling to follow. Why is it you think I might be your father?' I said.

Her expression didn't change. Shy, meek even, as if she were there against her will. 'I've been thinking about how to put it so it wouldn't come out as bluntly,' she said, leaning forward slightly. 'It doesn't seem to matter which way I turn the phrases over. You are my father.' She coughed awkwardly into her sleeve. 'I thought it would be better to tell you straight rather than dancing around it, if that makes sense?'

The planes of her face were smooth. It was an open face, an honest one. Her eyes were green, wide and bright. Her hair fell over her face occasionally and she had to push it back – a kind of tic, I supposed.

'Actually, it's a relief to tell you,' she said, giving me a watery smile. 'I've tossed this around for ages, sitting in your lectures, knowing all the time you're my father and that you had no idea. It got so I couldn't bear it. I felt like I had to tell you.'

Her voice, though tentative and soft, had the earthy guttural of the North in it. Because of all the reading and research I'd been doing recently, it made me think about those American soldiers during the Second World War stationed in the various towns of Northern Ireland – Coleraine, Ballycastle, Portstewart – and their unwritten legacy: the ones who left behind sons and daughters they might never have known about, while others were sought out later in life by their offspring. I had always thought this a joyful, if complicated, legacy – an ancillary tributary to the river of the past – an enriching one, even.

Still, I became annoyed at the vagaries of my own

mind and the distraction the girl had brought to my day: her prank, the articulations of an unsound mind, whatever it was.

I picked up my notebook, drew myself up from the chair, and walked to my desk. I felt the short fuse of my temper fizzle. 'Again, what makes you think I'm your father?'

The smile fell from her face. She reached into her bag for a tissue. I could tell she was struggling to maintain her composure. Perhaps I had been too curt. I had, after all, a duty of care to her as a student. She was young, lost; it must have been very difficult for her to pluck up the courage, however misguided, to come in to talk to me.

'Listen,' I said, 'you're clearly upset. And, believe me, it's not the first time I've had a student here in tears. University life can be daunting. People struggle. But there is help out there, if you ask for it. Let me give you the number of someone in Student Services you can call.' I went behind my desk and wrote the number on a Post-it. Claire O'Rourke, a counsellor on campus, was an old friend. As I scribbled the note, I wondered briefly what she would make of the girl's claims.

Ripping the page off the pad, I went to hand it to her but she didn't reach out for it. She didn't look at it at all.

I returned to my desk. 'If you don't want the number, that's your call,' I said. The situation had grown tiresome. I had work to do. 'I'm trying to offer you help, but I can't force you to take it.'

I tapped the space bar on my keyboard, stirring the computer to life. The monitor brightened and the image of Robbie and Holly dissolved.

'My mother's name was Linda,' the girl said, and my hand released the mouse. 'Linda Barry.'

Linda Barry . . . Hearing her name again was like having an unhealed wound prodded. I had not heard it for so long that I felt as if I was dreaming, or as if time was playing tricks. My mouth dried up.

'Linda Barry?' I said and, just like that, I was transported to another time, another place. It was as if her name was a secret password to the past – to my past, to a younger, more feckless and passionate man, and the time that went with it. A password that contained pain, too. I felt winded, and all at once on guard.

I looked at her again for any signs of resemblance when the figure of another student appeared in the doorway.

'Dr Connolly?'

'Not now,' I said testily. 'I'm in the middle of something,' I switched off the monitor. 'Come back later.'

'A little over a year ago, she told me about you,' the girl said, her voice barely a whisper.

'She told you about me?'

'She thought I needed to know,' the girl said, pulling at the strands of her sleeve.

I could tell she was waiting for me to say something, while the possibility of what she had revealed began to ghost its way through my mind.

'She told me when she was a student at Queens, you were her course tutor,' she said. 'She told me you had become friends, and that, for a while, you were lovers.'

It felt wrong – listening to a student discussing me and Linda, describing us as *lovers*. Could it be true? Had Linda had a child?

I thought about the weekend we'd spent in Donegal before we split up. Three days in a remote part of the countryside. I had felt as if I were shrugging off my previous life, the years of study, the immersion in academia receding from memory, like waking from a long dream. Beneath the surface, there had lingered the knowledge of a parting. Soon I would be returning to Dublin to take up a position in the university from which I had graduated three years before. The life I had lived in Belfast, at Queens, would draw to a close. And this relationship, this love affair – I had no idea how much it meant to me – it, too, would be laid to rest. We both knew it, although neither of us had said so.

The girl held a hand to her lips and I saw there in the rounded shape of her face a resemblance. A simplicity that might have been plain were it not for the liveliness of her eyes – Linda's eyes, or were they? I couldn't be completely sure.

'I don't see how . . .' I began. 'I can't understand . . .'

'She said your affair was brief. Afterwards, she went abroad to do a master's degree. That was when she discovered she was pregnant.'

I had, by then, completed my PhD and returned to Dublin. I had met Caroline again and our relationship – broken for those three years in Belfast – had resumed. After Linda, after the swirling highs and lows, I felt ready for something solid, stable and dependable. 'But she never said. She never told me . . .'

I remember what a relief it was to climb into marriage, to feel the safe, firm structure of it form around me. But with this girl in my office, I was again all at sea, the roar of waves in my ears drowning much of what she was telling me. I kept thinking of Linda with a baby – *my* baby. How could she not have told me? How could she have gone through all of that alone?

'This must be difficult,' she said, regaining her composure. 'It's got to be a lot to take in.'

With a slim frame, all wrists and knees, jeans clinging to thin legs, heavy oxblood-red boots, there was something vulnerable about her – even if she had just lobbed her grenade and set me reeling. 'A lot to take in? Yes, you could say that.'

'I know,' she said, an uneasy smile spreading across her face. 'But you have to know that I don't want anything from you.'

'You don't?'

'Nothing!' she said, laughing nervously. 'It's just I thought you should know.'

'And that's all? There's nothing else?' I asked.

She shrugged, and started to pick again at her frayed cuffs. 'Just to talk, I suppose.'

'To talk?'

She squirmed, grew sullen. The shield of hair had fallen over her face again. She made no effort to push it back. Quietly, from behind it, she said: 'I just wanted to get to know you a little.'

It was a reasonable request, I supposed, but I resisted. 'Did Linda put you up to this?' I asked. 'Does she know you've come to see me? Did she tell you to come?'

In retrospect, I see how foolish I was – how ridiculous I must have sounded – to think an old girlfriend had spent the last eighteen years hatching a plan to bring about my undoing.

'My mother's dead.'

Dead? Said so matter-of-factly, and with such certainty that there was no room for doubt. Still my initial and irrational response was to contradict her, even though I had had not one scintilla of contact with Linda since I had seen her last. Linda, my old flame, dead. I couldn't quite believe it. Briefly, I remembered, without wanting to, the first time I had kissed her: she had dared me to. 'Go on,' she had said that night, as I walked her home from an evening guest lecture. 'You know you want to.'

I had played dumb, but all the time, I was stepping closer to her, and she was stepping closer to me, until her hands gripped the pockets of my coat and my hands found their way to her waist. It had not been a lingering kiss. She had pulled away quickly, and I followed her, feeling I had been on the brink of making a terrible mistake but not knowing if the mistake was to follow her or to let her slip away.

And now she's dead? I was stunned by the revelation, numbed. How strange and unreal it is to hear of an old lover who has passed away. To think that the time you shared is no longer a common memory between you, no longer a testimony subject to agreement and dissent, no longer a space of contested but cherished moments already gone – like the rising smoke from a bonfire on a Hallowe'en night that we'd stood beside in Belfast. Gone – like the fading autumn light at sunset. It's like a sudden pull in the heart, a brief awakening, and the realization that their life has continued all the time you were apart, all the time they were forgotten; still they remained, creating their own history. A sudden burst of memory, the brush of old and tender feelings, then it fades.

'I'm so sorry,' I told her. 'What happened?'

'Ovarian cancer. It's just coming up to a year.'

Now it made some sort of sense to me: a young woman whose mother has just died seeks some kind of replacement to make up for her loss. It's possible. Psychologists might call it transference, and stranger things have been known to happen, certainly, on this campus. But I was curious. 'And when did Linda tell you about me?' I asked.

She pushed back her hair. 'It was towards the end.'

'Is that why you came to this university?'

She blushed, shifted in her chair. 'I dunno. Maybe. I've always liked history and, with Mam gone, I just wanted to get away, you know. Start again somewhere new.'

Whatever the truth of her claim, I couldn't help but admire her a little, the curious tilt of her chin, the bravery in her optimism.

A sudden rap on the open door startled her. She stood up quickly. Another student appeared. 'Dr Connolly.'

'Just a moment,' I said.

The girl was already fixing the strap of her satchel over one shoulder. 'I should go,' she said.

Awkwardly, beneath the gaze of the other student, we said goodbye to one another. I turned back into the room, went to the window and waited for the young man to sit. Below in the courtyard, staff and students sat at tables among the birch trees; the sound of their conversation rose in a barely audible hum. Shadows moved overhead, the day darkened. The student behind me cleared his throat.

'Would you mind waiting?' I said, making for the door. 'I'll just be a moment.'

She was at the stairwell by the time I caught up. Hair falling over her shoulders, strolling away. I called to her and she turned. A door opened and a flurry of students drifted out, passing us in a noisy group.

'I wanted to ask you,' I said, 'have you told anyone else? Any of your friends? Anyone in the class?'

'No,' she said.

'Can I ask that you don't? Please. Not yet, not until I've had some time to take it in.'

'Don't worry,' she said, her voice flat and unreadable. In her eyes, there was a flash of pity. I felt a nudge of something, too: shame, perhaps. However foolish, I still believed I could contain whatever it was that had been released.

'I won't say a thing,' she said, slipping into the stream of students passing, leaving me there, sweat on my palms, holding on to the rail, conscious that I was about to be swept up by something more powerful than I understood, something dangerous and beyond my control.

# 3. Caroline

I can remember when it began.

One afternoon in early autumn, I had been called away from the office unexpectedly because of David's mother, Ellen. There had been an incident.

I was just settling her with her tea-tray, the telly on, when my mobile rang, David's number appearing on the screen.

'Caroline?'

'I was just going to call you.'

'Why?' he asked. 'Has something happened?'

Something in his voice: a scratch of irritation or a wrinkle of concern.

'Who is it?' Ellen asked, her voice still quavering with nerves.

'It's David.' I turned up the volume of the telly, then closed the door gently behind me. In the hallway, I sat down on the stairs and felt the carpet rough at the back of my legs, a musty smell rising from it. 'Your mum,' I told him. 'She went wandering again.'

'Oh, Christ.'

'She's fine –'

'What happened?'

I told him about the phone call I'd received – Ellen's neighbour Marion, sounding breathy and rushed: *You told me to call if ever something happened.* I listened as she told me how she had found Ellen in Tesco, crying in the frozen-food section, not knowing where she was or how she would get home. It was not the first such occurrence. 'I've settled her now,' I said. 'I gave her some beans on toast.'

'Should I come over?'

Ellen was just beginning to get over her shakiness. The last thing she needed was to relive it for her son. 'Leave it until the weekend, David. Give her a chance to recover.'

'Okay,' he agreed. Then he said: 'Caroline?'

'Yes?'

He hesitated. 'Nothing. It can wait.'

But it was there in his voice – a note I couldn't identify.

I knew it at once: something had happened.

She came into our lives, into our home, at an awkward time for me, a time I think of now as being filled with nerves and self-doubt. I had, after a fifteen-year hiatus, returned to work at the advertising agency I had left when Robbie was born. Everything felt changed, like foreign territory I had visited once but of which I retained no memory. Nothing was familiar.

The decision to give up my career to raise my children was not something I regretted, even though it had been a strain at times: the boredom, the loneliness. There was a deep need within me to create for my children a warm and loving environment where there would always be someone making sure they did their homework, putting dinner on the table, checking on them when they were in

bed at night. I did it gladly. My only continuing contact with the agency was a calendar arriving every year at Christmas, each month headed with a sleek image of a car or an alcoholic drink or whatever product they were being paid to push. When the calendar arrived and I read all the names signed on the inside flap, I confess I felt a pang, a twinge of something close to envy. Fleeting, but I was aware of it nonetheless – a seam of uncertainty or regret that could be tapped into whenever I was reminded of what I had given up. When I met Peter by chance and he mentioned that one of the girls in the office was taking ten months' maternity leave, the idea took hold. My children were old enough. I had time on my hands. Although I had been out of the game for so long, I felt the pull of it, the undertow of a distant longing. I hadn't counted on Zoë. I hadn't even known she existed.

That evening, after I'd left Ellen, I drove home through heavy traffic, the image of my elderly mother-in-law crying next to cabinets full of fish fingers and frozen peas still alive in my mind. Opening my front door, I heard noise from the sitting room, movement upstairs. I kicked off my shoes in the hall, pausing briefly to enjoy the relief. Having hung my coat over the newel post, I went into the sitting room.

Robbie was sitting on the couch with his legs tucked up under him. On the telly a woman was sobbing in front of a studio audience, the man beside her mortified.

'Hello, sweetheart,' I said. 'Sorry I'm so late.'

'Hey, Mum,' he answered.

'I was at Nan's,' I told him, although he hadn't sought an explanation for my absence. 'Where's your dad?'

'Upstairs.'

He was still wearing his school uniform and, after shooting a quick smile in my direction, went back to staring avidly at the screen, the room dark apart from the light cast by the flickering images. The studio audience were hissing and booing, the presenter advancing through them. Robbie shifted under my gaze and I caught a glimpse of an empty crisps packet stuffed down the side of the couch beside him.

'You didn't eat a whole bag, did you?'

He smiled again and pulled a face. 'Sorry, I was hungry.'

'Robbie . . .'

'Sorry!' he said again, still smiling. At fifteen, he was at an awkward transitional stage, trapped in the hormonal no man's land between child and adult. At moments like this, when his roguish grin surfaced, he was my little boy again. I let it go.

Climbing the stairs, I could hear music coming from Holly's room – some tinny pop – and beneath it, the sweet, faltering accompaniment of my daughter's voice. I stepped past her door, opened ours softly and saw David stretched out on the bed, eyes closed, a glass of wine in one hand resting on his chest. I stood over him watching, his handsome face serious, even in repose, lines from laughter and concentration hardening now into permanence. He stirred a little.

'You'll spill that.'

His eyes shot open and he sat up quickly. I reached forward and rescued the glass, put it to my lips and drank.

'I didn't hear you come in,' he said, blinking and running a hand across his face.

The wine warmed the back of my throat. I set the glass on the nightstand, and sat down on the bed beside him. He lay back, locking his hands behind his neck and I felt a brief, surprising nudge of desire. I could lie down on the bed next to him and, with the dinner drying out in the oven, we could slip off our clothes and forget the troubles of the day for a while. It seemed so risqué, the thought of sex at this hour of the evening with the children in the house, the telly on downstairs. I put my hand on his shirt-front, traced a line down to his belt. This kind of spontaneity still felt unnatural in the wake of what had happened between us. His eyes closed and he shifted under my touch, tacitly agreeing to my unspoken suggestion.

Holly's bedroom door opened, her footfall in the hall outside. My hand paused and David opened his eyes.

'What do you think?' I asked.

He sat up and swung his feet to the floor. The moment had passed. He reached for his wine glass on the nightstand, and said: 'Come on. Let's go and eat.'

In the kitchen, he flicked on the radio while I got the lettuce from the fridge. A drive-time show was on, the presenter's voice, her forensic questioning, filling the space between us as she took some politician to task over the failed attempt to legislate for abortion in the case of fatal foetal abnormality. A year or so before, we had undertaken a major renovation of our home. Besides an attic conversion, a large extension had been built on to the kitchen, the additional space allowing room for a sofa and a stove as well as a large dining table and a kitchen island. The work had been costly and we couldn't have afforded it were it not for a small inheritence from my parents, who had passed away some years before. A loan from the credit union topped up the funds needed.

It was David's habit on evenings when he was tired after work to throw himself on the sofa, the two of us chatting while I prepared the dinner. On this particular evening, however, he leaned against the counter while I rinsed the salad leaves in the sink, and asked me about Ellen. I was tired but answered his questions, and he took it all in, his arms folded. Something needed to be done about her deteriorating state of mind, and we batted ideas back and forth, although we were reluctant to get into it.

There was something else I needed to tell him. I was weighing up whether to say it now or wait until the kids had gone to bed. David seemed distracted and I had the beginnings of a headache. I asked him to pour me a glass of wine while I spun the salad. When he went to call the others for dinner I decided just to say it, to get it over with quickly before the kids came into the room.

'There was an email from the school,' I said, taking down the plates and spreading them along the worktop. 'Robbie's parent-teacher meeting is next Tuesday. Are you free?'

He put the empty bottle into the crate by the door. 'Next Tuesday?'

'Yes, in the afternoon.'

I took the lasagne from the oven, placed it on the trivet and began separating it into segments. He was standing next to me, waiting to take the plates to the table. 'Can't you go?' he asked.

'It won't last long. Just an hour or so. You can take those ones.' I nodded at the first two plates, and he picked them up but didn't move away. I could feel him waiting for something more from me. I put food on the other plates, then opened the oven and returned the dish to keep it warm.

'Caroline –'

'Please, David. It's just one afternoon.'

'It's not that. You know it's not.'

I could feel the colour coming to my cheeks. I picked up the other plates and waited for him to let me pass.

'It's been a year,' he said, his voice soft but firm. 'You can't keep doing this. You can't stay away from there for ever.'

On the radio, the presenter was affecting a heavy sigh, the one she used to signal the end of an interview. The kitchen door opened.

'Please don't make me,' I said, as I stepped past him. I put the plates down hard on the table.

Over dinner, Holly talked about a school trip to the Burren that was planned for the end of October. Cheerfully animated, she spoke of caves and calcium deposits, bog-land and its varying plant-life. Robbie lolled in his chair, one elbow on the table, picking at his food. David was quiet. The children, no doubt, put it down to work. We used to joke about it, the kids and I. 'Dad's gone over to the dark side,' we would say, whenever he became distracted and vague. His silence that evening seemed heavier than usual and I attributed it to the parent-teacher meeting. I knew he was thinking of what had happened the year before, the whole awkward business at the school rearing its ugly head again. To combat it, I recounted the drama of my afternoon, the phone call at work, the confused state I'd found Ellen in.

'First thing tomorrow, I'm calling Dr Burke,' I announced.

'Poor Nan,' Holly said, drinking her water, her eyes behind her glasses perplexed.

'She'll be fine,' David told her, the firmness in his voice a kind of warning.

He was put out over the school thing, and I suppose he was entitled to feel resentful, but still. I had spent all afternoon taking care of his mother and I had yet to hear a word of thanks. 'Are you going to eat any of that?' I asked Robbie.

He seemed tired, pressing his fork against the raft of pasta hardening on his plate. 'I'm not hungry.'

David dropped his cutlery on to his plate with a clatter, making us all look up. 'Maybe if you hadn't shoved a whole bag of fucking Doritos down your throat you'd be able to eat,' he snapped.

Robbie's mouth opened, as if he were about to say something, but no words came out.

'David, please,' I said sharply.

He stared at me across the table.

My husband is a sulker, not an exploder. He wears me down with his stubborn silences. We made a point of not arguing in front of the children – even when our marriage was under strain. The fights had all been held in private, and we maintained a strained civility whenever the kids were around. The quality of his discomfort this time was different from before. I realized that it wasn't about the school at all.

'Let's just eat,' he said.

Addressing his plate again, he speared some pasta with his fork. We had forgotten about the salad, still sitting next to the sink, but neither of us made a move towards it. The jingle of the drive-time show was playing on the radio, its cheerful beat pounding through the speakers while we sat together without talking until the meal was done.

Whenever I try to remember how it all started, I don't think of the morning I found out, or the first time I saw the haze of yellow hair, the feline stare. I think of David that evening, the coiled rope of tension within him, the shiftiness of his irritation. I didn't know it was because of her – Zoë. I didn't even know she existed. But that was when I first felt her shadow fall over me. The first time I felt the ripples of a new presence within my home, like a dye entering water, already changing its chemistry.

# 4. David

I woke up the next morning to the thought *She is dead.* Linda is dead.

It wasn't grief I felt. How could it be? She had not been in my life for a long time. But, still, there was sadness, and the shock left me feeling out of sorts, on edge. I got up, threw water on to my face, shaved, showered and pulled myself together as best I could. Over breakfast, my world solidified around me. Robbie and Holly were absorbed in their cereal while Caroline got their lunches ready. I finished breakfast quickly, leaned in to Caroline to say goodbye and felt the warmth of her kiss on my mouth. I told myself, Everything is going to be all right.

I pedalled away from the house, my lungs filling with air, and flew past the traffic while trying to convince myself that, even if Linda had passed away, what this girl had told me was some kind of joke, an elaborate student prank. A student's life is full of mad-cap behaviour, full of stunts and dares. That was why there was no reason to tell my wife what she had said. Maybe somebody had put the girl up to it. Maybe I wasn't her father.

On campus, I spent the first hour going through my inbox. What struck me initially was the amount of non-college work I had taken on: media commitments, interviews, op-ed pieces, book reviews, as well as board and committee duty. I replied to as many emails as I could before I rushed to a tutorial with my third-years, followed by coffee, then seminars until one. My first-year lecture was after lunch, and as the time approached, I grew twitchy. My palms became sweaty, my stomach churned. I told myself to stop being paranoid and walked into the theatre, down the steps, swung my bag on to the bench and hooked my laptop to the projector. When I raised my face to the students, my heart was beating hard. A hush came over the auditorium. As I talked, I scanned the room for her, but drew a blank. Twice, late-comers interrupted. I looked to the swinging door only to find it wasn't her. During the last few minutes, I opened up the lecture to questions: it was another chance to search for her among the sea of faces. By the time it ended I was sure of it: she wasn't there.

Throughout that day and the next, I couldn't help thinking about her, despite my best efforts. Caroline's new job, and the discussion that had started between us over what we should do about my mum – home-help or sheltered accommodation – acted as something of a distraction. But the girl was there, in my thoughts, the entire time.

I didn't do anything about it, about her, until Friday. I was in a meeting with my most promising PhD student, Niki Agsten, and her co-supervisor, Dr Anne Burke. Niki's subject was the role of women during the First World War, and she was telling us about something she had stumbled on during her recent research. 'It was in the court records,' she said. 'I was going through the year 1918 when I came across this.'

Anne and I listened while she read out a statement from a witness detailing an account of a woman giving birth and subsequently taking the life of her newborn baby. 'It's strange,' Niki said, 'but since I read the account in the court files I can't stop thinking about her. She tried to strangle her own baby with a sock. When that didn't work she crushed it beneath the weight of a window frame. What made her believe that letting her baby live would be so much worse than having its death on her conscience?'

Anne made some answer but I was lost to the conversation, my mind tumbling back through my own history. An image came to me of Linda sitting hunched in a bathroom, her cheeks flushed with heat, the test in her hand, a line on a stick. My imagination ran riot. I thought about the panic she might have felt, the loneliness. I wondered again why she had never told me. That was, if what the girl had said to me was true, which I still didn't know. And if it was true what it might mean to my relationship with Caroline, and the challenges that already faced our marriage, not to mention how it might affect our children. Too many what-ifs crowded my mind, and too many unanswerables made it impossible for me to concentrate.

'David?' Anne was waiting for an answer.

What would she think if I told her about Linda, about Zoë?

'Sorry?'

'Next Thursday – are we agreed?'

'Yes,' I said. 'Yes, of course.'

They left. I stood and thought of how I had buried the girl's words, transformed them into a joke, reduced what she had said into a student spoof or the workings of an unsound mind. It occurred to me that there was something desperate in the way I was trying to blot out those words. Blot *her* out.

I went to my desk, stirred my computer to life and clicked on to the internet. It didn't take long to find it. Still, I was surprised. DNA testing seemed so foreign, a product of a more litigious society than Ireland's, but there it was in black and white: a company in Dublin that carried out paternity tests with a 99 per cent accuracy assurance, discretion guaranteed.

What did I need? A swab from the inner cheek was best, but there were other sources: a hair (with follicle, preferably), a toothbrush. I must have spent twenty minutes working out all the ways I could capture her DNA without her knowledge.

While I trawled through the DNA sites I was all the time weighing up whether or not to discuss the paternity test with Zoë. I thought about asking her permission, telling her I needed to get the test done – but every time I included her in the conversation my imagination tangled the possible outcomes into something messy and complicated. The minutes ticked past. My thoughts grew more confused: a sudden flash of how crazy this situation was made me close down the DNA page I was on. I told myself to get a grip. When Alan put his head around the door and asked if I'd join him in the common room for coffee, I was more than relieved.

Alan has been my friend and mentor since I was an undergraduate. A wise soul, with a gruff exterior, he had offered me my first post-doctoral post after Queens. I owe him a lot, and have a firm affection for him, despite our differences. He's an old-school historian, and is baffled sometimes by my approach to history. My adventures in the media irk him in particular. That afternoon, as we strolled to the common room, he took a pop at my latest article.

'The sports supplement!' he said. 'What are you doing writing about sports?'

I laughed. 'You don't think sport is relevant to history? What about the 1933 Olympics?'

'Come on. He's hardly Jesse Owens, is he?'

'Can you think of a more controversial figure in Irish sport?'

'I just don't see why you're wasting your time mixing it with the polemicists and writing such –'

'Go on, say it. You think it's drivel.'

'I was going to say journalism.'

'You were not.'

He laughed.

'Sport, the arts, popular culture, all of it informs the national consciousness,' I said. 'It makes us who we are as a nation. All of it is history in the making.'

We picked up our coffee and sat. Alan was smiling at what I had said. I could tell he was not in the mood for argumentative banter today. 'I'm supposed to go to this conference in East Anglia next month,' he said, leaning forward and examining his cup. 'To give a talk . . . I was wondering if you would go in my stead.'

'Really?'

'It would be good for you,' he replied. 'And your CV.'

How often had it been said to me that if I did a favour for someone it would advance my career at a later date? I didn't mind standing in for Alan, but it wasn't like him to duck out of a commitment. 'Sure, Alan. Is everything all right?'

'I've been doing some thinking,' he said seriously. 'My health is not good – a problem with my heart. They tell me I should have surgery, but I don't know if I want that. At my age . . .'

'You're only sixty-two.'

'Well, exactly. That's my point. I want to live a little while I still have time. So I've decided to take early retirement.'

'Early retirement?'

'What? Did you think I'd be here for ever, David?'

'Yes,' I said. A kind of sadness was pulling at me. I've never been very good at endings or goodbyes.

'This time I really do mean it,' he said.

He didn't need to spell it out for me. There was an unspoken understanding. If Alan left, there would be a position for a new professor. This was my chance. I couldn't help feeling a spark of excitement. The way he suggested it, it almost felt like favouritism. His kindness had always, it seemed, extended itself beyond a professional duty of care.

The possibility of the professorship stayed with me all the way back to the office, my mind brimming with ideas, rushing a few months ahead, to the interview board, the presentations. I began making a mental tally of the papers I hoped to publish that year, including the book I was finishing, wondering how my research output would compare to the other candidates'. The idea was so consuming that I almost didn't notice the slip of paper on the floor as I opened the door to my office. As I shut it behind me, the paper fluttered in the draught. I leaned down to pick it up, and read the words quickly.

All my excitement vanished. The lead weight was back in my heart.

It was a short note written in an elegant hand, signed with a flourish, her name a slash across the page.

*Meet me this evening? Madigans, after work. Say 6.30 p.m.*
*Zoë*

I placed it carefully in my wallet.

Friday evening, and there was a sense of expectancy in the air. The collective relief that the end of the week had arrived presented itself in a frenetic busyness on the roads and pavements. The wind had whipped up and I pedalled slowly to Donnybrook. Traffic was thick, people hurrying to get away from the working week, their desks, bosses and obligations.

By the time I got there, the pub was heaving: office workers, students, mechanics from the nearby bus depot, their voices blending together in a dense cloud of talk. I found her sitting on her own at the back, a bottle of beer in front of her. One elbow on the table, her head was resting on her cupped hand, her face blank as she fiddled with her phone. For just a moment, before she saw me, she looked so young, so harmless, that I couldn't help but feel sorry for her.

'You came.' She smiled, getting to her feet.

'Zoë,' I said.

'I saved you a seat.' She gestured to a stool. 'I'm so glad you're here. I wasn't sure you'd come. Let me get you a drink.'

'No,' I said.

'Please. It's the least I can do.'

'I'll get my own,' I said, catching a barman's attention. I ordered a pint and another bottle for Zoë.

She leaned on the table, one hand wrapped around her beer, her face open and expectant. About us, voices rose. Laughter rang out, and brass instruments played boisterous ragtime through hidden speakers. We almost had to shout to be heard.

'I had no idea this place would be so busy,' she said. 'I'd have picked somewhere quieter.'

The truth was, I felt protected by the noise and the clamour of people. Somehow, I didn't want to be cloistered in some quiet snug with a student, a stranger. I couldn't tell who might be watching.

'I just thought that, as it's close to college, it would be convenient.'

Our drinks arrived, and before the glass had reached my mouth, she was raising her bottle. 'Cheers.'

'*Sláinte*,' I said, with a strange premonition of how I might have taken Robbie for his first drink, to a dark pub, where a father and son could bond. Instead, here I was with a girl I barely knew.

'I wanted to apologize,' she began, 'for the other day. Taking you unawares like that. It was unfair. I'm really sorry,' she said, small creases appearing at the sides of her eyes.

She wore a plain red sweater, and I wondered briefly

whether those big army boots were still on her feet. 'You're not mocking me, Zoë, are you?'

'God, no!' Her eyes became round, but the anxious smile hovered at the corners of her mouth. 'I just think we got off on the wrong footing.'

'What you're saying about me . . . about me being your father, it's very serious.'

'I know, I know.' She looked down at the table, shaking her head.

I drank deeply and waited. I had prepared something to say, but I wanted to get it right. However, she spoke next and what she said surprised me: 'I want you to know that you don't need to be afraid . . .'

'Afraid?' I said.

'Of me,' she said, in a small voice. 'I don't want to hurt you. I don't want to get you into any trouble.'

'What sort of trouble could you get me into? I haven't done anything wrong.'

'No, I know. I meant that I don't want to make things difficult for you with the university, or with your wife.'

'My wife?'

'Yes,' she said. 'Have you told her about me?'

It had been nearly a week. Not a long time in the scale of things, but it had been a painstaking week of concealment and circumspection. All that time I had been keeping it from Caroline, telling myself I was protecting her, but what I was really doing was protecting myself. I hated keeping secrets. In fact, as a couple, I'd thought we were done with all that. The past had already taught me one thing: secrets will out, and by keeping them, there are always repercussions, but I had ignored my own hard-learned lesson. Right then, not telling Caroline seemed like a big mistake.

'I haven't told her about you, no,' I admitted. 'Not yet. Not until I'm sure . . .'

'Until you're sure?' she queried. 'That I'm not making the whole thing up?'

'You can't blame me. It's a shock, and I still have to establish the veracity.'

'"Establish the veracity",' she said, under her breath, reaching for her bag. For an instant I thought she was going to leave. Instead, she rooted in the tartan canvas satchel until she found a tatty envelope. She reached into it and placed a document on the table in front of us. 'My birth certificate.'

I ran my fingers over it. The date read '3 March 1995'. My eyes sought the details of paternity, but there was nothing conclusive: 'Father Unknown'.

Before I could say that the document didn't prove anything, she said: 'You might recognize these.' She placed a strip of photographs on the certificate. 'They were taken in May 1994. If you look at the back, you'll see Linda's handwriting.'

Four square photographs from a booth in a railway station. My youthful face beaming back at me. A set of different poses – two students larking around. I'd sported a beard that year – strange to see it now. It wasn't just the beard that was different: my eyes seemed wider, my face more open. There was humour and fun in it, and for a second I was back in that booth, Linda on my knee, my arms feeling her tremble with laughter as she half turned to me, her face against mine, telling me to be serious now.

I remembered how she had held me close, our smiles captured as the flash startled us, hanging on to each other, it seemed, for dear life.

'I do remember . . . It's just that it's difficult for me,' I said, hardly daring to touch the photographs. I wanted to say something else. I wanted to tell her that, if she really was my daughter, everything would be all right. We would sort it all out. But the words wouldn't come. Instead I ended up sounding like the uptight academic I didn't want to be, a supercilious father-figure. My phone rang. It was Caroline. I hadn't told her I was going out. I'd have to say I was working late, or taking the external examiner out for a drink.

Zoë said: 'Answer it if you need to. I have to run to the loo.'

I didn't relish the prospect of having to lie to Caroline. Extenuating circumstances, I reasoned, letting the phone ring out before putting it back into my pocket.

In the dusty half-light, I saw the glint of golden hair on Zoë's jacket. Without thinking I reached out for it. I ran my hand down its back and sleeves, my fingers reaching for the golden strands below the collar, and just like that, without any forethought or premeditation, I wound the hairs around my fingers and put them into my pocket.

I felt a rush of adrenalin, the excitement of doing something illicit, and then Zoë reappeared, smiling quizzically, asking me why I was holding her coat.

'I thought I could walk you to the bus or whatever . . .' I said, going to help her on with her jacket.

'We're leaving?'

'I have to go,' I said. 'I'm sorry . . . There's a minor emergency at home.'

‘Oh,’ she said, disappointed. ‘I hope it’s not too serious?’

‘It’s unfortunate, but I do have to go . . .’ I said, glancing at the photos again.

I put on my coat and held out my hand. Zoë ignored the gesture and embraced me, her arms wrapped around my neck with a kind of desperation. I stood awkwardly, willing her to step away.

People could see: a woman from the next table glanced in our direction, the barman caught my eye and grinned. Who else had seen us? I wondered, with intense unease. I took her arms in my hands and, forcibly, placed them by her sides.

She looked so crestfallen, so hurt, but I had to go.

‘Good night,’ I said, and walked away.

# 5. Caroline

I'm not the first person whose marriage has been rocked by an affair. Every day millions of people all over the world are unfaithful to their loved ones. I don't know why I was so surprised when it happened to me. But one of the things I learned during the crisis is that people can find different paths back to each other. Not every journey is the same. For me, the only way to deal with all that hurt, anger and resentment was to seek counselling. Talking things out, examining my life and some of the choices I had made, helped me come to terms with what had happened. David was supportive of the therapy, although when I suggested that we attend some sessions together, he balked at the idea. I'm not saying he didn't make an effort to mend things between us but his response was different from mine. I needed to talk it through, to pick over the past in order to understand what had happened. David's response was to buy a new kitchen. For a man who has made a career out of examining and understanding the past, his reluctance to plough through the history of our marriage to fix it was baffling to me. I'm not saying I didn't recognize the love underlying the renovation project. It was just another example of how, after twenty-odd years of being together, there are times when my husband still seems unknowable.

The crisis in our marriage happened quickly – a lightning

bolt – but resolved itself slowly, seeping away, like water finding a drain. I have learned that there are several steps – significant markers – along the path to reconciliation. The first time you have sex after the betrayal has been discovered (for us, it was four months later). The first time you share a joke, laughing together in a way that feels unencumbered by the wrangling and negotiations surrounding your decision to stay together. The first time he comes home from work and leans in to kiss you hello in a way that feels meaningful rather than dutiful. Slowly, the different elements of your life together are reasserted, carefully put back in place. At times it feels difficult, awkward, even fake, like you're just playing at being married to each other. At other times the pieces fit naturally into place, giving you hope.

When Zoë came into our lives, a year had passed since the affair. Even though we were well on our way to patching things up, the fissure in our marriage was still there. I wonder now, if that fault-line hadn't existed, would things have been different? If our marriage had been stronger, would we have been able to resist her?

Most of our friends don't know about the affair. Chris and Susannah were the only ones we told, but I'm sure others must have wondered, because for a whole year we slipped off the circuit. It was easier to avoid other people than to present a united front. We turned down invitations to dinner, to drinks, to the theatre, emailing apologies for not showing up at Christmas parties, fortieth birthdays, housewarmings. Neither did we issue any invitations of our own, which must have seemed unusual – before it happened, we regularly entertained at home. We used the house renovation as an excuse, but really it was because neither of us felt able to go through the choreographed dance of host and hostess when we were still, to an extent, tiptoeing around each other.

On that particular Friday evening – the Friday I'm remembering – it was the first time we had invited friends round since our marriage had unravelled. A significant marker in the knitting together of our relationship. I had invited Peter, my boss, an amiable man, and his wife, Anna, whom I didn't know very well. Chris and Susannah completed the party.

That evening the rain was coming down in sheets, streaking the windows, the umbrella stand in the hall filling as everyone arrived. David was late. The guests were in the sitting room and I was pouring drinks in the kitchen when he came in and stripped off his rain gear. 'Sorry, I got held up at work,' he told me, bundling his stuff into a sodden mass and coming towards me, kissing me hello. 'Sarah had her viva today, and the extern stayed on.'

'Have you been drinking?' I could smell the beer on his breath.

'A quick one in the common room.'

I snapped open a can of tonic and began pouring it into the gin.

'I had to take the man for a drink – out of courtesy, Caroline. He'd come over from England to do the viva as a favour.'

'I tried calling you.'

'Did you? I must have had the phone on silent.'

He moved past me to the sink, filled a glass with water and gulped it down.

'You forgot, didn't you?'

He put the empty glass on the draining-board. 'I'll run upstairs and change.'

For a Friday-evening supper, I had decided to go for something fairly casual – mussels in white wine to start, then lamb chops and a fennel salad with some crusty bread. A cheese board, and for dessert, toasted brioche with figs and pistachio ice-cream.

Throughout the meal the conversation pitched and rolled between various topics: the water charges, local politics, gossip about a shared acquaintance whose prurient misdeeds had recently made headlines. David, having recovered from his lateness – or perhaps in a bid to make amends – was lively and animated, steering the conversation, never allowing it to flag. Repartee sparked back and forth between him and Chris, with Peter joining in from time to time. It was, on the whole, a very male-dominated discourse. Anna seemed the type of person who was more interested in listening and agreeing, laughing in all the right places, rather than adding much by way of her own opinion. Susannah was unusually quiet. Chris is always the heart of the party – mocking, grandiose – and when things are good between them, Susannah is his perfect partner, taking his cues, matching his quips with barbs of her own, softened by the tongue-in-cheek manner of her delivery. They are the perfect dinner guests – funny, engaging, interesting. But that evening, from the tightness in Susannah's face, the way her eyes narrowed over her glass as she looked at him, I knew it wasn't going to be like that. At first it was just casual sniping, nothing major, but gradually over the course of the meal, as she emptied her glass, then emptied it again, she seemed to withdraw into a troubled silence.

After the coffee was finished, over whiskey and port, talk turned to a recent case where photographs of schoolgirls in Northern Ireland had ended up on a voyeuristic website regularly trawled by paedophiles. Anna's niece was one of the girls whose image had been stolen. 'It's shocking,' she told us. 'A fifteen-year-old girl, having her image abused in that manner.'

'What was the photo of,' Chris said, 'if you don't mind me asking?'

'Of nothing! Girls playing around, messing. It was innocent stuff.'

'Hmm.' Chris looked sceptical, and I saw a flare of colour appear at Anna's throat.

'Why? What are you saying?'

'Well,' he said, shrugging. 'Teenage girls messing around? It may seem innocent to you, but let's be completely honest here. A lot of girls have shed their innocence by the time they're fifteen. You see them hanging around in packs – they're well aware of their power –'

'Their power?'

'Yes! They understand inherently the power they wield over boys and men. What they possess – youthful bodies, burgeoning sexuality – it's highly potent. My God, you just have to look at how they're dressed to see they flaunt it. And why shouldn't they?'

'It's one thing for a girl to wear a mini-skirt on O'Connell Street,' Anna countered, 'but it's quite another for some pervert to steal her photograph and put it up on his grubby little website for all his friends to lech over.'

'Do you know what annoys me?' Chris said, leaning forward with a new intensity. 'It's these people who take photographs of themselves with their smartphones and post them on Facebook or whatever, send them to their friends, then whine when someone else views them.'

'Hang on a minute.' Anna sat up a little straighter.

'It's the same with these celebrities and their nude pics. For Christ's sake, who could be stupid enough to post those shots of themselves, and then be shocked when they enter the public realm?'

'It's hardly the same thing,' Peter said reasonably.

'No, just listen to me,' Chris continued, warming now to his subject. 'Caroline, does Holly have a smartphone?'

'Yes, but we monitor her use of it,' I hastened to add. 'She understands we can access her phone at any time, read her texts, her IMs, her Facebook posts, everything.'

'Okay. And does she ever use her phone to take pictures?'

'Of course, but they're very innocent. She's eleven, for God's sake! And she doesn't post them online – she's not allowed to put pictures up on any social networking sites.'

'Not now, maybe. But how long are you going to be able to police it?'

'For as long as we pay her phone bill,' David interjected, grinning and taking a slug of whiskey.

'What if she's staying at a friend's house?' Chris went on. 'That happens still, right?'

'Yes,' I agreed, cautiously, not liking where he was going with this.

'A sleepover with a group of girls. Giddiness sets in. The tone of the conversation changes. They start talking about boys they fancy. Someone gets out a smartphone. Pictures are taken. Someone – a girl whose parents aren't as vigilant – posts them on Facebook. And next thing you know, you've got a picture of your daughter in her nightie doing the rounds of the internet.'

'Christ,' David said, shaking his head.

'So what are you saying? That it's inevitable?' I asked.

He shrugged. 'Maybe it is.'

'My niece wasn't pictured in her nightie,' Anna added. 'I'd just like to make that clear.'

'I heard there was flesh shown in those pictures,' Chris countered.

'That doesn't mean they were having a pillow-fight in their underwear!'

'Now there's a thought,' Chris said, grinning and winking at Peter.

Peter stiffened. I looked at Chris and wondered how much he'd had to drink. It had been a few months since I'd seen him and there was a new fleshiness to him, shadows around his eyes that suggested ill health or unhappiness. He was a bit of a shambles, what with the weight he'd put on, the doughy pallor of his complexion. He had always possessed a kind of louche charm, relaxed good looks and a face enlivened by humour, but in the half-light thrown by the lamps and the candles, he looked washed-up, bedraggled, lost.

'I think you're making too much of this,' David told him, adopting a friendly, reasoned approach. 'The photos were probably of girls in their hockey gear, or something equally innocent. The fact is the trolls and sickos trawling those websites will corrupt even the most innocent image into something titillating, but it's a perversion in their own minds, nothing these girls are projecting.'

Chris laughed then, a honk of disbelief. 'Oh come on, Dave!' he said, slamming one hand on the table, still playful although a hardness had entered his voice, his eye. 'Can you hear yourself?'

'What?'

'You make it sound like they're all angels! You, of all people, should know about the scheming ways of teenage girls!'

David paused, just briefly, his glass halfway to his mouth. Then he laughed. 'What the hell is that supposed to mean?'

But something had entered that pause. A shiver of uncertainty. A cool doubt I had felt of late.

Chris was off now, explaining how David, as a university lecturer, must rub shoulders every day with teenage girls, harlots, as he described them, calling into his office, batting their eyelids at him in a bid to up their grades or be excused from a tutorial or whatever. Good-natured banter, I suppose, but most of it flew straight past me. I couldn't stop looking at David. The change was so subtle that only a wife would have noticed. The flush of colour in his cheeks from the drink had faded, most of the blood leaving his face. His lips had thinned slightly, and a new sharpness entered his eyes. He seemed wary, shaken even. I stared at him and it came to me then: my husband was keeping something from me.

How long did the moment last? The opening out of that realization within me, everything falling into place: his recent behaviour, the silences, the sudden snapping, the forgetfulness. I had put it down to the pressures of work, the consuming nature of his passion for history. Now I saw it was something else. I knew all the signs of concealment – we had been there before. I saw it and felt the heat of sudden anger flare within me. I wasn't afraid – not then. That would come later, when I knew her, when I felt the insidious creep of her presence through our lives. What I felt more than anything was shock.

I don't know what Chris said next – I missed it in the storm of my own private feeling – but whatever it was, it made Susannah snap.

'Oh, my God,' she said, the disgust in her voice hauling me out of my reverie. 'Do you even listen to yourself, Christopher? Have you any notion at all of how ridiculous you sound? How sad and creepy you come across?'

'It's called honesty, my dear,' he replied, his voice elevated and a hard smile on his face. 'Something you wouldn't recognize in your line of work.'

Susannah is a corporate lawyer, openly acknowledged as the real breadwinner of the two. Chris, who worked for a newspaper in a sub-editorial role that matched his whimsical nature, liked to refer to himself as a kept man, often joking how work for him was like a hobby. There were no such jokes that night.

Turning to Peter and Anna, who seemed increasingly uncomfortable, he explained: 'Oh, I know she looks like a woman, but Susannah is actually a shark.'

Susannah is striking, with strong dark features and a sharp angular haircut. On that occasion, her features appeared even more pronounced than usual, lipstick in a deep plum, her mouth a grim slash in her face. 'Listening to you talk of teenage girls in such a manner, you're just another drunken lech,' she said. 'God, when I hear you say these things, it makes me so fucking thankful we never had children.'

His eyes grew small. 'We never had children, Susannah, because I didn't want them. I knew any child I had with you might be born with a dorsal fin and several rows of teeth.'

There was a moment of silence, like a held breath, before Susannah stood up so suddenly her chair swung backwards and Peter had to grab it before it fell. Without saying a word, she left the room.

Chris broke the silence. 'Oops,' he said, and tried to laugh, but it came out as a gasp.

'Are you all right?' David asked.

Chris picked up the dessert spoon from his plate, turned it over, then put it back. In the hall, the front door slammed.

'One of us should go after her,' I said.

Looking at his plate, Chris said: 'Be my guest.'

The rain had stopped, water pooling in dips in the paving.

I could see Susannah striding down the street and shouted for her to stop, but she didn't slow and I had to run to catch up with her.

'Please come back,' I said, when I finally reached her.

She kept on walking, holding her coat closed with one hand, her handbag clenched in the other. There was something terrible in her balled-up anger, her refusal to speak until she reached the corner where our avenue meets the main road. 'I'm so sorry, Caro,' she said. 'We've ruined your evening, haven't we?'

Her eyes flicked past me to a taxi slowing as it neared and she stepped out on to the road with her hand held aloft.

'Please don't do this,' I said, but her mind was made up.

I watched the taxi drive away, saw the sharp silhouette of her haircut through the rear window, and knew that what had happened between them could not be undone.

Peter and Anna were at the front door when I returned, already in their coats, full of smiles and words of thanks for a lovely evening, then hastily departing. There was no sign of David. I watched them hurry away into the night, before closing the door on the darkness and returning to the kitchen. Chris had his head in his hands, David pouring him another whiskey.

'Chris is staying with us tonight,' he told me.

Normally, I am the one to offer comfort, to know the right words to say. 'I'll go and make up his room,' I said.

As I closed the door, I saw them clink glasses, solemnity in the gesture rather than any measure of cheer. At the same time, I felt my jaw tighten.

An idea had got its claws into me: that David might be having an affair. A dalliance with a colleague or some post-doctoral student. Some silly girl looking for excitement with an older man, the thoughtless facilitator of his midlife crisis.

We might have been able to weather the storm of such a crisis, but what was to come – the slow erosion caused by her destructive presence – proved far worse, a dark cavity that would open up and suck each one of us in.

# 6. David

'Who is Zoë?'

I turned and saw Caroline staring at me.

I had been rinsing the wine glasses from the night before, dog-tired and hung-over. Chris had just left. Her words startled me out of a daydream – a memory of Linda wearing a shirt of mine, her feet bare on the hard tiles of that kitchen floor in our Donegal cottage all those years before. Those same feet, the night before, had pressed into the small of my back, the soft curve of her heels. We'd had so little time left. I'd traced a finger over her temple, along the sloping curve of her cheek, and told her it was all going to be okay. I drew her close enough to feel her body against mine, caught in the green haze of her stare. I kissed her, the tenderness of her lips against mine. A sense of certainty had come over me – the sure knowledge that we were safe, that no harm could come to us. I had been twenty-four, my whole life ahead of me.

'David?' Caroline said. In her hand was a piece of paper, and she held it up to me. 'I found this in your wallet.'

It was the note Zoë had slipped beneath my office door, the one asking me to meet her in Madigans.

'Why were you looking in my wallet?'

'It fell out. I was doing the laundry.'

I put the tea-towel, which had been slung across my

shoulder, on to the draining-board and took a deep breath. 'Close the door,' I said. 'We need to talk.'

Caroline looked both confused and upset. She shut the door, and the chatter from the television in the next room became an indistinct hum. I gazed out into the garden where everything, for a moment, appeared to be moving in slow motion – the russet leaves falling from the trees, and above them a dense body of clouds rippling by in waves. In the distance, there was the dull sound of a car starting.

'Do you remember me telling you about Linda Barry?'

Caroline seemed to steel herself. 'Yes, I do.'

'Zoë is her daughter.'

'Her daughter?' she repeated.

I pulled at my earlobe. 'She's also one of my students. She came to see me because she thinks I'm her father.'

Caroline put the note on the table, but she kept her eyes on me. 'She said that?'

'She said she was pretty sure because her mother had told her who I was, and she had her birth certificate with her.'

Caroline pulled out a chair and sat at the table. 'A birth certificate?' she said.

Her resolute calm and steady nerve disarmed me. It would not have been unreasonable for her to raise her voice, to display some outrage. Instead there was a steely, implacable propriety. I should not have been surprised. Caroline had always demonstrated a degree of strength and inner resolve.

'It didn't actually name me as father . . .'

'Then how can you be sure she's your daughter?'

'I can't, not categorically. But there was a resemblance

to Linda, I suppose, and the dates match up. She had some photographs . . .'

'Photographs?'

'Of myself and Linda.'

Caroline looked about her as if to reassure herself, to check that she was where she thought she was – that the kitchen, with its stereo on the counter, the glass fruit bowl, the children's assorted books and computer games, the black-and-white framed pictures of us as a family on the far wall, were all there. I thought for a moment she might reach out and touch something – the need in her appeared so real.

'And where is Linda now?' she asked evenly.

'She's dead,' I said, and it sounded like a vindication, though I hadn't meant it to.

Caroline's eyes widened. 'Dead?'

I took the chair opposite her and went on to tell her what I knew of Linda's passing.

She reached for a napkin from the holder on the table. 'When did this happen? When did the girl tell you?' she asked.

'I found out at the start of the week.'

'The start of the week? Why didn't you say something?' Caroline said, a little more worked up, annoyed now. 'Why did you wait to tell me?'

'To be honest, I needed more time.'

'More time?'

'It was a shock to have her walk into my office and make that claim. I needed time to think it through before telling you.' I remained calm, pragmatic. 'I wasn't trying to keep it from you.'

'You should have told me straight away,' Caroline said.

'I wanted to get things clear in my head.'

'And are they?'

I hesitated. In my head there was an image of the whitewash of water whipped up by the wind on the beach in Holywood, breaking relentlessly, wave after wave, against the shore, where Linda and I stood hand in hand.

'I don't know,' I said in answer. 'The girl makes a convincing case . . .' I meant Zoë, but I was thinking of how Linda and I had tripped down Botanic Avenue on those evenings on our way to the pub or a poetry reading at Oxfam.

'But we need to be sure,' Caroline said. 'We need to know for certain whether she is your daughter or not.'

'I know,' I said. 'I've thought about it and there are several ways of finding out.'

'What? Like a paternity test?' she asked, with a grim laugh.

'Why not?' I answered, reaching out to her to try to reassure her, but her hand remained motionless.

'All these years . . .' she said.

I wanted to say what a relief it was to tell her, but I didn't. Something stopped me – the strange mix of emotions I was feeling, at once frightening and painful.

'You never suspected?' Caroline said.

'No . . . never.' As I watched for her reaction, I noticed something else, something within me, a disbelief at my own words because, to put it quite simply, they were not true. *I had suspected.* But it was a buried, unconscious suspicion. You see, ever since that weekend in Donegal, the seed of possibility had stayed with me. Had we been careful? Linda had asked me back then. Careful: up until then, we had always been careful. In fact, care was what had defined our relationship. We'd had to be both careful and circumspect. Nobody knew we were there in Donegal. Nobody knew we were together. Nobody knew we were even lovers. She was my student, after all.

'It's hard to believe . . .' Caroline said, bringing me back to the present. 'What will you do if it's true? What will we do if she really is your daughter?'

'If she is, she is. It doesn't have to change everything. It doesn't have to disrupt the lives we have. We'll adjust, get to know her, try to make room for her in our family.'

'As simply as that?'

I said: 'Why not?'

'Have you thought how this might affect Robbie and Holly if it's true?' she said. 'If they find out that they have a half-sister?'

I had thought about it. I was worried about how they might react. There had been enough disruption in their lives, and God knew I didn't want to see them hurt. But I really did think we could make it work.

'We'll manage, but first let's get through this next step.'

Caroline considered what I had said, and asked: 'What's she like?'

'She's young . . . bright, a little shy. She has all the gaucheness of a teenager and at the same time enough nerve to walk into my office and introduce herself as my daughter . . . Whether it ends up being true or not, I have to take it seriously.'

Caroline listened, concentrating on what I had said,

trying to process it all. 'The DNA test,' she said. 'That's what you mean by "paternity test", right?'

'Yes.'

'How are you going to do it?'

I thought about how I had met Zoë in the pub, how my hand had found the loose strands of hair on her coat and clutched at them. 'A hair follicle.'

'Just like that?'

'I've done it.'

'You've done it?'

'Zoë doesn't know. I took some strands of hair from her coat.'

'You're kidding me?'

'No.'

'But that's not ethical.'

'I suppose not. I thought it was the best thing to do at the time,' I said, my voice wavering.

'But, David, that's dishonest – it's underhand,' she said, appealing to my reason.

'And you're an expert on honesty now?' I snapped. Caroline was more disappointed than hurt. I apologized, but the awkwardness was back, as well as another worry, another fear I couldn't name as yet.

'Would it not be better to be upfront with Zoë and say to her that this has been a shock and would she mind if we had a professional check it out, just to be sure?'

'I know as a first measure it's not ideal,' I said. 'But I've thought about it, Caroline. The assertion Zoë is making, it could be a complete fiction. We need to know if she's telling the truth.'

'So when did this take place?' She gestured to the note discarded on the table – *6.30 in Madigans.*

'Yesterday. I met her at the pub before the dinner party.'

'You told me you were taking a visiting professor out for a drink.'

'Well, I didn't. I met Zoë.'

'Why didn't tell you me? Why did you have to lie?'

'We had guests in the next room, Caroline. Do you really think that was the time for me to bring this up with you?'

Her fingers tapped the table. 'And you're not going to tell her about the test?'

'I'm not, no.'

'I see. I just wish you'd come to me earlier,' she said. 'Your whole plan . . . it makes me uneasy.'

I said nothing. What was the point? I had no plan, but the wheels of whatever it was had been set in motion. Caroline held her hands to her face. She was deep in thought – weighing everything up. I stood up and looked back to the sink, the wine glasses refracting the morning light. I thought of that morning in Donegal and, just like that, she was there, a ghostly presence in the background, my old flame, Linda. And when I missed her, when I wondered what might have been, when I had been with someone else, or when I was with my wife, she still seemed to be there, in the shadows, and – it happened more than once – when I made love to someone else, I felt in some strange way as if I were still making love to her.

'Send the test off,' Caroline said. 'Get the preliminary results. But promise me you won't seek the girl out or spend any time with her that you don't need to. Not until we know for sure.'

'I promise,' I said.

The radio was playing in the background: a listener was complaining about the impending water charges. Another demonstration was being planned in town, he added, and as he did so, it occurred to me that within this house, within the confines of what we called our home, a real and indelible crisis was going on, which would disrupt our family unit irrevocably, but outside, beyond the boundaries of our home, life carried on – people were up in arms about water charges, about employment, about governance and corruption, but the very same people were going about their daily business. Life carried on – no matter what.

'What are you two talking about?' Holly said, standing in the doorway with her coat on. I don't know how long she had been standing there or how much she had heard.

'I'll be with you in two minutes,' Caroline said, and Holly went back to the living room. 'No contact with the girl,' she said to me. 'Not until we find out more.'

'Agreed,' I said.

She stood up stiffly, as if the truce she had made with me was unsatisfactory, but one she had to accept whether she liked it or not.

Without looking at me again, she called to Holly, 'Come on, love. Time to go.'

Holly kissed my cheek before she left and, it occurred to me only then that I had made a promise to Caroline that there was no way I could keep.

# 7. Caroline

My husband is not a vengeful man. Yet that Saturday morning when he told me about this daughter, about Zoë, as I sat and listened to him talking of DNA tests and establishing parentage, one distinct notion kept rising to the surface: this was David's way of getting his own back.

It was all so unsettling, so worrying. Who was this girl? What did she want from us? I had no way of knowing how it would impact on our lives. No idea to what extent she would want to become involved with our family. Would she expect to be treated in the same way as David treated Robbie and Holly? Would she expect us to provide for her? Pay her college tuition? Her rent?

I said nothing of this to Holly as we drove west of the city. Instead I allowed her to chatter on as she switched from one radio station to another, a happy buzz of excitement coming off her at the prospect of our shopping trip to Ikea. Since turning eleven, she had developed a pressing desire to assert her own taste and I had promised to buy new furniture for her bedroom. It was late morning by the time we had finished pushing through the showrooms and I was downstairs in the warehouse, a little weary and looking forward to coffee and a scone, when it happened.

Holly had returned to the bed-linen department, having

changed her mind about the pattern she had chosen, so I was alone in the aisle, scanning the stacks of brown boxes for the one I wanted. Having found it at last, I pulled it out and hoisted it on to my trolley. I was just straightening up when a woman came towards me and slammed her trolley into mine. Instinctively, I gripped the handle and looked up at her. Her eyes bright with fury, she was staring at me. Before I could say anything, she slammed her trolley into mine a second time and I let out a cry. The force of the impact caused some of her items to clatter on to the concrete floor. I didn't move, the suddenness of the aggression, the sharp focus of it, shocking me into inaction. She was a woman of my own age wearing jeans and a grey turtle-neck, dark hair drawn back into a ponytail. I had seen her occasionally at the school gates before the time of my indiscretion, but not since. Now she was fixing me with an expression of venom as if she wanted to slam me with her trolley, to push me back against the shelves stacked high with boxed furniture and watch as it all came crashing down on my head. There was something electric about it, the snap of current passing between us. It lasted no more than a minute. Then she drew back from me and turned, half walking, half running, struggling with the heavy trolley as she rounded the corner. The items that had slipped from her cart – a set of mixing bowls and some magazine files – remained on the floor where they had fallen.

Shaken by the encounter, I glanced around to see if anyone else had witnessed this strange assault, and there was Holly. She was holding a different set of bed-linen under her arm. She came towards me, and – this is the part that really kills me – she put the package on top of the boxes and, without looking at me, without uttering a word about what she had just witnessed, she said, in a small, flat voice, 'I think that's everything.' Then she walked towards the checkouts.

Holly has always been the more resilient of my two children, even though she's the younger. She lacks the sensitivity of her older brother, which has worried me from his infancy. I suppose because she is the baby of the family I sometimes underestimate her strength of mind, her astuteness. But every now and then she surprises me with her maturity. Did she know somehow what I had done? Who this woman was?

'Holly,' I said in the car. 'About what happened back there –'

'Please, Mum,' she interrupted. 'I don't want to talk about it.'

Throughout the journey home we were silent, but I kept thinking of her reaction – the coolness of it. Was it possible she knew? It made me wonder at how much she had been exposed to, my daughter with her steady gaze, her father's cool demeanour. The guilt was stirring within me again. It was never far away.

More than a year before Zoë came into our lives, I became involved with a man whose son went to school with Robbie. The word 'affair' seems wrong – a false name for what occurred between us. I don't think you can properly call it an affair if there was never full-on sex, can you? A fling, perhaps, although that makes it sound so throwaway, as if I'm the type of woman who whimsically forgets her marriage vows whenever the fancy takes her. I'm not that type of person. His name was Aidan – *is* Aidan, for he hasn't died, he's just not in my life any more; we met through the Parents' Committee. This 'fling', for want of a better word, lasted three, maybe four months. It wasn't love, never that. When it ended, Aidan and his wife took their son out of Robbie's school and the family moved to a different part of Dublin. David and I made the decision to keep Robbie where he was. In hindsight, I think it was a mistake.

I thought David had forgiven me but, in the aftermath of his revelation, I began to suspect he had actually been biding his time, waiting for the right moment, the right opportunity to present itself. Revenge had come in a way I had never imagined: in the form of a teenage girl.

I didn't say it to him. How could I? There was a time when I could have spoken my mind to David about anything. I never used to be afraid of confrontation. But something had happened in the aftermath of my indiscretion – a change in the dynamic between us. It was true that he had taken me back without punishment or reproach. But ours was no longer a relaxed home. An undercurrent of tension ran through everything. Even though we never told the children what had happened, what I had done, it was impossible to shield them from the atmosphere that developed between us. They regarded me with cautious eyes as if anxious I might plunge them back into a time of uncertainty. David acted with the same calm exterior, the same cool-headed thinking I had known of him. We carried on. We got through it. But I had lost some of my power. It had slipped away, relinquished because of the debt I owed him for his forgiveness.

On that Saturday morning, we made an agreement, David and I. We would put the matter of Zoë to one side until we had definitive proof. For the two weeks it took to decode the strands of DNA, identify a pattern, an affinity between David's genes and Zoë's – or none – we would try to live our lives as best we could. Everything would continue as before – work, the children, the house, our relationships. Just for those two weeks.

Easier said than done.

For the first week there was a buzz in my brain, a low-grade headache. I put it down to poor sleep. I tried to kill it with paracetamol so I could focus on my job but still it persisted. Going back to work for a company I had once been a part of was not the triumphant return I had secretly hoped it would be. It was disconcerting how far things had moved on in the past fifteen years, making the landscape almost entirely unrecognizable to me. I willed myself to become absorbed in the challenge, however difficult I found it. All the while, in the back of my head, there was this hum: *Zoë*.

I don't think I even recognized her as a person then. Instead I saw her as a problem I didn't know how to solve. Work allowed me to drown out the hum in my brain. It was in the evenings, after dinner, the kids occupied with homework or friends or TV, when David and I were alone together, that the sound was amplified.

'What does she look like?' I asked him.

It was night, and we were lying awake in the dark. Somewhere down our street, a car alarm was going off.

His gaze moved from the window to the ceiling, and I felt him smoothing the duvet around him. 'Much like any other first-year student,' he said, his voice flat.

'Come on, David. They can't all look the same. She must have some distinguishing features.'

'Her hair,' he said then, and I found myself grow tense. 'She has this shock of blonde hair. Long springy curls – almost white, it's so blonde.'

'She doesn't sound like you.'

'Linda's hair.'

Linda. Her name spoken in the darkness of our bedroom. I thought of her, all those years ago, and imagined David running his hands over those blonde curls, knitting his fingers up in them, marvelling at them, loving them. I had conjured up the image and now wished I hadn't.

'And boots,' he said then.

'Boots?'

'She wears these boots – military-looking. Doc Martens, I suppose. Oxblood in colour. They look enormous at the end of her skinny legs. She's such a little slip of a thing. Shy.'

The way he said it, I couldn't help thinking he felt affection towards her.

He lay there for a moment, staring into the dark. Outside, the car alarm had stopped, and silence came into the room, like a sudden intrusion. He turned over, flattening himself in preparation for sleep.

But I didn't sleep. It was as though each of us – in separate and distinct ways – had been plunged back into the past. Fragments of old memories were coming back at unexpected moments. I wondered, as David's breathing slowed, if his last waking thoughts that night were of Linda. As for me, I found myself going back further to another time, another meeting. A decision made. The weight of its seriousness pressing on my young shoulders. *You don't have to come with me*, I had told him. *I can go on my own.* Trying to sound brave while inside I was dying. Did he remember that conversation, my sleeping husband? Was any of this coming back to him, too? Old ghosts awoken, stirred angrily into life by this new girl, like a wasp's nest struck with a stick.

It was a flare in my brain – her golden hair. Everywhere I looked there were girls with blonde hair, hanging loose down backs and over shoulders, swinging in ponytails, with flicked fringes. I found myself staring at teenage girls, calculating their age, anxiously assessing their likeness to David, to Holly. She could have been any one of them.

I didn't intend to seek her out. But one morning when I was driving along Morehampton Road, running an errand for Peter, it occurred to me that if I kept on driving I would reach the UCD campus.

I rang the History Department office while driving, saying my niece was a first-year student of history; she had been visiting me last night but had left her phone in my house. I had no way of getting in touch with her, I said, and wanted to drop it into the university.

All I wanted was to get a look at her. I had no intention of approaching her. First-years had American History in Theatre J that morning, I was told. All I needed was to see her. Once I had done so, my fear would subside, or if not my fear, at least my curiosity.

The possibility of bumping into David, going from his office to a lecture, had crossed my mind. If I saw him, I would make something up. Part of me wondered what his reaction would be. Students were already streaming out of lecture theatres as I ran up the steps and into the Arts building, the corridors and foyers becoming momentarily clotted with them. When I got to Theatre J and looked around at the empty seats, the vacant space awaiting the next influx, I felt a small stab of disappointment.

*What are you doing?* I asked myself. *Foolish woman.*

Outside the lecture hall, students were drifting sluggishly along, like hung-over cows. I felt conspicuous among them, dressed in a black trouser suit and kitten heels, my shoulder-length brown hair flicked out at the ends. I didn't look like a lecturer, let alone a student. To them, I probably looked like an accountant or a management consultant on campus to give a presentation. I would call on David. Surprise him. Make a serious attempt to bridge the gap we both knew had opened between us since his revelation. Pushing myself away from the wall, I looked towards the stairwell, and it was in the act of turning that I saw her.

Blonde hair, just as he had said, luminous under the fluorescent strip-lighting. Her face small and pale. A skinny girl, and not very tall, but she held herself well, shoulders thrown back, a long, straight neck, her bag slung over one shoulder – a casual, relaxed pose. And the boots he had mentioned lent something firm and inflexible to her otherwise waif-like appearance.

She was standing by a marble and limestone sculpture known to generations of students as the Blob. I had wanted to catch a glimpse of her, nothing more. Well, I had done that, yet still I lingered. She didn't look remotely like either of my children. The lightness of her hair, the milky-whiteness of her skin were at odds with the darker colouring that unified the four of us. I looked her over and felt doubt trickling in.

She broke away from her friend and walked through the thinning crowd of students towards the exit. I watched her narrow back, her skinny legs, the careful manner of her walk – no slouching or dragging feet with this one. Reason told me to let her go, but impulse led me to follow her, and soon enough I was outside again, feeling the chill of the air, following her up the paved walkway towards the pond by the Engineering building. All the time, I was trying to keep my distance, trying to walk as if I had a purpose other than stalking her.

She took a seat on an empty bench on the deck around the pond. As I neared, the sound of my heels rang out and I slowed my step. She was sitting with her eyes closed, her head tilted to the sky, soaking up what little heat there was. Her pose was perfectly still, like a cat basking in the sun. I stopped, looked down at her, and slowly she opened her eyes. Green eyes, a little widely spaced, short dense lashes. They looked up at me in an assessing way, but she didn't say anything.

'You're Zoë,' I said.

'Do I know you?'

Still so composed, so unfazed. A Northern flavour to her voice.

'I'm Caroline,' I said. 'David's wife.'

Her face cleared in recognition, eyes narrowing a fraction, then a slight flicker as she took me in, her interest piqued. She smiled, a slow, lazy smile and, it seemed to me, a little sly. 'So he told you.'

A bristle of anger went through me. Of course he told me, I wanted to say. I'm his bloody wife. 'Do you mind if I sit?'

'Sure.'

The bench felt cold against the backs of my legs. My gaze followed the curling path of a moorhen, gliding through the reeds. That pond hadn't been there when I was a student. I could feel Zoë looking at me with that little smirk.

'You thought you'd come here and give me the once-over for yourself,' she said.

A statement, not a question, and I could see how it was going to be between us. She had no notion of treading softly with me. Whatever charm she had reserved for David, it was clearly not going to be employed here.

'You can't blame me for being curious,' I replied.

'True.'

She turned her face to the sun, her shoulders thrown back, and closed her eyes again. I examined the planes of her face, looking for some trace of David, but there was nothing. She was completely unfamiliar to me. David's words ran through my head: *A little slip of a thing. Shy.* Was that really how he saw her? Some vulnerable waif? The unfazed stillness of her pose made her seem so sure of herself, so self-contained, nerveless, where I was rigid and tense.

'What made you decide to seek him out now?'

'I don't know. I was always going to get in touch, wasn't I?'

'Why now, though? Why not before?'

'Now, before, later – what difference does it make?' She shrugged, then added: 'I'm here in the college, after all. It seemed stupid to avoid it any longer.'

'It's come as a shock,' I said, 'for David and for me.'

'Hmm.'

She said this in a ruminative, matter-of-fact way that infuriated me. There was no hint of her taking this seriously – it was all a game to her.

'I suppose I wanted to meet you so I could find out what your position is.'

'My position!' She laughed thinly, sounding insubstantial, lacking in conviction, although when she spoke, the words were sharp and precise.

'Yes, your position. I wanted to see where you stood on this.'

'You make me sound like a politician.'

'Well . . .' My voice faded. The truth was I didn't know what I wanted from her. Except, perhaps, for her to turn around and say it had all been a stupid joke: none of it was true. When I had made the decision to sit down next to her, I still thought if I just spoke to her – confronted her, I suppose – she would crumble, break down. There would be tears and an admission to a foolish spoof, some desperate grab for attention. But looking at this cat preening herself under the sun, I was the one close to breakdown.

'Does David know you're here with me?'

I looked at her sharply. 'Yes,' I said, the lie coming quickly to my mouth.

It was instinctive, the need to align myself with my husband in the girl's eyes. Something told me that if she knew the truth she could use it as ammunition.

'I see.'

'He's my husband,' I said. 'I don't want him to get hurt.'

She flicked back her hair, opened her eyes, leaned forward to pick up her bag and got to her feet. Standing in front of me, she blocked the low-lying sun, her face in shadow, but I could see her gazing down on me with those cold eyes. Without a word, she swung her bag over her shoulder, and turned away.

'My position,' I heard her say again, amusement in her voice.

Her laughter rang out as she walked back towards the Arts building, and it stayed with me – the mocking ring of it. Sitting on the bench, I felt a shiver of nerves cross my shoulders. All those years I'd spent thinking about Linda, wondering what she might have been like, trying to imagine her, now I felt as if I had finally met her. And I didn't like her. She unnerved me.

I told myself I was being ridiculous. Zoë was just a girl. A teenager. There had been no ghostly visitation. And yet I felt shaken by the meeting – unsettled.

Within my line of vision there was a bronze statue of two people reaching, leaping upwards with arms outstretched, limbs entwined – a man and a woman – lean, youthful, athletic, their fingers splayed as if trying to catch the sun. I looked across at that piece of art in the wake of Zoë's departure, and read within it energy, vitality, joy. It reverberated with optimism and boundless possibility which made me feel a little sad because I couldn't feel any of those things, not then. That day, staring at the bronzed figures in the coolness of the October sunshine, I felt hollowed out, as if something had just been taken from me. She was a thief, come to steal from me all that I loved. I knew it then: I would have to guard myself against her.

I wished I hadn't met her. I had taken the measure of her and didn't like what I'd found. I wanted it undone.

When David got home from work that evening and I heard him in the hall, I stirred the spaghetti in the pot and felt a tightening beneath my ribs. From upstairs came the sounds of Robbie practising his cello, a long drawn-out note, like a plea. David found me in the kitchen and asked: 'Any news?'

I could have told him then. Instead I lifted my face to receive his kiss, smiling right back at him. 'No. Not a thing.'

# 8. David

By my calculations, the results were due to arrive any day, and so it was that I found myself hurrying to campus the next mid-semester morning, my lungs filling with the heavy autumn air, a mixture of dread and excitement running through me.

As I free-wheeled past the water tower, and the sports centre, I saw the stirrings of a student demonstration. I cycled past it, locked my bike, walked up the steps to the Arts building and went to my office. I turned on my computer and scanned my inbox. A slew of emails confronted me, including a number of questions from Administration, Admissions and the student council. After I had responded as efficiently as possible, but before I had tackled my teaching preparation, I went to the common room for coffee. I needed the jolt. Alan was there with another colleague of ours, John McCormack, the two of them sitting in the corner, sipping tea and chatting.

'Good morning, gentlemen,' I said. 'Setting the world to rights?'

'What else?' McCormack said.

He was four or five years younger than me: prolific, brilliant, with an international profile to envy. In history circles his books on the belle époque and the poets of the Russian Revolution were considered sexy, if anything in history can be considered such. Rather than academic publishers, he had commercial publishing deals. He had an agent, and his books were shortlisted for prizes where they competed with other non-historical titles. As a historian, he was a rising star, as another colleague put it.

'Join us,' Alan said, and I sat. 'John was just telling me about the conference at Birkbeck later this month.'

'Will you make it?' McCormack asked.

I told them I hadn't planned on it this year. McCormack mentioned some of the presenters at the conference and how it was going to be a very full, but fulfilling weekend. In many ways, McCormack was everything I was not – we were both ambitious, but in different ways: he blazed trails where I dug ditches. I liked the dirty work, so to speak, and my pedagogic focus was, to the best of my abilities, student-focused; I don't know how important McCormack considered the students in his overall plan – teaching, to him, was a necessary evil, something he was obliged to do so that he could do what he really wanted, which was to write those critically acclaimed books. I had been asked the previous year to take on some of his teaching so that he had more time to focus on his research. I didn't mind. Neither did I begrudge McCormack his success – but I will admit to wondering about his professional integrity.

Those were the kind of things I worried about at the time.

We talked more about the conference before Alan stood up. 'I'm afraid I have a meeting. Duty calls,' he said, and bade us farewell.

McCormack brought up the dean's suggestion for a

week-long festival of teaching and learning. 'For whose benefit?' he wanted to know.

'Our students could get a lot out of it,' I said, but McCormack detailed how he thought it could end up only as more work for us, thereby swamping us in greater administrative duties.

'By the way,' he said, in a confidential whisper, 'I thought you might prefer it to come from someone you know rather than anyone else, but a colleague told me she saw you having a drink with one of the students. She did say it looked like a *compromisingly intimate encounter*.'

'Who saw me?'

'It's not important who saw you, David, it's that you were seen.'

I lowered my voice. 'It's not what you think.'

'It doesn't matter what I think.'

'She only wanted some advice.'

He smiled as if to say: That's what your office is for, not the pub. 'I suppose one needs to be careful these days,' he said.

I felt my temper simmering.

'It's best I told you. You know these things can spread if allowed to . . . escalate.' He stood up and tapped his newspaper on the table. 'I'd better go.'

I tried not to let what McCormack had said bother me, but as I got up and left the common room without the coffee I had come in for, I wondered which colleague had seen me and Zoë. Did people have to worry about this kind of thing in other jobs? The thought made me ponder my life in academia: how might I have fared in what people call the real world? I used to balk at the description of the university as an ivory tower. The older I got, though, the more I wondered. I once heard a visiting poet say hello to Alan as we met in one of the warren-like corridors in the Arts building. 'You're still here?' the poet said to Alan warmly.

'Me? I'm a *lifer*,' he replied, with a broad smile directed at me as if to say, And so are you.

The thought of being institutionalized, even by a university, genuinely frightened me. It seemed to me that I spent more and more time in meetings rather than researching my own books or, God forbid, teaching the students.

When I got to my postbox, I was glad to see it was there – a discreet letter, unassuming, aside from 'PRIVATE AND CONFIDENTIAL' printed on the envelope, which was nestled next to the UCD magazine and other anonymous-looking material. I swept up the lot, lodging the letter in my jacket pocket, and walked back towards my office, a shot of panic pulsing through my veins. I hurried along, imagining the possible content of the letter, playing a variety of scenarios in my head. As I pushed through the swinging doors and around the corner on the second floor, there she was, waiting for me, leaning against the wall, the cords of her pink earphones trailing over her shoulders and into the phone she was holding, one foot tapping to whatever she was listening to.

'Hello,' she said too loudly, struggling to remove the earphones. 'I wanted to ask you about the essay.'

'Of course,' I said, unlocking my office door. She followed me inside, and I asked her to sit. As she put her bag down and took a seat, it became apparent to me that

Linda was her mother. They were so alike – the hair, the eyes. I thought of the letter with the DNA results in my jacket pocket and felt a pang of regret, as if having the test done were an act of betrayal to Linda and the love we had once shared. Linda had clearly believed I was the father, so why should I doubt her?

'What in particular did you want to discuss?'

'I'm sorry, but I didn't submit it in time. The essay.'

'Oh,' I said, a little annoyed. 'Why not?'

'I wasn't feeling well,' she answered shyly. 'And then the book I needed wasn't in the library. It wasn't on the shelves and it hadn't been checked out. The staff had to put a search on it,' she ended, rather hopelessly.

'You should have come to me before the deadline.'

'But I was ill . . .'

'Too ill to pick up the phone?'

She started to justify her non-submission, but I stopped her. 'It doesn't matter what you did or didn't do. I'm telling you what you should have done.'

She looked at the floor. I had upset her by being too brusque. I felt bad, tried a softer tack: 'There are procedures. A form to fill out for mitigating circumstances.'

'Mitigating circumstances?'

'This is far from ideal, but we'll try to come up with a solution.'

My peace-offering was met with a timid shake of the head. Something of me within it, a hint or trace of who I was, my parentage, my lineage. I feared she was on the brink of tears. 'It's not the end of the world,' I said.

'It's just that I found it so hard to concentrate.'

'These things happen. You mustn't take it to heart.'

She looked so crestfallen, so fragile, that I wondered if something else was going on. 'Is anything else wrong?' I asked.

'It's just . . . It's nothing.'

'Zoë,' I said, as reassuringly as possible. If she needed to confide in me, I wanted her to feel comfortable enough to do that. 'You can tell me.'

'It's Caroline,' she said.

'Caroline? My wife?'

'She came looking for me . . .'

'What are you talking about?'

'On campus . . .'

'Caroline was on campus? But when?' I asked.

'On Tuesday. She said you knew.'

I closed my eyes, rubbed them with my thumb and forefinger, and steadied myself.

'You didn't know?' she asked innocently.

'No,' I admitted. Caroline had never said anything to me about coming to campus. But why wouldn't she? We had seen each other every day – it's not like we were ships in the night. What had she to hide?

I have to be careful, I thought. I didn't know this girl at all, couldn't be sure whether she was telling the truth about Caroline, or about anything else, for that matter. There was still the possibility that what she was saying was part of some elaborate mischief.

'Oh,' Zoë said, still upset.

I needed to calm her. I definitely did not want her leaving my office angry and upset, especially after McCormack's comment. I couldn't afford to have people talking. 'It's been very busy at home,' I said. I thought about

Robbie's cello vibrating through the house, Holly's studious introversion – the busy activity of family life. 'Perhaps it slipped Caroline's mind.'

'Perhaps,' Zoë said, a little forlornly.

Outside, the sound of a drill rose and fell in intensity. Its bright hum seemed to fill the room. I wasn't sure yet about who Zoë really was. I might have been talking to my daughter or to a perfect stranger, but right then, I didn't know, which made me circumspect and hesitant. I thought about the sample of hair I had sent off to the DNA lab without her knowledge and, of course, the letter in my pocket. 'I don't understand why she would have felt the need to come here to talk to you,' I said, betraying my confusion.

'Maybe she was trying to warn me.'

'Warn you?'

'I was sitting on a bench by the pond outside the Engineering building and she just came up to me. At first, I didn't even know who she was. It freaked me out, the way she confronted me.'

'Confronted you?'

I could tell she was trying to remain calm in her account, but still her voice trembled. I wasn't sure whether I should apologize or question the veracity of her claim. Either way, I was dumbfounded by the idea of Caroline acting surreptitiously behind my back, sneaking about campus without my knowing. I thought about the conversation I would have with her later. Losing my temper wouldn't achieve anything, but I had to let her know that her behaviour was unacceptable. If she wanted to meet Zoë, she should have asked me: that would have been the mature and responsible thing to do.

'It's just that I thought I had done everything . . . correctly,' Zoë said. 'I thought I had approached the matter in the right way.'

'Did she tell you why she wanted to speak to you?'

'She asked what I wanted, and how long I was going to chase after you, and when I would leave you alone. And had I thought about the effect I had exerted on your other children, and on her.'

'Jesus.'

'And she wanted to know if I'd considered the consequences of my actions and what I was going to demand.'

'Demand?'

'Those were her words. I don't want anything, David. I'm not demanding anything. I never wanted to upset anyone, you or your wife, or your two children.' She spoke clearly and calmly, but I could tell it was an effort for her. 'She said she had come with your express agreement and . . .'

'And what, Zoë?'

'And didn't want to see you hurt . . . as if I . . . as if I . . .'

The tears came. I was torn between sympathy and suspicion. Here we were again, thrown together – not in the crush of a pub but alone and, more worryingly, in my office.

'I know you don't want to hurt me,' I said.

There was a swift and sudden knock. I looked up and noticed, too late, that I had accidentally closed the door shut behind us; in so doing, I had broken one of the cardinal rules. McCormack's face appeared around the door.

'Sorry, I can see you're busy,' he said, gazing at Zoë and

raising an eyebrow in surprise. 'Perhaps you can ring me when you get a chance. Nothing urgent . . . A departmental matter, that's all.'

He smiled, and left the door pointedly ajar. Zoë wiped her tears, blew her nose and picked up her bag. 'I should go,' she said. 'I'm sorry to have sprung this on you. It didn't occur to me that you might not have known.'

She walked out, and I was left again with the uncomfortable sense of being on the receiving end of another awkward revelation, something to remind me yet again of how life could be so unpredictable and perplexing.

This time, I didn't run after her. Instead I went to pick up the phone to ring McCormack, but stopped. He could wait. I pulled the envelope out of my jacket and cut it open with a paperknife, which was lying on the corner of my desk. I scanned the document and found the results printed in bold capitals at the bottom of the page. My heart sank. It was the worst possible outcome. Neither one thing nor the other. It didn't tell me whether I was or was not Zoë's father. Above a blizzard of qualifiers and small print, the word 'INCONCLUSIVE' glared back at me.

Another test would be necessary, the report said. That, and a ream of information on why the results had come back as they had. The strand of hair had not been enough for definitive confirmation.

What to do now?

I folded the report, put it back into the envelope and stuck it in my desk. Already, I was thinking about what I would tell Caroline when she asked. I would not show her the actual report. That was one thing I had decided quite quickly. I could tell her it had been delayed. Or, and this was how I discovered that one deception breeds another, I could tell her what she didn't want to hear, but what I suspected by then to be the truth: that, whether she liked it or not, Zoë was my daughter. Even if my latest deceit felt like kind of a punishment to Caroline, well, I thought fleetingly, after her intimidation of Zoë, after her affair with Aidan, maybe she deserved it.

# 9. Caroline

Take the time back, and I wouldn't approach her again. Had I known the heart beating in her chest was cold, I would have left her sitting alone at the pond, the sun warming her face. If I had known what was to come, the violence it would lead to, I wouldn't have said a word. Curiosity led me to it. Curiosity over a dead woman. Linda. A woman I had never met. I would be lying if I claimed I'd never thought of her, though. Throughout the years of our marriage, she was alive in some part of my imagination. The truth is, she was there from the very start.

David never liked talking about Linda. Whenever I probed him about her, he grew sullen. He didn't love her, he said, when I pressed him. It was never love, he maintained, and for a long time I believed him.

It was a lie, though. He did love her. I found that out in the end, on my fortieth birthday. A weekend away at a farmhouse in Crookhaven, stunning views of the west Cork coastline – it should have been perfect. David and I, Chris and Susannah. 'It's like Russian roulette, going away with those two,' David had remarked, on the way down, but he'd said it good-naturedly. We were both in high spirits, looking forward to the break, some time away from the kids.

It happened on the second night. Dinner in a lavish

country house, a lot of wine, and one too many suggestive comments from Chris about the attractive young waitress – and Susannah snapped. They were off in their own whirl and tumble of conjugal battle, passion and principle tangling together in a barbed and nasty way. David and I glanced at each other across the swathe of white tablecloth, unwilling to intervene, but not wishing to bear witness either. The taxi journey back to our accommodation was icy and silent. Susannah went straight to bed, and I followed suit, leaving the two men downstairs with an open bottle of whiskey.

Some time in the night, I heard their voices. The drink, rather than mellowing them, had made them garrulous – confessional. I got out of bed to use the bathroom and at the top of the stairs I stopped to listen.

'I don't know how you do it,' David said, his voice sluggish and heavy with booze. 'The constant bickering. The full-scale rows. Doesn't it exhaust you?'

'Completely.'

'I don't get it. How do you put up with it?'

'Because I love her.'

'Is that enough?' Disbelief crept into David's voice.

'Honestly, Dave, sometimes I think it's over between us – that I've had enough. God knows how many times I've resolved to leave her. But,' Chris's voice softened, 'it's always been Susannah. From the first time I set eyes on her. I can't not be married to her. She's the love of my life.'

'Maybe sometimes you're better off not marrying the love of your life.'

The way he said it, thoughtful and quiet, I knew it was deeply personal to him, something he'd given thought to.

'Are you telling me you regret marrying Caroline?'

'I'm not talking about Caroline,' he answered quickly, and I felt myself stiffen.

'Ah,' Chris said, as the penny dropped. 'Linda.'

Her name seemed to bloom in the air before me – a sudden burst of red – and I felt my hands grow cold. Understanding came quickly: David must have talked of her to Chris, confided in him in a way he had never confided in me. What intimacies had he spoken of? What admissions of love and regret had he made? That he had done this without my knowledge, behind my back, seemed to me a marked failure in our marriage. But worse than that – far, far worse – was the realization of how deeply lodged she was inside him. *The love of his life.*

'Do you ever hear from her?' Chris asked.

'No.'

'Ever wonder where she is? Who she's with?'

'Sometimes. The odd time I'm reminded of her.'

'Tell me,' Chris went on, his voice more incisive, 'do you ever wonder how things might have turned out if you'd stayed together?'

The question chilled me. I found myself turning away from the possible answer.

David gave a hollow laugh. 'We'd be like you and Susannah – an endless series of fights and reconciliations. I wouldn't have the energy for it.'

'But you'd have passion,' Chris countered.

'Yes,' David said, in a tone of wistfulness. 'We certainly had that.'

'More than you have with Caroline?'

'Yes.' The answer was immediate. He didn't even need

to think about it. 'Caroline is different. She's dependable, safe.'

I'd heard enough. Sickened by this new knowledge, I had turned away, returned to the bedroom, wishing I had never left it. I slipped away to bed, and when David came up later, I held my body still, feigning sleep. He didn't try to touch me.

How to explain the quiet devastation caused by those words? Every time I remembered the wistfulness in his voice when he recalled his lost passion, something dark opened inside me. Like the unfurling of a shadowy new fern, I felt the opening out of doubt within me. Had it all been a mistake? Our marriage, the life we had built together, our children? Everything I valued and loved, everything I had worked so hard for, I saw now it had been built on a foundation of regret. He had given up his great love. With the cool detachment I knew him to be capable of, he had weighed up his options: passion and instability versus the safe warmth of marriage to me. No matter how hard I tried, I couldn't escape from the knowledge that I was not the love of his life. That title was claimed by a woman I had never met, a woman whose face I had seen once in a photograph I'd found hidden among his possessions.

I think that night in the cold darkness at the top of the stairs, overhearing the conversation, was when it started for me. The moment when things began to unravel. Unhappiness swept in like the arrival of autumn on a September day. I tried to rationalize it, telling myself David had been drunk when he'd said those words, he hadn't really meant them. But the truth of it continued to niggle at me. I told myself to be satisfied with what I had: a good husband, wonderful children, a comfortable home. It was more than a lot of people had – an enviable life. But the rot had set in. My husband had no passion for me. In marrying me he had chosen to settle. A pinched, mean voice inside me whispered: *If you're not the love of his life, what makes you so sure he's yours?* I'd never thought of myself as a woman who would have an affair. But by the time I met Aidan something had changed within me. Like a stone dislodged deep inside me, I felt the structure of my being start to crumble.

After my affair ended, David and I went through a difficult patch. Our bedroom, once a place of refuge and comfort – of love – became the arena for our hissed arguments, the to-ing and fro-ing of whispered accusations, of denial and blame. We tried to keep it from the children, remaining civil in front of them, a tight cordiality that seemed stilted and formal. Slowly, things got better. The atmosphere lightened. I still felt obliged to explain my absences, however innocent they were. I was careful of my behaviour in front of David. I found that I censored my comments when speaking of other men – friends, colleagues. I tried to find happiness again within my marriage, within my home. The stone inside me that had been dislodged slipped back into place. I was returning to myself. Normality resumed. But then Zoë had come along.

I thought about her constantly. At work, at home, in the evenings when I went out running, she was always with me, shadowing my thoughts, clouding my emotions.

I considered telling someone about her – confiding in a friend – but the only person I might have told was Susannah and she was locked inside her own conjugal disaster. Any time I spoke to her on the phone, she sounded on the brink of tears. It was disconcerting, given how commanding she normally was. She had separated from Chris, finally moving out, and under the circumstances I felt I couldn't burden her with my own domestic turmoil. Instead, I kept it to myself.

'What is it, Mum?' Holly asked one evening, over dinner. David and Robbie looked up from their plates. 'Why do you keep staring at me?'

'I'm not.'

'You are! Every time I look up, you're staring. It's freaking me out.'

Scanning my daughter's face, interrogating it for traces of Zoë. Was there something in the slight flatness to her cheeks, the small nose, the wide, thin-lipped mouth revealing a straight row of small teeth?

An expression sprang up from childhood: *The cat can look at the queen.*

'Just eat your dinner,' I said.

While we waited for the DNA test results, it seemed as if David and I were living within an unarticulated argument. We were cordial with each other but we took a measure of care when moving through our conversations, both of us cautious not to touch on the subject. We talked about the children, about work, exchanged words about shopping, cooking, household tasks. Any thoughts or doubts I kept to myself, and if he had any misgivings he didn't confide them to me. Then one evening he arrived home from work and I felt a change in him straight away. When he came in from the garden, taking off his jacket as he closed the door behind him, I felt his muted anger in the way he seemed to shrink from my gaze.

'Glass of wine?' I asked, and he said sure, moving past me to hang his jacket from the hook on the door.

From the sitting room came a burst of laughter – Holly and two of her friends were watching the One Direction film. Beyond the window, the trees were dripping from a recent downpour, but it was warm in the kitchen, the mellow trumpet sounds of Kenny Durham coming through the speakers.

'Cheers,' I said, and we clinked glasses. I sat on the sofa and watched him lean back on a barstool across from me, wondering what was pulling at him. 'You okay?' I asked, solicitous, concerned.

'Why didn't you tell me you met Zoë?' he asked quietly.

My breath caught in my throat. 'David, I'm sorry. I should have told you. I'm not sure why I didn't.'

He kept looking at me, a baffled expression clouding his face.

'I suppose I thought if I could just see her, get a look at her –'

'How did you even find her?'

'I rang your department,' I said, shame creeping up through me as I admitted it. It occurred to me that the methods I had employed, the way I had sneaked about, were like the actions of a suspicious wife trying to catch her husband in the act of adultery. If David saw the irony, he didn't say so. He was swivelling the barstool slightly from side to side, the movement channelling some of his anger.

'Don't you think that's a bit creepy?' he asked. I had the sense that he was choosing his words. For all the care he took, I could hear the accusation behind them.

'You're right,' I agreed, wanting to smooth things over, even though the need to talk it through was still there, the angry pulse of it running through everything. 'I'm sorry. It was impulsive. I didn't think it through properly.'

He drank from his glass, turned and put it on the counter behind him. I thought he was going to let the matter drop. But then he looked back at me and said: 'Have you any idea how freaked out she was?'

A match striking tinder. The sudden spark, his concern for the girl, seeing how it overrode my apology, my discomfort. The anger I had been holding at bay came to life inside me. 'How freaked out *she* was?'

'Yes. She was in a state when she came to my office today, in tears over what you had said to her—'

'What did I say? Tell me. What did I say to upset her?'

Still quietly, he went on: 'She said you demanded to know what she wanted from me. She felt threatened, intimidated—'

'I didn't intimidate her. The way you talk of her, you'd swear she was this shrinking violet.'

'She's just a kid.'

'She's old enough to know how to manipulate, David. Believe me. Clearly, she has you all figured out, turning on the waterworks so you'll feel sorry for her.'

'Do you even hear yourself, Caroline? Do you know how harsh you sound? How bitter?'

'Well, what do you expect from me?'

He was making the barstool swivel harder now, his anger growing.

'Come on, David. Tell me how you think this should work. Should I just take it on the chin? Say, "There, there, dear. Never mind about all this", open my home and my heart to this girl – this stranger – without checking first to see if she's real, if what she says is true?'

The chair stilled and he said: 'You should have told me.'

'I know. I know I should, and I've apologized for that.'

'We agreed to wait, didn't we? Until the test results came back.'

'Yes,' I said, my voice cool and firm. 'We did. And you also agreed that you wouldn't have anything to do with her outside class – remember?'

'She came to my office. What was I supposed to do?'

'Tell her you were busy. Have her make an appointment.'

'I couldn't. She was upset—'

'Oh, David, please. She sheds some crocodile tears and immediately you cave.'

'Don't be like that,' he said.

'Like what?'

He thought for a moment, then alighted on the word. 'Hard.'

I stood up and walked past him to the counter, threw the wine from my glass into the sink, a burgundy splash over the white surface. 'That wine tastes too sharp.'

I turned on the tap and watched it sluicing down the

drain, took the dishcloth and held it under the water, then flicked off the tap and wrung it out. I started to clean the plughole, the taps, the area around the sink.

'Why are you angry with me, Caroline?'

I wiped down the granite counter-top.

'I haven't done anything to you,' he went on. 'I haven't been unfaithful.'

He must have seen the way I stiffened, for he continued in a tone of irritation more than apology: 'I didn't mean it like that. What I meant was, it happened a long time ago, when I was free and single. I didn't screw Linda behind your back – we weren't together then. I never knew she was pregnant.'

'Didn't you?'

'Of course not!' His voice rose, for the first time a note of real anger in it. 'She never told me. I never knew there was a baby. Not until Zoë came into my office that day. Caroline, none of this has happened to hurt you. It just happened, that's all.'

He was so maddeningly rational. I had reached the end of the counter and pulled out the pestle and mortar. I saw a mark left on the counter. I went at it with the cloth, the perfect black circle it had made so stark against the natural veins running through the stone.

'I feel like you blame me for all this,' he said, 'and it's not my fault.'

'I know it's not your fault.'

'It was just a mistake.'

'I know.'

'You're going to rub a hole in the granite, the way you're going.'

I flung the cloth into the sink. 'It's because of the baby.'

'What baby?'

I turned, leaned back against the counter and gazed at him. 'Our baby, David. The one we didn't have.'

It took a moment for his expression to clear and I saw, with a shock, that he had pushed that whole painful episode in our history out of his mind. He had moved on.

'Oh. That.'

'You'd forgotten, hadn't you?' I asked.

His fingers went to the stem of his glass – there was still some wine in the bowl, which he began to swirl in a slow, meditative way. 'I hadn't forgotten. I just don't think about it any more. It was so long ago, Caroline.'

I felt the counter behind me, the hard surface of it there to steady me. 'She would have been twenty-one now,' I said. 'Or he.'

He put his glass down, his brow creasing with a pained expression.

I waited where I was – I wouldn't go to him – and after a moment, he got up off the barstool, came over and put his arms around me, pulling me into his embrace. I don't know how long we stood there, holding each other, and all the while I was trying to feel the warmth of his hug – the sincerity within it – but I kept thinking, He's trying to silence me. Trying to close down that avenue of conversation.

He drew back, looked at me, our faces close to each other. 'You okay?'

'Yes. I'm fine.'

He held me there for another moment, then reached for the wine bottle and turned away.

'Is that it?' I asked.

'What?'

'Is that all you're going to say on the subject?'

He stood at the other side of the counter, filling his glass again, the look of forbearance on his face making me want to scream. Patiently, he said: 'It was a long time ago. I thought we'd put it behind us.'

'You tell me about this girl – this daughter you fathered back when you were a student – and you never once think about our baby? The one we got rid of?'

My voice broke and I had to stop, feeling the rising commotion inside me. I wanted to tell him that when I met Zoë – when I looked at her – all I could think of was the pregnancy I had terminated. After so many years of holding it at bay, controlling it, never allowing it to cast its shadow over my life, here it was in front of me in the shape of that girl. All the memories of what had happened seemed stored up in her. I'd looked at her and felt myself being dragged back to a time when I was sick with fear and uncertainty, overwhelmed by the mistake we had made and the decision we'd had to face. Sitting alongside her in the sun, I'd felt as if I was back in the waiting room, a form attached to a clipboard on my knee, the deep-pile of the carpet underfoot, the crisp receptionist behind her wall of Perspex, and all the while my legs wouldn't stop trembling. Twenty years old, in my final year at university, my whole life ahead of me. I had thought that once it was done I would feel relief. That I could forget. And I did. But there was also the slow advance of dread crawling up from that empty place, the awkward rumblings of conscience.

'Anyway,' I said, giving myself a shake as though to dispel the chill from the past. 'It's just nerves. All this waiting – it's making me jumpy.'

He glanced up at me with a guarded expression.

'Once those test results come through, we can put this whole wretched business behind us.'

I still remember the forced optimism with which I said those words.

'Caroline,' he said slowly, and I saw at once how clearly I had been counting on it being false, her wild claim proven to be the troubled fantasy of an attention-seeker. The long, awful time of not knowing was about to end, and my throat grew dry and stiff.

'Tell me,' I said.

He didn't need to say it. The bitter truth was written all over his face. 'I'm sorry,' he told me. 'I know you hoped it would be different . . .'

I hardly heard him. I kept thinking back over the words he had used to defend himself. *It's not my fault.* Like a schoolboy pleading innocence. *It was a mistake.*

A mistake he had made twice.

That was what was so unforgivable. The very mistake we had made together – the baby we had accidentally started – he had repeated it with another woman. How maddeningly stupid of him. How unbelievably careless. For a man so self-controlled, composed and careful almost to the point of coldness, it seemed wildly out of character. His Achilles heel, perhaps. Reckless with passion, he had fallen into the same trap a second time. Linda had kept her baby, though, and neither of us could have foreseen the consequences of her decision.

He continued talking about the test results – the science involved – using cold clinical terms, and I thought of these strands of DNA and imagined them to be threads escaping their spools. She was a thread that ran through the fabric of our family. In the same way each of my children was a thread – including the child that was never born – woven into a complex tapestry. Love, trust, fidelity: these were the strands that bound us together.

Families don't come apart because a thread has loosened. The break, when it comes, is sharp, brutal. It takes ripping and hacking to tear the tapestry apart.

# PART TWO

# 10. David

It was nothing to be ashamed of. That was what I told myself at the time. This daughter who had parachuted into my life out of nowhere didn't need to be covered up or explained away with a mixture of apology and discomfiture. If a mistake had been made, it was the mistake of a younger man. What is youth without the odd indiscretion? The important thing, I reminded myself, whenever I felt the doubt creeping in, was how I handled it now. It was a situation requiring calm and maturity. I needed to be honest, upfront, and offer no apologies: there was nothing to apologize for.

Not everyone shared this view. Caroline, for one, shrank from the notion when I informed her I was going to tell the children.

'What?' she asked, clearly aghast.

'They have a right to know,' I told her. 'And a right to meet their half-sister.'

'Wait a second. Telling them about Zoë is one thing, but meeting her? What is it you intend to happen?'

'They ought to have some kind of relationship with her,' I argued. 'Get to know her for themselves.'

'Have you thought about the effect it might have on them?'

'Of course I have,' I answered, a little irritated by her response. 'They're not babies, Caroline. Robbie is fifteen, and Holly has always been older than her years. I think you're doing them a disservice, suggesting they might not be able to handle it.'

'It's not that,' she answered. 'It's what they might think of you once they find out. That's what I'm concerned about.'

She had a point. Even though I was openly dismissive of her concerns, when the time came to sit down with Robbie and Holly, Caroline looking on watchfully, I felt an inner trembling at what I was about to admit. In my mind, I had rehearsed my little speech over and over, explaining as gently as possible about a relationship I had had before they were born, the consequences of which were only beginning to play out now, and even though my words were as I had planned, they came out sounding colder and more matter-of-fact than I would have liked. In truth, even though I had reasoned with myself that I had nothing to blame myself for – it was a mistake that could happen to almost anyone – my explanation to my children came out sounding defensive.

'A half-sister?' Robbie asked, with a mixture of amusement and disbelief.

'Yes. Her name is Zoë. She's eighteen.'

'What the fuck?' he had exclaimed, laughing to cover his shock.

'Robbie,' Caroline said in partial admonishment, but mostly to steady him.

'How come you never told us about her?' he asked me.

'Because I didn't know about her myself until a couple of weeks ago.'

'You didn't know?'

'Her mother and I had lost touch.'

'Who was her mother?' he asked.

'That doesn't matter,' I replied quickly, unhappy with where his line of questioning was going. 'She was someone I went out with for a little while. It's not important.'

Immediately I regretted that statement. For one thing, it seemed to imply that I had been the type of person in my youth who slept around without any thought to the consequences – not the message I wanted to send my children. Also, I couldn't escape the feeling that Linda was somehow watching me, her spirit present in the room, witnessing my offhand dismissal of a love affair that had been both powerful and precious.

Caroline glanced out of the window. Holly shifted a little on the couch.

'So what?' Robbie asked. 'Is she going to move in with us?'

'No, no,' I assured him. 'But I would like you to meet her. I was thinking of inviting her over for lunch one Sunday. How would you feel about that?'

'Yeah, okay.'

'And you, Hols?' I asked.

She said nothing, gave a noncommittal shrug. The whole time I was talking, she had sat there quietly, watchful, absorbing everything I was telling them. But now I saw her eyes flicker over me briefly in an assessing glance, the kind I had never received from her before. I saw at once that Caroline was right. This revelation I wanted so desperately to make normal had already altered our family bonds. Beneath my little girl's gaze, I felt myself changing, becoming a different kind of father from the one she had known and relied upon until then.

*

Later that week, I was mulling all of this over in a meeting with Alan. We were discussing a funding bid to a government scheme attached to the Peace and Reconciliation Committee. Alan was supportive of the concept, agreeing to add his name to the proposal. 'Even if I won't be here to see it through,' he said, referring to his intended retirement. I made no reply. He was in good form that day, brisk and cheery, and once our business had been concluded, he capped his pen and flipped his notebook closed, expecting me to do the same.

'Actually, there's something else I wanted to speak to you about,' I told him.

'Yes?'

'It concerns a student. One of my first-years. Her name is Zoë Barry.'

I felt nervous about telling him. It was as if I were readying myself to own up to a transgression that had only just happened, rather than something that had occurred almost twenty years ago.

'The thing is, Alan, it turns out that I'm her father.'

He put down the pen he was still holding, realizing that our conversation was going to last longer than he had planned.

'It was when I was at Queens – I had a relationship with the girl's mother. I never knew she had a child. This all happened before I was married . . . I've only just discovered.'

'Good Lord,' Alan said.

'I wanted to let you know – let the department know. She's my student, after all, and I didn't want there to be any . . .' I hunted about for the right word '. . . any misunderstanding.'

'Right,' he said, sounding slightly fazed. His eyes darted over my face and I wondered if he was making some kind of mental reassessment of me, some private speculation as to my personal life. A bead of sweat rolled down my back.

'Have you mentioned this to anyone else in the department?'

'Not yet,' I answered, wondering whether I should tell him what McCormack had said.

'Because she's one of your students, we'll need to declare a conflict of interest when it comes to grading papers, assessments, exams . . . fulfil all the necessary protocols.'

'Protocols?'

'Inform the registrar, the ethics committee, and let me see who else . . .'

'An ethics committee?'

'It will only have to be noted. Nothing to worry about.'

'What about confidentiality?'

'It's assumed.'

He picked up his notebook and pen and got to his feet. I understood the meeting was over. At the door to his office, he spoke a few words of reassurance, making me feel even more as if I'd done something wrong. In fact, the bureaucratic minefield I was walking into was tinged, the way Alan put it, with a moral code, which it appeared I had unwittingly broken.

I had confessed to Caroline, owned up to my kids,

revealed all to the university, but where was the expiation of whatever guilt I had felt? When would the burden of the past lift? My wife's shock was one thing, my children's surprise another. I could deal with those twin pressures, given time, but the university's way of punishing me was soul-destroying – all the paperwork that would need to be filed, the ethics committee, the protocols and standards that were required to be met – like a figurative black mark against me, like ash on the forehead, or a scarlet letter.

That Sunday, there was the usual flurry of activity in the morning, but this time the day's machinations held a certain edge, a serration to the light of early afternoon and the energy that went with it. Zoë had accepted my invitation to come for lunch and, with her arrival imminent, I felt an air of nervous anticipation hanging in the house.

The doorbell rang.

I called out that I would get it. Behind the frosted glass, there was the outline of a slight figure, hooded, waiting, expectant. I pulled open the door. She had been glancing back at the garden, surveying the clumped hydrangeas, the wine-red spread of acers, and as I said her name, she turned and her eyes met mine. An uncanny tremor of *déjà vu* passed through me, and with it a fleeting memory of Linda on my doorstep on one of those feckless nights in Belfast, her voice emerging from the past: *You said I could drop by.* The answering kick of my heart.

'I hope I'm not late,' Zoë said, smiling nervously. 'I was in town and lost track of time.'

'Not late at all.' I stood back so she could enter.

I closed the door and turned to find her looking around

the hall, her eyes travelling upwards. She was a little flushed. She was holding a bottle of wine and a small bouquet of flowers. As if suddenly remembering them, she held both out to me. I took them from her and thanked her. For a moment we simply stood there.

'Zoë, hello,' Caroline said brightly, coming out of the kitchen and wiping her hands on a tea-towel.

They shook hands, exchanging some pleasantries I didn't quite catch. I was still a little shaken from the *déjà vu*. I felt as if I had asked not just Zoë into our lives, but the shadowy aura of Linda, too.

'I hope you're hungry,' Caroline said, hanging Zoë's jacket in the hall, then ushering her into the kitchen. 'David's been toiling over a hot stove all day.'

'She's joking, by the way,' I said, but the truth was I had gone to some lengths in preparing the dish, making extra effort. Earlier that morning, Holly had made a passing comment about how I was fussing. 'It's goulash.'

'Something the soldiers ate in the trenches of one or other war, isn't that right?' Caroline jibed. She gestured for Zoë to sit on one of the barstools and started cutting the foil from the neck of a wine bottle. 'Red or white?' she asked Zoë.

'I'd prefer white, please.'

If Caroline was feeling the strain, she hid it well. I noticed she had taken care with her appearance – she was wearing a smart fitted dress, high heels, and diamond earrings winked beneath her neatly curled hair. While there was no doubting her attractiveness, next to Zoë's casual beauty there seemed something over-formal and made-up about her. She poured the wine into three glasses.

Jazz was playing on the stereo – easy listening, nothing to distract us from getting to know each other, but if everything did break down and go quiet we wouldn't have to cringe in our own silence. Above the low melody, I could hear the rumble of feet on the stairs. Robbie came in.

'Zoë, this is Robbie,' I said. He held up his hand in a gesture only teenagers can pull off – a kind of salute.

All morning, the notes from his cello had filled the house. Not the beautiful sonorous sounds of performance, but the harsher false starts of practice. Still, there had been something familiar and reassuring about them.

'Hi,' Zoë said, a little apprehensively. She smiled and took a timid step back as if to fully observe her half-brother.

Holly followed, but positioned herself behind one of the kitchen chairs before saying hello. She had been unusually withdrawn in the days since I had broken the news about her half-sister, not her usual ebullient and confident self. I felt a jab of uncertainty. All of us seemed unsure how to negotiate the terms of these newly discovered relationships. In some respects, we reverted to the buttoned-up awkwardness of polite exchange that had marked the time after Caroline and I had patched things up post-affair, when we talked to each other in front of the kids with a forced civility, maintaining the pretence for their sakes that our marriage was solid. I imagined it to be how distant relations talked after having being introduced for the first time – awkward, circumspect and full of artifice.

That being said, Caroline remained resolute. She took command of the situation, enlisting Holly's help with putting out the food, instructing us all on where to sit.

'You have a beautiful home,' Zoë offered politely, albeit with a wavering voice. Her eyes were casting around the kitchen and family room. Light flooded in through the glass doors and the skylight. The weather was unusually fine for October.

Robbie asked Zoë where she lived, and blushed a little when she answered.

'I rent a small flat in Rathmines. Just a bedsit, really.'

'What made you want to come to Dublin?' he asked.

She shrugged, 'I've always liked it, since I was a child.'

'Did you come down much?'

'I have cousins in Greystones, so sometimes we'd stop off in Dublin on the way to visiting them. Mam and I used to go shopping on Grafton Street.'

I tried to picture it: Linda holding the hand of a little girl, gazing in the windows of Brown Thomas or Marks & Spencer. Dublin is a small city. Would it have been so far outside the bounds of possibility that I might have bumped into her? Would she have introduced me to her daughter if I had? Told me the truth, or tried to pretend Zoë wasn't mine? Would she have said anything at all?

'How are you finding UCD?' Caroline asked, once we had started eating. I was afraid all the questions would make Zoë feel she was being interrogated. She was nervous enough as it was.

'It's good. I'm still finding my way a little,' she said, smiling shyly. 'But I'm enjoying it.'

There were further questions about her lectures, what clubs she had joined, the part-time job she had picked up in the students' union shop. She answered them all patiently, and politely, even if there was a note of hesitancy in her voice, as if she did not trust herself completely to say what she thought was expected of her. We were distracted by the food, passing bread and dipping into the salad. To all appearances everything was going well, but beneath the small-talk there was something else, an unspoken tension – a kind of undercurrent of suspicion so that, no matter what Zoë was asked, I heard the subtextual rip-tide, the undercurrent of what was really meant: *Why are you here? What do you want?*

It was a relief to hear her ask a question of her own and deflect some of the intense scrutiny she must have felt: 'Who plays the cello?' she asked.

She had finished eating, making a neat cross of her cutlery on the plate. The cello was leaning against the wall to the side of the sofa.

'That's mine,' Robbie told her.

'He's in the National Youth Orchestra,' Caroline said proudly. 'You should hear him play some time.'

'He thinks he's Yo-Yo Ma,' Holly said, with a smirk.

Robbie told her to shut up, and she pushed her glasses back up to the bridge of her nose. It was the first time she'd spoken since Zoë had entered the house.

'I love the cello,' Zoë told him. 'Can you play that Elgar piece?'

Robbie leaned his elbows on the table and gave her a half-grin. 'Not really. I'm trying to learn it but it's, like, super-hard.'

'We played it at my mam's funeral – not a live performance, just on the stereo. Still – it was beautiful.'

No one said anything. I had a groundless feeling at the

thought of Linda dead in a box, the room swelling with the sound of those melancholy strings.

'Sorry to hear about your mum,' Robbie said quietly.

'Thanks.'

'It must have been shit,' he added.

'It was,' she said, a little distressed, 'but I've been busy since it happened, moving down here and starting college.'

'What about your family in Belfast?' Caroline asked.

Zoë brushed the hair from her eyes, 'Well, there's just Gary – he's my stepfather.'

'He must miss you.'

'I don't think so.'

'Oh?' I asked, surprised by the change in her manner. 'Why not?'

'We don't really get on.'

'You don't?'

She thought about it, no doubt aware of the weight of our stares. 'I dunno. We never kind of hit it off.'

'When did he and your mother marry?' Caroline asked.

Zoë shifted in her chair: 'When I was six.' She picked up her fork and fiddled with it. After a moment's hesitation, she continued: 'He was nice at first – always buying me sweets and toys and that. But after a while, he just got bored of me.'

'That's awful,' I said.

Caroline asked: 'He and Linda had no children together?'

'No. I think Gary really wanted to have kids of his own, but when it didn't happen, he just grew despondent. Kind of jealous, too.'

'Jealous?' I asked.

'Of me and Mam. Our closeness. Especially towards the end, when she was sick.'

'It must have been very difficult for you,' Caroline offered, but I was more interested in the jealousy she had mentioned. There was something beneath the strained politeness, something she wasn't saying that worried me: I didn't like the sound of Gary one bit.

'Your stepfather,' I said, 'do you hear much from him?'

She shook her head. 'Not since I came down to college. I think he's glad to have me out from under his feet.' Then, almost as an afterthought: 'I'm glad to be out from under his feet, too.'

'Really?' I asked.

'The way he used to go on sometimes, his temper . . .'

'His temper?'

The question startled Zoë, as if she hadn't realized she had spoken her thoughts aloud. 'Maybe "temper" isn't the right word. It's more subtle than that. Oh, I don't know,' she said, dismissing her words with a wave of the hand.

'Passive aggressive?' I suggested.

She made a remark about how delicious the food had been. It was clear she didn't want to discuss the matter further.

Caroline got up to make the coffee while Robbie cleared away the dishes. The topic was dropped, but I didn't forget it, even when the conversation returned to safer subjects: Zoë and Robbie discussing the various bands they were into, what films they liked, Holly answering to what her favourite subjects were in school. All seemingly congenial chitchat, but there was still an almost palpable tension running through the blood of the conversation, like a contagion. Nothing, it seemed, not wine, light-hearted chat, or even dessert, could dispel it. Or maybe that was just the way I saw it because what she had said about Gary's jealousy and temper stayed with me, and brought out in me a kind of protective zeal I had not expected to feel for her.

We finished our coffee, Robbie saying, 'Can we go sit in the comfy chairs?' and everyone got to their feet.

Caroline, clearing the last of the table, was reaching across to take Zoë's cup when her hand brushed against the stem of my glass, which I had recently refilled. It toppled, sending out a splash of Burgundy, some of which hit Zoë's midriff, the rest spilling over her placemat and dripping on to her lap. She leaped to her feet.

'Oh, Christ!' Caroline exclaimed. 'I'm so sorry!'

'Here,' I said, handing Zoë a paper napkin.

'It's fine,' she said, dabbing at her T-shirt.

'God, I'm so clumsy,' Caroline said. 'Here, let me get you some soda water.'

'It's all right – really,' she said, laughing to show it was no big deal. Her cheeks had pinked and she put the napkin on the table.

'Do you want to borrow one of my T-shirts?' Caroline offered.

'Ah, no, thanks,' she said, then gestured towards the door. 'I'll just go to the bathroom, give it a bit of a scrub. That'll be enough.'

She left the kitchen. I picked up the napkin and began to mop up the spilled wine. Some of it had dripped on to the floor and I bent to wipe it away.

'I can't believe I did that,' Caroline said, in a half-amused kind of way.

Her response annoyed me. It was almost as if she took some kind of pleasure in what had happened. As if it was a small triumph for her.

'Unfortunate,' I commented.

'Shall I open another bottle?' she asked, oblivious to my prickliness.

I stepped past her and threw the sodden napkin into the bin. 'Hardly worth it now, is it?'

'Oh, God. You're not angry because I spilled your wine, are you?' Her voice still held that slightly mocking tone.

'Her first time here . . . I don't want her put off by us knocking wine over her.'

'It's not the end of the world, David. No point crying over spilled Burgundy.'

Caroline's efforts to defuse the situation made me more agitated. 'Maybe I should check on her. Make sure she's okay.'

Caroline made a little noise of irritation at the back of her throat. 'You stay here and finish tidying up,' she instructed. 'I'll check on Zoë.'

She disappeared out of the kitchen and Holly joined Robbie on the couch. The TV was on, and the two of them were absorbed. I continued with the clear-up until I heard feet on the stairs. Coming out into the hallway, I saw Zoë descending. When she caught sight of me, she smiled broadly. 'Thanks so much, David,' she said, reaching the bottom step and taking her coat from where it was hanging on the newel post. 'This has been really lovely.'

'You're not going already?'

'Afraid so,' she said cheerfully. 'I've an essay to hand in tomorrow, so I need to go home and work on it.'

Caroline was on her way down the stairs.

'Let me give you a lift,' I said, helping Zoë into her coat.

'I can walk home,' she said, laughing at my offer. 'I don't want to put you to any trouble.'

'No worries,' I said, and she rewarded me with a grateful smile.

While Zoë turned to thank Caroline for the meal, I put my head around the door and told the kids she was leaving. Robbie came out to say goodbye, but Holly remained on the couch. I decided not to make an issue of it.

'Sorry about the wine,' I said, once we were alone in the car. 'Caroline isn't normally that clumsy.'

She told me not to worry, laughing it off.

I felt real affection for the strength she had shown: it was no mean feat to walk into another's family home and join the established rhythms of their life as seamlessly as she had. It showed real maturity. 'I know that can't have been easy,' I said.

'It was really nice to meet everyone.'

'I hope you didn't feel we grilled you too much.'

'Not at all,' she replied. 'It was nice getting to see another side to you.'

'How do you mean?'

She shrugged. 'Outside college, the private you, that's all. How you are with your family.'

'Well, I hope you can get to know all of us better.'

'I'd like that. Holly and Robbie are lovely. Robbie's so like you.'

I wondered had she been hoping to see traces of herself in his or Holly's face, some linking traits that marked them out as her siblings.

Neither of us spoke for a few minutes, the car filled with silence as I drove through Rathgar village towards Rathmines. While the afternoon had passed off well, I still felt a lingering sadness. It had started the moment she mentioned Linda's funeral. Briefly, I thought about how different our lives might have been had Linda made contact: a phone call, a letter – that was all it would have taken. Instead, she had decided to raise Zoë alone. What was so terrible about me that she'd felt she couldn't get in touch?

We turned the corner into Rathmines, passed the neon shop-front signs blinking in the dark, the fast-food joints, then a charity shop and the church with its copper dome. She directed me down a side-street and we turned on to a terrace of Georgian houses that had seen better days. I pulled the car up alongside the kerb.

'Can I ask you a question?' I began tentatively. 'Did Linda ever talk about me?'

She considered her answer carefully, as if she were remembering something difficult and painful: 'Towards the end, when she was dying.'

'But not before then? Not when you were growing up?'

'Not really,' Zoë said hesitantly, gazing out of the window. Her hand was on the door-handle, and I sensed her need to go. All the questions she had been asked that day – it must have been exhausting. But, still, I wanted to keep her there, to find some kind of resolution to the problem that had been bothering me from the moment she had come into my office and made her revelation: why hadn't Linda told me?

'Well, there was one time,' she said shyly, as if reluctant to divulge the information. 'I must have been eight or nine. We were in Greystones with our cousins, and she took me on a special outing, as she called it, like it was something secret just the two of us were to know about and no one else. She borrowed her cousin's car and drove up to Dublin, to Belfield. She took me on to campus. It was the first time I had ever been to a university.'

'She took you to UCD?' I asked, confused.

'Yes.'

'But why?'

'I don't know. We just sat in the seating area near the Blob. I don't know how long we were there – an hour, maybe. She told me someone she knew worked there – someone who had once been important to her. The whole time we were there, she kept looking around, as if she were waiting for someone. Then, eventually, it was as if she gave up. We went back to the car and drove away. She never said anything more about it.'

I had the feeling that she was telling me this to make me feel better, but as I sat there, one hand still gripping the steering wheel, I felt an enormous sense of loss. The wasted opportunity, cruel Fate. Of all the hundreds, no, thousands of times I had walked past that very spot . . . Had I only done so on that day, had I spotted them there together, seen the face that had once been so familiar to me, so well loved, everything might have changed. Everything might have been different.

Perhaps she saw my reaction to her story. Awkwardness came into the car and she pulled the door-handle, a chill air entering the space around us.

'If it helps at all,' she said, one foot out of the car, 'I could tell that she had never really forgotten you.'

She stepped on to the pavement, pulled up the collar of her coat and walked down the darkened laneway. I closed my eyes and breathed in the last traces of her presence. When I looked at the street again, it was quiet, orange pools of light shimmering in the darkness.

I started the engine, pulled the car away, and above the white noise of the engine, emerging from the deep tangle of my thoughts, one phrase shone clear of all others – the thrill of them: *I could tell she had never forgotten you.*

# 11. Caroline

'I think it went well. Don't you?'

It was almost midnight. Hours had passed since he had dropped Zoë back to her flat, and still David's voice retained its buoyancy, the same optimism that had imbued the whole afternoon.

'Yes. I suppose.'

I was in bed already, reading my book, while he moved about the room, changing into his pyjamas, getting out his clothes for the morning. There was an energy about him, as if the day had bolstered his spirit, whereas I felt drained. I tried to concentrate on the words in front of me, but his jittery presence was a distraction. Putting down my book, I watched him fumbling at the back of his wardrobe for something he couldn't find.

'What are you doing?' I asked, a note of irritation in my voice.

'Looking for my climbing gear. Have you seen it?'

'David, you haven't climbed in years.'

'I know. But I thought I'd go down to the sports centre tomorrow, give the climbing wall a go.'

'Why?'

'Why not?' he replied cheerfully, with no indication that he had picked up on my annoyance. 'It's probably in the attic.' He disappeared on to the landing.

For a few minutes I sat there, fiddling with the page of

my open book, listening to him overhead. Where had the sudden urge come from to revisit a sport he had long forgotten about? Zoë, of course. I thought again of the two of them disappearing down the driveway into the evening. Ever since his return he had been upbeat, happy in a way I hadn't seen for a long time.

'Find your gear?' I asked, when he came back into the room.

'Yep. It's a bit dusty, but not beyond use.' He set about restoring order to his wardrobe.

'What was it like?' I asked. 'Zoë's flat.'

'Oh. I don't know. I didn't go up.'

'I thought you might have. You were gone a while.'

'Was I? There was traffic.'

'What's it like from the outside?'

'It's a quiet enough street – a terrace of brown-bricks in Rathmines, behind the swimming pool.'

'The rent can't be cheap.'

'A poky room in a freezing attic, Caroline. I don't think she can afford much else.'

'I imagine it's all incense sticks and posters of Morrissey,' I said, picking at the corner of my book.

'Her taste is a bit retro. What was it she told Robbie she likes? The Cure and Massive Attack. I mean, those were from way back in our day.'

'You make it sound like the Dark Ages!' I said, the ice inside me beginning to thaw. The way he'd said it – *back in our day* – reminded me of our shared history, and all the joy that lay within those memories, a joy she couldn't touch. Putting aside my book, I pulled back the covers and moved across the mattress to where he was sitting, looped my arms around his neck, bringing my cheek alongside his. He reached up, grasped my wrist, and I could feel his face against mine, smiling.

'I still remember you dancing around a bedsit to the Smiths,' I murmured.

He laughed. 'Me too.'

It was nice, the warmth between us – the sudden intimacy. After the day that had passed, it felt fortifying to have him in my arms, his body against mine, as if I were reclaiming him.

'I must dig out some of my old CDs,' he said. 'See if Zoë wants them.'

One mention of her name and the mood between us evaporated. Where I was bathing in the warmth of an old memory, he was focusing on a future neither of us had bargained for. There was a frisson of excitement in his voice. Subtle enough, but I caught it. I could tell how pleased he was with this daughter, taking pride in her originality, her desire to separate herself from the crowd. With the mention of her name it was as if, somehow, she had crept into our room.

'She's very beautiful,' I said tentatively.

It was true. She had the cool beauty of a glassy lake on a cold day – you wanted to stare at it, to take it all in, but you wouldn't want to touch it. A coldness that seemed biting. I said it to test him, I suppose. A childish need to hear him dismiss it, or make some comparison. *Not as beautiful as Holly. Not as beautiful as you.*

'She's like her mother.' His tone was matter-of-fact but still I felt a pang.

'You like her. Don't you?' I said. 'I mean, as a person.'

He turned in my embrace so that he could face me, and I let my arms drop. He held on to my wrist, his thumb idly stroking the inside. 'There's something about her,' he began cautiously. 'I think it was brave of her, coming here today, meeting all of us. It must have been daunting.'

'Daunting?'

'To her mind, we must seem this fully formed machine, this tight unit,' he explained. 'I'm sure she must have felt nervous.'

I thought back to the moment just after Zoë had arrived and the introductions had been made. The way she had held out her hand to shake mine, giving me a shy smile, and said: *I hope we can become good friends, Caroline.*

It was not what I had expected.

The smile was bright, but the handshake weak. It was like trying to grip water. I couldn't dispel the sense that the words used had been carefully selected, well rehearsed. *I hope we can become good friends.* David looking on with a hopeful expression. The words said to me, but for his benefit. There was something very adult in the phrasing, a hint of archness in her tone. Quite unlike that of any eighteen-year-old I had met. In advance of her visit, I had wondered if anything would be said about our conversation that day at the university, whether I should broach the subject with her, maybe even apologize. As soon as she said those words, I understood that it was her way of opening and closing the subject. It was, I felt, the most subtle of put-downs.

'I feel sorry for her,' he said, rousing me from my private thoughts.

'Do you?'

'Listening to what she was saying about Linda dying. How lonely she must have been. And as for the stepfather . . . He sounds like a piece of work.'

'We're only hearing her side of the story, you know,' I said, thinking of the way she had bowed her head and looked up at David with those big eyes. The coyness of it – the *faux*-shyness, the manufactured vulnerability. How readily he accepted it. With Robbie and Holly, he was impenetrable to their appeals for sympathy, often demanding proof to back up their complaints.

'What are you saying? We shouldn't take her word for it?'

'She's a teenager. They bend the truth to make it match their own view of the world.'

'That's a little harsh, Caroline.'

'Haven't you said as much about Robbie in the past?'

'That's different,' he said, letting go of my hand.

'How is it different?'

'Because Robbie hasn't lost a parent.'

I kept my anger in check. 'Okay. She's obviously grieving for Linda, but I'm sure Gary is too. People don't always communicate well when they're trying to cope with loss.'

He took off his watch and put it on the nightstand. Turning to get into bed, he said, not unkindly, 'Shove up,' and I scooched over to my side of the bed, while he settled back against his pillow. 'The kids seemed to handle it well, don't you think?'

'Yes,' I said carefully. I thought of Robbie's shy enthusiasm, the way Zoë seemed to draw him out with talk of music and film, shared cultural references. Holly had said little throughout the meal, and from the thinness of her mouth, the way her eyes caught mine, I could tell she was bothered by the other girl – a little threatened, perhaps.

'Robbie was great,' David continued. 'They seemed to hit it off – him and Zoë. Did you notice?'

'Holly seemed quiet.'

'Did you talk to her after Zoë left?'

'I tried to, but she was being cagey. You know Holly. She likes to process these things first.'

'I suppose it's natural for her to feel put out. Until now she's been the only daughter.'

She's still *my* only daughter, I thought, a surge of anger rising out of nowhere. 'You should tread carefully with her,' I told him, a gentle warning. 'She might be feeling displaced.'

'I will. Thanks for today, love,' he told me. 'I know it hasn't been easy for you – all of this. It's early days, but I think it'll be okay. When she first walked into my office and dropped that bombshell, I was sure our lives were about to be turned upside-down. But after today I feel heartened. Optimistic.'

Now was the time to tell him, the opening I needed to voice my doubt, to express how unsure I was of the girl, wary. There was something about the way the situation was unfolding that was not right. I should have said it – I would have, but for the look in his eye when he turned to me.

'I think we could get through anything,' he said, 'you and me.'

A quiet conviction in those words, which instantly summoned up the difficult work involved in mending the split between us. I felt the pressure of his grip and squeezed his hand in return.

He let go just long enough to turn out the lights and was back with me again, the two of us sliding under the covers. For a few moments everything else dissolved around us, the world narrowing to this room, this bed, this breath, this touch.

Afterwards, he fell asleep with his arms around me. A short while later, I gently moved away, and he settled into a deeper sleep.

I stayed awake, listening to the noises of the house around me – the creaking of wind in the gables, the ticking of pipes deep in the recesses of the house, and the soft breathing of my husband next to me. I thought about Zoë, her weak handshake, her behaviour towards me. With the others, she was all warmth and charm and interest, but I got cold politeness. She hardly even looked at me, her eyes always sliding away from mine. I thought about it now, and realized the subtlety and slyness of it.

The spilled-wine incident had chilled me. I remembered again her laughing refusal when I offered to lend her one of my T-shirts, the way she warmly shrugged off any apologies, making light of the matter. 'It's not a problem,' she had said, of the splash across her T-shirt, like evidence of some act of violence, while she smiled and laughed, and then excused herself to use the bathroom. David mopped up the wine while I cleared away the dishes. Together we set the room to rights. Zoë was in the bathroom for at least ten minutes and we both assumed she was rinsing the wine from her top.

'I'll go and see if she needs help,' I told him.

The cloakroom off the hall was empty, and as I climbed the stairs, I heard the sound of running water coming from the bathroom. I knocked on the door and said her name.

'Come in,' was the reply and I pushed the door open to find her leaning against the sink, attempting to wash out the stain from the T-shirt she was still wearing. It seemed an awkward task, and she didn't look up from it, her mouth set in a thin line of determination. As she wrung water from the hem, the T-shirt rose a little higher from her waist and I could see a band of pale flesh at her midriff, so thin she was almost concave.

'I just came to see if you needed help,' I said. 'Did you manage to get it out?'

'No.'

'Perhaps some salt would help?'

She let go of her clothing and turned to me, her face a small pinched mask. 'It's fucking ruined,' she said.

The words seemed to bounce off the cold surfaces of the room.

'Zoë, I –'

'Don't bother,' she snapped, pushing past me, taking the stairs two at a time.

I remained in the bathroom, trying to make sense of what had just passed between us. The ferocity of her words had taken me aback, the speed at which she had swung from warmth to hostility leaving me reeling.

There were voices in the hall, and as I came down the stairs, I saw David helping her on with her coat.

'I can walk home,' she was saying, laughter slipping easily between her words. 'I don't want to put you to any trouble.'

'No worries,' he answered, and she beamed back at him.

Then, seeing me on the stairs, she directed her smile at me, as if nothing had passed between us. As if the ugliness of our encounter in the bathroom had never happened.

'Thank you so much for a lovely lunch, Caroline,' she said warmly. 'I really enjoyed it.'

I must have mumbled some kind of goodbye but, for the life of me, I can't remember what. It was breathtaking, the way she turned on the charm in front of David, reserving her cool hostility for the occasions she and I were alone together.

I could have said something to David – but what? That she had snapped at me? Told me her T-shirt was ruined? He would say I was reading too much into it, that I had misinterpreted her tone. To his mind, the whole time she was with us she had been polite, friendly – charming, even. He would think I was being unfair. Still, I regretted having let it pass with no mention at all.

I lay in bed listening to the patter of rain on the roof, the wind strengthening. Soon enough it was howling around the eaves, lashing against the windows. David stirred in his sleep but didn't wake. I lay there in the darkness, staring at the ceiling long after the storm was spent.

My unease after that first visit faded as the days passed. There was work, a dental check-up, the usual household obligations. Before I knew it, Sunday blew in and she was among us again – Zoë. I hadn't thought she would return so soon, but when David put it to her that she was welcome to join us, she apparently accepted eagerly.

Just like that, it became a pattern – a set-piece that

bookended the week. November passed, the weeks studded with these curious occasions. Curious because, although they became more relaxed as we got to know her, I still felt there was something stagey about them.

Each week now tilted towards Sunday, as if all the other days were just treading water to make time pass. That day, those visits were taking on a significance that made me feel uncomfortable. I could see it in the behaviour of the others. Come Sunday morning, a bounce and vigour would enter Robbie's step, and at the same time I could see a tightening in Holly's face. As for David, it used to be his Sunday treat to take himself off alone to our local for a quiet pint and to read the papers for an hour or two in the afternoon. Since Zoë's arrival, that had stopped. Instead he would drive to Rathmines to collect her, and after lunch, he'd drop her back again, like some kind of shared custody arrangement after a marital separation. Only Zoë was not a child. And if David was in any way put out by this, he didn't show it. In fact, he appeared happy.

Another thing: those Sunday nights, after she had left, after we had all settled down to sleep, he would reach for me in the darkness, drawing me to him, fingers exploring the plains and declivities of my body, meandering lines traced over my skin. There was something different about our lovemaking then. It seemed to gain a new charge, a new intensity. I put it down to a release of tension. Sex on those occasions was rather like sex after a long and bruising argument – the sweet resolution of our bodies finding each other, the unspoken forgiveness in the dark. While there was something restorative about it, a small part of me was troubled. I worried that while for me it was a release of tension, for David it was something else.

I used to believe that when you embark on an affair you lose interest in sex within your marriage. I have learned since that desire can be a blind, grasping thing. In those months when I was seeing Aidan, I would often turn to my husband with the most ferocious passion, the desire within me like a little ball of electricity, charged and directionless and constantly seeking an outlet. When I made love to David, it was with a blend of passion and guilt, desire and remorse, and afterwards I had to resist the impulse to curl up under the sheet at the furthest side of the bed from him, my back turned so he couldn't see my shame.

On those nights after Zoë had left, when David reached for me in the darkness and I felt his intensity, it crossed my mind more than once that he was like a man in love.

# 12. David

Timing is everything, isn't it? Had Zoë come to me earlier, when she was still a child, when I had a chance to be a proper father to her, would things have worked out differently? The irony is that when she arrived in my life I actually thought the timing was perfect. My mother was dying. There had been no official prognosis, but I could see for myself the steep decline she had slipped into, the steady corrosion of her thoughts and memories that brought a corresponding weakening in her body. Within those short weeks, it was like witnessing a shrinkage in her, not just her brain growing porous, but her body diminishing to a frightening degree. When I helped her into or out of the car, I noticed with alarm the thinning of her limbs. I began mentally to prepare myself for what was imminent. While the sadness of my mother's decline was in my thoughts, I found some consolation in my growing relationship with a daughter I had not known existed. Zoë coming into my life at that time seemed a natural exchange – where one light was dimming, another had begun to glow.

She came to us every Sunday, and as the weeks progressed, I noticed with a touch of happiness how she relaxed, opening up a little more each time. I felt a corresponding loosening within myself. At college, it remained awkward, and our dealings there retained a note of professional distance. But at home I could be myself, and so could she. As the days of the week passed, I would find myself looking forward to Sunday.

I knew that Caroline wasn't happy about it. She had made some noises about Robbie and Holly feeling displaced but I couldn't help thinking that at the back of her words lay a petty meanness, a sort of jealousy over the time and attention I was giving to Zoë. Whenever we came close to discussing it, the conversation would teeter on the threshold of argument. Mostly we went around it in circles, avoiding anything too combustible. I promised to do something with just *our* kids, and managed, on a couple of occasions during those autumn months, to spoil Robbie and Holly. Those events passed off peacefully enough, but still I had the niggling feeling that such gestures towards Caroline and the kids were a lame effort at ameliorating the disruption I'd caused by introducing Zoë into their lives.

She didn't come to the house every Sunday. Sometimes I took her to my local for a pub lunch, just the two of us – partly as a sop to Caroline's mood, partly because I felt it important that we spend a little time alone together to get to know each other better.

'How's the studying coming along?' I asked one Sunday.

We were sitting in the corner snug, surrounded by wooden panelling adorned with tinsel, a rugby match on the telly above the bar, two lasagnes sitting in front of us.

'Okay, I guess.' She took a forkful of food, spitting it out quickly, her tongue burned. 'God, that's hot!' She laughed, looking flushed and youthful.

'Here, take a drink.' I pushed her lager towards her, drinking from my own pint while she raised the bottle to her lips.

'I can't wait for the exams to be over,' she admitted. 'Any hints you can give me about your paper?' she added jokingly.

'Nice try,' I said drily, enjoying her playfulness. 'You know I won't be correcting yours. Undue influence, and all that.'

'Sure. I know.'

I was relieved that she didn't argue: I didn't want to go into the protocols of an ethics committee. Besides, any mention of McCormack made me feel queasy; he had been given the task of grading a tranche of my papers, Zoë's included, and to reciprocate I had agreed to take some of his students' scripts. It had been an awkward moment, but Alan had dealt with it perfunctorily at the exam board. It was enough to gloss over it with Zoë.

'You must be looking forward to Christmas?' I asked.

'A break, yes, Christmas not as much.'

'Bah, humbug,' I joked, and she laughed.

'No, it's not that. It's just weird now, without Mam.'

'Of course. I'm sorry, I wasn't thinking.'

'That's okay,' she said.

'What are your plans? Will Gary be expecting you?'

'Gary,' she replied, disdain creeping into her voice. 'Who knows what he's expecting?'

I'd been giving the idea some thought for a while, even though I hadn't discussed it yet with Caroline. The thought of Zoë spending Christmas in the chilly company of a stepfather who had little affection for her was troubling. I hadn't intended broaching the subject with her that day, but while it was on my mind, I decided what the hell.

'Maybe you don't have to go to Gary for Christmas,' I ventured.

'How do you mean?'

'You could come to us.'

'David, I couldn't, but thanks.'

'Why not?'

She put down her knife and fork, and wiped her mouth with a napkin. I had the impression she was stalling. 'You should spend Christmas together, the four of you,' she said eventually. 'I'd feel I was intruding.'

'Don't be ridiculous. We'd love to have you.'

'Even Caroline?'

'Listen,' I said, 'Caroline will be fine. I'll square it with her.'

She frowned at her plate, half the food untouched. 'I don't know. She really doesn't like me. I don't want to cause any trouble for you – especially not at Christmas.'

I could have tried explaining to Zoë that she shouldn't take Caroline's perceived coldness to her as something personal, but she was so despondent that the words would have sounded hollow. I weighed up the situation in my mind – perhaps, in hindsight, I should have been more cautious – then said: 'When I told Caroline about you, back in October, it was difficult for her, but not for the reasons you might think.'

She was listening now, her despondency replaced by curiosity.

'She got pregnant, you see, when we were students. This was before I knew your mother.'

I told her everything. About the pregnancy, the abortion, our subsequent break-up. She took it all in. Only when I had finished did she sit back. 'Now it makes more sense.'

'It's hard for Caroline, you see. She still feels regret about what happened. And when you came along . . .'

'I was a painful reminder,' she said, finishing my sentence. 'Did you ever regret it?'

'No. No, I didn't. We were young. It happened. I never really think about it.'

'Do you wish Linda had done the same?'

Her question shocked me. She held herself still as she waited for my answer.

'Of course not,' I said. Instinctively, I reached for her hand, held it there on the table. With a flash I thought of Linda that day in the Oarsman pub when I had told her about accepting a post-doctoral position in UCD. *You're leaving Belfast?* she had said, her voice small and shocked. It was the same day she had given her lecture on Walter Benjamin's 'Angel of History'. A doomed creature, she had called it: 'It wants to make whole what has been destroyed.' I thought about how Klee's painting *Angelus Novus* had been projected on to the wall of the lecture theatre. How beautiful it was, how beautiful she was. I thought about how she had given me exactly the same look as Zoë had just given me, her hand in mine, the same plunging feeling in my heart.

A cheer went up from the rugby supporters – Leinster had scored. I let go of Zoë's hand and we both sat back.

'Come to us for Christmas, Zoë.'

She thought about it for a while. Then, smiling up at

me, a bashful look on her face that couldn't disguise her pleasure, she said: 'Okay, then, I will.'

'What's this?' Caroline asked.

It was Christmas morning; Robbie and Holly were in the next room, still exploring their newly opened gifts while I was making coffee, readying myself for the Christmas lunch preparations. Caroline had arrived downstairs, festive in a red wrap dress and black heels, her hair loosely curled, and now she stood there, holding up the little silver box.

'A present for Zoë,' I answered, adding sugar to my cup. 'Coffee?'

'Please.' She turned the box over in her hands. 'Mind if I look?'

'Go ahead.'

I poured her coffee while she prised open the lid and looked at the earrings. A pair of freshwater seed pearls, silver threads curling around them in the shape of looping petals. I had spied them in a jeweller's window in Powerscourt and thought at once of Linda, the one Christmas we had spent together, tinsel draped over the windows in her flat, a plastic Santa on the mantelpiece, looking at the earrings I had given her in the cup of her hand, saying: 'You do it.' How vivid the memory remained – my knuckles grazing the skin of her cheek, the whorl of her small ear against my hand, the feel of the soft fleshy lobe as I held my breath and pressed the sharp point into it. That moment seemed to me more intimate, more erotically charged, than the half-hour we had previously spent tussling with each other under the sheets.

'They're lovely,' Caroline said, her voice quiet and contemplative, betraying, I sensed, what might have been a touch of resentment. She closed the lid and returned the little box to the counter, while I gave her her coffee, all the time hoping she wouldn't ask how much they had cost.

'What time did you tell her?' she asked.

'One.'

I hadn't liked the thought of Zoë waking up on Christmas morning alone in her flat – especially when we were at home together as a family – but it would have been a step too far to ask her to come first thing, too disruptive to the routines we had already established as a family over the years.

After coffee, the four of us walked around to attend Christmas Mass in our local church, then I left Caroline and the kids at home while I drove over to my mother's to pick her up. She seemed bright that morning, sprightlier than I had seen her of late, but the vagueness was still there as she glanced about her house, as if trying to remember something she didn't want to leave without. Whatever it was eluded her, and I coaxed her gently into the car. At home, we settled her into an armchair close to the fire, and I left Holly chatting to her while I joined Caroline in the kitchen.

She was wearing an apron over her dress, and there was a high colour in her cheeks as her heels clacked over the kitchen floor.

'Can I help?' I asked.

'You do the spuds,' she said briskly. 'But first, be a love and pour me a glass of wine. It'll make tackling this goose a lot easier.'

I plucked a bottle from the rack – a Margaux I had been saving – and poured her some. Without commenting, Caroline lifted the glass to her lips and drank. She let out a sigh and it felt like the tension between us was lifting, as if a temporary truce had been declared. My hope was that it would last beyond the day itself – that some kind of normality might return, a gentle remoulding of our family to allow for the newest member. Glancing at the clock, I saw that it was half past twelve. Zoë would be here within the half-hour. A tingle of nerves passed briefly over the back of my neck.

'We're on schedule,' Caroline said, putting on an oven glove.

Holly came in and set the table, and I sat for a while in the living room with my mother. *My Fair Lady* was on the telly and Mum watched it with glazed eyes and a smile. I kept glancing at my watch, growing a little agitated as it crept past one, and then towards two.

Caroline stuck her head around the door. 'Any sign of Zoë?'

'Not yet.'

'Maybe try calling her. The goose will be ready soon.'

I dialled her number and listened while it rang through to voicemail. I left a message, and then, just to be sure, sent a text as well, trying to word it to appear casual.

Robbie came downstairs and announced he was starving. 'Is Zoë here yet?' he asked.

'Any minute,' I said, with an optimism I didn't feel.

In the kitchen, I asked Caroline if we could hold off for a little longer. She continued stirring the gravy, but didn't look happy.

I went upstairs and tried Zoë's number again. There was no answer. I considered driving around to her flat in Rathmines but because I had already had a drink I decided against it. Standing at my bedroom window, I craned my neck to see down our road, searching for her blonde hair above the hedgerows and gates.

By half past two, she still hadn't arrived.

'We'll have to start without her,' Caroline said.

Reluctantly I agreed, and we all sat down and began tucking into the terrine Caroline had made. A festive runner lay down the middle of the table, pillar candles lit, encircled by sprigs of holly and ivy. Christmas choral music came softly through the speakers. I knew I was lucky. I was surrounded by my family in our comfortable home, enjoying the spoils and privileges of hard work and a professional salary. Yet part of me was thinking about the dingy flat in Belfast, the plastic Santa, Linda and I eating, plates balanced on our knees, and it seemed to me, when I thought about it, that I had felt much happier then. I had been unburdened, my whole life still ahead of me, with the joy of the new love that filled me in a way I couldn't measure. I ate the terrine, clearing my plate, with a degree of discomfort and guilt.

We finished off the Margaux and I opened a Châteauneuf-du-Pape. After the goose, there was pudding, and we all agreed that we were too stuffed for cheese. Outside the window, the sky had darkened. No one said it, but it was clear that Zoë wasn't coming.

'No word?' Caroline asked, as we cleared away the dishes.

'No. I wonder what happened to her.'

'Maybe she went up to Belfast after all.' She put the detergent tablet into the dishwasher and flipped the door closed.

'You'd think she'd have rung,' I said.

Caroline gave me a sidelong glance that seemed laden with wry weariness, but didn't say anything. All day she had seemed to be giving off something – a kind of relief that Zoë hadn't turned up. It wasn't anything she said *per se*, just the relaxed relish she took in the day without Zoë, as I perceived it.

'I just hope she's okay,' I added, prodded by anxiety. It wasn't like Zoë, no matter what Caroline was implying.

'I wouldn't worry,' came her sharp reply. She wiped her hands on the towel, then threw it on to the counter with a flourish. 'I'm sure she'll be in touch when she needs something.'

As it happened, it was not Zoë who got in touch, but someone else.

Christmas Day passed and I dropped my mother home the following morning. Afterwards, Caroline and I took the kids for a hike up around the Three Rock Mountain – a St Stephen's Day tradition. I walked with a hand in my pocket, clutching my phone, waiting to feel it vibrate with an incoming call or text, something to explain Zoë's absence. I had left several messages, dropping any pretence of casualness as the time passed and there was no response from her.

Back home, I went straight through into the kitchen, putting on the kettle for tea, my hands and feet still numb from the bitter cold of the mountain air. I didn't hear the phone ringing in the hall. It was only when I heard Caroline's voice saying, 'Is she all right? What happened?' that the rigour of her questions and her polite but worried tone alerted me to trouble. I stood in the kitchen doorway, watching her speaking into the phone, growing more anxious as she said: 'Of course. I'll let him know immediately. He'll be over right away.'

*My mother*, I thought.

But it was not my mother.

'It's Zoë,' Caroline told me, her eyes fixed on my face, choosing her words carefully. 'She's in hospital.'

'*What?*'

'She's fine, David. She's out of danger.'

'What happened?'

Lowering her tone, so the children in the next room wouldn't hear, she said: 'She took an overdose.'

Weakness came into my legs. The numbness left my extremities and I felt the stinging pain of pricking needles all over my feet and hands as the blood came rushing into them. 'She tried to kill herself?'

Caroline didn't answer that. Instead she told me which hospital and named the ward where Zoë was. I grabbed the keys from the hall table where I had left them and went back outside. My hands were trembling as I started the engine – it was still warm.

It's something no parent ever wishes to see – their child lying helpless in a hospital bed. Even though Zoë had been a stranger to me only months before, even though I had missed all the birthdays and Christmas mornings of her childhood, the first day at school, the hockey matches and end-of-year plays, as soon as I saw her lying there, tubes travelling into her veins, I felt a rush of protective love so strong that I had to stop and collect myself, lest all that emotion might break inside me and flood out.

She was lying on her side, a blanket covering her body. She was not fully awake – sedated, perhaps, or deep in a depression. A bruise blossomed on her hand where an IV had been inserted. I wanted to reach out and touch her, but I was afraid of disturbing her.

As I approached the bed, her head turned. As soon as she saw me, the mask fell away, her face contorting with tears that seemed to gust through her, savage and raw.

'Zoë,' I said softly, pulling a chair up next to her.

She was trying to cover her face, hiding her brokenness from me, but the sobbing and shaking spoke of her fragility. 'I'm so sorry,' she said, the words coming out liquid and halting, spoken between gulped breaths.

'Sssh,' I whispered. 'You don't need to apologize. I'm just glad you're all right.'

She continued to cry but the sobbing had lost some of its raw edge, and while she was still upset, I could see she was calming. Passing my eyes over her, I noticed how pale and gaunt she was, skeletal under that harsh lighting. All the colour had drained from her – even her hair looked drab and lifeless. She was wearing a hospital gown, her bare arms emerging from the printed cotton. I was so used to seeing her swathed in baggy jumpers, or long-sleeved T-shirts, the cuffs tugged down over her wrists and hands. With a shock, I saw the markings on the inside of her arms – a series of vicious little cuts, as if a cat had clawed her, over and over. Some were fairly new, the scabs still present, while others had healed into fine pink lines, and a few had faded almost completely. I saw those lines and felt emotion inflate within me, tears of shock and pity coming unexpectedly. I swallowed them, taking her hand.

'What happened?' I asked gently. 'You can tell me.'

'You must wish you'd never met me,' she said hoarsely.

'Not at all. In fact, quite the opposite.' It surprised me how much I meant those words. 'Please tell me, Zoë. I promise I won't judge. I just want to understand.'

She turned over so that she was lying on her back, staring up at the ceiling. Her face looked flatter, her eyes dulled. She had let go of my hand but still I sat close, leaning towards her, waiting.

'It just got too much,' she began. 'Everything got on top of me. I felt like I was drowning.'

I nodded encouragement. When she didn't go on, I prompted her: 'Was it your studies? A lot of students struggle in the first year. It's very common.'

'Yes,' she agreed, but I could sense the tug of reluctance within her and knew there was something more.

'There's still plenty of time to catch up,' I offered. 'It's only the end of Semester One.'

'Time,' she said drily. The tears were gone now, and what remained was dry deflation. 'That's part of the problem. I have no time.'

I knew that she had a part-time job to help pay her rent, but as she detailed the jobs she had and the hours she needed to work to pay her bills, it became clear to me the burden under which she was struggling, and how little time remained for her studies.

'What about Gary?' I asked, feeling somewhat awkward at mentioning his name. 'I had the impression that he was helping you financially, paying your fees at least?'

Even as I said the words, I felt fraudulent. I was Zoë's father, not Gary. Why did I expect a man I had never met to pay for my daughter's education?

'Gary has made it obvious that he wants nothing more to do with me.'

She enunciated the words clearly, hardness entering her tone. There was a warning there to keep away, not to prod the sore too deeply. For now, I resolved to leave it be.

'How do you manage?' I asked. 'With all these part-time jobs, you must barely have time to go to class, let alone study.'

In a voice still scratched from the recent tubes down her throat, she described to me the various uppers and downers she took to get the work done, how she used medications to keep her awake through half the night when she needed to study, and then to induce rapid sleep. It was depressing listening to it, hearing the dry clack of her tongue against the roof of her mouth, her tiny frame dwarfed by the bed, the hospital cubicle, the austere reek of disinfectant in my nose.

'Well, that has to stop,' I said, a fatherly, instructive tone creeping into my voice. 'You can't keep that up. Look at what it's doing to your body.'

'I know.'

'Zoë, something must have prompted you to do this now,' I said, as calmly as I could. 'What was it?'

She tried to prop herself up, but had hardly the strength to do so. Reaching for a bottle of water on the side table, she took a sip, then settled back against the pillow. She appeared sullen, a little ashamed, perhaps. 'It's stupid,' she admitted. 'I'm such a cliché. Trying to kill myself on Christmas Day. The psych nurse they sent around to talk to me told me they get more suicide attempts at Christmas than any other time of the year.'

'I suppose that makes sense. A lot of people find Christmas hard.'

'Yeah. And without Mam, it's just . . .' Her voice died away.

'What about us, Zoë? We wanted you to have Christmas at the house. We were all expecting you. Robbie was really disappointed –'

'You won't tell him, will you?' she asked quickly, panic in her eyes.

'Zoë –'

'Please? I couldn't bear it.' She started to cry again, and I put my hand on her arm to reassure her.

'It's okay, sweetheart,' I said, the endearment slipping out as easily as it would were Holly lying in the bed needing comfort.

She settled back, the fright going out of her eyes, but she remained uneasy. 'I've let you down,' she stated.

'No, you haven't.'

'It was kind of you to invite me for Christmas. But as the time drew near, I just knew I couldn't come. You were only inviting me because you felt sorry for me.'

'That's not true,' I argued, feeling a warm breath of anger. 'The only person feeling sorry for you was you. I asked you because I wanted you to be there. Because you're my daughter and that makes you part of my family.'

'David, you don't even know me. There are things I've done . . .'

Her voice trailed off and she turned her face away. The words spoken, she seemed more lucid than she had since I'd sat down. It chilled me to hear them.

'Listen,' I said. 'As soon as you're discharged, I want you to come and stay with us. There's a spare room in the attic. You'd be comfortable. Safe.'

She didn't answer. Already her eyes were closing, as if she were locking me out, wanting to be alone again with her troubled thoughts, her guilty secrets.

'Live with us? Isn't that a bit rash?' Caroline said.

'She tried to kill herself. I'm her father – it's the very least I can do.'

She was preparing dinner and I watched as she sliced an aubergine, placing each sliver carefully in a colander and sprinkling it with salt. 'I know,' she said softly. 'It's hard to take in, that's all. What she did. It seems unbelievable.'

'I just think if we can get her back here, provide her with some stability and support, help her get back on her feet again, it will be better for everyone.'

Caroline turned on the tap and rinsed her hands. 'What should we tell the children?'

'Zoë doesn't want them to know what she did.'

'David –'

'Please. She's ashamed.'

'Are we to lie to them about it?'

I shrugged, a mean thought entering my head: *You've lied to them before. You've lied to all of us.*

'I feel very uneasy about this – all of it,' she said,

wiping her hands on the towel. 'She's clearly unstable and vulnerable, and I'm not sure she's a good influence on Robbie and Holly. I mean, what if she tries to do it again?'

'I don't think that's going to happen.'

'But what if it does?'

'You know what, Caroline? If it were anyone else – the child of a friend of ours, one of Robbie's pals – you'd be flinging wide the doors, laying down the red carpet for them.'

She turned away and hung the tea-towel over the rail of the cooker. Her back still to me, I heard her say: 'She makes me uneasy.'

With her admission, the air between us seemed to deflate, the tension easing.

I went to stand behind her, put my hands on her shoulders and leaned in so the side of my face was close to hers. 'She needs us, love,' I said gently. 'She has nothing, no one. Only us.'

A brief hesitation, and then her hand reached up to cover mine.

'I'll go and make up her room,' she said.

I stood in the corridor by the lifts, waiting for Zoë. There was a window looking on to the tops of the trees, the rooftops of Merrion and Ballsbridge. Outside, the evening was cold and still. I felt a stirring of nerves in my chest. The sky was a bright blue, so clear I could see as far as Howth Head beyond the bay. Seagulls called loud and clear. My fingers tapped impatiently on the sill.

It was back with me again, the *déjà vu* – the nervous energy in my body fizzing. Something had changed between us, and even though I felt as if I were carrying all the giddy expectancy of a younger man, the solid mass of our bond lay underneath. The hours I had spent with her at the hospital over the past few days, holding her hand, listening to her, comforting her, I had felt it announce itself so strongly that I wondered how I had ever questioned it. I thought of the DNA test I had ordered, the deceitful manner of it, and felt ashamed.

A door opened and I turned to see her carrying her bag, shoulders slumped forward in her grey hoodie, but she gave a half-smile when she saw me and I felt a bloom of hope.

'Hey,' she said shyly, and I took the bag from her.

'Plenty of rest, the doctor said,' I told her, as I pressed the button to call the lift.

I put my arm about her shoulders. She felt so slight against me, enclosed within my embrace as the lift doors opened, but I could see our reflections in the mirror and she was smiling. For the time being at least, she was safe.

# 13. Caroline

That first night, David spent a long time up in her room, his low, sonorous tones coming down the narrow stairs as I stood on the landing, looking up at the closed door. I kept thinking of the dark shadows around her eyes and mouth, lending an austere grace to her beauty. The tragic princess. Afterwards, when he came downstairs, he said little of what they had talked about.

'She's calm,' was all he said, as if that was his primary concern.

One by one we went to bed.

I lay awake staring at the ceiling, thinking of her in the room above us. I couldn't tell if David was asleep beside me. Perhaps he, too, was listening for noises overhead, light footsteps across the floorboards, the gentle creaking of the bed as she turned over. I was listening attentively, every nerve alive to the sensation of this stranger in my home.

Some time before midnight, I heard her voice, words muffled by their passage through floor and ceiling. She was alone up there and I pictured her sitting on the bed, knees drawn up to her chin, talking on her phone to a friend or a boyfriend, filling them in on the new turn her life had taken. I thought of the room surrounding her – the pitched ceiling under the eaves, the paint still fresh and gleaming from the attic conversion completed in the last year. I thought of the striped bedding, the lamp plugged in on the floor, the wall of plastic storage boxes containing some of the children's old toys and clothes that I couldn't bring myself to throw out. Boxes of nostalgia, things that were precious to me, now a part of her domain. I tried to tell myself that this was just a temporary arrangement, a fleeting stay until she had recovered. But as I listened to her voice, the high, light note of her laughter coming from up there under the roof, I felt a trickle of doubt. She didn't sound to me like a girl who wanted to end it all. She sounded relaxed, as if she were settling in. 'Make yourself at home,' I had told her, when really I meant nothing of the sort.

I woke up early on the first morning of the new term, and was out of bed, showered and dressed before anyone else had stirred. David came down some time afterwards, his eyes still puffy, wordlessly fixing a pot of coffee while I sat at the counter, eating toast and making a list on my iPhone.

'Are the kids getting up?' I asked, after he had taken his first sip.

'There's movement. Robbie's in the bathroom. Zoë's not going into college so I don't expect we'll see her until this evening.'

It was disconcerting – already he was including her in the collective 'kids'.

Holly came downstairs, followed by her brother, the volume of noise in the kitchen rising with their presence – the clatter of spoons and bowls, the low-key grumbling – and soon enough it was half past eight and we were gathering in the hall, packing lunches into school bags and pulling on coats.

'Should we check on her?' I asked David, as he came downstairs with his bag, taking his cycling helmet from the coat-stand.

'She needs to rest, Caroline, after what she's been through.'

The kids were piling out of the door now, getting into the car, and David was wheeling his bike down the path. I stood there, looking up the stairs, feeling uneasy. I didn't like the thought of her being alone in my house. I imagined her tiptoeing down from the attic as soon as we'd driven off, nosing around our bedroom, picking over my things.

I ran up the stairs, making sure my footfall was audible. Knocking sharply on the door, I heard her call, 'Come in,' and pushed the door open.

She was lying on her side, propped on one elbow, her head resting on her hand, reading *Madame Bovary*.

'Did you sleep well?'

'Yep.'

'Well,' I said, as she glanced up from her book, a hazy look on her face as if her attention was still with the novel, 'I just wanted to let you know that we're going now.'

'Right.'

She appeared pale and slight, the long sleeves of her nightdress pulled down over her wrists. I hesitated a moment, my eye caught by the coverlet over the bed. It took me a moment to recognize it – a patchwork bedspread, triangles of blue and grey cotton stitched together into geometrical patterns. I had bought it in Thailand years before when I was not long out of college. Zoë must have found it among the storage boxes up there, which meant she had been snooping through our things. It wasn't as if there was anything secret or valuable hidden away, but I still felt angry and disheartened. It was another incursion by her into our lives, another presumption on her part that she was entitled to take possession of whatever she found. I considered saying something, but instinct told me it wasn't worth it.

'How're you feeling?' I asked.

She didn't answer, just shrugged, her attention on the book again.

'You know, if ever you want to talk,' I began, 'about what happened . . . about what led you to . . .'

She looked up sharply.

'. . . I'd be happy to listen,' I finished.

'Right,' she said, bemused, before she returned to her novel and lazily turned a page.

I backed out, stung by her dismissal of me. It wasn't that I expected her to accept my offer, but a small show of appreciation would have been nice. It occurred to me that, by attempting suicide, she had got exactly what she wanted – her foot in the door – which made me doubt whether she had ever intended killing herself at all. By the time I got downstairs, David was already gone, so I left a key on the hall table, took one last look back up the stairs, and closed the door behind me.

The rain started that morning and continued all week – heavy, blistering downpours, monsoon-like in their unrelenting ferocity. The air in the hallway was heavy with the odour of damp clothes. Condensation on windows, heavy traffic, leaves clogged in drains pooling with water.

Every day, when we left the house, she was up there in

her room. When I came home in the evening, I'd find her curled up on the sofa with her book, eating a carrot, or watching TV with the others. She'd look up briefly when I came through the door, greet me with a wan smile, then return her attention to whatever she was absorbed in at the time. She wasn't hostile, or even cold, but there was a mildness to her, a lack of engagement, that I found maddening. From what I could tell, she had reasonably recovered from her blip at Christmas. There was no evidence of lingering depression, no black moods. She seemed so docile, so willing to fade into the background, that it made me wonder had she any desire or intention to find an alternative place to live. Not that I mentioned it. Even after she had returned to college, David made it clear that she remained too fragile to live alone.

The month passed in a flurry of storms interspersed with unseasonably warm weather. It was as if the meteorological elements were somehow mirroring the uncertain climate within our home. As the weeks progressed, I felt Zoë's position solidifying in the house, growing unquestionable. She was making more of an effort to help out and was, I suppose, largely unobtrusive. Tidy, hers was a quiet presence, but a presence nonetheless. And when the others were not around – when it was just me and her – she allowed the mask to slip, her polite charm vanishing, replaced by cool remoteness.

The precariousness of our situation was made clear to me one weekday evening – the occasion of our first serious argument about her. We were clearing away the dishes after dinner, David scraping plates into the bin and handing them to Holly, when Zoë stood up and, without a word to any of us, left the room. In her wake, I heard the dull thud of the salad bowl being brought down hard on the counter. 'Why is she allowed to get out of the dishes?' Holly demanded.

'Until she's well –' David began, but Holly cut him off.

'There's nothing wrong with her! Why do you keep tiptoeing around her?'

David put down the plate he was holding.

From upstairs came the jagged strains of Robbie's cello. He, too, had been excused household chores but Holly wasn't interested in that. 'How much longer is she going to be here?' she asked, her whole body stiff with tension. I could see how frustrated she was.

'Sweetheart –' I began, trying to calm her.

'I'm sick of her!' she declared, her voice rising to a screech.

'Holly!' David said sharply, but she was already turning from him. Seconds later we heard feet thundering up the stairs, the slam of her bedroom door. We looked at each other.

'Well?' I said.

'What?'

'She has a point.'

He turned from me, picked up another plate and continued scraping, but with a more committed air.

'Can't we talk about this?' I asked. 'Holly's not happy.'

'Holly's behaving like a spoilt brat.'

'I think you're being unfair, David. This is her home and she's feeling marginalized.'

'I'm not saying Zoë should stay here indefinitely,' he said, putting the plate and knife down, 'but it's only a few weeks since she tried to kill herself. I'm not comfortable at the thought of her taking care of herself yet.'

'Have you talked to Zoë about it? About how she's feeling now, within herself?'

'A little. I mean, she's doing better but she's still vulnerable. I think she needs our support.'

'Shouldn't she be getting professional help?'

'How is she supposed to afford that?'

'What about the university? Haven't they got counsellors?'

'I don't think that's the answer, Caroline.'

I could see I wasn't going to get anywhere. Turning back to the worktop I began scraping leftovers into a Tupperware box.

'I'll do something with Holly,' he said, to appease me. 'Something to make her feel special.'

'Fine.' I put the box into the fridge. Still I could feel him watching me. When I glanced at him, it was obvious there was something else on his mind. 'What is it?' I asked.

'I've been giving some thought to Zoë's college fees,' he began. Instantly my defences rose. 'She hasn't said it outright, but it's clear that she hasn't got much money. Gary isn't exactly supportive and the part-time jobs barely pay her rent. I have the impression it might have been a contributing factor to what she did on Christmas Day.'

'Where are you going with this?' I asked, unable to keep the coldness from my voice.

He was standing opposite me, looking at me squarely. 'I want to pay her college fees.'

A laugh escaped me, and I could see it startled him. 'With what?' I asked. 'A big chunk of your salary goes to pay the mortgage. Have you forgotten the loan we took out to do all this?' I gestured with one hand to take in the new kitchen, the extension, with its wall of windows, revealing the garden beyond. Despite the bequest from my parents, our house renovation – the renovation of our marriage – had put pressure on our finances.

'We'll manage,' he said, standing his ground.

'What about all the other outgoings? Car payments, school fees, health insurance, not to mention cello lessons, piano lessons and the other after-school activities? It all adds up, David. How are you going to make your salary cover all that as well as college fees?'

He began to look shifty.

'Can't you pay for some of that stuff?'

I didn't say anything, just stared.

'Now that you're working, you could cover the kids' activities and the school fees. Maybe the health insurance, too.'

I could hardly believe what he was suggesting. 'You want me to pay for Zoë's college fees?'

'I didn't say –'

'That's what it amounts to, though.'

'For God's sake, Caroline. Is it so much to ask that you contribute a little? All these years, I've been shouldering the entire financial burden. Is it unreasonable to ask you to share the load now?'

Anger shot through every muscle and fibre. It was outrageous. All those years I had worked in our home, raising our children, keeping things running smoothly on the domestic front, leaving him free to pursue his career, all that time it had felt like there had been a pact between us, a mutual appreciation of the other's endeavours. Now, with the sweep of his words, he was devaluing all the years I had put into our family, our home, as if there were some kind of debt I needed to repay him. His suggestion that I should pay for Zoë's education – and that was what it was, no matter how he tried to dress it up – was like a slap in the face.

'I am not paying for that girl's education,' I said emphatically.

'Hang on –'

'No, David.'

I stepped past him quickly, unwilling to spend another second discussing it, and as I went into the hall, I felt it. The slightest movement of air coming from the top of the stairs, the faintest creak of a floorboard overhead. I moved into the middle and looked up, hoping to catch a glimpse of whoever had been listening.

Perhaps I had imagined it. All the bedroom doors were closed. Robbie's cello was silent. I thought I heard laughter drifting down from his room. Still, I couldn't shake the feeling that someone else had overheard our entire conversation in the kitchen.

A little later in the week, I was in the office when out of the blue I got a call from Robbie's school asking me to come at once. There had been an incident.

'What happened? Is Robbie all right?'

'He's fine,' the school secretary told me. 'He's in Mrs Campbell's office at the moment.'

I had not seen Mrs Campbell, the headmistress, since the business with Aidan, and even hearing her name now brought a prickling to my skin, like thousands of nerve-endings sitting up in fright.

'I'm at work,' I said, flustered. 'I mean, is he hurt?'

'Oh, no. *He*'s not hurt,' she said, and my heart sank as she went on: 'If it's difficult for you, perhaps Robbie's father could come. Either way, Mrs Campbell wants this sorted out immediately.'

There was no way I could ask David. He'd made it clear after the parent-teacher meeting in September that I needed to get over my humiliation.

'I'll be there in half an hour,' I told her.

A short time later, when I parked my car outside the school and climbed the granite steps, I was filled with dread at going back there. Dread mingled with a niggling sense of annoyance. Why hadn't I stood my ground at the time, insisted on moving Robbie to a different school? The whole staff knew what I had done. Did David get some kind of satisfaction from that? His petty revenge meted out piecemeal with every parent-teacher meeting for the next three years? Every school play, every sports day, every end-of-year Mass: did he quietly enjoy my humiliation at every occasion?

'I'll be brief,' Mrs Campbell told me.

Ever the professional, she sat behind her desk and filled me in on the campaign of aggression that my son had been waging against his French teacher, Miss Murphy. It had been going on for some time, apparently, but Miss Murphy – in her twenties, this her first teaching job – had kept quiet on the matter, hoping it would resolve itself without her having to involve anyone else.

At first it was small, silly stuff: using the face of his

watch, he would reflect sunlight from the window into Miss Murphy's eyes as she faced the class; he made a popping noise every time she finished a sentence; he would hum constantly, then deny it was him. Stupid stuff, the kind of petty misdemeanours that drive every teacher mad but not enough to warrant serious disciplinary steps. Lately, however, things had escalated. He had started throwing pens at her whenever her back was turned. When she came into the classroom, someone had drawn her likeness, breasts bared, on the whiteboard, with the caption 'Come get it, boys!' in a speech bubble from her mouth. She couldn't prove it had been Robbie, but her suspicions leaned in his direction.

The incident finally prompting her to tell Mrs Campbell had happened that morning. Having grown exasperated with his constant baiting, she had ordered Robbie to stand up by the whiteboard for the duration of the class but as she proceeded to give the lesson, he began slowly inching towards her. At first, she didn't notice, until some of the other boys began sniggering and she turned to find him almost upon her. Shouting at him to get back against the wall, she had put a hand to his shoulder to propel him. Instantly Robbie had swiped away her arm and putting both hands to her chest he had shoved her roughly back. Miss Murphy, stumbling over the leg of a table, had fallen awkwardly and banged her head against the seat of a chair. She was still in the sick bay, apparently, shaken.

'It goes without saying,' Mrs Campbell went on, 'that a violent assault on a member of staff is absolutely insupportable and must be treated with the utmost seriousness.'

'Of course,' I said, reeling from all she had told me.

'The most worrying part in this sorry affair is how targeted the attack was,' she said. 'In every other class, Robbie is well behaved. None of the other teachers have any complaints about his behaviour.'

'I don't understand it,' I said. 'I have no idea why this has happened, or what he has against this teacher. He's usually such a gentle boy.'

Her eyes narrowed, and her voice softened. 'Is everything all right at home? When a student is disruptive in school, it's often because of some difficulty he's experiencing at home.'

Neither of us mentioned my year-long absence from the school, my previous indiscretion. I'm sure it must have been on her mind, though.

'Everything's fine,' I said quickly.

Robbie was suspended for a week.

How strange it had been, going back to the school. Just standing within those stone walls again had touched old memories alive, and I found myself thinking back to that time as I drove in silence, my son staring sullenly out the window.

If you saw Aidan, the word 'handsome' would not come to mind. A tall, thin man, with a longish face and blue eyes, he was affable and self-effacing. His son was in Robbie's class and we were both on the Parents' Committee. It was not love at first sight, but from the start we'd got on. Sometimes, after a committee meeting, a few of us would go for a drink in the pub around the corner. On occasion, it was just the two of us. All we did was talk, but it was such talk! Small things and big things, from school gossip to our own individual parenting concerns. Idle chitchat, that was all, but a constant pleasurable flow of it.

We had been flirting with each other for some time – harmless enough – but on one night, a night where we stayed behind for a third drink after the others had left, it began to grow more serious. He told me his wife was a very neat and organized person – there was never any question of them leaving a trail of clothes along the floor on the way to the bedroom as seen in movies: everything had to be neatly hung up and put away before lovemaking could commence. 'I bet you're not like that,' he said, keeping his eyes on me over the lip of his glass.

Outside, he waited while I unlocked my bike from the railings, and when I turned to say goodnight, he kissed me long and hard on the mouth and I let him. I remember standing in my kitchen a short time later, my hands to my hot cheeks, horrified by what I had done and yet thrilled by it, too.

The next day I felt silly and ashamed. I had let things go too far and resolved to stop before it got out of hand. A text from Aidan in the late afternoon and I, foolishly, responded. We began texting every day and soon we were meeting outside committee nights – for coffee during the day and, when we could swing it, at night. We met in dingy pubs I'd never heard of in rough parts of town. We sat in the back row of art-house movies, necking like teenagers, discreetly fumbling in the dark.

We never actually had sex, although we probably would have, eventually, if we hadn't been caught. And, yes, I did feel guilty about it, desperately guilty, but something kept driving me on, refused to let me stop. The seed of anger planted inside me – *She was the love of his life, not me.* Somehow it opened out and grew shoots, tendrils sneaking out to grasp forbidden pleasures. Such a heady time. Between the elation of the illicit romance and the crying fits in the privacy of the bathroom when the children were at school, my husband at work, I would think of what I was doing and grow frightened and depressed.

At the end of the committee meeting one night, while the others were tidying away the coffee cups, Mrs Campbell made a neat stack of her paperwork and said: 'Caroline, Aidan, a word, please?'

She hid it well – I'll give her that much. Throughout the meeting she had behaved as if she was entirely without suspicion that two of her committee members might secretly be fucking. It was only when we went into her office and Aidan closed the door behind us that she addressed us in a tone of icy fury, her eyes bright with disgust. 'I think one of you had better tell me just what is going on.'

At first, we feigned ignorance, even hilarity at the suggestion, followed by indignation when she would not be put off.

'You were seen!' she told us, and I felt a twang of fear.

Aidan refused to go gently, challenging her assertions, demanding to know the details behind the allegation – where had we supposedly been seen (Conways on Parnell Street), when (three nights ago), by whom (she refused to say).

'You have children!' she said, with exasperation. 'How could you be so reckless with their happiness? So selfish and stupid?'

I couldn't look at him afterwards. We both knew it was over.

Still I thought I could keep it secret, hide it from David, from my children.

At the school gates, in the days that followed, I began to notice the nudging and staring, the whispered conversations I was not party to. Then a phone call from another parent on the committee.

'You've heard the news? Aidan's left. He's taking his son out of the school.'

It took a moment for it to sink in, my mind spinning off in all directions.

'What about you?' she asked then.

'Me?'

'Do you still want to be on the committee?'

'What do you mean, Olivia?'

All that time, she had been speaking in her usual brisk manner. Now her voice dropped, taking on a confidential tone. 'I think you know what I mean, Caroline.'

Just like that, I knew I would have to tell David.

And when I did tell him, later that night, it was like watching a coldness come over him, like a thin sheet of ice forming over his skin. I had expected anger, indignation, some kind of volatile reaction. Instead he just sat there, his breathing heavier as I gave my sorry account, made my shameful confession. Then, in a quiet voice, he had said, as if addressing his words to the table and not to me: 'The children must never know.'

Robbie refused to speak the whole way home. I tried various methods of coaxing information out of him but he wouldn't answer and after a while I gave up. The journey took longer than usual, traffic from a rugby match clogging the streets. As the wheels of the car crunched over the gravel in our driveway, I felt exhausted and troubled. Every single book or magazine article I had read about the adolescent male had warned of sudden fits of aggression, yet still I hadn't believed it. Not my Robbie. Not my gentle boy. Had arrogance led me to think like that? The blindness of a mother's love? He had always been softer than other boys, easily hurt. I had worried that he might be the object of bullying. To learn he was the perpetrator of violence had thrown me completely. I turned off the engine.

'Robbie,' I began carefully. 'I know things have been strange lately. I haven't been around as much now that I'm working again. If I haven't been there for you, then I'm sorry. Perhaps you feel that I've let you down, but –'

'I don't. I think it's good you have a job.'

'Then what is it, love?'

He shook his head then pressed it back against the headrest, unhappiness filling his face.

'What you did to that teacher . . . It's so unlike you. What's the matter? Has something happened?'

He didn't answer.

A thought crossed my mind. All those evenings, the two of them up in his room, talking, whispering. 'Does this have something to do with Zoë?'

He put a finger to his mouth, biting at the corner of a nail.

'I know you two get on well, Robbie. But I think it best if you spend less time with her. She's older than you are.

The long chats you have in your room – I don't think they're a good idea.'

He gave a small exasperated sigh and shot me a look of disgust. 'Miss Murphy was the one who saw you together – you and Jack's dad. The one who ratted on you.'

Something hard caught in my throat, like a cold stone wedged there. The shock of his admission and all the realizations that flowed from it. He knew what I had done. *He knew.* I felt it, like a fist around my heart.

'Oh, Robbie . . .' I wanted to explain it, to make it better. I knew, though, that nothing would, just as I knew he had lived with the knowledge all this time. David and I had secretly been congratulating ourselves on shielding the children from what I had done, and all the time he'd known.

He opened the car door and clambered out, and I sat there, watching him march to the front door, put his key in the lock and disappear inside. I thought of all the small triumphs of motherhood – teaching him to read before he started school, recognizing his musical ability before anyone else did, finding the instrument that best suited his temperament, remembering the flush of pride when the librarian remarked on how many books he got through each week for such a small boy. I thought of all these things and felt how flimsy they were, how paltry in the face of the pain I had caused.

It was a few moments before I could get out of the car. Then I locked it, straightened myself and followed him slowly into the house.

# 14. David

It happened that around this time I was invited to speak at a conference hosted by my old stomping ground, Queens University, Belfast. On the morning I was due to leave, I got up early, before Caroline's alarm went off, and wandered downstairs. It was one of those surprising February mornings when the frost sparkles beneath the hard sunlight, crocuses spearing up through the frozen earth, and you sense the real possibility that spring has arrived. I took my coffee and the notes for my talk and went to sit in the garden on the wooden bench by the back wall.

I read over my notes, but the words kept blurring on the page, my attention pulled elsewhere. It had been years since I had been to Belfast, and while it was nice to receive the invitation, the thought of going back to Queens only served to stir up buried memories, and awaken old ghosts.

Earlier in the week, I had taken it upon myself to track down the contact details for Zoë's stepfather, Gary. Of course I could have asked Zoë for his number, but she was so closed and defensive – almost frightened – any time he was mentioned that I chose not to. Instead I went through the university registrar. In the end, it was all straightforward enough. A brief phone call suggesting we meet, which he accepted without question, although I noted the surprise in his tone. I told myself that I just wanted to outline for him my plans to become actively involved as Zoë's parent, paying her tuition fees as well as taking her into my home. I didn't know whether or not to tell him about her suicide attempt, weighing up his need to know versus her desire for privacy. It was still unclear to me what responsibilities towards her Gary felt still existed in the wake of Linda's death. I suppose that was why I set up the meeting rather than discussing it over the phone.

Another question on my mind was whether I ought to tell Zoë about my planned visit. I didn't like going behind her back. Part of my intention to see Gary – a big part – was the hope that he might help me get to the bottom of the question that had dogged me since Zoë's arrival: why hadn't Linda told me? Any time I had tried tackling Zoë on it, she'd become evasive and withdrawn. I had the impression she didn't know.

I was so lost in these thoughts, my notes put to one side, that I didn't notice Robbie until he was almost upon me.

'Mum says you'll miss your train,' he remarked, his hands in the pockets of his school trousers. I noticed a new eruption of spots across his chin. He looked particularly gloomy that morning.

I glanced at my watch. 'There's time. Here, sit down for a minute, will you?'

There was room enough for two or three people on the bench, but rather than taking the seat next to me, he chose to perch at a distance on the armrest – an awkward solution, but one that drove home to me the distance he had been putting between himself and the rest of us since his school suspension the previous week.

'How's school?' I asked, and he shrugged, not answering.

'Everything all right?' I probed.

'Yeah. Why?'

'You seem tense.'

'No, I'm not.'

I suppose I might have put his defensiveness down to hormones. But ever since Caroline had sheepishly admitted the reason behind Robbie's violent outburst at school, I had worried his withdrawal had deeper roots than teenage disaffection. It upset me that my son had been aware of his mother's wayward behaviour, that he had carried the burden of this knowledge in secret for more than a year. I had tried talking to him about it, hoping to squirrel out some information over what repercussions he had had to deal with – bullying at school? Teasing? A change in any teacher's behaviour towards him? But every time I tried to draw him on the subject, he clammed up. At home, the mood was fraught. He barely spoke to either of us, and even though this incident had served to fire up my anger towards Caroline over what she had done, I felt a duty, nonetheless, as a co-parent to rein in Robbie's attitude towards his mother, which was verging on disdain.

'Listen, go easy on your mother while I'm away, will you?'

'Sure,' he said, with marked disinterest.

'I know you're angry with her but, Robbie, she's your mother. She loves you. She only wants what's best for you.'

He got to his feet and began moving towards the house.

'Robbie.'

He turned to me with a withering stare. 'How can you stand it?' he demanded. 'After what she did?'

'Marriage is complicated,' I said, but already he was stalking back towards the house, uninterested in my reply.

So that was how he saw me: a cuckold, a worm, spineless and ineffectual.

Back in the house, I put my coffee cup on the draining-board, my notes in my bag. Without saying a word to anyone, I took my things and left.

The conference was well attended and lively, a buzz about the university as the lectures attracted students and those outside academic life who had an interest in the history of the world wars. By coincidence, an old pal of mine from my Queens days – Giancarlo – was also attending. He had become something of a star in academic circles in his native Italy, but to me he was the same mischievous, irreverent student I had known twenty years before. On the first night of the conference, we headed out together to revisit some old haunts around Belfast and it was late when I got back to my hotel room, a little the worse for wear. There was a missed call from Caroline, but I chose not to return it. I was still peeved over my conversation with Robbie in the garden that morning, and I guess I blamed Caroline, tracing the roots of his grievance back to her fling.

My lecture took place on the second morning and passed off well. Afterwards, there was a lunch in the dining hall alongside some of my old professors. I enjoyed their company, and we talked about the passing years, as well as engaging in a lively discussion about the rise of Islamic fundamentalism in the West, so it was with some reluctance that I excused myself, found a taxi outside the main entrance and instructed the driver to take me to an address in Holywood, outside the city.

I sat in the back of the cab, staring out at the massive yellow Harland and Wolff cranes, the concrete bridges under which the road passed, the verges becoming green and lush as we left Belfast behind us. I thought of Linda, curious to see how, where and with whom she had lived all those years without me. It was hard to imagine the Linda I knew – flighty, scornful of formal commitments, loath to be tethered to anyone or anything – succumbing to marriage, an institution she had roundly derided in the heady days of our love affair. I felt a little nervous, unsure as to what I wanted to happen at this meeting. I hoped to smooth things over, let Gary know that I was on the scene now, and that whatever kind of relationship he had with Zoë, the role of father-figure he might have played, it was different now.

The taxi stopped at a terrace of houses with pebble-dashed walls and small gardens, facing out on to a green. Some of the gardens were well maintained, while others were strewn with kids' bicycles and plastic slides, dustbins shoved alongside breeze-block walls. A group of sullen teenagers were sitting on a wall, staring as the taxi approached. I tried to imagine Zoë playing on the green as a child, cycling along the road.

I paid the fare and stepped out to a house at the end of the terrace, purple and blue hydrangea bushes in the garden, a green Volkswagen Golf in the driveway. I imagined Linda coming home from work every day, pushing a buggy along that footpath, opening the door every morning to take in the milk.

Holywood, I knew, was an affluent town, part of Ulster's gold coast, but there was something down-at-heel about this street. Not that there were flags hanging from the lampposts or kerb-stones painted with the Union Jack. But for all its neatness, there was an impoverishment. I used to think all of Belfast was a bit too small to contain Linda, let alone this choked suburb.

I rang the doorbell, and after a moment's wait, a shadow appeared behind the frosted glass. The door opened and I was met by a tall, gaunt man. He was, I guessed, in his early fifties. In brown cords, a black knitted cardigan and horn-rimmed glasses, he reminded me of a geography teacher I might have had at school.

'David,' he said, extending his hand to shake mine.

His voice was deep and his handshake was strong. At his request, I followed him inside. He led me through a narrow hallway into a kitchen at the back of the house. 'Coffee?' he asked.

'Please.'

The kitchen was long and narrow, lined with white cabinets, a butcher's block surface that was almost entirely free of appliances apart from a red Gaggia next to the sink, which Gary began fiddling with.

'Please, make yourself at home,' he urged, directing me to a light-filled room that opened out of the kitchen.

What I had seen of the house so far had seemed fairly mundane – even characterless – but when I stepped into the sunroom, I understood I was in its heart. Floor-to-ceiling windows gave on to an immaculate garden, and even on that gloomy afternoon, light poured through the skylights in the ceiling on to honey-coloured wooden floors. The walls were filled with books and prints, shelves stacked with paperbacks in haphazard arrangement, a reading lamp sitting on top of a neat tower of magazines. There were framed photographs everywhere, photographs of weddings and parties and visits to foreign cities – some with Gary, some of Linda alone, one or two of her among a group of people I didn't recognize. My eyes were drawn to them, searching for her. How strange it was to see that woman with her careful smile, her monochrome clothes, and realize she was Linda – *my* Linda. It was a shock to see her hair cut short, tamed into a neat bob, still blonde but dark at the roots. I suppose she might also have been surprised at how I had aged – the young man she had fallen in love with had grey hair, a forehead furrowed with age-lines.

I picked up one of the framed photographs from the side table. It was of Linda, standing outside Belfast City Hall in a yellow dress, holding in one hand an umbrella, in the other an oversized hat.

'We thought it was going to rain,' Gary said, coming into the room and putting a tray on the coffee-table. 'Our wedding day. I insisted we bring an umbrella,' he said, smiling. 'Linda was holding it up because it hadn't rained.'

'When was that?'

'Twelve years ago in March. I'll let you help yourself to milk and sugar.'

'Thanks,' I said, putting the photograph back where I had found it, but not without wondering where Zoë was when the picture had been taken. In my mind's eye I saw a six-year-old girl in a blue dress, hair in plaits, gaps in her teeth showing as she smiled for the camera. But she was not in that picture, or any other. As my eyes took in the room, I found there wasn't a trace of her anywhere.

'The last time I saw Linda,' I told Gary, as I took my cup and sat in the armchair opposite his, 'she was preparing to go to Canada to do her PhD.'

'Yes, well, she did go, but things happened. She dropped out and came home.'

Things happened. Pregnancy. Motherhood. I listened for the trace of unspoken accusation in his voice but there was none.

'She never finished her PhD?'

He shook his head, adding: 'That's not to say she never studied again, though. Quite the opposite. She was always working away at something. City and Guilds courses, Open University. Night classes in creative writing or women's studies. One year she decided to learn Italian, another she took up Mandarin. "Mandarin?" I said to her. "Sure, what would you want with that?" I used to tell her she'd be better off learning how to drive, but she wouldn't hear of it.'

Something snagged in my brain. 'She couldn't drive?'

'No. Preferred to get the bus. Or a taxi, when she was feeling flush.'

He filled me in on the scant details of their life together: she had worked in a book-shop; he taught at a local school, taking a leave of absence when his wife became sick. I thought of Linda and all those night courses, desperately seeking an outlet for her busy intelligence, and heard the wild flapping of wings tossing against a closed window. An exotic bird trapped in a room.

'I was so sorry to learn of her death,' I told him. 'It seems wrong. She was too young.'

He nodded slowly, growing solemn, and neither of us spoke.

'Linda's mother also died in her forties,' he said after a minute. 'Did you know that?'

'No, I didn't.'

'The same type of cancer.'

'So it was hereditary?'

A frown-line became pronounced on his forehead while he considered that.

'They couldn't say so for sure. And, you know, our lifestyle . . . Well. We weren't exactly health freaks.'

I heard the scratch of cigarettes in his voice, and thought of Linda smiling mischievously at me over her glass of wine. The air in the room had changed, the sadness within him dragging at me. I had an urge to get out of there and thought it best to get to the point, and address the purpose of my visit.

'About Zoë,' I began. 'I just wanted to let you know that she's living with us now – with my family.'

'Right,' he said, as if the information didn't weigh too heavily on him.

'Also, I'm going to be paying her tuition fees from now on, just in case you felt any responsibility in that department. I'm happy to step in now.'

A pucker of confusion around his brow. 'Her fees? But she has money for that.'

'No, I don't think so.'

'She does,' he said firmly. 'Linda left Zoë money specifically to pay for her education. Believe me, I know. I put the cheque into Zoë's hand myself. Six thousand pounds.'

I stared at him, unsure what to believe.

'She failed to mention that, did she?' Gary said drily, reading my confusion.

'She did.'

He gave a brief, mirthless laugh. 'She has a loose association with the truth, that one.'

The way he said it only served as a reminder of all the hints and intimations Zoë had given of this stepfather with whom she didn't get on. Suspicion rolled over in my mind.

'God knows what she's told you about me,' he added.

'She said you two never hit it off.'

Another laugh, more a quick exhalation of air through his nose. 'That's putting it mildly.'

The hardness of his manner faltered a little as he ran a hand over his forehead as if to rub away the tension there. Adopting a softer tone, he said: 'It's not all her fault. I suppose I'm partly to blame. It was such bad timing, you see, her coming along when she did, just after Linda's diagnosis.'

'Sorry, what do you mean?' I asked, confused by the turn the conversation had taken.

'You asked me about Linda's cancer,' he said patiently, 'was it hereditary or lifestyle or just pure misfortune? Perhaps all three. But the one thing that keeps me awake at night is the thought of all the hormones she pumped into her body. We couldn't have kids, you see. Unexplained infertility. We did IVF seven times,' he went on, with a brief shake of his head. 'Seven times. All those hormones, all those tests and procedures.'

All those disappointments, I thought. I tried to imagine how they managed on their salaries – fertility treatment wasn't cheap. The house, the estate, it began to make sense to me.

'All those hormone injections she'd had,' he said. 'I couldn't help but think they contributed in some way. That was how I felt when the diagnosis came. And when Zoë showed up on the doorstep like that, the child she had given up all those years before, well, the timing of it . . . It felt like a cruel irony.'

I stared at him blankly. A buzzing feeling had started in my head, the room seeming to dip and sway around me. There was a radio on in the next room and I wished, irritably, that he would turn it off so that I could think. 'I don't understand,' I said. 'What do you mean, the child she had given up?'

He scrutinized me again, in a way that suggested he was still making up his mind about me. 'Yes. After she was born. You didn't know?'

'No,' I said, hardly trusting myself to speak with all the emotions and questions clawing around inside me.

'It was the one real regret of Linda's life,' Gary continued. 'She never forgave herself for it.'

He was talking now about a letter that arrived, indicating the girl's desire to reach out to her natural mother, the subsequent meeting and how euphoric Linda was afterwards, but all I kept thinking about was Zoë, sitting in my car, the orange glow of streetlights outside as she told me about Linda bringing her to UCD – *driving* her there – when she was a little girl. *I could tell she had never forgotten you*, she had said, and I had latched on to those words. But Linda never learned to drive. Was it all lies? Was there truth in anything she had said? Other accounts came back at me: the Greystones cousins, shopping trips to Grafton Street, occasions that my mind had fixed upon, imagining the scene had I happened upon them – had I rounded the corner at the Blob that day and spied my Linda and a little blonde-haired girl, had I stopped dead on Grafton Street, Linda holding a child's hand, walking towards me saying, 'Hello, David,' the memory of her voice saying my name coming to me in a painful jab. All of it lies.

'At first, she seemed sweet,' Gary said of Zoë, his words shaking me from my confusion. 'She used to come around here and sit for hours, the two of them talking, swapping stories. In a way, it was a bit like watching a love affair unfold.'

Hard as it was, I tried to imagine it: Linda and Zoë sitting in those chairs, their eyes and voices locked on each other, anxious to make up for all the lost years.

'When Linda suggested that Zoë move in, I wasn't too sure. It all seemed to be happening so fast – and Linda was quite sick, the treatment taking its toll. She loved having Zoë here but was always exhausted afterwards, you know? Still, I couldn't object – Zoë was her daughter, after all. She moved in, and it was fine for a while. Then things began to change.'

'What things?' I asked, my coffee cooling in my mug.

He crossed his legs, frowned a little, staring not at me but at some spot on the floor, his mind casting back through memory. 'Small things, at first – she'd tell Linda that I'd done something or other to upset her when I hadn't. Making out that I was being cool with her or trying to shut her out – Linda became upset. When she confronted me, I denied it – tried to explain to her that Zoë was imagining it or, worse, making it up. It was ridiculous – the poor woman was in and out of hospital, as thin as a stick, and here we were arguing over silly little lies a teenager had told.'

An icy dread flowed through me: had she been doing the same with Caroline and me, playing one off against the other, working at pulling us apart?

'There wasn't much I could do about it,' Gary went on, 'not without upsetting Linda. So I put it on the back-burner, said I'd take things in hand once Linda got the all-clear. But she kept getting sicker, and the situation at home was growing worse. I mean, on the one hand, I felt sorry for Zoë. She was this messed-up kid who just wanted to get to know her mother. On the other hand, I felt she was trying to shut me out so that she could have Linda to herself.'

He leaned forward and returned his coffee cup to the tray. 'Even saying that now sounds ridiculous – like I'm jealous of her, this school kid.' His voice hardened again. 'Still, it's difficult to accept what she did. Those last few months with Linda – she poisoned them.'

Poisoned them? Was this the same girl whose hand I had held while she lay in a hospital bed, the life-blood drained from her? What was it she had said to me? *You don't really know me. There are things that I've done . . .* While the girl who was living under my roof might be my daughter that didn't mean I had any real idea who she was.

After that, the conversation dwindled. I could hardly remember the purpose of my visit, let alone try to question him further. He, too, grew taciturn, perhaps regretting how much he had admitted, and after I'd thanked him for the coffee, we both stood up and he led me to the door.

It was only when I had stepped outside, and was turning to say goodbye, that I felt the push of the question that was lodged inside me. 'Why did she never tell me?' I asked him. 'Linda. About the baby. Why didn't she get in touch?'

He looked beyond me to the rough green grass covering hillocky ground, bald in places, growing long and clumpy in others. 'Leave sleeping dogs lie,' he said, returning his gaze to my face and I saw that, behind the flatness of his features, judgement lay.

Dissatisfied with his answer, but knowing I would get no more from him, I turned to go.

'Watch yourself,' he said after me.

It was a colloquial goodbye I remembered from my Belfast days, one I had heard many times. Yet when I walked away from him that day, the words remained stuck in my head in a way that felt uncomfortable. Perhaps it was the shock of what I had learned or the cold manner of our parting, but the words and the way he had said them kept repeating inside my head: *Watch yourself, watch yourself.* As I raised my hand to hail a taxi, it occurred to me what was so troubling about them. I felt as if, far from saying goodbye, they had been intended instead as a kind of warning.

# 15. Caroline

David was gone for two nights, and for the duration of his absence, we didn't communicate. Not in any way. From the distance of a hundred miles, I could feel him sulking.

There wasn't time to dwell on it. Life was busy with school runs and extra-curricular activities, not to mention work. There was a trade fair running all that week, hosted in City West Hotel, where our firm had a stand, hoping to attract new business. I was pencilled in to attend with a couple of colleagues. It was a frenetic few days, the throng of the crowd ringing in my ears long after I'd left the building, my feet aching from standing for hours. Occasionally there were lulls in the day, and I would find myself at the stand, my eyes glazing over, thoughts turning inevitably to the uncertain atmosphere at home. I thought about Robbie's sullenness, his trouble at school and his refusal to discuss it with me afterwards; about Holly and her obvious unhappiness at how things had changed. I thought of David and how every conversation between us lately had seemed loaded and dangerous, as if a wrong word spoken would tilt us into argument. And all the while Zoë retained her occupancy at the top of our house.

Her presence was constant – at the dinner table, in the evenings when we were watching TV. In the mornings when we were rushing about she'd sit there calmly, eating yoghurt. Even when the house was empty, I could find traces of her recent presence – the bathroom steamy and warm from her shower; a coffee cup cooling on the draining-board. Occasionally, I would pass the stairway to the attic and catch the faint scent of cigarettes wafting down. Our home had been invaded by her presence, and despite my unease, I couldn't think how to change it.

'Caroline?'

A voice drew me out of my reverie, the din of the crowd coming back at me suddenly. I turned, my gaze clearing, and as soon as I saw him, the blood came rushing to my cheeks.

'Aidan,' I said, as he leaned forward with a half-smile and gave me a chaste kiss on the cheek. 'This is a surprise.'

Over a year had passed since we had seen each other, the last occasion that excruciating meeting in Mrs Campbell's office. The memory of it flitted through my mind and that alone was enough to stir up feelings of humiliation. We talked for a moment about the trade show, the company I was working for, and then he asked if I wanted to grab a coffee. We were two adults no longer involved with each other. It seemed churlish to say no.

Standing together at a tall table in the hospitality tent, two lattes between us, I told him about my return to work, the pressures and challenges as well as the rewards. He filled me in on his recent promotion. It was strange, being there with him, carefully restricting our conversation to safe topics while the commerce continued around us. We had to raise our voices to be heard and lean in to listen, and while we talked I was taking in the changes that had occurred in him. His hair seemed thinner under the bright spotlights, and there were crows' feet shooting

out from the sides of his eyes that I hadn't noticed before. He was wearing a suit – his tie was fractionally askew and the jacket a little crumpled beneath the pockets. Small things, but they added up to give the impression of tiredness, sadness perhaps, which made me wonder about the health of his marriage.

I enquired how his son was doing; he asked after Robbie. My automatic reply was that Robbie was doing well, but after a moment's hesitation, I added: 'There was an incident at the school recently. Some trouble with a teacher.' I explained what had happened, about the intimidation, the bullying, the assault. It was only when I revealed Robbie's motivation that his eyes widened.

'The French teacher? It was her?' Then he grinned. 'What the hell was she doing in Conways? It's such a dive!'

'I know!' It felt good to be able to talk like that with the benefit of distance from the event itself.

He was still smiling at me, a note of fond recollection coming into his voice, saying, 'When I think of some of the places we used to meet. I mean – the Three Sisters? Jesus! You must have thought I had no class at all.'

I laughed, and his eyes seemed to flicker over me, the smile dying on his face. 'You have a lovely laugh, Caroline,' he said, more serious now. 'I always thought that.'

The moment had passed, and I felt the creep of shame again.

'I've missed it,' he added.

'How have things been with you?' I asked, uncomfortable beneath the weight of his stare. 'With your wife, I mean?'

He rotated his coffee cup a fraction, his weight shifting to his other foot. 'Okay. These things take time, I guess.'

I wondered had she told him about the incident in Ikea. I had a sudden recollection of the ferocity of her trolley bashing into mine, her face stripped of everything except the purest anger. I almost said it to him, then changed my mind. Instead, I told him about Zoë.

'A daughter?' he asked, interested. 'From another relationship?'

'One that predated our marriage. She's eighteen, almost nineteen.'

His eyes opened wider in disbelief, and he exhaled out of the side of his mouth. 'That must have been a shock to the system.'

It occurred to me that I hadn't told a soul of Zoë's existence – not a friend or a family member, not even a colleague. It was as though I had been trying to contain it, hoping it would somehow go away. Talking to him about it was a relief, and once I'd started, it was hard to stop. Aidan listened carefully, interjecting with questions and opinions of his own.

'Does she look like David?' he asked.

'Not that I can see. A little like his mother, perhaps, but no, not really.'

'What do the kids make of her?'

'Holly can't stand her. She almost comes out in a rash whenever Zoë's in the room.'

'And Robbie?'

'They're closer in age, and they've more in common. I can tell that he likes having her around. It's just . . .'

'Just what?'

'I'm worried about him. He's been acting up lately – and I know he's a teenager and that's what they do, but the way he's been behaving seems out of character. They spend so much time together, him and Zoë. In the evenings, at weekends. Sometimes I find them talking in his room late into the night. I'm worried about the influence she has over him.'

'She's living in your home?' he asked incredulously. 'Whose idea was that?'

'David's. There was an incident over Christmas. It seems she tried to kill herself –'

'It seems? Do you not believe her?'

'I don't know what to believe, Aidan. She can be two-faced. After the overdose, David wanted her to move in with us and I felt I couldn't say no.'

'Why not? She's not your responsibility.'

'Not mine, perhaps, but David feels responsible. He is her father, after all.'

His expression was sceptical.

'Listen, he gave her his DNA, that's all. And in the great big scheme of parenting, that doesn't amount to much. Where's the mother in all this?'

'She's dead.'

'Any other family?'

I shook my head. 'A stepfather, but he doesn't seem involved.'

'So you're left with a cuckoo in your nest.'

There was dry humour in those words but his gaze was serious. I felt a chill cross the back of my neck, like some unseen person had just breathed across it.

I picked up the sugar sachet next to my cup, turned it over. 'I don't trust her,' I said quietly.

'How come?'

'She's always perfectly polite to me, but for David's benefit. There's no real connection between us. It's like she doesn't want it. Every effort I make in that direction just seems to wash over her.'

'She's freezing you out.'

'That's what it feels like. David thinks she's great. He doesn't see what I see.'

There had been incidents over the past few weeks – nothing major, but enough to stir up trouble. Once, returning laundry to her room, my hand had accidentally brushed against her laptop, awakening the screen. At that particular moment, Zoë had walked in. Later, she told David she had caught me snooping through her emails. Another time, she had come down to breakfast wearing a blouse that was mine – grey silk, scoop-necked. It had been hanging at the back of my wardrobe. I hadn't worn it in months.

'You're wearing my top,' I had said, surprise in my voice.

'Am I?'

She had looked down at it, pulling it between fingers and thumbs to examine it in a pantomime way. 'So it is,' she replied, laughing. 'It must have got mixed up with my clothes in the wash. I thought it was mine!'

She was all charm and politeness, David in the background observing. She had offered to run upstairs and change, but somehow that made things worse. I tried to feign a casualness I didn't feel, told her to put it into the wash at the end of the day when she had finished with it. I wasn't as good an actress as she was, and despite my efforts, suspicion leaked into my tone. I couldn't prove it, but I knew she had been going through my things.

'Thanks, Caroline,' she said, those shallow green eyes of hers briefly finding mine.

I recounted the incident for Aidan, but what I didn't tell him was that when I looked at the grey silk skimming her slender curves, I realized, with a pinch of envy, that it looked far better on her youthful frame than it did on me. I knew that I would never wear it again.

'Have you spoken to David about your misgivings?' Aidan asked, regaining my attention.

'Any time I do, we just end up arguing.'

Sympathy entered the look he was giving me, and when he spoke again, his voice was softer but firm. 'You need to think about what it is you want, Caroline. It's all very well flinging wide the doors and welcoming her in, very noble, but it shouldn't be at any cost. You're not the girl's mother. Have you thought about what kind of relationship you want to have with her? What you expect from her in return for welcoming her into your family?'

'Not really.'

'Take my advice and think it through properly. Work out exactly what you're prepared to live with and what you absolutely cannot accept.'

He drained his coffee and returned the cup to the table with an air of finality. 'Work it out and then stand your ground. You can't let this interloper walk all over you with her poor-little-orphan side-show.'

I checked my watch and said I'd better get back to my colleagues. He came around the table and we hugged awkwardly, each of us feeling the strangeness of contact after all that had passed.

*

when she was right there in the room. What got into you? Didn't you see how upset she was?'

My eyes widened. 'How upset *she* was?'

'Oh, Christ, don't do this now,' he said, turning away from me and sitting down at the table.

'Don't do what?'

'Don't make this into a competition between you and her.'

'*What?*'

He lifted his palms with an air of surrender. Then he picked up his sandwich and began to eat.

How had things spiralled out of control so quickly? I thought of Chris and Zoë sitting in the warm conviviality of our local pub, sharing a joke over their pints, and felt a twinge of envy. Inside our kitchen, it felt very cold. I could tell from the way David was hunched over his sandwich, a hardened look about him, that I would have to pull back, tread a little softly, if I wanted to persuade him.

'Listen,' I began, as I sat opposite him. 'One of the girls at work has a place free in the house she shares. All young girls, in their early twenties. It's in Ranelagh, close to UCD. I was thinking Zoë might be interested. What do you reckon?'

'She couldn't afford the rent,' he replied, taking another bite.

'Well, we could help out there.'

'A few days ago you were losing the plot over my suggestion of paying her college fees. Now you want to stump up for her rent?'

I ignored the barb. 'This was never supposed to be a permanent arrangement, David. It was just a stop-gap until she found somewhere new to live. Robbie's going to be doing his Junior Certificate in a few months. He needs to be able to concentrate on his studies. Her presence at home is unsettling for all of us – a distraction.'

'Robbie will be fine.'

'Really? I'm worried about him.'

'You're overreacting. He's fifteen. Teenage boys act up from time to time. And I'll talk to him about his homework, get him to knuckle down a bit.'

'Will you?'

He must have heard the doubt in my voice, for his gaze narrowed, his mouth settling into a grim line. 'I just said I would, didn't I?'

'You've been so distracted lately. You keep brushing aside Robbie's behaviour, instead of tackling him about it. I can't help but feel that you've stepped back a bit from him – from Holly too. They need your attention as well, David, your love.'

'Hang on a second. You're the one who's been out until all hours, doing trade shows and what-have-you, and now you're giving *me* a hard time about not being there for the kids?'

'What are you saying?' I asked. 'That I shouldn't have gone back to work?'

The swing of the argument took over, each of us drawing on the peculiar accounting involved in parenting, trotting out all the hours each of us spent with the kids versus the time we had to ourselves. Revisiting old ground, we criticized each other's parenting styles: I accused him of being too hands-off, then jumping in at the last minute with harsh discipline; he argued that I was too soft on them, too wrapped up in their lives, that I didn't give them the space and freedom to make mistakes and learn from them. The whole thing was exhausting.

David finished his sandwich and got up.

'What about Zoë?' I said, determined not to let him walk out of the room without reaching some kind of agreement.

He put his plate into the dishwasher, then straightened up. 'I'll talk to her. Tell her she can stay here until the exams are over.'

'That's not until the end of May.'

'It's a natural break, Caroline. End of semester. She'll probably be heading abroad with her friends anyway – she mentioned something about a J1 visa for the States. We can make it clear that when she gets home after the summer she'll no longer be living here.'

There was a degree of sense in what he was suggesting. Still, I felt a niggle of worry.

'Happy now?' he asked coldly, and without waiting for my answer, he left the room.

The house was empty when I got up the next morning, having waited for the others to leave. The days spent at the trade show had taken an unexpected toll. Peter had given us leave to come in late that morning, and as I lay there watching the time tick by on the digital clock, I felt the passage of dull pain around my body, tenderness at the bridge of my nose a warning sign I was coming down with a cold. I had left my phone downstairs in the kitchen the night before, and it was a relief not to be able to check for emails from the office. After a while, I got up and stood for a long time under a hot shower, feeling the heat permeating my skin. I thought of David and our argument, which was still unresolved. We had lain in bed alongside each other, not speaking. Some time after midnight, I had heard the front door open and close, Zoë's light footfall on the stairs. I know he heard it too. The end of May, I thought, mentally tallying the weeks and months that would lead to that date, to a time we could finally be rid of her.

After my shower, I felt better. Wrapping my hair in a towel, I went downstairs in my bathrobe to make tea.

Zoë was in the kitchen, her hair pulled back in a ponytail. She stood perfectly still, looking straight at me. My phone was in her hand. 'I'm sorry,' she said. 'It beeped and I thought it was mine.'

It was true that our phones were similar, and that we had the same text alert, but still I was annoyed. I moved forward, and she handed it to me. Her bag and coat were on the counter and she picked them up, then said a stiff goodbye.

The door closed, I looked down at the screen and saw the text message that had come through. It was from Aidan and it was open. I read it quickly with a growing sense of alarm: *When I said I missed your laughter, I should have said that I missed your lips, your lovely mouth, you. You're in my head again, Caroline.*

'Shit,' I said out loud.

The front door was open when I stepped into the hall and said her name. She was pulling on her jacket and made no sign of having heard me.

'Zoë,' I said again, and grabbed her arm.

She wrenched it away, tripped on the step and steadied herself against the wall of the porch.

She hurried away from me, her ponytail swinging as she went down the path. Weak sunlight came from overhead, filtered through a canopy of fresh spring leaves. I held my robe closed with one hand and called again, but she didn't look back, her step quickening now as she pulled her jacket tight around her. I thought about her reading that text and something loosened within me. Gazing after her helplessly, I watched as, armed with that new knowledge, she hurried away from me, rounded the corner and was gone.

# 16. David

It was late that night when she came home. I was sitting at the writing desk in the living room, darkness pressing against the window, the only light thrown by the angle-poise lamp on to the notes spread in front of me. The rest of the household was sleeping when I heard the crunch of her feet on the gravel outside.

I could have stayed where I was, working out my thoughts for the radio interview I was scheduled to give early the next morning. All week, I had been meaning to prepare for it, but what with my trip to Belfast, the time had got away from me, and despite my good intentions, here I was on the eve of the interview with very little done. In hindsight, I often come back to this moment, and wonder had I chosen to remain at my desk, not got up from my chair and gone out into the hall, would things have turned out differently. So much of what went wrong in the ensuing days and weeks seemed to stem from that night's events. But hindsight is not my friend. It never will be.

The argument we'd had in the kitchen the night before had been on my mind all day. There was a bad taste in my mouth from how we had left things, and I suppose it was for that reason – a desire to smooth things over – that I went out into the hall to see her. She was hanging her coat on the newel post, her back to me, when I said her name and she turned around.

'Christ,' I exclaimed.

The left side of her face, from eye-socket to cheekbone, was badly bruised, swollen and grazed, with a dull purple stain of dried blood.'What happened to you?'

'It's nothing,' she said, letting her hair fall over her face.

'Let me see.' I stepped towards her.

I reached out to touch her chin, and she allowed her face to be angled towards me, her eyes bright and large in the light's glare.

'I fell. It's not serious.'

'That cut is close to your eye. We should get it checked out.'

'It looks worse than it is.'

'Who did this to you?' I asked, shocked by the livid wound.

'I told you, I fell . . .'

'I know you didn't.'

Her eyes moved quickly towards the top of the stairs. 'Can we not talk about it here?' she asked. 'I don't want the others to hear.'

'Come into the kitchen, then.'

Meekly, she followed me and watched as I drew open a freezer drawer, emptying ice-cubes from the tray on to a towel.

'Here,' I said, gathering it all together. 'Put this against your face. It will help bring the swelling down.'

She did as I asked, wincing as the cold compress touched her cheek.

'What happened, Zoë?' I said, my voice softer now that I was getting over my shock.

'I can't tell you,' she answered, and then she began to cry.

Gently, I moved her towards the kitchen table, and sat next to her, taking her hand in mine, trying to appear calm in the face of her obvious distress. 'Please tell me, Zoë. Let me help you.'

'If I tell you, she might get angry with me again.'

'Caroline?' I said, reading between the lines. 'Are you saying she did this to you?' I couldn't keep the disbelief from my voice.

Zoë said nothing, just stared down at the table-top, holding the compress to her face.

While it was no secret that Caroline wasn't happy about Zoë's presence, there was no way she would ever physically attack her. I knew my wife. I understood her boundaries. I couldn't help but think this was some ham-fisted attempt on Zoë's part to get back at Caroline for the things she had said the night before.

'I'm sorry, Zoë, but I find that very hard to accept.'

She took the compress away, stared down at the towel, soaked through now, then said in a small voice: 'I knew you wouldn't believe me.'

'Keep that against your face,' I instructed, partly because I felt a little queasy – the violence of the wound, the swollen flesh, the seeping cuts – and partly because I was annoyed at being drawn into another of her dramas. The whole thing was exhausting.

'It was my fault,' she said, in that same quiet voice.

'What?'

'She didn't mean to do it. She wouldn't have, if I hadn't . . .'

The sentence was left to drift. *Just spit it out*, I thought irritably. My notes, abandoned in the other room, would probably remain unread now. I'd just have to wing it during the radio interview in the morning.

I asked her to tell me exactly what had happened.

'I mistook her phone for my own, you see,' she began. 'I read one of her text messages by accident. It was private. That was what she said. I tried to tell her it was a mistake. That I wasn't spying on her or anything like that. But she didn't believe me.'

'Go on,' I said, listening now.

'Some guy had sent her a text,' she said again. 'I probably shouldn't tell you –'

'Saying what?'

She hesitated, putting the compress to one side, a little crease of a frown appearing between her eyebrows. Her reluctance was apparent, but I was curious now.

'It's okay, Zoë. You can tell me.'

'Something about how he missed her. He missed her lovely mouth, or something.'

She said the words and my irritation fell away.

It's a funny thing – trust. Trust and love, the foundation stones of a marriage. When I found out about Caroline's little romance, it was like someone had taken a hammer to that block of trust and begun pounding at it, causing cracks to run through it, like veins. We had spent the past year and a half working to mend those fissures, sealing them up with gestures and promises. I still loved her, still felt grateful that she was my wife, but cracks like those can be hard to fix, and when Zoë said those words – *he missed her lovely mouth* – all at once I was thinking about another man pressing his mouth against my wife's, prising open her lips, exploring with his tongue. It was an image I had tortured myself with at the time, but had learned to suppress. It was back with me now, and suspicion sprang to life. The sealing cement was falling away to reveal the cracks in our trust in all their ugliness.

'I know I shouldn't have read it,' she was saying, 'but you have to believe me – I would never have read it if I'd known it was her phone.'

Keeping my voice carefully neutral, I said: 'So what happened next?'

'She was so angry . . . She snatched the phone back and she pushed me against the wall.'

The image snagged in my brain. It didn't seem quite right. 'Are you sure about this, Zoë?'

'I don't think she meant to hurt me. Not really. But the way I fell, my face kind of hit the wall and I know there's a bruise, and it throbs a bit, but it looks worse than it is . . .'

She started to cry again, and while I was full of conflicting emotions, I couldn't stand seeing her upset like that, her face damaged and sore.

'I'm sorry,' I said, even though it was not my fault. My thoughts and feelings were opaque, torn between wanting to believe her and my natural instinct to back away from the hard knowledge of my wife's infidelity.

'It's okay,' she said, getting up from the table.

She was going to say goodnight, but before she did I reached out and held her wrist.

'I'll talk to Caroline,' I said, feeling her pull away.

'No, please don't. I don't want her thinking I've been telling tales.'

'Zoë,' I said gently, trying to calm the nervous agitation within her. 'She's going to see your face. We need to talk about this – all three of us.'

'No, please. Not after last night.'

'We have to sort this out. You're my daughter and I want you to feel safe here. But Caroline is also my wife. This is her home. Whatever has happened, we can't just ignore it.'

'I need to sleep,' she said, twisting her arm from my grasp.

'What will you do?' I asked, suddenly worried that she would pack her bags and leave.

'I don't know,' she said, moving towards the door. 'Stay out of her way, I suppose.'

She turned – something about her defiance reminded me sharply and painfully of Linda.

After a while, I switched out the light and went upstairs to bed. Caroline didn't move as I climbed in next to her, and for a long time I lay there, staring at the outline of her body, her hair spread over the pillow next to mine, with the uneasy feeling that even though she was my wife and the mother of my children, even though I had known her half my life, she was still a stranger to me.

My radio interview was scheduled for 8 a.m., which meant leaving the house earlier than normal. As it was, Caroline had a breakfast meeting, so we were all up early – all of us except Zoë.

'Pour me a mug there, will you?' Caroline asked, and I felt a flare of irritation.

I had resolved to talk to her once we were alone, but

with Robbie and Holly slumped over their breakfast, conversation was impossible. I had promised to bring Robbie with me to the radio station after he voiced an interest in the media, and now I found myself quietly regretting it. I wanted to spend more time with him, but I had slept badly and my nerves, made worse by my lack of preparation, were getting to me.

'Pass me the milk, Zoë,' I said.

Both Holly and Robbie looked up.

'You called me Zoë,' Holly said, as if I'd slapped her.

'No, I didn't.'

'You did, Dad,' Robbie said.

'It was a slip of the tongue,' I said, a little crossly. 'Could one of you please pass me the milk?'

Holly stood up and left the room.

'Forget it,' I snapped, not in the mood for histrionics. I took my black coffee and left the table, going into the living room where I found my notes, just as I had left them the previous night, spread out on the desk. There was little point in going through them now, so I swept them into an untidy sheaf and stuffed them into my briefcase.

'Are you all right?'

Caroline had come into the room behind me.

'Fine,' I said tersely.

'You seem nervous.'

The anger jumped alive inside me. How dare she just swan in here, playing the attentive wife, when only the day before she had been texting an old lover?

'Are you seeing him again?'

'What?' she asked, puzzled.

Not who? Because she knew who I meant. She knew exactly what I was talking about.

'Well, are you?'

Comprehension flashed across her face, and I caught the movement behind her eyes – artifice, deceit, the realization she'd been caught out. I could see her thinking quickly about how to explain it away.

'It's not what you think,' she began. 'I bumped into him by accident at the trade show. I had no idea he would be there.'

'So? How was it?' I said, in a mean voice, standing straight in front of her, my arms crossed, making a show of outer strength and indignation. Inside, I was trembling.

'David –'

'Did you feel the spark again?' This was a low blow. In one of our earliest arguments post-fling, Caroline had admitted to feeling a spark between herself and Aidan. I had latched on to it then, using it as a recurring motif in the rows that raged. To bring it up now was like touching alive an old sore. Caroline's eyes briefly flared, but she chose to ignore it.

'Zoë told you,' she said flatly. Then, almost to herself: 'I knew she would.'

I picked up my bag. 'Yes, she told me. She also showed me her face.'

'Her face?'

'She said you shoved her up against a wall. Her cheek is a mess. I'm surprised she didn't need stitches.'

Caroline didn't say anything, just stood there gaping at me, open-mouthed, like a fish.

'I'm going to be late,' I said, moving past her to the door.

'David, I didn't push her.' She came into the hall after me. 'I don't know what you mean.'

The confusion on her face was annoying. It seemed over-dramatic. Fake.

'Robbie!' I called. 'Let's go.'

'David, please. This is serious,' Caroline said. 'What kind of accusation has she made?'

Robbie was in the hall now, a slice of toast clamped between his teeth as he attempted to put on his jacket and school bag simultaneously.

She didn't wish me luck and I didn't kiss her goodbye, didn't say goodbye at all, I just pulled the door shut behind us with force, felt the slam of it reverberating through the air as I hurried down the driveway to the car, where Robbie was already waiting.

The show's producer had sent a brief outline of what the interview would entail and it had all seemed fair-minded and reasonable. Even though I had not prepared as much as I would have liked to, when I took my seat in front of the microphone, I felt there was nothing to be concerned about. Behind the studio's internal window, I could see Robbie sitting alongside the producer. I gave him a wave and he smiled back.

The show's presenter, Des Earley, introduced me to Sean Kelly, a local councillor, who was to give an opposing point of view. I hadn't been informed of this, and thought it a bit haphazard and hastily arranged, but in hindsight I see more clearly what it was: a set-up, an ambush.

'The 1916 centenary celebrations are fast approaching and figures leaked last week show an astonishing level of government overspend. Many are reading this as both a political stunt and a calculated measure to impress the populace in advance of a general election and thereby boost their votes,' Earley said for his opening salvo.

Kelly piped up: 'Buying votes!'

'As a member of the expert advisory group, Dr Connolly, can you justify the kind of money that has been earmarked?'

'Well, first of all I would say that those figures are not entirely accurate,' I began, 'and I couldn't comment on something that isn't official.'

'Why not?' Earley wanted to know. 'After all, many people in Ireland think the amount of money being discussed is eye-watering. Surely it would be better spent on tackling the homelessness crisis or the problems in the health service rather than spending it on commemorating an event that is largely irrelevant today.'

'Well, I wouldn't agree that it's irrelevant,' I argued. 'For many people, the 1916 Proclamation and the circumstances under which it was made . . .'

The words were coming out of my mouth, but they were somehow disconnected from my brain. I had a flash of memory to the night before and the words *lovely mouth* sprang up before me.

'It's all cant, isn't it?' Kelly was saying. 'Why else would the Relatives Association have boycotted the launch of the plan?'

I tried to answer as evenly as I could, but my thoughts were muddled and I muttered something about not putting a price on history.

'You don't think twenty-two million too much to

spend on what, after all, is simply a slap on the back to republican-minded people out there?'

'No, no, I don't . . . It's a chance to re-imagine the future,' I stammered.

I was tired, I suppose. Stressed. Here I was, the history expert, yet I couldn't even get to grips with the events of my own past, couldn't see or understand the history of my own life. A little voice in my head whispered: *You're a fraud.*

'You're just a mouthpiece for government ministers,' Kelly sneered.

'You're taking the whole thing out of context,' I said. 'The purpose of the commemorations is to –'

'I'm not one of your students, Dr Connolly.'

'For Christ's sake, will you let me finish?' I said sharply.

'Okay, briefly now, before we finish up,' Earley interjected, trying to bring the conversation back on track. But Kelly was leaning in, his face reddened with fury.

I hardly heard what he said, some acerbic remark about academics in their ivory towers. I thought about Caroline in Aidan's arms, his mouth on hers. Hers on his. I thought about Zoë's battered face.

'You're talking complete *shite*,' I said. 'Is that plain enough for you? You ignoramus.'

The words flew out of my mouth. I could almost see them flapping around the studio like birds. Earley went straight to an ad-break, and Kelly sat back, arms crossed over his chest, a smile of satisfaction on his stupid face. 'I can already see the headlines,' he gloated.

I took the earphones off and left.

*

I hurried to my car, Robbie half running to keep up with me. There was a storm in my brain, fury coursing through my body. If I had come across Kelly in the car park, I'd have decked him, but in truth it was myself I was furious with. We got into the car, slamming the doors. I leaned my head on the steering wheel and let out some of the breath I had been holding in a long sigh.

'Are you okay, Dad?'

I closed my eyes. It seemed like everyone lately was asking me was I okay. And I knew I wasn't. I was trying to hold it together, but inside I was quaking. 'I'm sorry, Robbie. I wish you hadn't been a witness to that.'

'It's okay,' he said.

I sat back in my seat. 'I shouldn't have lost my temper.'

'The guy was a tosser.'

'Still. It was wrong.' I pressed my fingers against my eyelids, felt the throb of a nerve at the back of my eye. 'Christ, what a disaster.'

'Don't worry about it, Dad.'

'I don't know what came over me.'

'Sometimes it just happens,' he said. 'Something snaps and you just see red.'

I took my fingers away from my eyes.

'Once I thought I was going to lose it, big-time,' he began, his voice a bit timorous – no doubt he was finding it strange to offer comfort to his father rather than vice versa. 'It was at a rugby-club disco. I was outside, in the bleachers. And I saw this guy I knew – and something kind of snapped in me. You see . . .'

He went on, but I wasn't really listening. My nerves were back with me again, anger replaced now with a stomach-churning dread at the thought of all those listeners, what they must have thought. My mind was racing ahead to media reaction at my outburst, the possible consequences within my academic circle. Which of my colleagues might have heard me? What about members of the interview board? My students? There was no way to erase my performance. The interview had been broadcast. It had been put into history, and there was no way of expunging it from the record.

'. . . and the thought that I might have done something like that – it was really scary,' Robbie was saying.

'Right,' I said distractedly, slotting the key into the ignition and starting the car. 'Let's get you to school. The last thing you need is to be late after your suspension.'

His eyes were on me while I reversed; there was no mistaking his disappointment. Then he looked out of the window, and hunched against the passenger door.

I dropped him at school, neither of us saying another word.

As I walked up the stairs to the History Department on the third floor, my phone began to ring. It was Caroline.

'I suppose you heard that,' I said, referring to my disastrous radio performance.

Instead she said: 'David, I've just seen Zoë's face.'

I trudged up the final few steps and turned down the corridor.

'You can't believe I did that to her? My God . . .' She sounded hysterical.

'Calm down,' I told her. 'We'll talk about this later.'

'She must have done it to herself,' she went on, as if she

hadn't heard me. 'She must actually have smashed her face into a wall *on purpose*, David.'

'I can't deal with this now.'

'It's frightening,' she said. 'That she would do something so violent . . . I don't think I can go into the office today. I'm all over the place.'

Caroline was normally so together, unflappable. It was disconcerting to hear her so agitated, admitting to her own insecurity. 'Please, love,' I said, softening my voice, 'try and pull yourself together.'

I was passing Alan's office, the door open, and heard him call my name.

'Listen, I have to go,' I told her. 'I'll call you back shortly.'

Before she could stammer a reply, I hung up.

My head was like a jar of bees with what-I-should-have-said and what-I-should-not-have-said scenarios. I knew, entering Alan's office, that he had listened to my interview and was about to reprimand me.

To my surprise someone else was there, waiting, it appeared, for me to arrive.

'Niki?' I said.

She sat rigidly, her hands clasped, a little startled, though she must have known I was coming. Alan told me to take a seat.

'Niki came to see me about something,' he told me, 'and, rather than me feeding you the information second-hand, I thought you'd like to hear it from her for yourself.'

I could tell Niki was intensely uncomfortable from the way she shifted in her chair, as if trying to avoid my gaze. It was obvious she didn't want to be there. Alan prompted her with a gentle cough.

'I'm withdrawing from the PhD programme. I'm sorry.'

PhD students have been described to me by Alan as 'the holy grail': the more quality PhD students we 'complete', the better it reflects on the institution's reputation and on our chances for funding. Losing Niki was not just a personal defeat, it was an institutional failure.

'But why?' I asked.

'I've been offered a fellowship at Trinity.'

'You never said anything about applying elsewhere.' It seemed to me that Niki had grown shifty, not meeting my eye.

'I'm sorry, David. I was at a Royal Irish Academy meeting in January, which you were supposed to be at. Afterwards I was approached by a professor from Trinity. It's not that I went looking. I've been unhappy for some time, but whenever I wanted to discuss it with you, you seemed too busy or distracted.'

I don't think, even with hindsight, that I was too busy or distracted to talk to Niki about her work. To me her argument was self-serving. 'I think you should reconsider, Niki. You've made good progress on your work here. By all means accept the fellowship, but defer. Finish your research here first.'

'I'm sorry,' she said. 'I don't really want to do that.'

Alan dropped a sheaf of papers on to his desk as if he were swatting a fly. 'Niki says she tried to meet with you, but you didn't make yourself available.'

'Well, there was that one time I couldn't see you,' I said to Niki, then turned to Alan: 'I had to cancel, but it was only the once.'

Niki said, her voice gaining a little strength, 'There

were other times when you were unavailable. And it's not just that. I was hoping to be more included in the research unit, and to play more of a contributing role in the department.'

'But that's all to come,' I said.

'I just don't feel I'm getting the support I need,' she said in response.

I said, in my defence, 'I'm sorry to hear that, but a good deal of research is self-led independent learning.'

'I need regular rigorous feedback,' she said, as if she had rehearsed it.

'Can I ask you to reconsider? We've already made some excellent progress.'

'I've made up my mind,' she said, avoiding my eye.

We talked for a few minutes more, but nothing I said seemed to appease her. Finally, she stood up, and Alan nodded his assent. She held out a hand and I shook it, with some annoyance.

'I'm very sorry about this, Alan,' I said, when she had gone. 'Is there no way of persuading her to stay?'

'I tried. I explained the process, how it makes us look.' He sat down heavily. 'Of course we'll have to carry out an internal investigation.'

'Is that really necessary?'

'She was the vice-chancellor's fellow, for God's sake!' He spread his hands across the desk. 'We'll have to form a committee and formally sign off on her release from her research with us.'

'I don't know what to say . . . I can't believe she didn't come to me before.'

'Apparently, she tried.'

'I can check my emails but, really, I don't think I missed anything.'

'It's disappointing,' Alan said. 'I just hope we can make up for her departure in some way.'

'We'll certainly try,' I said, in an effort to sound positive.

He appeared distracted, and I took it as my cue to leave.

'One other thing,' he said, as I got to my feet. 'The radio interview this morning . . .'

'You heard?'

'I'm afraid I did. What on earth came over you?'

'I'm sorry, Alan. I was very tired. I slept badly last night . . .'

My voice petered out, silenced by the weight of concern in his stare.

'The timing couldn't have been worse.'

I apologized again.

'I'll have to speak on your behalf to the dean. I'll explain the pressure you're under at home.'

I dropped my eyes, uncomfortable at the unspoken assertion that I had allowed problems in my personal life to pollute the working environment of the department.

'How are things at home, David?' he asked, his tone changing, becoming avuncular. 'How's your mother doing?'

In one of our informal chats over coffee, I'd told him that she had moved into a nursing home for palliative care. 'She's not so good. It's only a matter of time now.'

'Time is precious. I often think time is the commodity we deal in, as historians. An examination of its passage . . .'

Alan's patter began to sound perfunctory, and I lost focus on what he was saying.

He must have noticed my wavering attention, my despair: 'What about taking a break?' he asked.

I protested, but only mildly.

'Take a few days,' he said. 'Spend them with your mother. With Caroline and the kids. A break will help you get your affairs in order, and let matters blow over here.'

'What about my lectures? My seminars?' I asked.

'Don't worry about any of it. I'll ask John McCormack to cover for you.'

Great, I thought, as I left his office. McCormack to the rescue.

# 17. Caroline

April started out as a difficult month. After a bruising client meeting one afternoon, in which I presented with incorrect data, Peter called me into his office and informed me that, once the maternity leave I was covering was over, my employment with the firm would end.

'It's not just today,' he said, in response to my craven apology, my pathetic attempts to explain myself. 'You've been distracted for a while now – missing appointments, turning up unprepared.'

Like an idiot, I began rattling on about another client, a proposal I was putting together, plans I wanted to run past him. I felt like a child again, needing him to be pleased with me. He held up his hand. 'I'm very sorry, Caroline,' he said with cold civility. 'We have limited resources, and I need someone who is at the top of her game, not distracted by her domestic situation. I'm happy to write you a good reference, but that's the best I can do.'

He meant well, but I left his office ungraciously, barely making it to my car before the tears came.

Whatever disappointment I felt had to be put on hold once the news we had been waiting for came. On 14 April, a week shy of her seventy-fifth birthday, Ellen passed away. David, who has always had a knack for compartmentalizing, held himself together well in the days before the funeral, making the arrangements, taking calls of condolence, dealing with the nursing home and the undertakers. Even on the day of the funeral, he managed to control his emotions, appearing sombre but composed, his voice only cracking once during the address.

Outward displays of grief are not part of his make-up but in the days that followed he seemed to turn in on himself. He became enervated, his sadness surfacing in a kind of lassitude. He moped around the house, saying little to anyone, while the rest of us tiptoed around him.

A week or so later, I suggested we take a hike in the Wicklow hills – all of us. All this hanging around the house in gloomy silence wasn't doing us any good. It had been a long time since we had undertaken a family outing, and a trek over muddy terrain in the fresh spring air was just what David needed to blow away the cobwebs of his depression.

'All right,' he said. 'Why not?'

It was a sharp, clear day, the air crisp with new life pushing up through cold ground. We took the car as far as Tibradden, then got out, lacing up our hiking boots, a brisk breeze whipping at our anoraks as we pulled rucksacks on to our backs. There were five of us that day as Zoë had chosen to come with us. The bruising on her face had faded, and in the days since Ellen's death, she had seemed calmer, more acquiescent. Her manner had changed: the threat seemed to have left her. Or maybe the change had occurred within me. I was tired of feeling suspicious and angry. I was sick of myself and the constant negativity Zoë inspired. All of a sudden, it didn't matter to me – her insidious presence, her lies, the self-inflicted wounds. She was a silly little girl with her own problems, none of which seemed important after Ellen's death.

We set out, David taking charge of the map, pointing out the route we would take. He went ahead, Holly at his side, while Zoë and Robbie trudged through the mud together. I was happy to take up the rear. It felt good to be silent in the great vastness of the Wicklow hills. We splashed through water and trudged through gorse and heather, floundering occasionally in unexpected boggy dips.

'You okay back there?' David called to me.

'I'm great!'

And I was. Seeing him smiling down at me, his face ruddy, I felt hopeful that the last few months were behind us. My failure at work, the struggle over Zoë, none of it seemed to matter, such was my optimism that day. No harm could come to us in that beautiful place.

After an hour, the climb steepened, and we found ourselves scrambling up a craggy path, slippery with scattered rocks and gravel. Trees grew tall on one side – Norwegian spruces, pines – and the shadowy ground was soft with layers of brown needles.

'Will we stop soon?' I called, and David pointed to a clearing on one side a little higher up. A space cut into the rock-face, shelter from the wind that had whipped up as we made our ascent.

We reached it and set about emptying our backpacks of provisions. My hands and feet were cold. The temperature was lower up there than it had been when we set out.

'What about a campfire?' David asked.

'Is that allowed?' I asked, thinking of gorse fires spreading rapidly over the county.

'Don't be such a wimp,' he said, teasing me.

Robbie was eager to help and they set off in search of firewood, with Zoë. Holly clambered up over the hill to explore and I was left alone.

For a while, I just sat there, kneading warmth back into my fingers. The others had disappeared. It was very quiet and the rock beneath me felt hard and cold. Clouds scudded across the grey sky, and the outline of the trees along the horizon was jagged and harsh. I wanted the others to come back and break the silence, which seemed vast and watchful, like a presence. But no one was there – only the rocks and thicket growing over the windblown hill.

Impatient, I decided to set off after Holly, up over the hump of gorse, the scrabble of a rutted mud path. It was hard going and I was beginning to sweat under my clothes, my legs tired from the strain of the climb. A copse of trees lay ahead, the ground between thick with nettles and briars. I scaled the perimeter until I rounded the corner and found myself almost at the brink of a sheer drop into a quarry, yellow machinery far below lying idle and unmanned. I peered over the edge, birds wheeling above, and felt my heart pound at the plunging depth. It must have been a drop of ten metres or more. My fear was chased by indignation – how dangerous! No fencing, no warning signs – if you were to stumble up there in poor light or a heavy fog, you could easily fall to your death.

I stepped back and looked to my left, my eyes caught by the bright colours of Holly's anorak. Her feet were placed almost at the lip of the drop, wind whipping her hair out from her hood as she peered over. She hadn't seen me, her body inclined slightly away from me.

That was when I saw Zoë edging through the periphery of my vision. She seemed to be stepping carefully, stealthily. Her jacket was grey, camouflage against the craggy stones of the quarry. A wave of nausea came up suddenly from my stomach and I opened my mouth to shout a warning but fear gripped my throat and no sound came out. I watched her creeping up, Holly oblivious to the approaching threat. I watched as she put out a hand, and all the danger in the world seemed to come alive in that moment. Maternal empathy meant that I saw the push before it happened, felt the hands as if they were to my own back, the sickening shove, the terrifying moment as the ground falls away and there's nothing but the air around you and the bone-breaking impact of the ground – no escape. I watched that hand reach out, and forced the word up the blind tunnel of my throat: 'No!'

A shot to my heart, Holly turning, my eyes all the while fixed on Zoë's hand as it gripped Holly's shoulder and pulled her back.

Even now, after everything that has happened, and with all I know, I still look back to that moment with uncertainty. If I hadn't followed Holly up there and shouted out, would Zoë have pushed her? Or was that my feverish imagination, powered and warped by my intense distrust of the girl? But that is the rational thought of hindsight again. For at that moment it was pure instinct. I had seen the violence Zoë had done to herself; I had recognized her ruthlessness in getting what she wanted. The truth is, I was afraid of her.

Holly stepped back from the edge, came towards me and I wrapped my arm around her, shooting Zoë a look.

'What?' Zoë shouted after us, because I had already turned away, ushering Holly down the hill, away from her half-sister and the danger she represented. 'I was just trying to help her!'

That night, going up the stairs to bed, I passed Holly's door and heard crying. I found her lying in the darkness, hugging a tatty old bunny that had been consigned to the bottom of her wardrobe for the last couple of years. Seeing her clutching it to her chest – an old talisman against night-terrors – set off an alarm bell in my head. 'What is it, sweetheart?' I asked, sitting on the bed next to her, my weight on the mattress drawing her towards me.

'Oh, Mum,' she said, reaching up and throwing her arms around my neck.

That physical demonstration was so unlike Holly. She was normally self-contained, eschewing outpourings of affection. I could feel her thin body against me, shaking.

'I was so scared,' she whispered, her mouth close to my ear.

I knew she was talking about Zoë and something hardened inside me – a resolve forming. 'It's all right,' I told her gently, trying to sound calm and firm. Drawing back so I could look into her eyes, I said: 'I would never let anyone hurt you – you know that, don't you?'

'But you're not always there, Mum. You don't see what she's like – the things she says to me . . .'

'What things?'

'When there are other people around, she's nice and sweet to me, but it's all an act! When we're alone, just the two of us, she's horrible!'

'Why? What does she say to you?'

'She says I'm nothing.'

'*What?*'

'That I don't matter. That no one will miss me when I'm not around.'

'Holly, that's not true. You know it's not.'

'Dad wouldn't notice,' she said, her voice dropping a little.

'Of course he would! Your father loves you and Robbie more than anything.'

'More than Zoë?' Her eyes, still wet with tears, held mine.

'He's known you your whole life, sweetheart. Since before you were even born. That makes things different. Special.'

'It doesn't feel that way,' she said. 'It feels like *she*'s all that matters to him now.'

She ran her fingers along the battered ear of her bunny and I remembered a time when she couldn't sleep without him, how loved he was, and felt a twinge of sadness that she had outgrown him. Tonight was just a blip. Very soon, that bunny would be consigned to a box in the attic along with the other relics of her childhood, and somehow, I didn't feel ready for that.

'I'll talk to Dad,' I told her.

She lay back, turning away from me, but she was not comforted. 'It won't make a difference,' she said, resignation – not reassurance – in her tone.

I think that was when I decided to take matters into my own hands. I couldn't rely on David for help, so I resorted to a deception of my own. The danger was alive and living in my house. Necessary evils were called for.

I bided my time, remaining watchful, until early one morning when Zoë was in the shower, the others downstairs having breakfast. I moved quickly and quietly up the steps to her room, finding her mobile phone lying on her bureau. My heart beating wildly, I scrolled through her list of contacts before finding what I needed: *Mam Mobile*. I scribbled the number on a Post-it, and fled before I could be caught, the hiss of the shower jets coming from the bathroom as I hurried downstairs, my pulse beginning to slow.

My motives for meeting Celine Harte were unclear. I wasn't so naïve as to think she could solve my problem by whipping her daughter out of my house and dragging her back to Belfast. I suppose I was seeking evidence of sorts, some confirmation of the fear I felt. Part of me was afraid that I was obsessed with the girl, and maybe losing perspective. Was I right to suspect her of meaning harm towards me and my daughter? Or was she just a mixed-up kid, meddlesome but benign, who would, with time and support, settle down and find her place within the family? Either way, some poor unfortunate had been landed with Zoë as their kid, and I wanted to meet them to find out what exactly I was dealing with.

We met in AppleGreen – a service station on the M1 between Dublin and Newry. Sitting at a plastic table, the coffee cooling, Celine Harte, bundled up in a quilted jacket even though the day was warm, looked at me flatly, her eyes like two inky-black pebbles. 'Why don't you tell me what you want?'

Her candour took me aback. The world-weariness of her demeanour gave me the impression that this was not the first time she had been called to such a meeting. I answered with candour of my own. 'It's Zoë,' I said. 'I want her out of my home.'

If she was surprised by that, she didn't show it.

'She's come between me and my husband,' I went on. 'She has some sort of vendetta against me, like she wants to get rid of me. I'm worried about the influence she's having on my children, my son in particular. I'm afraid she's a threat to my daughter.'

Celine took it all in, her expression unchanging, then looked down at her cup, a pale skin forming on the surface of the coffee.

'I'm sorry,' I said. 'I didn't mean to shock you.'

'I'm not shocked.' She brought her eyes up to meet mine, tiredness in the heavy lids. 'It's what she does.'

The dryness of her tone bordered on cynicism. I expected her to go on – it was a shocking thing to say of your own daughter – but rather than qualifying her statements, she just stared at me in stony silence.

'I don't know what to do,' I admitted. 'Am I imagining it, or does she want to tear us apart? So much has happened.'

'Why don't you tell me what she's done?' she suggested, and I thought I detected a trace of sympathy entering her voice. Resignation, perhaps, or maybe it was pity.

I told her everything, about Zoë's behaviour when alone with me and how markedly different it became when David was around. I told her about the lies, the deception, the inflicting of damage on her face, then blaming me. She listened to it all without betraying any emotion, except when I told her about Zoë's suicide attempt. Briefly, she closed her eyes, then was back with me, having pushed down whatever pain had surfaced at the catalogue of trouble Zoë had brought upon my family. I told her everything, except the part about Holly – the incident at the quarry. For some reason I was reluctant to discuss it – to suggest her daughter was capable of a cold-blooded killing might overstep the mark – and I wanted Celine Harte to share with me what she knew and understood of Zoë. I didn't want to risk her growing defensive.

She finished her coffee, pushed the mug to one side, then leaned her clasped hands on the table in front of her, as if she were about to pray. The words she spoke to me then had the rehearsed quality of a prayer, or perhaps a parable, the telling of a story, one she had told herself or others many times over. There was no pleasure in the telling, no spark in the tale. Rather, a kind of bleakness, as if she had learned long ago that, no matter how she told it, the outcome would always remain the same.

She began by telling me about a family whom Zoë used to babysit for while she was still at school. 'Every Saturday night, religiously, for over a year. Then it just stopped. I asked her about it, but she said it was nothing, told me to mind my own business. I let it go. But then,' she continued, 'one afternoon, the mother comes down the road to me all distressed. She tells me that Zoë has been pestering her husband, hanging around his workplace, calling him at all hours of the day and night. The wife had found out about it – she'd looked at his mobile phone, seen the lewd texts Zoë'd been sending him. She showed me some – disgusting things – not to mention all the poison written about his wife. Zoë believed this man was in love with her, you see, that he was going to leave his wife for her. The way she got between them . . .' She leaned forward. 'She was fourteen years old.'

She kept on watching me to see if I took in the significance of that. *Fourteen.*

There were others, she said. A crush on a teacher that had bordered on obsession. The son of a friend, his girlfriend harassed until she complained to the police. The duplicity, the relentless nature of her intent, her consuming passion for one person leading her to isolate and eliminate anyone who might stand between her and her prize. On and on she went. It was depressingly familiar, as if our story had been written for us long ago and we were merely acting out a foregone conclusion.

'She wasn't always like that,' Celine said, drawing back now. I could see her account had drained her. She summoned the energy to paint a picture for me of a bright little girl, pale and beautiful, vivacious and energetic, always dancing and singing, the centre of attention – the centre of their world. As she said it, I thought of my baby – the baby I might have had – a child who could have given happiness, fulfilment. And if I had kept that baby, would David have gone to Belfast? Might there have been no Linda? No Zoë? A jab of regret came at me and in a bid to swallow it, I took a sip of my cold coffee.

Somewhere along the line, Celine told me, Zoë's childhood energy became restless. Adolescence came on and spikes appeared in her personality. The vivacious child became a cunning and devious teenager. Unrelenting, refusing to be appeased or cajoled, her restless energy meant they could never relax, always jolting from one crisis to the next.

'The one thing that bothers me,' she said, 'the one thing I've never been able to understand, is what brought on the change in her. It wasn't always there – I'd have seen it. If I could just know what it was . . .'

She had plucked a sachet of sugar from the saucer beneath her mug, and was turning it over in her hands, nervous energy overtaking her, like a sudden itch.

'Something she told us,' I began, carefully because I was on uncertain ground here. 'About your husband. She said . . . at least she implied . . . that something may have happened . . .'

The pain that came over her face was unmistakable. It stopped me saying what I had been about to add. Her hooded eyes opened a little wider as if in surprise. But she was not surprised. Dismayed, perhaps. 'She told you that story?'

I nodded, a feeling of shame coming over me as if I had invented the story of abuse, not Zoë.

'You don't know my husband, but he's the kindest, gentlest person you could meet. To make those claims about him – it was the worst kind of hurt. Those allegations left him reeling. He was never the same afterwards. And the worst part . . .' Her voice broke for the first time. 'The worst part was the cleverness of her lies, the way she worked on me over those few days . . . For just a short while I began to doubt him. I began to question my own husband, who wouldn't harm a fly.'

She looked down at her hands. She had twisted the sachet in two, sugar spilling on to the table. 'My doubts didn't last. But the damage was done.'

The air between us seemed to deflate. All the stoicism had gone from her now and I sensed our conversation closing down.

'Did you ever meet Linda?' I asked.

'No. I never wanted to. What would have been the point? And besides,' she said, hardness pinching her lips into thin lines, 'I knew that once Zoë found her birth mother, all her attention and love would be transferred from me to her. That I would be discarded. That's how it is with Zoë. Once you've outlasted your use, you become expendable.'

Bitter words to speak of your own daughter. I tried to imagine an occasion when I might speak of Holly or Robbie in that way, but could not. She had grown quiet, and I could see what it had cost her, the lengths to which Zoë had pushed her.

'You still love her,' I said, an observation not a question.

She smiled for the first time, a smile that didn't reach her eyes. 'That's the thing about love,' she said. 'It doesn't matter if they knock you down, abuse you, push you to the brink. You still love them, don't you? You'd forgive them anything.'

After that, things deteriorated. I made no secret of my wariness towards Zoë, and she, in turn, maintained an air of injury. Over dinner one evening, she announced that she had found a part-time job as a waitress in town. She was out more than ever now, and I had the feeling she was avoiding me. Her occupancy of the attic continued, but a new coldness had entered her presence. The days and nights continued as they had before, but something had changed between us, and I came to believe it had as much to do with the day of the hike as anything else. She knew I suspected her of something, though at the time I couldn't name it, and I certainly didn't mention it to her again. But whatever it was, it was foul, and underhand – whether she was, on that day, willing to hurt Holly or simply wanted to plant the notion in my head, it meant we kept our distance from each other. It was noticeable, I suppose. Robbie would often ask me where she was when he got home from school, and when I said I didn't know, he looked peeved, as if it were my fault that she wasn't waiting for him.

What she did next, though, I hadn't expected. Even though it wasn't yet May, the end of semester still weeks away, she moved out.

I had been in Tesco, doing the weekly shop, the evening light fading as I returned home and parked in the driveway. As soon as I stepped inside the hall, I heard raised voices.

Leaving my bags of groceries by the door, I began to climb the stairs towards the attic.

'You can't be serious?' I heard Robbie say, his voice querulous and shrill.

Zoë, sounding more controlled, said: 'Please, Robbie. Don't be like this.'

'I think it's disgusting.'

'Don't be so dramatic!'

'He's old enough to be your dad!'

'So what?'

'That beer belly. How can you let him touch you?'

'What's going on?' I asked.

Robbie stood with his arms folded over his chest, while Zoë turned back to the bed. I saw the open suitcase, clothes flung inside. The drawers of her bureau lay open and empty. She began zipping her laptop into its cover.

'Are you leaving?'

'That's what you want, isn't it?' she replied, a little petulantly.

I didn't deny it and she put the laptop into her bag, squashing down the clothes, and zipped up the suitcase.

'Where are you going?' I asked.

When she didn't answer, Robbie spoke up. 'She's moving in with *him*.'

'Who?'

'Tell her,' he said to Zoë.

'Tell me what?'

She stood at the other side of the bed, her eyes trained on her bag. There was something shifty in her manner. At last, she straightened up and looked at me, her gaze growing more defensive. 'I'm moving in with Chris.'

'Chris?' I asked, momentarily confused, scanning my memory for some recollection of a Chris in her conversation. 'You don't mean *our* Chris?'

'It's a joke,' Robbie said.

'It's not a joke,' she countered, her forehead creasing with annoyance. 'We care about each other.'

'Oh, please,' he said. 'I'm going to throw up.'

I couldn't explain the feeling of betrayal that arose.

The thought of Zoë and Chris together. It was not just shock that I felt, but something with a harder burn: she was creeping into every area of our lives.

'Aren't you going to say anything?' Robbie asked me.

'How long has this been going on?'

She shrugged. 'A couple of months.'

'The night Chris called over,' I murmured. 'You both went for a drink.' The pieces fitting together in my head. All those nights she hadn't come home, her withdrawal from the household. Of course someone else was involved. It made perfect sense.

'He was really kind to me that night, when I was upset. He made me laugh.'

'He's, like, Dad's best friend!'

'So what? He's fun. He understands things.' She lifted the bag from the bed and it occurred to me how young she was – the bag, a monstrous thing, seemed more than she could handle.

'Are you going now? Right this minute?'

'Why?' she asked. 'Do you want me to stick around for a long, slow farewell?'

I ignored that. My mind was leaping all over the place. Yes, I wanted her gone, but not like this. Not to him. 'Have you thought this thing through properly? Don't you have some friend your own age whose couch you can crash on for a while?'

'What do you care, Caroline?'

'Don't get me wrong, Zoë. I love Chris dearly. He's a kind, funny, caring man. But he's a lot older than you. And his marriage has just broken down – his emotions are all over the place.'

'So?'

'Aren't there boys in college you'd be more interested in dating? Boys your own age? A girl like you – you could have your pick.'

She rolled her eyes, a strand of hair falling across her face, which she made no attempt to push back. 'I like Chris. He's fun,' she said. I saw the mischief come into her eye, a hard gleam of trouble. 'And he's great in bed.'

Robbie looked at her in amazement.

I rubbed my hand along my brow, the throb of a headache starting in my temples. 'Does David know about this?' I asked.

She shrugged. 'I haven't told him.'

'I'm not sure this is a good idea. It's a big step.'

'I know what I'm doing. It's best for everyone if I go. You'll be happier without me.'

On a rising note of exasperation, I said: 'Is this a permanent thing? Are you moving in together or are you just going to stay with him until you get something else sorted?'

'I don't know. I'll see how it goes.'

Lowering my voice, I said: 'Zoë, please. This is serious. You might get hurt.'

'I'll be fine,' she said.

All those weeks of her being in the house, the dread that announced itself every time I walked through my front door. All those meals sitting across from her, the careful way she ate, pulling her hair into a twist over one shoulder. Those nights listening for her voice on the phone upstairs, or for the sound of her key turning in the lock. All the time, I had been waiting for her to leave, willing it to happen so that we could be free of her constant presence. Now that it came to it, I found no sense of satisfaction or relief.

'Please just stay until David gets home.'

Part of me couldn't quite believe I was saying those words. She met my eyes, the corner of her mouth curling up into the slightest of grins. 'Thanks for everything, Caroline,' she said coolly. 'You've been so kind – all of you.'

The formality: it was like we were right back to that first Sunday lunch. *I hope we can become good friends, Caroline.*

'Help Zoë with her bag,' I told Robbie.

'Is that it?' he asked in disbelief.

'I can manage. Really.'

'Here.' He took the bag from her arms, pounding down the stairs with it. Zoë followed and I closed the door to what had been her room and would now go back to being David's office. When I reached the bottom step, she was already at the door, her bag slung over one shoulder.

There were no embraces, no goodbyes. Robbie and I stood together, watching her go.

'You could have stopped her,' he said quietly. 'You blame her for what happened to Holly, on the hike, don't you?'

'Robbie . . .'

'That's why she left. You drove her away. You could have made her stay.'

I looked at him, my son, his face narrowing with contempt, and said to him the same words I would say to his father some hours later when he returned from the office and I gave him the news that she had gone: 'I'm sorry, love. I tried.'

He turned from me, disgusted, and soon I was standing alone in the doorway, staring down our road, empty of traffic, watching, as if she might change her mind and come running back.

# 18. David

Caroline and I sat side by side in the darkened auditorium, waiting for the music to start. I've always loved that hush, the rush of nerves and excitement that comes with the dimming of the lights, the last few coughs as people prepare themselves for the performance. But that night, as I sat in the National Concert Hall with my wife, looking up at the orchestra full of youthful, expectant faces, I felt no excitement.

The low hum of muted percussion started, the plucking of harp-strings, and slowly, elegantly, the rising progression of the melody above the droning bass as Debussy's *La Mer* filled the room, little ripples and waves as the string section took over and the brass joined in. I felt Caroline straining beside me to catch a glimpse of Robbie, and there he was, pale-faced under the lights, bowing away at his cello. Dimly, I recalled the chords and melodies I had heard him practising for weeks – how disjointed and odd they had sounded, but now a piece fitting neatly into a puzzle, surrounded by the flow and harmony of the other instruments. I watched him, aware of my paternal pride – his concentration, his seriousness, the way the conductor and the musical score in front of him held his attention. I tried to focus on this fatherly love, hoping it would drown the shock and indignation I continued to feel forty-eight hours after Caroline had broken the news to me that Zoë had moved in with Chris.

In the past couple of days I had made several efforts to contact Zoë, leaving messages on her phone, texting her, all to no avail. I had pointedly not been in touch with Chris. He had been at my mother's funeral and, whatever the time or place, I found it hard to believe that no one had said anything to me about the two of them being an item. I felt the onus was on him to seek me out, and offer some kind of apology for his behaviour.

At the interval, when we streamed out and found our pre-ordered drinks waiting for us, I said to Caroline: 'So when Chris finally does decide to make contact, what do you think he'll say?'

'I don't know,' she said, with an air of mild resignation. 'I expect he'll say something to appease you.' She sipped her gin and tonic.

'What sort of explanation could he possibly give?'

We were leaning against a pillar. People were milling past. She shrugged.

'However you look at it, he's taking advantage of someone vulnerable.'

That caught her attention. 'I'm not sure I'd describe Zoë as vulnerable.'

'She's a teenager. Her mother recently died.'

Caroline wasn't buying it. 'She's nineteen and pretty savvy – and, whether you like it or not, she didn't know Linda all that well.'

'That's not the point.'

'Well, what is the point?'

'Doesn't it sicken you – the thought of them together?'

'There was fifteen years between my parents.'

'That's not the same,' I snapped. 'When I think of them together, sleeping together . . . Chris, of all people! I had no idea he was capable of doing something like this. Doesn't he realize he's betraying me and our friendship?'

'I doubt very much you're on his mind when he's in bed with her.'

'I suppose not,' I said.

'You know, for a second there, you sounded a little jealous, David.'

'Don't be ridiculous.' I took a large slug of my drink, felt the tonic creeping up the back of my nose.

'Anyway, all of this has very little to do with the reason we're here, which is Robbie. I hope he's okay,' she said. 'He looked nervous.'

'It sickens me,' I continued. 'Right to the pit of my stomach. If he tries to tell me he's in love, I think I might punch him.'

She put her glass on the wooden ledge with a sudden angry clink. 'Could you please stop?' she said, in a loud whisper. 'I know you're upset about this, but it's all you've talked about for the past two days and now I'm the one who's sick of it!'

The force in her voice silenced me, and for the next few minutes, we stood glancing about at the other audience members, sipping our drinks. When the bell finally rang to signal the end of the interval, it was a huge relief. We could escape each other's company and return to our seats.

*

The Arts building was quiet at that time of year, the swell of students on campus having fallen after lectures ended. The libraries were still busy, but a kind of hush had descended as exams began. I spent a good deal of time in my office, gathering together the papers I had published in the previous twelve months to read them before my interview, which had been scheduled for the following week. On that particular day, I was reading through the latest minutes of a student-staff consultative committee when the phone in my office rang. I picked it up and heard Chris at the other end of the line.

'I'm not going to apologize.' The first words out of his mouth, which might have been defensive and provocative, but he said them with a kind of casual serenity.

'No one's asked you to,' I said evenly, putting aside my papers and swivelling my chair so that I faced the window.

'I know you're upset.'

'You can't know what I'm thinking or how I feel, so don't pretend to, please.'

'I know it's not ideal.'

'She's my daughter, Chris.'

'It's not something I planned –'

'I'm not even going to get into the age-difference thing,' I said, 'because I think you know already how wrong it is. I mean, she's a teenager, for Christ's sake –'

'She's a grown-up, David.'

'Only barely!'

'You don't give her enough credit. She's very mature and knows her own mind.'

'It's you I'm not giving credit to. What the hell are you thinking?'

'That I'm in love with her.'

I leaned forward in my chair, as if I'd been punched in the stomach. Through the window, I could see a couple below in the courtyard. She was sitting on his knee playing with his hair. They were only kids. Love at that age – it retained a sort of innocence. But not this. Not what he was suggesting. 'This isn't love, Chris. It's a midlife crisis.'

'It's love,' he insisted.

'Answer me this,' I said. 'Why didn't you tell me? Why did I have to hear it from Caroline that not only were you dating my daughter but that you two have moved in together? We've known each other for *twenty-six years*, Chris. I would have thought the least you owed me was the decency to tell me to my face.'

'You're right,' he said, trying to sound reasonable and accommodating. 'I should have told you sooner.'

'So why didn't you?'

A pause, as if he was trying to find the words. 'This might sound crazy, but I was afraid that if I talked about it, the spell would be broken. The magic gone.'

I couldn't believe it. The guy was talking like he was in a Disney movie.

'From the start, I knew she was special. That first evening, the way we talked, the way we seemed to connect, not just on a sexual level but –'

'No,' I said, cutting him off. 'I can't go there, I just can't.'

'Okay, fine. I understand that. But the connection we have, the bond, it's so much deeper than anything I've ever experienced before. Even with Susannah –'

'Does she know about this?' I cut in. 'Susannah? Have you told her?'

'Not yet.'

'Have you thought about how hurt she'll be?'

'Susannah has it in for me,' he said, sounding aggrieved.

'She's going to hit the roof when she finds out,' I went on.

'You know what, David?' he snapped, his tone changing. 'Since Susannah and I split up, I've hardly heard from you. Barely a phone call to see if I'm okay. I could have been at home busily killing myself or losing myself in a bottle, and you'd have had no idea.'

I shifted in my chair, the truth of what he was saying making me uncomfortable.

'Zoë has been the one person to take an interest in my emotional wellbeing since this whole break-up happened. Not you, not Caroline. You ask me why I didn't tell you earlier? Maybe if you'd been more interested in how I was, I might have confided in you.'

'You're right,' I conceded. 'I should have been there for you, and I'm sorry. But I still don't think that's a good enough reason to seduce my daughter.'

'I wish she wasn't your daughter, but the way we've connected, it feels real. It's not some immature infatuation or midlife crisis. It feels like this is something . . .' he struggled to find the right word '. . . inevitable.'

I hated him then. He seemed so sure of himself. Here he was, one of my oldest friends, trying to conduct a conversation with me in reasonable tones and all the while he'd been sharing his bed with my daughter. My daughter fuelling his blood with desire. My daughter satisfying his flesh. It was too much. I told him I had a meeting, then hung up, dropping the receiver on to its cradle.

Too distracted to continue reading, I went instead to the common room for a mid-morning coffee. I shouldn't have been surprised to see McCormack on the couch in the corner – I saw him almost every other day – but I was. He had on a formal suit, not the casual garb he wore for the day-to-day grind of university work. The pin-stripes and tie made him look more like a banker than an academic. I noticed his hair had recently been cut and he was freshly shaved. Engrossed in reading from a thick folder, he did not see me approach.

'McCormack,' I said. 'You're a little overdressed for the kind of scrutiny you're giving those documents.'

He smiled. 'Dr Connolly,' he said, examining his watch. 'Aren't you up before me?'

'Up?'

'Interview day. I'm just glancing over my presentation.'

Two things startled me: interview day, and presentation. Neither made sense to me, but already I was sweating with panic.

'I've chosen not to do a PowerPoint,' McCormack said, 'I hate the damn things.'

'What are you talking about? The interviews are next week.'

'They changed the date, and added that we should present. It was all in the letter.'

'I never had any letter.'

'Are you sure? They sent one out about two weeks ago.'

How had this happened? Was it possible that I had received the letter and simply forgotten about it? Or had

Caroline picked it up and failed to pass it on? My heart-rate doubled, and my mind began to race.

'I've already seen two of the other candidates,' McCormack said. 'Barnes from London, and Gillis from Edinburgh. You're on at twelve. Are you sure you didn't get a letter?'

I looked at my watch. It was eleven thirty. I excused myself and ran back to my office. I rang Alan, but the interviews had already started. I explained what had happened to his secretary, Mrs Boland, but she insisted the letters had gone out. 'By registered post. They were all signed for.'

I explained that I had not signed for anything, then listened to her rustling among paperwork for a minute or two before she identified what she was searching for.

'Here we are,' she said, then read out: 'Signed for by C. Connolly.'

*Caroline.* A warm rush of anger went through me.

'Shall I tell the panel to expect you?' Mrs Boland asked.

I had little choice but to go ahead. 'Of course,' I said. 'I'll be right there.'

It was too late to dash home for a change of clothes. I was wearing an old shirt, a worn pair of corduroys and a jacket that had seen better days. So much for first impressions. I combed my hair, took up my papers, and wondered what on earth I would make a presentation on. My mind went blank. I had to run up the two floors to get to the dean's office, and when I walked into the room, out of breath, four serious individuals sat at the large oval table before me. Alan was the only one smiling. Acting as chair, he welcomed me and asked me to take a seat. I sat down and poured myself a glass of water. I drank it straight away, parched.

I made an attempt to explain the lost letter, how I had only just found out that the interview was to take place that day. Alan was sympathetic while the others looked askance, their eyes on my attire. Either way, I'd opened the interview on the back foot with apologies and excuses. It was not the start I had hoped for.

They asked about my publications, which conferences I had attended recently, if I would consider creating a symposium at UCD for combatants and veterans. Alan smiled his encouragement, but the others were tougher. The external examiner asked about enrolment, post-application conversions for our graduate programmes, possible interdisciplinary degrees that could be developed, and PhD completions.

I offered some platitudes about a personal-development programme for doctoral students and a mentoring scheme I hoped to initiate. It was bread and butter to me – until the extern asked his next question. 'That's all very good,' he said. 'But what about the actual retention of your students?'

All I could think of then was Niki. How she had walked out on me. My star student. He must have found out. Alan would have had to divulge the unfortunate fact of her departure and with it the reasons.

When it was time for my presentation, I rehashed the last paper I had written on the relationship between Roger Casement's humanitarian work for the British Crown and his role as an Irish nationalist. Suffice it to say,

I did justice neither to the research nor to the subject matter. The questions were routine, until Professor Mary Sinnott took up the reins. She asked about my doctoral work, and brought me back to Belfast. I talked about the Irish Battalion in the First World War, the so-called South Irish Horse, how I had developed my dissertation into my first book.

'And your media profile, Dr Connolly, how does it impact on your contribution to university life?' she asked.

I faltered. This is so unfair, I thought. I should have had time to prepare, just like everyone else. The radio interview came back to me, with a flush of shame and irritation. The letter of reprimand was no doubt still being drafted. I waffled, and stuttered, but ultimately re-focused my efforts. I wanted that professorship, after all. I talked about the media's relationship with history through the years – the chasm between ethical reporting and sensational press. A vagrant image of Chris and Zoë entered my mind. My own daughter, living with him. *Sleeping* with him.

'The position of professor is not just another rung on the ladder,' the dean said. 'It is a position of leadership. We're looking for someone with the necessary charisma and sang-froid not to be rattled in situations of intense or unpredictable pressure.'

He could not have disguised his disapproval more thinly. I told him I had learned a great deal about pressure in the previous academic year, and how, all things considered, I was learning to use it to my advantage. But that was not true. Look at me now, I thought, struggling to answer these questions, my life falling apart around me. Zoë – taken from me by my best friend.

I thought of Linda, her last lecture, her Angel of History: 'From Paradise a storm is brewing, and this storm has so much violence that it catches in the angel's wings and the angel cannot close those wings. The storm grows in intensity, picks up and propels this celestial being into the future.'

Alan ended the interview by asking me what history meant to me – what was history?

A line from Ambrose Bierce came to me: 'History is an account, mostly false, of events, mostly unimportant, which are brought about by rulers, mostly knaves, and soldiers, mostly fools.'

I said something else.

At home, I asked Caroline about the letter. She was adamant she had not received it.

'You might not have noticed actually signing for it,' I suggested. 'You could have been distracted by something else.'

'I'm telling you, David, I never signed for it.'

'It was your signature,' I insisted.

We rowed, and she accused me of not believing her, of not trusting her.

But I couldn't let it go, my temper flaring. 'Well, what did happen? If you didn't sign for it, who did?'

I asked Robbie and Holly, who both denied any knowledge of the letter.

'It must have been Zoë,' Caroline said, and I turned away from her, enraged.

'For God's sake,' I muttered. 'Everything is her fault,

according to you. Why on earth would she sign your name?'

'Because that's what she's like, David. You know it, and I do too. She's capricious, destructive, cruel.'

We rowed some more, but it was pointless. Whoever's fault it was, the damage had been done.

I waited for an email, a letter, a phone call, but there was nothing.

In the meantime, my mood plummeted. I felt loneliness come over me – as if, until then, I hadn't realized how important my mother's presence in my life had been. She had been taken from me, and so had Zoë. It was a desperate week, one in which the hope for promotion did not diminish but, if anything, heightened. As if the professional advancement could somehow counteract the losses I had suffered personally. To say I was unsettled when Alan finally called me into his office is probably something of an understatement.

'I wanted to follow up with you on your interview,' he said. 'An official communiqué will follow, but I'm sorry to say that this time you have been unsuccessful.'

I sat down. The energy seeped out of me. The extra committee work, the substitute teaching, the journalism and research, all for naught. I couldn't help thinking it had been a colossal waste of time.

For Alan to talk to me like that was professional courtesy. But, with the bitter taste of defeat in my mouth, I explained to him how surprised I was about the interview date change, and that I had not received official notice. He told me rather matter-of-factly that these things happen all the time, that the letter had been sent, and that all of the other candidates had appeared, and, besides, he insisted firmly, I had not missed the interview.

I thought again of what might have happened to the letter, Caroline's accusations creeping into my head. Had Zoë signed for it, then secreted it in her room, shredding it before she left? Laughing at me. Making a fool of me yet again. Her cruelty echoed and added to how Linda had left me in the dark all those years ago – some inexplicable disdain had been handed down from one generation to the next.

'David, I know it has been a difficult time for you.' The line between mentor and manager was sometimes a blurred one with Alan. He invited you into his confidence, but I was never sure whether it was for professional motives or personal altruism. It occurred to me that maybe he didn't know the difference. 'My condolences again for the passing of your mother.'

I thanked him.

'This business with your new-found daughter, it must be taxing, not to mention distracting.'

'It's not entirely pertinent to whether I got the job or not. You know that,' I said, noticing the deep grooves of age on his forehead.

'The panel was very impressed with your showing.'

I felt like saying, 'It doesn't matter. I wasn't good enough. No need to sugar-coat the truth.'

'It's also beholden on me to tell you that they have selected Dr McCormack for the position of professor.'

Anyone but him.

'We realize that you'll be disappointed, but for the moment, can I say that your research outputs are strong, teaching and learning are also strong . . .'

'Why didn't I get it?' I asked, although I had a good idea of the answer – I was playing along with this charade of feedback. 'You can be honest with me.'

Alan was back at the window. A flock of seagulls swooped by. Behind them, I could see the two red and white Pigeon House chimney stacks at Poolbeg.

'We're relying on anyone hoping to gain the professorial grade to secure a minimum of external funding each year . . .'

'McCormack is bringing in more than I am?'

'In a word, yes. I want this to be an ongoing conversation. We don't have to hash out the whys and wherefores right now.'

'How much?'

'David, it's not the time for those questions, or for disclosing actual figures.'

'You know I've been in talks with the Royal Historical Society, who are in the process of securing commercial funding . . .'

'How is Caroline? How are the kids?' He hadn't disguised his desire to sidetrack me.

I lied: 'They're all good, Alan. Tip-top.'

'I'm glad to hear it,' he said, sounding utterly unconvinced. 'Perhaps you should get away. Take a break.'

'I took a week off after the radio interview.'

'I mean a holiday,' Alan said, trying to sound upbeat, the words scraping across his throat in a husky cough. 'A proper one. Abroad.'

Was the department trying to sideline me, to get me out of the way? 'I'm not sure that's a good idea,' I said.

'I have a place in France,' Alan said. 'A villa on Île de Ré, not far from La Rochelle. Small but comfortable – a winding road that brings you down to a very quaint village. It's a place of tranquillity.'

'It sounds idyllic but –'

'There's enough room for you to bring the family . . . It's really rather lovely.'

'That's very kind of you, Alan, really, but I couldn't . . .'

He suggested July. 'Please,' he said, 'just consider it.'

There was no point in returning to my office, no point even in remaining on campus. As I packed my bag and locked the door to my office, I thought that, for the first time in my life, the university seemed hostile to me. For years I had been stitched up in the cocoon of academic life, blanketed by the security of tenure, but now, as I walked through the corridors with their tiled floors and characterless breeze-block walls, I felt the hardness of every surface, the smugness of the cliques in their cosy coffee groups. It was like a giant country club that had just refused me membership. What had once seemed a friendly, liberal environment now seemed elitist, unforgiving, archaic.

I had no intention of going home. The thought of hanging around an empty house waiting for Caroline to get back so I could give her my bad news just filled me with despair. Instead I cycled into the Dublin Mountains and the Blue Light, where I sat with a pint of Guinness and gazed out over the city, bathed as it was in a great burst of sunshine that had arrived without warning on that May day.

I was exhausted, and on edge. I felt the torpor of my mother's death in my limbs. Everything was falling apart. The university had rejected me. My wife was barely speaking to me. I had lost the knack of communicating with my children. And now there was that other daughter – a grandchild my mother had never known – who, despite my best efforts, I had somehow managed to push away.

I drank another pint, and decided about France. Alan was right. I needed to get away. I needed to sort things out, and gain some perspective. I finished my drink and free-wheeled home to tell Caroline, but as soon as I came into the hallway and rested my bike against the stairs, I knew all was not well. I heard her through the open kitchen door. She was crying.

'What is it?' I asked, and she looked up from where she sat at the counter, a glass of wine in front of her, tissues scattered on the counter.

The skin around her nose and upper lip was red, as if she had been crying for some time. A lurching feeling came over me. *The children.* She must have seen the panic in my eye: 'No, it's not that. They're fine.'

My heartbeat calmed a little. I approached her nervously. Whatever it was, I wasn't sure I had the energy for it. Already I was assailed by the feeling that I was somehow at the root of her misery.

'It's everything else,' she said.

Just saying those three words seemed to threaten what little composure she had summoned. She took a deep sip of wine. 'I'm forty-one years old,' she said quietly, 'and on the surface of it, my life is just fine. I'm married with two wonderful children, a comfortable home, friends. So why do I feel utterly useless? Completely expendable?'

Her job, I thought. Of course: today was her last day. I heard the bitterness in her voice, as if she had been conducting a kind of accounting of her life, looking over her achievements with a critical eye, withdrawing from what she had seen.

'I don't seem qualified to do anything. I'm at the mercy of my husband, a kept woman.' She enunciated the words in a way that brought home to me the dangerousness of her mood. 'And my husband hardly speaks to me. Can barely stand to be in the same room with me, in fact.'

'That's not true, Caroline.'

'Isn't it? I can't even remember the last time we made love.'

I sat down so that we were facing each other.

Her expression was flat and unreadable. She took me in as if I were a stranger. 'I haven't a clue what you're thinking any more, David.'

It was not acrimonious, the way she said it. It was not an accusation. It was said more out of exhaustion than anything else – a last-straw relinquishment, a reluctant capitulation – and despite my earlier thoughts in the same direction, I felt a growing sense of panic. It felt as if she had almost surrendered, and it occurred to me that I hadn't realized she had been fighting so strongly, or for so long, for herself and for us.

It might not have been the right time, but I told her then about being turned down for the professorship.

'I'm sorry,' she said.

I couldn't help thinking that if I had received the

letter, with the revised date and time, it might have changed the outcome. I didn't need to say as much to Caroline. It was as if she could read my mind: 'We have to do something, David. She's pulling us apart. Our family, our marriage.'

'You mean Zoë?'

'You don't actually think I hurt her, pushed her against a wall, like she said?'

'No,' I answered truthfully.

'She scares me.' She took my hands.

'Scares you?'

'All the lies, all the deception . . . I really think she's out to destroy us.'

I almost said that her words were too strong, but I didn't: a part of me agreed with her.

'We have to do something, David.'

'We will,' I said, trying to reassure her. I lifted my wife's hands to my lips and told her everything was going to be okay. I told her about Alan's offer of the villa in France: it would be a chance not only to get away from the disappointments and confusion of life at home, but an opportunity to address, without the obstacle of Zoë's presence and probable intervention, all the marital difficulty we had found ourselves in. Caroline seemed genuinely relieved, and over the coming weeks, our discussions returned again and again to France, the tickets and travel, the villa and what would be, we hoped, time to reconcile our differences, a chance to heal, a holiday to remember.

And all the while we talked about it, I felt, beneath my excitement, an undercurrent of uncertainty. A month had passed since Zoë had left and in that time I hadn't heard a word from her – not a phone call or a text – let alone seen her. As the days slipped towards summer and our holiday grew close, I began to realize, with a sadness I had to keep hidden, that I had lost her. And whenever the realization crept over me, another thought would surface: *perhaps she isn't my daughter.* I had kept the inconclusive test results to myself and even though I told myself they didn't prove anything, secretly they bothered me. From time to time, I thought about telling Caroline. But as the days slipped towards summer and our holiday grew close, I kept the information to myself, protecting her, or so I believed. Reasoning with myself that it didn't change anything and what harm could it possibly do to keep it from her?

# PART THREE

# 19. Caroline

The sun was beginning its splendid descent when we crossed the long stretch of bridge to Île de Ré. We had journeyed overnight by ferry to Cherbourg and spent the day in the car, making our way steadily south. By the time we reached the island and found the village of Loix, the air had grown cooler and the sky was starting to turn pink. The house lay on the outskirts of the village, tucked down a small alleyway too narrow for the car to navigate, so we parked by a square, each of us taking a piece of luggage, and walked the rest of the way.

The villa, like its neighbours, was low and squat, with whitewashed walls, a terracotta roof, and olive-green shutters closed over the windows. A six-foot-high perimeter wall masked it from view, but once through the wrought-iron gates, we found ourselves in a pretty courtyard lined with bursts of lavender. A heavy burden of tangled clematis hung low over the front door. The humble exterior masked a warren-like tumble of rooms, and narrow, twisting staircases rose to hidden bedrooms tucked away in the attic. The floors were covered with slate tiles and it was a relief to kick off my shoes and feel the coolness beneath the soles of my hot feet. Robbie and Holly, having dumped their bags at the door, had gone ahead of us, and I could hear the excitement in their voices at each new discovery.

'Mum! Come out here – quick!' I heard Robbie call, and I followed his voice through the now-dark kitchen and living room, out through a set of French windows to a garden at the back with yew and olive trees. A limestone terrace glowed in the half-light. In the midst of it all was a pool – long and narrow, a little wider than a lap-pool, the water appearing purple-grey in the dusky light.

'You didn't say there'd be a pool,' I said to David, coming to stand next to him.

'I thought I'd surprise you,' he replied, looking genuinely pleased. It was the first sign of real delight he'd shown in months.

'I'm going for a swim,' Robbie said.

'Hang on,' I called after him, as he hurried back to the house. 'Isn't it a bit late for that?'

'Let him,' David said. 'He's happy.' I felt his arm go around my shoulders, drawing me to him. Tentatively, I put mine around his waist. I couldn't remember the last time we had stood together like that.

Holly had taken off her shoes and was sitting at the edge of the pool, her feet dangling into the cool water. Behind her, the grass grew in long, dry clumps, feathery flowers peeking through. I could hear the low hum of nocturnal insects rising around us, and from one of the neighbouring houses someone's laughter rang out.

'So what do you think?' David nodded back at the house.

I thought of the cool peace within those rooms: was he asking if I thought that here was a place where we might reconcile? Within the confines of this island, might we find some kind of healing after the difficult months we had endured? Perhaps it was the relief of arrival after a long journey or the unfamiliarity of his body against mine, but I felt an answering optimism in my heart. 'It's perfect,' I told him.

His smile broadened, and just then Robbie came running past and launched himself into the air, his hands clutching his knees to his chest. We watched as he plunged into the water, Holly shrieking and turning aside to avoid being splashed. I remember thinking I must freeze this memory and hold on to it: the beauty of the garden, the coolness of twilight after a long journey, the weight and warmth of my husband's arm around me, and the rocking waters of the pool as my son surfaced, gasping for air, laughing, triumphant.

The first night, we wandered out into the quiet village square and ate outside a bistro while men played boules on the red clay beside the church. By the time we got back to the house it was late and we were all exhausted after the journey. We said our goodnights and it was not until the next morning that I had a chance to explore the house properly. David and the kids had gone out to the market to buy provisions, while I was left alone to wander through the quiet rooms, accustoming myself to the particular sounds and odours they held.

There was a masculine feel to the place – the furniture dark, although comfortable enough. The walls were hung with framed maps of the island and various sepia-tinted photographs – studio portraits of Victorian women with strong jaws and crinolines; moustached men with books lying open on their knees. Indeed, there were books everywhere in the house – stacked in piles behind doors, towers of them leaning against walls. I imagined Alan sitting alone in the long stretch of the evening, sipping a glass of wine and getting lost in his reading, not noticing the hours ticking by. I was surprised at his gesture of kindness, offering us the use of his holiday home in the wake of David's disappointment.

We hadn't talked much about David's failure to gain the professorship – he was reluctant, too, to discuss the difficulties in our marriage or the death of his mother – but I knew it had affected him deeply. It was more than just a professional disappointment. To him it was an indictment of his whole career. 'You'll get another chance,' I had told him. 'There'll be other opportunities.'

'That's just it,' he had said, looking at me in a despairing way. 'There won't be. This was my one chance and I blew it.'

He had always tended towards seriousness, but when we were first married, he would sometimes catch himself becoming morose or pessimistic, and pull the corners of his mouth into a cartoon face of misery that made me laugh. Just like that his mood would lift. Somewhere along the way he had lost the knack of it.

As for me, I was still smarting at Peter's parting words: 'I need someone who's at the top of her game, not distracted by her domestic situation.'

Standing in the darkened living room, running my finger over the gilded titles of those old books, I considered our professional humiliations and the injured pride that went hand in hand with them. I thought about the chasm that had sprung up between David and me over the past six months. I could blame a lot of it on Zoë, but the first fissure had appeared long before that – the first time I'd kissed Aidan, or when I'd stood in a darkened hallway and listened as my husband named another woman the love of his life. Perhaps it went further back to the ghost of a baby. That fissure had been there a long time, but how easily Zoë had caused it to widen and deepen, ripping through our family, pushing us apart. I looked around the room and felt the strain of my hope that in this house we might find solace, a renewal of love, a way back to each other.

The iron gate jangling on its hinges pulled me back into the present. At once the cloistered atmosphere in the house changed as the others came in, bringing with them the energy of the marketplace, the triumph of their purchases. There was a flurry of activity as bags were emptied, contents spread over the table.

'Hungry?' David asked, holding up a bag of pastries, the brown paper translucent with grease.

'Famished.'

Those first few days, I remember in a haze of lightness, like shrugging off your winter clothes and stepping into the sun. We hired bikes and cycled across the salt flats, along the coastal paths. We went to Saint-Martin-de-Ré and marvelled at the wealth of pleasure-boats and yachts clustered in the harbour. On our way back to Loix, we discovered an oyster bar with an ocean view and spent a couple of hours there under the shade of parasols, feasting on seafood, David and I getting nicely sozzled on a chilled bottle of Chinon. The village itself hadn't much to offer by way of entertainment – a café by the market, the bistro and a bar on the village square – but it didn't bother us. We were content to spend our days on the beach, our evenings dining on the terrace, reading our books as the sun set.

The kinks and bruises of the past few months faded a little more with each passing day. The tension that had stiffened David's shoulders dissipated, and he relaxed, whistling to himself in the mornings as he made coffee, his face animated, no longer closed or drawn. Robbie was talking to me again, his exams completed without incident, the trouble at school behind us, as too was the fear I had felt for Holly's security and well-being. The village, and the island, felt small, intimate, safe. The kids were able to wander off on their own, exploring the area on their bikes, while David and I relaxed by the pool or took a stroll down to the seafront.

Towards the end of our first week, David and I were sitting on the terrace eating lunch when his phone buzzed. Shading the screen from the sun with his cupped hand, he said: 'A missed call.'

'Who from?'

'Zoë.'

I reached for my glass.

Since our departure from Ireland, her name hadn't been mentioned: an unspoken rule between the four of us – a rule that even Robbie had adhered to. We needed to get away from her, if only for a short while.

'Are you going to call her back?'

He began pressing keys with his thumb then seemed to think better of it. 'No. If it's urgent, she'll try again.' Putting the phone down, he reached for the bottle.

Later, we sat in a companionable silence, reading our books and finishing the wine. The afternoon stretched out long and lazy and there was no sign of the kids returning. I thought about walking down to the harbour, but when I suggested it to David, a slow smile spread across his face. 'I've a better idea,' he said.

The house was caught in the white glow of the afternoon sunlight, stillness and quiet filling the rooms. In our bedroom, we undressed with the shyness of new lovers. It had been months since we had made love and we were nervous, despite a long history of intimacy and the loosening of inhibitions brought on by the lunchtime wine. In the quiet of the late afternoon, as our bodies came together, I felt an enormous sense of relief. We held each other beneath the sheets, moving towards a new understanding, another layer of meaning added to the complexities of our bond.

We were dressed by the time the kids returned, tiredness quietening them as they slumped in the armchairs, their faces glowing from the sunlight, Robbie's arms tanned against the white of his T-shirt.

'There are pizzas in the freezer,' David told them. 'Your mother and I are going out.'

We set off hand in hand, still feeling the heat of our afternoon reunion. Something had sparked to life between us, passion rekindled. As we walked through the deserted streets, the noises of domesticity trickled out of open windows – saucepans clattering, voices raised in talk. His hand in mine, I basked in the renewed familiarity. Warmth from the sun still hovered in the air as we reached the square and took our seats at one of the tables outside the bistro.

I ordered *moules frites* while David had steak, and with a bottle of Sauvignon Blanc in an ice bucket between us, we talked of the village and of Alan's house, speculating as to how he had come to own it. Property on the island was phenomenally expensive – when we had peered through the window of a local estate agent, we had come away reeling. Conversation flowed easily between us. David voiced his opinion that Alan had inherited his house and this led on to a discussion about Ellen, David confiding his sense of loneliness in the wake of her death, that with his parents no longer alive, and no siblings, he had been cast adrift.

'You're not alone,' I assured him, and he reached across the table, placing his hand on mine.

'Being away like this,' he said, 'it's made me wonder whether I should look into taking a sabbatical abroad, maybe take Giancarlo up on his offer to do some research in Siena.'

'Are you serious?'

He shrugged. 'Why not? After Mum . . . I just need something to clear my head, take a break from UCD for a while.'

'What about the kids? What about school?'

'Robbie's got three years left until he finishes – there's time enough before he needs to start thinking about exams and university. Holly's still in primary school. Now might be the perfect time for us all to go.' He had finished his steak and pushed his plate to one side. 'I think it would be good for us, Caroline. It might be just the break we need.'

With the wine in my bloodstream and the heat of the

sun still in my bones, the idea made me giddy with excitement. 'Won't it take time to organize?'

'I'm sure I could square it with the university. We could be out there by Christmas. And it doesn't have to be for a whole year. Six months would do, don't you think?'

Six months in Italy sounded like a dream.

We leaned towards each other, talking excitedly about what would need to happen – arrangements with the school, perhaps let our house. It was all fantasy, really, and I think we both knew that. But for just a while, it was good to fool ourselves that we could live unfettered lives, shrug off the things that held us down. The conversation alone felt restorative, nourishing.

It was dark in the square as David signalled for the bill. Strings of brightly coloured lights reached across the boughs of the plane trees forming the perimeter. A hush had come over the gathered diners.

'What about Zoë?' I asked quietly. Even mentioning her name felt like a gamble. Our afternoon reunion, the flow of conversation between us, the warmth that had returned – it was still tentative.

He looked down at the receipt in his hand, folded it in half and pushed it into his shirt pocket with his wallet. 'I think she'll manage.'

His voice sounded heavy and I knew it was not just tiredness. He sat back, casting his eyes upwards at the lights looping through the trees. 'I thought it would be easier. It didn't seem like such a big thing to have her in our lives. Pretty naïve, huh?'

I waited for him to go on.

'It's not like having a child you've known from birth.

With Zoë, I don't feel I'm ever really going to get to know her.'

'You've tried hard with her, David.'

'And I'll continue to try. It's just that . . .'

'What?'

He shrugged, seeming a little sad in the half-light, a look of defeat coming over him. 'I'm here for her if she needs me, but she has to forge her own path.'

Hope bloomed in my heart. Words I had longed to hear. 'She can manage on her own, David. She's perfectly capable.'

'This thing with Chris . . .'

'It's a fling. She's nineteen. You have to allow for these things.' I didn't say what I really thought: that her relationship with Chris was calculated to get at us.

'I suppose.'

'Wait and see. By the time we get home to Dublin, it will probably be over between them.'

A chill had entered the air as we stepped away from the square, David's arm around me as we walked together. Buildings appeared chalky blue in the moonlight. We talked a little of our plans for the next few days. David wanted to visit some of the beaches on the south of the island where bunkers built by the Germans in the Second World War still existed. I had promised Holly a shopping trip to La Rochelle. Tired but content, we returned to the house, closing the gate behind us and crossing the courtyard.

As soon as I opened the front door, I felt a change. The house seemed alive in a different way – the air spiked with a new presence. David behind me, I pushed open the door to the living room and saw Robbie sitting with his arms crossed over his chest, his face dark and unreadable. Movement in the kitchen caught the corner of my eye, but before I could turn to look there, Chris was getting out of the other armchair, his face a mixture of hope and apology.

'What are you doing here?' I asked. He had been crossing the room to greet me, but the abruptness of my question made him stop.

'Caroline, Dave,' he said. 'I know this is a surprise, calling on you unannounced . . .'

He had a glass of wine, which he was passing from one hand to the other, as if unsure of what to do with it. He put it down on the coffee-table. Then, straightening up, he addressed us with a smile: 'We wanted to surprise you, didn't we, babe?'

She was almost at my elbow by the time I realized she was there. Wearing a sleeveless short blue dress and orange flip-flops on her lightly tanned feet, I was struck all over again by how slight she was. Without the boots, her winter armour, she seemed wispy and insubstantial, like a twig that might snap in a brisk breeze.

'It's my fault,' she said, the corner of her mouth pulling into a smile but her eyes were watchful, moving from me to David. 'We were in Paris, you see, when it happened, and I knew you guys were here. Chris said we should ring but I preferred to tell you in person.'

She stepped past me towards Chris. I felt David close behind me, but couldn't see his face. I was too caught up with these new arrivals. Her new way of dressing made her look younger rather than older. Next to her, Chris was like some trendy uncle. He was sporting new clothes too, clearly aiming for a look that was youthful and flashy. He'd had his hair cut differently – there was a sort of mussed artfulness about it.

'Are you sure it's all right?' Zoë asked, assuming a worried expression. 'It's a bit cheeky, I know, turning up out of the blue. It seemed like such a good idea at the time, but then, when we were driving over the bridge, it suddenly felt like a mistake. That you might not be happy to see us.'

'You're very welcome, Zoë,' I told her, thinking of the times before when I had uttered the same hollow statements. Gestures of hospitality, but they were empty of any truth. David said nothing.

'You see?' Chris told her, putting his arm around her, smiling with reassurance. 'Didn't I tell you it'd be okay?' Then to me: 'She worries about everything.'

Oh, please, I thought. Give me a break.

It was nauseating to watch him clutch her to his side, beaming down at her. How could she stand it? The suffocating benevolence. I had a glimpse of what it was like between them – the way he lavished her with attention, his cloying affection, Zoë enduring it with a patient smile. She looked up at him then and her expression changed, the two of them giggling. There was something shifty about it, as if they were sharing a joke that I wasn't in on. I knew this visit wasn't the whimsical decision they had made it out to be.

'What?' I asked. 'What's happened?'

They exchanged a look, then Zoë reached for a bag on

the table and pulled out a bottle of champagne. 'We brought this,' she said, and offered it to me.

I can still remember it, his hand on her shoulder, her almond-coloured skin beneath the reddened tips of his fingers, my eyes travelling the length of her arm to the orange label on the green bottle, the stones in her ring catching the light.

'Oh, my God,' I said.

I didn't turn to David, not wanting to see the slow shock that was surely coming over his face. Instead I kept my eyes fixed on hers. Brackish green eyes, gleaming now with excitement. Excitement, not nerves, for while Chris was sweating a little under the low ceiling of the room, she betrayed no anxiety. I thought again of when I had first met her – how nerveless she had seemed. She held out her hand to us – a queenly gesture – presenting us with her ring as if inviting us to come forward and kiss it.

Robbie shifted on the couch.

'I don't believe it,' I said.

'It's true,' Chris said, pulling her close to him, the two of them laughing as he kissed the side of her face.

It was only then that I looked at David.

I suppose there is a latent violence in all of us. It lies in the dark folds inside us waiting for the conditions outside and beyond to draw it out into the light. David is a man who goes quiet when enraged, his mood darkening. His anger internalized, he silently broods.

But when I turned to him that night, when I saw him take a step forward, I was sure – for that brief moment – that there was violence in his mind. It was in his hands, clenched at his sides, in the wild light in his eyes. The room had grown hot, but still I felt coldness passing over my neck and shoulders, like a sudden chill breeze. Even now, after all that's happened, I can't forget it. A memory that refuses to be erased. The weight and coldness of that bottle of champagne in my hand, and the look on David's face as if he wants to kill them. And in that sharp instant, I see that he could.

# 20. David

My working life has been the study of days – days and events. The marking of Time. But here's the thing: I have never really felt what it must be like to wake on the morning of one of these historic events, either big or small. I've paused to consider the leaders of the Easter Rising sitting in their cells as dawn broke on the day of their executions, but I've never *felt* it. In the same way I've never experienced the stomach-clenching fear of the trenches in the First World War or the sickening shock of a pilot knowing his plane has been hit. I've read about these emotions in the dry pages of books without ever having to experience them. Perhaps that is what I have been lacking all along – the peculiar empathy required to truly understand the past.

But I felt it that day – the last day. The portent of something in the atmosphere. I felt it from the moment I woke.

It announced itself as a heaviness in the air, like oppressive heat before a storm. When I flung wide the shutters, though, the sky was a brilliant blue, not a cloud in sight. There was a smell like smoke mingled with petrol – it was distant but I could catch it, the acrid tinge in my nostrils. The bed was empty, Caroline having left it hours before, but I had lain there, trapped within this uneasy heat. Something felt wrong. Sure, I was a little hung-over, still fuming from the night before, but this was something else. I'm not a superstitious man. I don't believe in signs or foreshadowing, none of that predestination claptrap. But when I consider all that happened that day, and remember how I felt upon waking, it makes me stop to wonder.

I threw on some clothes, my mouth tacky and dry, and stepped into the hallway. It was quiet, heat lurking in the darkened corners of the house, a murmur of unease running through my thoughts, like a whispered complaint I couldn't shake. The door to the kids' bedroom was ajar. I pushed it open and stuck my head inside. Holly's bed was empty, but Robbie was sprawled on his, forearms flung over his head against the pillow.

'Morning, son,' I said, and his eyes, which were open, flicked in my direction.

'Hey.'

'Sleep okay?'

'No,' he said pointedly.

This was a reference to his indignation the night before at having to vacate his room and bunk in with his sister to provide our unexpected guests with a bed for the night. His reaction when the arrangements were being hastily made had been incandescent fury and I could see that his anger still burned, albeit at a lesser flame.

'Thanks, Robbie. For giving up your room.'

'It's not like I had a choice.'

'Well, none of us knew they were coming.'

'It's a joke,' he said, one that he clearly didn't find funny.

'I agree.'

Propping himself up on his elbows, his brow darkening, he went on: 'I can't believe she's engaged to that twat!

I know he's your friend and all, but come on, Dad, he's ancient!'

I rubbed my eye, felt some crust lodged in the corner and wiped it away.

'It's bullshit,' he added and I agreed. It was.

'Can't you talk to them?' he asked. 'Make them call it off?'

'I can't make them do anything,' I said, laughing a little. There was something childlike and innocent in the way he still thought I had the power to effect that kind of change. I wondered, too, why he was so upset about it.

I muttered something about needing a coffee and turned away. Briefly, he called me back: 'Happy birthday, by the way,' he said.

July 8th – the day of the birthdays. It was something that marked us out as unique, I always thought, this shared event. What are the odds of a daughter being born on her father's birthday? In the twelve years I had shared the date with Holly, certain traditions had sprung up around it. One of them – perhaps my favourite – was the birthday hug, a long, squeezing clench like a physical acknowledgement of our special bond. With this in mind, I went downstairs in search of her.

As I reached the bottom step, I heard voices in the kitchen, and lingered for a moment, listening.

'I think it's ridiculous, Chris, to be honest,' I heard Caroline say.

She was clattering around in there, busying herself with some kitchen task, and I heard the lightness of Chris's laughter above her industry.

'I'm in love, Caroline! Aren't I allowed to behave foolishly?'

'You're in love,' she muttered, a little exasperated. 'And it's not the age-gap that bothers me, you know that, right?'

'What is it, then? Is it David?'

'It's Zoë. Have you seen her arms, Chris?'

He made a kind of tutting sound, clearly unimpressed, but Caroline was not to be silenced.

'And you know she tried to kill herself at Christmas.'

'Yes, I know,' he replied, his voice dipping. 'We've talked about that. I believe I can help her. I'm good for her –'

'For God's sake, Chris, you're only out of a marriage about five minutes! Now you want to nosedive into another – with *her*?'

'You don't like her,' he said, with the smugness of his own certainty. 'That's what's really the issue.'

I heard the dull slap of something flung on to the counter.

'I'm not sure you've really thought about what you're taking on. She's mixed up – vulnerable.'

Her tone had changed, caution tempering her forthright words.

I was still standing in the narrow hallway, my eye caught by the flash of movement beyond the French windows leading on to the patio. I saw the splash of water, an arm raised and then disappearing again, as Holly did her laps of the pool. I could have gone outside, joined her, turned my back on the low-grade argument rumbling in the kitchen. But I didn't.

Chris was sitting at the table, his iPad in front of him.

'Here he is,' he said. 'The birthday boy.' There was forced jolliness in his tone.

'Happy birthday, love,' Caroline said, with warm affection, briefly forgetting her annoyance with Chris as she came and put her hands on my chest, reaching up to kiss me.

'Thanks. Any coffee going?'

'I was going to bring you breakfast in bed.'

It was clear she had been to the market already, the counters and table littered with her purchases. I picked up a croissant from the plate and Caroline poured me some coffee while I took a seat opposite Chris. He eyed me warily. My mood the night before, my reaction to his preposterous announcement, made him unsure of me. No doubt he was thinking that, having slept on it, I'd have mellowed. He thought wrong.

'So how old are you now, Dave? Forty-two, forty-three?'

'Forty-four.'

He whistled.

'I don't know why you're so smug. You're only a few weeks shy of it yourself.'

He grinned, determined to be sunny in the face of my terseness. 'Forty is the new thirty,' he declared.

'Does that make nineteen the new nine?' Caroline asked.

'*Touché*,' he replied, but his smirk seemed to sag a little. I had a sudden urge to lean across the table and slap it off his face.

'When are you leaving?' I asked, not caring that it was rude. I wanted him gone, even if that meant Zoë leaving too, and I didn't care that he was stung. In truth, I wanted to hurt him.

'Actually,' Caroline said, pausing in her slicing of melon, 'there's a bit of a problem.'

'What?' Her eyes were fixed on me and I sensed she was reluctant to break the news.

'There's been an accident on the bridge.'

'What sort of accident?'

She put down the knife, wiping her hands on a tea-towel. 'An oil tanker crashed into the toll booths early this morning.'

'*What?*' I could hardly believe it, yet I had smelt the smoke when I'd woken up, even from where we were, on the far side of the island from the bridge.

'They told me when I was at the market. There's a massive fire. No cars can come on to or get off the island.'

'Here,' Chris said, offering me his iPad, which was opened on a French news page. 'My French is shit but from what I can gather they've sent in fire brigades from La Rochelle to try to tackle the blaze.'

I scrolled through the images of smoke billowing from the inferno, the long bridge snaking across to the mainland. 'How the hell did it happen?'

'Who knows?' Caroline said, returning to her task.

'Maybe the brakes failed,' Chris offered. 'Or it could have been a terrorist attack.'

'On Île de Ré? Hardly an obvious target for ISIS or Al-Qaeda.' The notion was absurd.

'Whatever,' Caroline said, setting the bowl on the table with a sharp clink. 'There's no way off the island. Not today, at any rate. Maybe not for a few days.' She didn't sound happy.

'I know it's not ideal,' Chris said, coming over all

reasonable, 'but let's try to make the best of it, hmm? Can't we use the time to try to reconcile our differences?' Caroline cast him a doubtful look but he went on: 'Zoë so badly wanted to come here, to tell you our news in person. If you'd seen how excited she was, how insistent on sharing this with you . . . Can't you please try to be happy for us? For her, if not for me?'

He went on a bit about how much we all meant to him and Zoë, but I had no interest in listening to the fairytale he was peddling – about how we were family, about mending the wounds – so I cut across him: 'What about Susannah?' I asked.

That took the wind out of his sails. He selected a strawberry from the bowl and popped it into his mouth. 'What about her?'

'Does she know about your engagement?'

'I haven't told her yet . . .'

'Chris,' Caroline interjected.

'And I'd thank you not to tell her either,' he added.

She was nonplussed. 'I don't get it,' she said. 'On the one hand, you're all lovey-dovey, buying rings, making your big announcement, and yet you're trying to hush it up.'

'I want to tell Susannah to her face, not over the phone.'

It was a cop-out and he knew it. I said: 'Your divorce could take years to come through. Why couldn't you have waited? Getting engaged while you are still married, it's not right.'

Before he could answer, Caroline said: 'She's not pregnant, is she?'

It hadn't occurred to me, but now that she said it, it seemed so startling and obvious, I was almost breathless.

Chris stared at her, injury settling on his face. 'No, Caroline, she's not.'

She put a hand to her chest, her relief instantaneous, then reached out to touch his shoulder. 'Sorry. No, really, I am sorry – that was crass. I don't know why I said it.'

'Is that really what you think? That the only possible reason Zoë and I might want to marry each other is because of an unplanned pregnancy?'

Neither of us said anything. The truth was that their relationship confounded us both. For my part, I believed he was in the throes of a midlife crisis. There was something sordid and desperate about the way he had latched on to Zoë. Caroline's thoughts, when she voiced them, tended towards conspiracy theory. She believed Zoë was using Chris as part of some game she was playing, that the girl was *getting her tentacles into every area of our lives* and that *not even our friends are safe from her.* I dismissed her theory, but I knew she hadn't let it go. The suspicion was written all over her face. If Chris saw it too, he didn't say.

'For years I've been sleepwalking through my life,' he told us. 'But with Zoë I can feel the blood rushing through my veins. The divorce might take a while. It's Ireland after all, but once it's done, Zoë has agreed to marry me.'

I couldn't listen to any more of it. Standing up, I announced I was going to find Holly. As I left the kitchen, passing through the hall towards the patio doors, I heard Caroline say in a low voice: 'You see how upset he is? You guys being here is the last thing he needs. His mother just died, for God's sake.'

I don't know how Chris responded, whether he nodded sheepishly or mumbled a reply. All I heard was

Caroline's voice, her instructional no-nonsense tone: 'As soon as the bridge reopens, both of you need to leave.'

It was mid-morning and sunlight was making progress across the back wall of the garden, throwing long shadows from the yew tree on to the terrace below. The pool was half in shade. I stood at one end where Holly's towel was neatly folded on the ground, her glasses sitting on top, and waited for her to finish her lap. She stroked evenly through the water, touching the end and squinting up at me.

'Hey there, Birthday Buddy,' I said, smiling down at her.

'Hi, Dad.'

She made no move to get out, just stayed there swishing around.

'What's it feel like to be twelve?'

'It's okay,' she said, impervious to my attempts at good humour. 'Did Mum tell you about the bridge?'

'She did.'

'It means we can't go to La Rochelle.'

'I know, sweetheart. We'll do something else instead.'

'Okay.'

Her heart had been set on a day in the city. Caroline had promised to take her shopping and we were going to have lunch, the four of us, in a swanky restaurant. In the wake of such disappointment, Holly was entitled to have a little sulk, I supposed.

'Your mum's been to the market. She's bought all manner of things. We're going to have quite the birthday feast.'

Taking her glasses from her towel, she put them on and said: 'I suppose *she*'ll be there.'

She, meaning Zoë.

'I expect she will be,' I said gently, 'and Chris.' I wanted to be sensitive to her mood but had to be firm too. It wasn't as if I was thrilled at the prospect either.

'Mum hates her,' she told me.

The word struck me like a physical object. 'That's a bit strong, Holly.'

'It's true,' she said. 'I do too.'

The blankness of her voice, the way she said the words so tonelessly, with such sincerity, was chilling.

I didn't say anything, just watched as she put her palms down on the poolside terrace and pulled herself out of the water. She reached for her towel and shook it out. She was still my little girl. I opened out my arms to her. 'Birthday hug?'

'I'm all wet, Dad,' she told me, turning away so she could dry herself.

The sun was hitting the water behind her, the shimmering light blinding. Her body was silhouetted against it and I saw, with sad surprise, the buds of new breasts beneath her swimsuit that I hadn't noticed until now. This change in her, coupled with her dismissal of my embrace, tugged sharply at my emotions, and I felt the shock of imminent tears. This was my first birthday without my mother. Somehow Holly's coldness and the understanding that she was shutting down the physical affection between us – a natural side-effect of adolescence, I knew, but still – drew out my grief in a new and unexpected way. The light bouncing off the pool made my head hurt. The heaviness I had felt in the air when I first awoke no longer seemed atmospheric. Rather, it had moved inside my head – an inner pressure pushing outward against the boundary of my skull.

Holly went inside, and I stood there, feeling wobbly, an unbidden thought entering my brain: *What if Linda had told me?* A dangerous thought. It conjured up images of a different life, a different holiday, a different wife – Linda in the kitchen now chopping fruit, rather than Caroline. A blonde version of Holly going indoors to dry off, a different son lounging upstairs in bed. And Zoë – how differently might she have turned out had her natural parents stayed together? Physically the same, but might she have been less mercurial, more grounded and together? In that scenario, I had no doubt that the insides of her arms would be free of scars, and there would be no middle-aged man sharing her bed.

And what about me? How different might I have been? I shied away from the thought, uncomfortable with the gnawing doubt it brought on. I slipped back inside, past the kitchen where Caroline was rinsing a salad. Her back was to me and I noticed the tension in her shoulders, a tightness that had come on overnight. Holly and Chris had disappeared, and as I climbed the stairs, I felt the quietness of the house all around me.

The children's door was closed. I had the impression that the room was empty. Walking past Chris and Zoë's, I heard low whispering. At least, I'd thought it was whispering. But as I lingered I realized that what I was hearing was not language but the fluency of movement. A subdued grappling, the tangle of sliding limbs, a moan so hushed I hardly heard it.

Recoiling, I hurried down the corridor to my bedroom,

the heaviness bursting in my head. I closed the shutters and lay down for a long time. But even though my body was present in the room, my mind was elsewhere. It was back down the corridor, hiding in a corner, scared and watchful in the darkness as they twisted and writhed together.

# 21. Caroline

Because of the fire we couldn't leave. Even though we couldn't see leaping flames or billowing plumes of smoke, the air above us became infused with the smell of it, as the day progressed and news reports told of a growing inferno. As our planned day-trip to La Rochelle was cancelled, I suggested we take the bikes and cycle along the paths that crisscrossed the salt flats leading to Saint-Martin-de-Ré. There were plenty of shops, though mainly of the tourist variety, but still, I was hopeful of finding something to please Holly. It bothered me when the others pounced on my suggestion, Chris and Zoë making a quick run to the marketplace to rent bikes. But it was part of the weirdness of the day, brought on by the haze of smoke, the heavy heat pressing down on us, so it didn't matter. Torpor suppressed my fear, making me disinterested. It was just one day, I told myself. We could get through it.

We were sitting around on the sun-loungers, waiting for David to come downstairs so we could leave, when Chris said: 'So, July, the eighth. What does that make you, Holly – Cancer or Leo?'

'Cancer,' she answered quietly.

The sun was rising high in the sky and I wanted David to hurry, the boundless heat making me restless.

'What about you, Robbie?' Chris asked, striving against the collective silence.

Robbie didn't answer. He didn't have it in him to be conversational that day. He was sitting halfway along the diving board, his feet dangling into the water. Since the lovers' arrival the night before, he had grown sullen, hardly speaking apart from the odd grudging reply when a question was put to him. If either Zoë or Chris was aware of his unhappiness, they hid it well, the two of them perched on the sun-lounger opposite me, Chris's hand resting on her thigh.

'Robbie's a Leo,' I answered in his stead.

'Like myself,' Chris said. 'Not that I believe in any of that astrology stuff.'

'I don't know,' I said. 'There are personality traits common to David and Holly.'

'That's because they're father and daughter, not because they have the same star-sign.'

'What about you, Zoë?'

'I'm Pisces.'

'What're they like?' I asked, keeping up the veneer of civility. I already knew what she was like.

'Spiritual, intuitive. The chameleons of the Zodiac.'

'Chameleons?'

'Yes, we're very adaptable. And our inner lives are important to us. Our secrets and dreams.'

Her expression was masked by large sunglasses; she might have been staring at me mockingly or with an empty gaze.

'In other words,' said Chris, winking at me, 'they have a hard time distinguishing fact from fiction.'

'We're watery types too,' she continued, ignoring the jibe. 'Just like Cancerians. Which makes us excellent swimmers.'

Robbie shot her a sidelong glance. 'You can't be a good

swimmer just because of your birthday.' His expression, though guarded, seemed quietly furious.

'Our sign is symbolized by fish,' she answered coolly.

'So what? You're a better swimmer than me just because you're a Pisces?'

Unfazed, she smiled sweetly: 'One way to find out.'

Instantly rising to the challenge, Robbie got to his feet.

'No, Robbie,' I said. 'We need to go.'

He ignored me, pulling the T-shirt over his head as he padded back along the board to the pool's edge. Zoë looked on with amusement although there was something mean about her smile, the corners of her mouth turning up in hard edges.

'Well?' he demanded of her. Then, without waiting, he marched to the far end of the pool.

She rose slowly from the sun-lounger, removing her sunglasses with a deliberate air and placing them carefully on the table. In a single movement, she reached down for the hem of her dress and pulled it up over her head, revealing a small mint-green bikini with orange laces tied at the back of her neck and below each hip.

Chris grinned. 'Here she goes!' he said, watching as she stepped to the water's edge. It was not pride or amusement I heard in his voice, but nerves.

I took in the curve of her hip, the crevice running the length of her spine. Shoulder-blades pronounced like wings, she was so thin. Her breasts were small but shapely, neatly cupped by the bikini. Narrow thighs, rounded calves tapering to narrow ankles. Her skin was smooth and lightly tanned, unblemished apart from a large mole the size of a one-euro coin just above her knee.

I was transfixed by her body and held by Robbie's expression as she took her place beside him. Bare-chested, his shoulders wide and square, his waist and legs skinny, there was something fierce about him, as if the challenge thrown down was far more than just a race. They stood at the lip of the pool, the sparkling water a backdrop to their lithe youthful bodies, and I felt a tug of sadness I couldn't explain or understand.

Robbie was first to break the water. Harnessing the power in those newly widened shoulders, he charged ahead, Zoë's strokes even and patient as she glided in the wake of all that froth and foam. They reached the end, tipped the side and turned back. The heat had sucked the life from my own limbs and I could see that once the first burst of his energy had been used up, Robbie was flagging, his strokes becoming more erratic, while Zoë continued calmly. When he reached the end first, he drew himself up, ready to express his triumph, but instead, as she caught up, she simply tipped the lip of the pool, then swerved in the water, kicking off for another lap. The race was not done yet.

He shouted: 'Hey!' then plunged after her, messy strokes, like an excited puppy, but she had found her groove, strong and steady. She swam with confidence, never looking back to check his progress, her face turning in the water, her mouth an O taking in air, clearly in control as she tipped the end and turned back for the final lap.

Reaching the finish, she didn't pause to raise her arms in triumph, or look back at her opponent. Instead, she pulled herself out of the pool, wringing out her hair, her face expressionless.

'Not fair!' Robbie shouted, when he reached the end. Standing in the water, he thrashed the surface with his hands in frustration. 'You never said two laps! I won that!'

She paused, and I saw the way she turned back to the edge of the pool, gazing down at him, towering and imperious. I watched my son looking up at her, the wet bikini gripping her breasts, the outline of two sharp nipples, water dripping from the ends of her hair and between her legs. There was another challenge in the way she stood looking down at him, this one different from the last. Her face was lost from view, but I saw his – the expression changing from outrage to something softer, more secret. He kept looking up at her. I watched as his hand emerged from the water and realized he was reaching out to clasp her ankle.

I don't know what he had in mind, but something within me reared up against it, seized by a cold revulsion. Don't touch her, I thought. Please don't.

She took a step backwards and his hand fell down into the water. Turning from us, she stalked towards the house. Robbie launched himself back into the water, swimming away from us and from his own humiliation. David emerged on to the terrace.

'Everyone ready?' he asked.

Chris ran a hand through his hair, momentarily undecided, before he followed Zoë back into the house.

'What?' David asked me, but I didn't answer.

I was thinking about the fire burning at the other side of the island, making prisoners of us. On the limestone terrace Zoë's dark wet footprints were fading beneath the sun.

*

We cycled in a row along the narrow white path, through the dead heat. We crossed swamps and marshes, the water glittering through the reeds and grasses. The wetlands, usually straining with life, were unusually quiet that day, no swish of tails in the water, no sudden flap of wings. As we neared Saint-Martin, the smell of smoke changed, became textured with the tang of burning rubber.

We stopped for lunch at the oyster bar and sat with glasses sweating in the heat. It was after midday but the heat was still rising. We ate in silence, the food tasting different now, flavoured with smoke. Looking out at the haze of blue sea and sky, the horizon appeared shimmery and indistinct. The wine had a soporific effect on the men, and they began to voice reluctance to travel any further, content to sit in their own uneasy silence gazing at the ocean. Robbie was locked within the grim confines of his defeat, and so it was that our group split along the gender divide as Holly, Zoë and I mounted our bikes after lunch and continued on to Saint-Martin.

We pedalled the short distance to the town, locked our bikes at the marina and set out through the narrow cobbled streets, Holly going ahead, now and then turning back to check we were still behind her. The air felt dry, the alleyways quiet, and there was a sleepy feeling in the town, as if everyone else was having a siesta while we trudged through shop after shop.

'Look,' Zoë said, holding up a black T-shirt she had found, white lettering emblazoned on one side: *Sweetness, I was only joking.* 'I'm going to get it,' she declared, clearly delighted. 'I'll wear it any time Chris and I have an argument. It will be my way of apologizing.'

I couldn't picture them fighting. The way he fawned over her, Zoë's sulkiness – it seemed an uneven match.

Holly, having picked out a few items of clothing, disappeared into the changing rooms while I went outside to wait. Zoë emerged with her purchase in an orange plastic bag and, for a few moments, we stood alongside one another on the cobbled street in the shade thrown by the awning overhead.

After all that had happened between us, small-talk seemed impossible. She had a way of standing still, her face impassive, as though she were waiting for me to say something, do something, an expectancy that I found troubling. I noticed she was twisting the ring on her finger and I glanced down at it – a trio of diamonds clustered on a white-gold band. It was an old ring, purchased in the Clignancourt markets outside Paris, they had told us, and both the size and the setting of the stones bore the veneer of age. It was not a very delicate ring – the diamonds looked heavy on her slender finger – more suited to a woman in her thirties or forties.

It was the first time we had been alone together since the announcement of their engagement. I suppose, with the incident at the pool that morning still troubling me, on top of what I already understood of her fickle nature, I couldn't help but wonder whether she was serious about it or whether her acceptance of the marriage proposal was just another strand to her elaborate game.

'Have you told your adoptive parents about your engagement yet?' I asked, thinking about Celine Harte, imagining her hooded eyes growing fractionally heavier at the weight of this news.

'No,' she admitted, letting go of her ring and looking around distractedly. 'They'll go nuts when they find out.'

'Oh?'

'When they hear I'm marrying a divorced man they'll hit the roof. Not that I care what they think.'

She leaned back against the window, her arms crossed, the plastic bag hanging from her wrist. I had the impression she was affecting nonchalance. Beneath the bravado there was uncertainty.

'What about your friends?' I asked. 'Have you told any of them?'

'Yeah, a few people. Mostly they didn't believe it.'

'I don't suppose there are many married students in your class,' I remarked.

'Nope, apart from the mature students.'

'It'll be something of a talking point, I imagine. Your engagement.'

She shrugged. 'For a little while, I guess. Until something else comes along.'

'How do you think you'll manage it?'

'What do you mean?'

'What about parties, nights out with your friends? Won't it be strange for you, having a husband or a fiancé you must return home to instead of staying for all of that? Won't you find it limiting?'

She looked at her ring, twisted it on her finger. 'Not really. Chris is cool – he doesn't believe that marriage needs to tie us to each other.'

'Did he say that?'

'Sure.'

I thought of how closely he shadowed her, the way his

gaze followed her around the room, and scepticism inflated within me.

'After all he's been through with Susannah,' she went on, 'he wants things with me to be different – more free and relaxed. She was such a head-fuck, constantly making demands on him. I'm like the exact opposite.'

'That's a little unfair on Susannah.'

'I know she's your friend. But she really did give him a hard time.'

'I'm not saying Susannah is a saint, but I wouldn't say that of Chris either. Marriage is complicated. Things go wrong – unexpected things. We all start off full of hopes and ideals, armed with the notion that our relationship, our marriage, is going to be a success, but no one can see into the future. Things come along to test us. Are you ready for that?'

She pushed her hair over her shoulder. 'Is that how it was for you?' she asked then.

'Yes,' I admitted carefully. 'When David and I got married, I believed we had faced our big trial. I was young and naïve. We both were.'

'And now?'

She had put on her sunglasses so that I could no longer see her eyes. I remembered her in my kitchen with my phone in her hand, having read Aidan's text message. I remembered Holly at the quarry's edge, the hand reaching out to push her. I remembered all those lies Zoë had told about me, the damage she had inflicted on her own face and then blamed on me, the corrosive way she had come between me and David, and with these memories came caution. I already knew she was dangerous to me.

'Now things are good,' I said.

A thin smile appeared on her face. Perhaps I imagined it, but it seemed to contain a grain of pity, which confused and angered me. Behind her through the window, I could see Holly returning the clothes she had tried on to their racks.

'One thing, Zoë, before Holly comes out. And please don't take offence.'

'What?' she asked.

'I hope you're being careful. That you're taking precautions.'

She laughed and shook her head, making a deliberate show of her mortification.

It had been on my mind since my conversation with Chris that morning. 'Seriously, though. Getting engaged is one thing. Having a baby is quite another.'

She ran her finger over her lower lip, the smile still there.

'You don't want to get caught out –'

'Like you, you mean?'

The venom in her voice was unmistakable. It came at me so suddenly it took me a moment to absorb it fully. Before I could answer, she spoke again, her voice rising with a little tremor in it. 'Or were you referring to my mother?'

The coolness of her sudden anger pooled in the air between us.

'Why would you say such a thing?' I asked, and thought of how it always was whenever I was alone with her – her iciness announcing itself abruptly, coming down on our conversation, like a blade slicing through air.

'Any luck?' she asked brightly, as Holly joined us on the street.

'No,' she answered.

We tried other shops but the offerings were overpriced, largely just souvenirs, which was not what Holly wanted. She became more despondent as the afternoon wore on and eventually declared she'd had enough.

'We can go to La Rochelle another day,' I said. 'Once the fire has burned out and we can escape the island.'

'Let's just go home, Mum,' she said, turning for the harbour and walking back towards the bikes.

We passed through streets of tall buildings with grand apartment blocks, clipped boxwood and lollipop bay trees standing sentry at the doors, the niggle of Zoë's words worming its way inside me.

*Like you, you mean?*

But how did she know? Had David told her? We had never discussed it with the children – or with anybody. That he might have shared something so intimate with her – a secret so deeply private to me – felt like the worst kind of betrayal. And if she knew, had she shared her information with Chris? Or with Robbie? The worry brought a new bloom of anger. When was she going to leave us? This was our holiday and the days were petering out – how much longer would we have to tolerate her company?

We were nearing the harbour, the air drenched with the smell of salt, smoke and petrol, when my eye was drawn to the draped folds of silk on a mannequin in a window and I stopped outside a bridal shop. An idea took hold. 'What do you think?' I asked Zoë. 'Shall we go in?'

I'm not sure what drove me to do it – anger pushing me towards meanness? Her reluctance served only to spur me on.

'Come on,' I said. 'It'll be fun.'

After the glare of sunlight on the street outside, we had to wait while our eyes became accustomed to the low-key lighting and plush interiors. The shop assistant, a woman I guessed to be my own age in a smart linen suit, pearls at her throat, came forward all smiles and greetings, switching from French to English once she realized we were not natives.

'Ah, but you are so young!' she remarked gaily, when we told her that Zoë was the bride.

She drew us further into the shop where velvet armchairs clustered in the centre of the room, a chandelier twinkling overhead.

'Have you anything particular in mind, *chérie*?' she asked.

Zoë chewed her lip, looking at the rails of dresses, each one encased in a zipped clear bag. 'Not really.'

The first dress she tried on was a lace gown with a slim silhouette and scalloped neckline, the skirts pooling around her bare feet on to the plush grey carpet. It dragged her down, her figure appearing curveless within the crusts of lace that clung to it.

'I have something better,' Madame suggested.

'I'm not sure about this,' Zoë said quietly, but I would not listen to her reluctance.

'Oh, come on!'

The hard kernel of anger was pushing me. *Let's play my game now*, I thought.

I made her try on five dresses in all, and with each one, she became increasingly withdrawn.

The last was a delicate thing made of white tulle, cinched at the waist with a band of nude pink satin. Beneath the whispery outer layer there was a glimpse of the same pink in silk beneath. Dainty lace appliqués adorned the bodice, which closed like a corset low on the back. Behind her a tiny train spread across the floor of the changing room.

'*Parfait!*' Madame declared. 'Look at yourself!' she demanded, turning Zoë towards the mirror. 'You are beautiful!'

'You really are,' Holly agreed, her voice coming out hushed with awe. Or maybe it was envy.

Zoë stood perfectly still, looking down at the reflection of her feet in the mirror, refusing to take in the full length of her body. 'I want to take it off,' she said quietly.

'One final touch,' Madame insisted, going to the glass cabinet and removing from it a small tiara twinkling with Swarovski crystals. 'Just to complete the picture, yes?'

She fixed the crown carefully into Zoë's hair, which fell around her shoulders in a deluge of curls.

'Such hair!' Madame remarked, oblivious to the brittleness of Zoë's mood, the shadowy look that was crossing her face. 'There!' She stood back to admire her handiwork. 'What a proud man your husband will be!'

I could see that Zoë was close to tears. Her cheerfulness over lunch, the sunshine of the day, her delight at her purchase, all of it had vanished. The weight of each dress had soaked through her, crushing any happiness inside her. On the floor, tossed to one side by the mirror, lay the orange plastic bag containing her T-shirt, its youthful sensibility forgotten amid these sombre dresses and the onerous responsibilities they symbolized. Beautiful as she was, there remained something ridiculous about her, in the same way that her ring was ridiculous – a little girl dressing up in her mother's clothes. She had no intention of going through with the marriage – she never had. I knew it and now I had exacted my proof.

'Get it off me,' she said, distressed now, reaching behind her to claw at the clasps holding the bodice together.

'Careful with that,' Madame said, coming alive to Zoë's fragile state, and going forward to assist. I just sat there, held back by the coldness of all she had done, her meddling, her manipulation, the memories making me cruel.

The clasps undone, Zoë wrenched herself free of the corset, her breasts, small and wide apart, visible for just an instant. The rings of the curtain sang out as she drew them swiftly across the cubicle rail.

Outside, the heat hung above the streets, the houses, down to the white shore, the boats clinking under the sparkling sun. Nearby on the bridge a fire raged. But in that changing room there was only cold.

Madame bent down and picked up the corset, fingering it delicately, the look she gave it bordering on distaste as if it had been sullied by the grubbiness of this exchange. There was no sound apart from that of weeping in the cubicle, and the clink of the glass cabinet as the tiara was returned.

The rest of the dresses were gathered up with a new alacrity, Madame saying, 'I will put these back if you are finished,' anxious now to be rid of us.

*

Sometimes, even now it is all over, I think I can hear her crying like she did that day in the dress shop. Her weeping echoes up from the corridors of the past, making me stop whatever I am doing, momentarily thrown by what has happened. And I think of the straightness of her back as she cycled ahead of me, back along the track, past the oyster bar, empty now as the sun dipped towards the horizon. I see her in my mind's eye cycling away from me, moving towards the evening and all that was to come.

# 22. David

The evening began with a change of plan. Caroline, agitated from the moment she returned, complained that it was too hot to cook.

'Let's go out to eat instead,' I suggested.

I was lying in the semi-darkness of our bedroom, waiting for the two Solpadeine I had taken to kick in. Caroline was hastily changing out of the clothes made grimy by the bicycle ride in the heat. 'I can't face going back to Saint-Martin,' she said.

'Did something happen?' I asked, made curious by her agitation. Something was clearly bothering her.

'Nothing happened. I'm just hot,' she muttered. 'That bloody fire. God knows what kind of toxins we're inhaling.'

I got up slowly, heaviness sucking at the inside of my head like a wet cloth. 'Have you got anything else I can take for a headache?'

She rummaged in her bag before handing me a sachet of white tablets. Normally I scoffed at her homeopathic remedies, but the headache had been building all day, blurring my thoughts and making me feel clammy. It had eased after the lunchtime wine, but now that it was wearing off, the pain had roared back to life.

'I'll ring the bistro in the village. I'm sure they'll have

a table free,' I told her, slipping two pills under my tongue, then went downstairs to make the call.

The house was quiet, but for the sounds of shuffling preparation coming from behind closed doors, the others having retreated to their rooms to dress for dinner. Passing Zoë and Chris's room, I heard him say: 'What about the little black number?'

Zoë's reply sounded unhappy: 'No. I don't think so.'

I didn't linger, still haunted by what I had overheard of their lovemaking earlier that day. In the kitchen, Caroline's half-hearted start at dinner sat forlorn and abandoned on the table. I took my phone and went into the quiet of Alan's study, rang the bistro and booked a table – indoors, because of the smoke still hanging in the air – then lay on the couch and closed my eyes.

Caroline's remedy was stronger than I'd thought it might be, pulling me under into a troubled sleep. I was caught in the tangle of a strange dream when I heard someone say, 'Dad? *Dad!*' in an urgent tone, and felt a pulling at my sleeve. Opening my eyes I saw Holly, gazing anxiously at me from behind her glasses. In her hand was a piece of paper.

'What is it?' I asked, pulling myself into a sitting position, a groggy feeling in my head, like I was under water.

'I found this.' She held up the piece of paper, still watching me with those big worried eyes.

I saw the blue and white insignia of the letterhead, and recognized it immediately. Panic crawled into my throat. 'Hang on, Holly. I can explain.'

'It says, "Test results are inconclusive."' She pronounced the words carefully, stressing each vowel, making it sound like a verdict of guilt or a fatal diagnosis of some sort.

My thoughts teemed with confusion. Where had she found it? I was sure I had left the letter, along with the other information on DNA testing, in my desk at the university.

'Robbie and I were playing Scrabble. We needed a page to keep score. Mum said there was paper here on the desk.'

She pointed to the old mahogany bureau, a sheaf of my documents in a blue folder alongside some journals and books. The letter from the clinic must have been slipped in among them. Holly was rattled and upset. I knew I had to act quickly, and carefully. 'Listen, sweetheart, it's not what you think.'

'It says she's not our sister.'

'No, that's not what it says.'

'It is.'

'No.' Her panic was winding me up when I needed to stay calm. 'All it says is that the samples they were given proved insufficient to make a match.'

'But she might not be our sister,' Holly said, stubbornly holding her position.

'Look, love, Zoë is your sister. I know that for sure.'

'How?'

'I just do,' I said, my voice rising a little, tetchiness creeping into it. I was in no fit state for this conversation and wished I'd destroyed the damn letter instead of keeping it. 'To be honest,' I told her, 'I don't know why I even did the test. It was foolish of me.'

'You mustn't have believed her,' Holly stated shrewdly.

'It was a shock, when I found out. But once the shock wore off, I saw plainly that she was telling the truth.'

'Does Mum know about this?' she asked. She was still holding on to the letter. I wanted to take it back from her but the way she was clutching it told me she wouldn't relinquish it easily.

'She knows about the test,' I said.

'She does? That it was inconclusive?' Holly sounded disbelieving, and rightly so. She knew her mother well.

'I know it looks strange, sweetheart,' I said, deflecting her question. 'I know it's a fright to come across a document like this, but what you've got to understand is that it is only one result.'

'But it's inconclusive, Dad. That means she could be anyone.'

'It's very common for these tests to come back inconclusive.'

'She doesn't feel like my sister,' she told me. 'She feels like a stranger. Like she doesn't belong.'

Upstairs, I heard a door opening, a voice on the landing.

'Listen, Holly, you have to promise me you won't tell anyone else.'

'Why not? Not telling anyone else makes it sound like a secret.'

'You don't have the full facts, Holly. If you'd let me explain –'

'But why does it have to be a secret? That doesn't seem right.'

'Please stop calling it a secret,' I said, as calmly as I could. She sounded a little frantic and my own mind was racing. 'It's not a secret. It's just that I don't want everybody to know about this piece of paper because it's meaningless in the great scheme of things.'

As if to prove my point, I took the document from her hands and scrunched it into a ball, tossing it into the grate. She followed it with her eyes, her brow creasing with thought.

'Now listen, Holly. It's really important that we don't upset everyone else by bringing it up,' I said, taking her shoulders and brushing the hair from her eyes. As reassuringly as I could, I said: 'It's not the time or place, okay, sweetheart?'

She didn't say anything, but continued to gaze at the ball of paper in the grate.

'You and I can sit down later and have a proper chat about it, I promise.' Outside, I could hear Caroline calling to the others.

'It's our birthday, remember?' I said, smiling, trying to chivvy her out of her mood.

'Fine,' she said, turning towards the door, but I felt her stubbornness nonetheless and knew she hadn't given in. My heart was hammering from the encounter.

'We're all set,' Caroline said, startling me. I was so lost in my own catapulting thoughts, I hadn't noticed her head poking around the door. 'Are you ready?'

'Sure,' I said, flustered but trying to mask it with busyness as I located my wallet and phone, and put them into my pockets. It was not until we were outside and halfway down the street that I remembered the letter pressed into a ball and left lying in the grate.

*

On the stroll down to the village square, our group separated, Holly and Caroline hanging back while the rest of us went on ahead. Zoë, wearing a blue dress and make-up, linked my arm as we walked. We talked about the day, the fire and the smoke, but my mind was elsewhere. I kept thinking about Holly, trailing behind with Caroline – of the new knowledge she possessed. Once or twice I glanced back at them, but the narrow streets were darker than usual, the shadow of smoke making the air gloomy. I couldn't tell if they were talking, let alone make out their expressions.

At the bistro, the tables outside were empty. For once, all the diners were indoors, cocooned against whatever poisons infused the air. Our table was at the back, and we made our way through the crowded room. The noise level was high beneath the stringed bulbs that swung across the ceiling, the smell of smoke already fading in memory, replaced by the scent of garlic sautéed in butter. At the next table, a group of young men – all ripped jeans and messy hairstyles – were enjoying a raucous meal. They glanced up at us as we took our seats, Zoë and I sitting alongside each other, our backs to the wall, Robbie and Chris opposite.

Things began to go awry when the others arrived. Holly was staring at Zoë. 'You can't sit there,' she said.

Zoë laughed, confused.

'We sit together,' Holly went on, 'me and Dad, on our birthday.' Her voice was cold.

'Oh.' Zoë began to get up.

I put a hand to her arm to stop her. 'Stay where you are, Zoë. Hols, why don't you sit here?' I indicated the seat next to me at the top of the table. 'That way you'll still be next to me.'

A frown came over Holly's face.

'It's not the same,' she said quietly.

'Sorry, Zoë,' Caroline intervened firmly. 'A family tradition, you understand.'

'Of course,' she said, getting to her feet, a little flustered.

'Here, come and sit by me,' Chris offered, patting the seat at the bottom of the table but Caroline had already put her scarf on the back of it.

'Caroline's sitting there,' Zoë said in a flat voice, and took the seat at the top of the table.

One of the guys beside us glanced over.

Holly sat in against me. Despite her small triumph, she did not look pleased.

'How about some champagne?' Chris suggested, seeking to lift the mood that had settled over the table. He ordered a bottle of Veuve Clicquot and I wondered, briefly, whether he was planning to pay for it. Diamond rings, a foreign holiday, eating out – did Susannah know about this, I wondered? And would she ultimately be footing the bill for Chris's generosity? The champagne, however, was a welcome distraction, all that faffing with corks and glasses, drawing attention away from Holly's brittle mood, Zoë's obvious hurt.

'Can I have some?' Robbie asked me.

'Go on then. Just this once.'

We raised our glasses to the birthdays, and turned our attention to the menu. There was some commotion as we gave our orders and baskets of bread arrived, a collective hunger voicing itself in the clatter of cutlery. I wish I could say that I became relaxed, that my fear over Holly's new knowledge subsided, that the evening passed off peacefully, but that was not the case. The first signal that Holly wouldn't let the matter go came when Zoë presented her half-sister with a birthday gift.

'I hope you like it,' she said, handing her a small grey box wrapped in a pink diaphanous ribbon, a sprig of dried flowers caught in the bow.

'Oh, thanks,' Holly said stiffly.

Inside the box was a bracelet – little shards of coloured glass strung together, a delicate thing in shades of lilac and purple.

'I found it in a little shop near the harbour in Saint-Martin, when you weren't looking. Aren't you going to try it on?'

'Maybe later.'

An uncomfortable silence stretched across the table. I felt annoyed at Holly's rudeness, even though I knew where it stemmed from.

'Say thank you,' I told her, in a forceful whisper.

Defiance in her eyes. For the briefest of moments, I wasn't sure what she would say. 'Thank you, Zoë,' she said, glancing across at her. 'You really shouldn't have gone to the trouble.'

'No trouble.' Zoë's voice had become small. After a moment, she drained her glass and sat back, casting her gaze around the restaurant. One of the guys at the next table – the same guy as before – looked over. The incident with the bracelet had disappointed her, I could see. The little box sat forlornly on its side, forgotten beneath the bread basket.

Our food arrived, and we began to eat, our conversation naturally turning to the events of the day Holly was born, reliving the details – reinforcing family mythology, I suppose. Chris, unaware of his fiancée's growing sullenness, her attention drifting to the next table, was an eager listener.

'So tell me, Caroline,' he said, 'this time twelve years ago, were you screaming your head off in the delivery ward?'

'Not a bit,' she answered, shooting Holly a smile. 'Easiest birth ever.'

'Bollox.'

'I'm telling you, it's true. Robbie, on the other hand, was a complete nightmare.'

I kicked him playfully under the table. 'Difficult from the start, weren't you, son?'

'Ha-ha,' he replied. Perhaps it was the champagne, but he seemed to have perked up a little, leaning into the table to be part of the conversation.

'Holly came so quickly,' Caroline went on, 'I barely made it up on to the bed. I just breathed her out.'

Holly stirred with pleasure – she loved this story.

'Tell them about the caul,' I said.

'Holly was born with the caul unbroken.'

'What's that?' Chris asked.

'It's a membrane that covers the baby's face and head in the womb. It tears during childbirth, except in rare instances, and in Holly's case it was unbroken.'

'They say it brings luck to the child,' I said, putting my arm around Holly's shoulders. 'Isn't that right, sweetheart? Or in some countries they believe the child has second sight.'

'Do you, Holly?' Chris screwed up his eyes and peered closely at her.

She blushed beneath his scrutiny, and shook her head.

'One of the midwives told us that sailors often use a caul as a talisman against drowning,' Caroline continued. 'She asked us if we wanted to keep it or even sell it.'

'Gross!' Robbie cried.

'It was David's birthday and I'd left his present at home, so I turned to him and said, "There you go, love. That's your present." '

'Please, Mum. TMI,' Robbie said.

'My mother kept my umbilical cord,' Chris volunteered, sending Robbie into fresh groans of revulsion. 'I found it after she died, this dry, shrivelled thing in a box. It looked a bit like tripe.'

I placed my knife and fork on the empty plate and laughed. 'Now that is gross,' I said. My headache had lifted – the champagne, the wine that had followed, the food, they had all gone some way to relieving the pressure.

'We kept the hospital bracelets the children wore, didn't we, Caroline?' I said. 'Tiny little things – they barely fit around my finger. To think that they were once around your wrist, Robbie, and your ankle, Hols.'

Zoë, who had been silent throughout this exchange, brought her empty glass down on to the table with a hard clink. 'Well, no one kept any mementos of my birth.' She wore a brittle smile but her voice was barely controlled. 'And whether Linda had a rough time at the birth or if she just *breathed me out*, I'll never know.'

'Zoë,' I began, 'we didn't mean to . . .'

She pushed her chair back: 'I'm going outside for a smoke.'

Chris followed her with his eyes, until Caroline asked him to pour the wine. I couldn't shake the feeling that something else was bothering Zoë.

'Is she all right?' I asked Chris.

'She's fine,' he said, sounding unsure.

Caroline sipped from her glass. Robbie and Holly were silent.

From where I was sitting, with my back to the wall, I could see Zoë through the window outside, leaning against a tree trunk, putting a cigarette between her lips. The guy from the next table was with her – I hadn't noticed him follow her outside – leaning in with his Zippo, her hand cupping the flame as she lit up. I glanced back at Chris. He hadn't noticed.

Our conversation had moved on to our college days by the time she returned, smoothing the folds of her dress against the backs of her thighs, taking her seat.

'You okay, hon?'Chris asked.

Robbie sat between them, making it impossible for any physical display of affection.

'Fine,' she replied, her eyes on the guy returning to his friends, tossing his Zippo on to the table and glancing at her. Chris followed her gaze. His expression darkened.

Caroline had brought with her to the restaurant the birthday cake she had purchased at the market that morning, and once our dinner plates had been cleared away, the waitress carried it out – a delicate cream-filled mille-feuille topped with candles, the lick and sway of tiny flames. We were temporarily the focus of attention in the restaurant, and to the eyes of the other diners, we might have appeared celebratory, happy even at the short burst of applause. They had no idea of the tangle of confused allegiances, the discontent crackling in the air between us.

'I sometimes think,' Caroline said, puncturing the air with her fork, 'that there should be particular-flavoured cakes for particular occasions. You know, chocolate cake for anniversaries, meringue for birthdays, something fruity for weddings.'

I decided she must be a little drunk.

'What sort of cake shall we have for our wedding?' Chris asked Zoë, smiling across Robbie at her.

Zoë put a delicate forkful of cake into her mouth but didn't answer. She had hardly touched her food all night.

'Come on,' Chris said, warming to the subject. 'What would you like?'

'I don't know,' she answered quietly.

'You must have a preference,' he persisted. 'What's your favourite?'

'I don't have a favourite.'

'Chocolate or lemon?'

Putting down her fork, she said sharply, 'I don't even like cake.'

Without any explanation as to where she was going, she got up and left the table again.

'Where's she off to now?' Chris asked, crestfallen. He turned in his seat and saw the guy at the next table calmly leaving the restaurant, Zoë turning to say something to him I couldn't hear.

'What the hell's she playing at?' he asked, almost to

himself, before he dropped his fork on to the plate with a little clatter and rose from his seat to follow them out on to the square.

'Don't get involved,' Caroline warned me, and for a few minutes we sat in an uncomfortable silence, while outside the window Chris remonstrated with Zoë, the guy smoking his cigarette, bemused. I couldn't make out what they were saying, but I could see Zoë's cross face, her body language growing hostile. As I finished my dessert, she pulled the door open and marched back inside, Chris following. He took his seat, smiling at us all, but the redness of his cheeks betrayed his real emotions. The dude at the next table also returned, remarking to his friends in French, which set off a low rumble of mocking laughter around their table. Chris pulled at his collar. I began to feel sorry for him.

'Shall we have coffee?' Caroline suggested.

'Perhaps we should just get the bill,' I said. The air at the table was spiky now with the threat of argument.

Jealousy is a terrible thing – I know what it's like. It's a grotty outcrop of insecurity and need. It eats you up inside, pushes you to do and say reckless things. Chris, I could tell, was on the brink of something drastic.

'What are you guys doing the last weekend in August?' he said, in an important way, making it sound like an announcement.

'August?' Caroline asked.

'Saturday the 29th,' he went on, leaning forward on the table knitting his fingers together. 'What about it, Zoë?'

'I don't know what you're talking about,' she said

sulkily, clasping her arms at the elbows and sitting back in her chair.

'An engagement party. Something to make it all official. We can invite all our friends.' He was smiling at her but there was hardness in his voice, a challenge in his eyes.

'Maybe now isn't the best time to decide on anything official,' I said, hoping to derail this line of conversation.

Chris ignored me. 'I thought it would be good to have a date nailed down.'

Zoë was clearly uncomfortable with the term. 'We're not nailing anything down,' she said, quietly insistent.

'Why not? Isn't that what we agreed? We'd tell Susannah, then have a party.'

'You told Susannah?'

'That's what you wanted, isn't it?'

'I thought you were going to wait until we got home. You said you wanted to tell her to her face.'

'Well, I changed my mind.'

'How did she take it?' Caroline asked.

Chris coughed. 'The main thing is she knows.'

Zoë had leaned forward, her face partially covered by her hands. Her defiance was replaced by shock, the blood draining from her face. 'Chris?' she said slowly.

'And the good news is,' he went on, ignoring the warning tone in her voice, 'she's agreed to fast-track the divorce!' He beamed at the rest of us as if expecting congratulations.

'Fast-track? There's no such thing in Ireland,' Caroline said.

Chris smiled. 'She's not going to contest it.'

The waitress arrived and left the bill in the middle of the table.

'I'm sorry,' Zoë said.

'Here.' Chris took a credit card from his wallet and tossed it on to the bill. 'This is on me.'

Caroline and I protested but he wouldn't hear of us chipping in. All the time he was punching in the numbers and smiling up at the waitress, Zoë sat there, patiently biding her time. What was coming was obvious. He was only putting off the inevitable.

'Chris,' Zoë said again, trying to hold his attention.

'Shall we go back to the house?' he asked, with forced brightness.

'I can't do this,' she told him.

'Or shall we go somewhere for a *digestif*?'

More insistent now, she said: 'I can't.'

Chris's smile faltered.

I felt Holly shift beside me. All this time, I had been waiting for her to pull the pin on her little grenade. I had not expected the detonation to come from Zoë.

At the next table, the guy stood up, this time openly gesturing to her to join him outside. Chris, seeing this, swung around in his seat and snapped: 'She's not going outside for another cigarette, so why don't you just *fuck off*?'

The dude raised his palms and told Chris to chill out in heavily accented English. Evidently, his ardour for Zoë did not extend to violence. He laughed and backed away, his friends teasing as he rejoined them, all shrugs and smirks.

'How dare you?' Zoë hissed across the table. Her eyes were lit up – I had never seen her so enraged.

'You're my fiancée,' he snapped. 'I will not be humiliated by your flirting with some tosser!'

She was on her feet, twisting the ring on her finger. As soon as he realized what she was doing, he was backing down. 'Now, come on, Zoë, just wait a minute.'

She threw the ring on to the table. It bounced off a saucer, landing on the salver that held the bill. 'You have no claim on me now,' she said. Her eyes flashed around the table at the rest of us. 'None of you do!'

She ran from the restaurant, Chris following an instant later.

'Fuck,' Robbie said, exhaling the word, as if he'd been holding his breath.

'What should we do?' Holly asked.

'Leave them to it,' Caroline advised. That feeling was back with me – the same feeling that had lingered all day, accompanying the pressure in my head: the sense of something about to happen, something bad.

I told Caroline to bring the kids, while I went after the others alone.

What to say of what happened next? When I look back on it now, in hindsight, it's from behind the shelter of raised hands, as if I can't bear to look at it directly. I hurried after them along the street, watching as he dragged her by the wrist, tugging at her fiercely whenever she fell back, their sparring voices like daubs of paint in the night. To a stranger, he might have appeared to be a father dragging his recalcitrant teenager home, not her jilted fiancé. Anger made her cruel and she lashed out verbally, calling him a washed-up, middle-aged man, a pervert, a predator.

I followed them without any fully formed notion of how to intervene or whether I even should. It was not until they reached the gate and I saw him slap her – a quick little swat at her mouth to stop the foulness pouring out of it – that I shouted: 'Hey!'

It's a strange thing, living in a world that presents you with violence every day – violence filtered through the screen of your TV or the medium of your newspaper. Film violence, video games – it's there in the cartoons we show our kids. You'd think we'd be inured to it. But when confronted with it in the flesh, as I was that night, it seemed to rise up as something not frightening but absurd – absurd in how easily it happened, that slap, the sound of it impacting on my own mouth. The simplicity of it and yet how it changed everything. Just like the blow I received a few seconds later when I pushed up against him – all the reason had gone out of him, leaving the blunt instrument of his fist. I didn't even raise a hand in self-defence. I was kind of amazed by it. I think that was the last lucid thought I had before the night unspooled around me. The thought of how easy it was to raise one's fist to a man's face and in so doing take a pop at your own pain.

I was on the ground almost instantly, brought to my knees, pain flooding in to replace thought. One thing shines clear: Chris's words spat at me in the darkness – 'Keep her then,' he said. 'The little bitch.'

What then?

Hands cupping my face. The warm run of blood from my nose. Someone saying: *Jesus Christ!* The rough edges of cloth pressing against my face and – oh, God – the pain. Pressure in my head unbearable now, ready to burst, like just before a sneeze only far, far worse. Vaguely, in the background, *He shouldn't drive. Someone should go after him*. More footsteps. I can hardly see. Asphalt under my feet, moving now, stumbling indoors where the lights are too bright and there's something very cold on my face, ice, a new and different pain. *Take it easy,* she says, and I try to focus. Concern in her eyes, the liquid softness of them. And I'm back there at the very beginning, in a place I have lost, a place I have longed for, where there's nothing, only time and love and endless possibility. And her, just as she was. *Linda*, I say and I kiss her.

# 23. Caroline

It was so dark that night. Not a star in the sky, the moon obliterated by the cloud of smoke blending into the blackness. As I stood at the side of the road, watching the red tail-lights of Chris's car in their wild dash away from me, I fancied I saw a glow coming from over the dark hump of the land – the dying embers of the fire on the bridge.

I had tried to keep him there, for his own safety, not out of any desire to see them reunite. I was glad they were done with each other – one of her tentacles severed – even if the manner of it had been ugly and hard.

'Lying, to her, comes as easy as breathing,' he had told me, bitter tears in his eyes.

He wouldn't be dissuaded and I didn't try.

'There's nowhere for you to go,' I had argued, meaning the closed bridge, the island cut-off. But his need to put distance between himself and her overrode my concerns for his safety. He listened to my pleas and warnings, my quieter regrets – 'I wish she had been gentler on you' – then muttered an apology about David and put the pedal to the floor.

I was staring after his car, exhaust fumes mingling with the night air, when I felt it. Something hard in my pocket. All the commotion in the restaurant, the lovers storming out, David hurrying after them, everyone had forgotten about the ring. I remember picking it out of the salver, slipping it into my pocket, then going out into the night with the others. Now I stood there, turning it over in my fingers like a worry bead.

The tail-lights were gone, but the hazy glow remained – a dirty orange smear on the horizon – and I imagined it to be the same colour as the pocket of hot air I felt inside myself. The sac of heat I had carried within me since the day I'd first heard her name. It wasn't anger, or jealousy, or resentment – those hard, robust emotions pushing outwards with defiance. Rather, it was something inward-looking, fragile, its membranes delicate. I had to carry it carefully inside me lest it break. It's a shy emotion, guilt. It cowers in the darkness, sits quietly for years, not bothering anyone, until something comes along – or someone – and pokes it with a stick. Then it swells, its membranes straining to hold it in, pressing up against your insides like another organ – a womb. For that was where I felt it. A pocket of hot air where a baby had once been.

*Like you, you mean?*

The venom in her words. A smirk pulling up the corners of her mouth, eyes glittering and hard. She knew. She knew what I had done. All afternoon and into the evening, I had kept it inside me – the knowledge of his betrayal. I had gone through the motions as I always do – the dutiful wife, the dutiful mother – locking away the knowledge of his betrayal so as not to ruin the evening. But it had leaked away inside me, like alkali seeping from a battery, the slow corrosion worming down through me, mingling with the pocket of hot air to produce something noxious. As I walked back towards the house, I felt the slosh of it inside me, dangerous should it get out. Lethal.

Holly was standing outside, her face caught in the light thrown by the kitchen window.

'Where are the others?' I asked, and she jumped, the sharpness of my tone giving her a fright.

'Inside.'

It was like entering a different house from the one we had left a couple of hours previously. All that busy energy, the sense of anticipation before a night out, gone now, replaced by an uneasy stillness. I found myself walking softly, as if wary of disturbing someone, but whom I could not tell.

The light was on in the kitchen, illuminating the undressed salad, the vegetables half-peeled and abandoned, spilling over the side of the chopping board on to the table. Straight away, I knew something was wrong. I knew it in the way Zoë seemed to have backed into a corner, her hands behind her on the counter, shoulders a little high and tense.

'What's going on?' I asked. Even from that distance, I could see her contracted pupils – small pinpricks in the green fabric of her eyes.

'Nothing,' she said. But I knew it wasn't nothing. I knew it from the way David was leaning against the counter, swaying slightly, as if he hadn't heard or noticed me. His nose was bloodied and while her pupils had shrunk to almost nothing, his had dilated. Two black discs fixed on her, like a drunk.

'Linda,' he said to her, and I just about caught her

reaction – that recoil of horror – before my eyes snapped in his direction.

'What did you call her?'

He slumped briefly against the counter, before pushing himself upright. He was still gazing at her in that sluggish way.

I said, louder this time: 'David, what did you say?'

My words seemed to hit the middle of his forehead, the way he winced, put his hand to his brow, briefly pinched the skin at the bridge of his nose. When he took his hand away he looked at her again. It was extraordinary the change that came over his face. Confusion cleared, replaced by an expression of naked disappointment. A hurt that went deep. He shook his head to rid himself of it and said: 'Nothing.'

He was coming back to himself, whatever delirium he had experienced trickling away, but the shock of it remained.

'You thought she was Linda.'

He looked around for something, then finding the towel, he picked ice cubes up off the counter-top and began filling it with them.

'Didn't you?' I insisted.

'I should go,' Zoë said, and started to move past me.

'No,' I told her firmly. 'You'll stay right here until someone tells me what's going on.'

Something had happened. The air moved differently between them.

'Mum?' I heard Holly say.

'Go to your room,' I told her, my tone brusque, my heart beating quickly now with the feeling that I was on the cusp of something – a hard truth.

She turned away, leaving the three of us alone. I had no idea where Robbie was – it wasn't important. Nothing was important right then except getting to the nub of the rot in our home. This weed that had taken root, growing and strangling all about her.

'What happened just now?' I said again, looking from one to the other.

'Caroline, my face is bleeding, for crying out loud.' He was recovering but he still sounded groggy.

'The way you were looking at her just now. You were thinking of Linda, weren't you?'

He took the towel from his nose, examined the blood on it.

'You told Zoë about the baby, about the termination, didn't you?' I said, changing tack.

That caught his attention. He put aside the towel, buying some time to think.

'Didn't you?' I pressed, my voice trembling with anger.

'I didn't think you'd react like this.'

'You stupid, heartless –' I stepped forward and he caught my wrists before I could reach him. I wanted to lash out, but his grip was strong and all I could do was pluck ineffectually at his shirt.

'Caroline, for God's sake.'

I was crying now, tears of rage and grief and helplessness. Tears over a decision made many years before. He held on to my wrists until the fight in me died and he let me twist from his grasp. Leaning against the table, I could feel her eyes on me, but I had no idea what she was thinking or how she might use this situation later against me. I was so tired of her, exhausted by her constant presence, trying to second-guess her motivation, bracing myself against her manipulation, feeling the waters closing over my head. One thought rose to the surface, a single piece of flotsam: *She must go.*

I told him then. Told him I'd had enough. Enough of her and the trouble she brewed up, enough of him and his wavering loyalty, his lack of trust. Enough of Linda. He blinked as I said her name, a raw nerve touched. I had read it in his inward stares, his lost thoughts – I had felt him summoning her memory, like the medium at a séance calling back the dead.

'It's her or me, David. One of us must go.'

My hands on the table, its hardness beneath my fingertips, the heavy warmth of the night air coming in through the open windows.

'You've never liked me, Caroline.' Her voice came almost as a surprise. For the last few moments, what was passing between David and me had felt so intensely personal it was as if no one else was in the room. 'I don't know why, but you've never liked me.'

Holly was at my elbow again. 'Please, love,' I told her. 'Not now.'

She was handing me something, and David said, 'No,' with an urgency that made me look.

A scrunched-up piece of paper put in my hand.

'Holly!' he said.

I opened it and read quickly, David saying, 'Look, I can explain.'

I looked at him, and it was dreadful the way he stood there in front of me, his nose bloodied but his face blank of all expression. He was simply waiting to see what I would do next. In my hands, the lie he had told. The thing he had tried to cover up.

'You told me it was positive.'

He swallowed, the noise of it audible in the silence of the room.

'How could you do that?'

'Because it doesn't matter. It doesn't prove anything.'

But it did prove something. It proved the measure of his want. I couldn't put it into words – it was more a feeling, an intuition about the need that lay within him, something untouchable and remote, a hole in his life that had to be filled. All those years I'd believed that our marriage, our children, his career were bringing him fulfilment. But it was still there inside him – that wanting, that emptiness.

'You had my DNA tested?' Zoë asked quietly.

'I'm sorry,' he told her.

'You didn't believe me,' she stated, hurt cracking the corners of her voice.

'I wanted to. But it was a shock.'

'You didn't want it to be true, did you?' she said, and the anger stirred in me, as I watched her turn it on, how easily she went to work on him.

'Zoë, please,' he said, stepping towards her, although he was standing close enough already. 'How many times do I have to say it? You're my daughter and I'm glad you are . . .'

She didn't believe it. 'Linda told me this would happen.'

I saw him slow and tense at the mention of her name. 'What?'

'Towards the end, when I told her I wanted to find you, she warned me not to.'

'She warned you?' He was hanging on her words, soaking them up, while I listened with growing scepticism.

'You asked me once why Linda never told you about me.'

'You said you didn't know.'

'Yes,' she said, but I could see something moving behind her eyes, some new deception being put into play. 'I didn't want to hurt you with the truth.'

Linda hadn't told him about the pregnancy or the birth of her baby because she'd known he wouldn't want it.

'It broke her heart, she said, but there was no point. No point in telling you. Because she knew that this had happened to you before and there was only one outcome you'd wish for.'

Half the things Zoë ever told us were lies. Even now, sifting back over these memories, I can't be sure of what was true and what was false. But if he had told Linda, then how had he told her? In what tone was his explanation couched? Heavy with regret? Or with a sigh of relief?

Or did it matter? Zoë would have twisted whatever it was. I knew that much, the way she had already drawn him in. There was something magnetic about her – you couldn't pull your eyes away from her. And I could see the way he was watching her, the way he hung on her every word, and for just a brief moment, I understood the power she had to hold you in her spell.

'No,' he said, 'it wasn't like that.'

'She thought you wouldn't want her to keep it.'

'No,' he said again. 'I would have wanted to . . . It was different, you see. I loved her.'

It was as if he had forgotten I was in the room. The hurt was instant, but not new. *The love of my life*. I had felt it before and still it had capacity to wound. She was a knot in the wood of our marriage, the grain of it forming around her. I was so busy focusing on his admission of love for that other woman that I failed to absorb the new truth – the real hurt – in what he was saying. It took a moment for my thoughts to catch up.

'You would have kept that baby?' I asked, disbelief curling up the end of my question. 'But you didn't want ours?'

I had asked the question but I didn't want the answer, I already knew it. It was there in his eyes. A sensation of deep and bitter regret rose in me. Somehow, for almost two decades, I had lived with a man who had kept one eye over his shoulder peering back at his past. And I had chosen to ignore it.

He was saying something now about timing and opportunity, but I was backing away. *Enough. No more*, I wanted to say. I needed to be alone, to be free of this house and the people in it. I caught the look on her face as I backed away – the narrowing of her eyes and the hard line of her feline grin. *There*, it seemed to say. *Now you see.* Her triumph over me was complete. There was nothing I could say, nothing I could do.

I stumbled against an ancient dresser in the hall, felt the crack of pain against the bone of my ankle but didn't stop, not until I was outside in the warm dark, the gate jangling some distance behind me, not glancing back to check if I could still see light from the house, or if any of them had tried to follow me.

It was better that I was alone. Hurrying along the little footpath, away from the lights of the village, walking quickly without purpose towards the welcoming dark of the coast, the gentle hiss of the sea greeting me. The sand running along the crescent of the beach was dark, bluish grey, no moon to cast it in a silver glow. The hulk of an abandoned boat lay rusting on one side, like a beached whale that had long given up the will to return, sinking to its inevitable ruin.

There was something inevitable, too, about the feelings stirring inside me, or so it seemed. The ring in my pocket, the hard roundness of it smooth against my palm. Feelings of an ending, I was sure of it now. Our marriage, that dry, desiccated thing, was a dead animal we had been dragging about for so long, both of us too cowardly to pronounce its demise. Or too blind. Willing ourselves to look away, to keep things going for the sake of the children. But I knew he would leave me once the kids were gone. All that love, the terrible waste of it.

I stood at the shoreline, listening to my breathing, waiting with no clue of what I should do next. Memory stirred uncomfortably. After what had just happened, I was vulnerable to it, helpless, and I remembered a narrow room with a high ceiling, a milk-white lampshade on a brass chain suspended above us, the shadow of dust gathered in its bowl. I remembered lying beneath it, the two of us, looking up at it, feeling the rise and fall of his head against my chest.

'I'm sorry,' he'd said, drawing away.

It was our first time after I'd come back. Our first time since the problem had been taken care of.

I needed his touch to make me feel healed. I needed him inside me again as absolution. But in the darkness of that room as we tried to find our way back to each other,

I had felt a third presence – a watchful eye inside me. Perhaps he felt it too. But when he rolled away from me, his hands going up to cover his face, moaning his apology, I felt ashamed. Contaminated. A failure. The ghost of what I had done watched me, like a fragment of glass mingling with the dust in the lamp above our heads.

I had not returned to that memory in years. The warm relief of our eventual reconciliation had pushed it down. Two further babies had helped to obliterate it. But now, as I stopped dead by the edge of the sea, with the blunt hardness of those old diamonds pressed between my fingers, the memory ripped through me as fresh and vital and cutting as a new blade of grass spearing the earth.

That night was a punctuation mark in my life, a pause between the love that had been before and the hard road of our parting. It marked the start of a three-year lacuna and, though I hadn't known it then, from that hole in our history came Zoë.

Out there in the darkness, something moved in the sea. A gurgle of water followed by a faint splash. I didn't move. Inside I had become very still. It was coming to me from a distance, a disembodied notion, a shimmering thought. A cancer had taken root in our family, a spreading tumour that needed to be cauterized. A reckless thought, but I didn't feel reckless. I felt very calm.

Surgical, clinical, my hand steady, my heart cold.

# 24. David

'I'm sorry,' I said again, but my apology sounded hollow even to myself.

Zoë regarded me coolly. 'Aren't you going to go after her?' she asked, picking up her cigarettes and tapping one out of the carton. As I watched her lighting up, her demeanour seem to change. She wasn't upset. Neither did she seem frosty. If anything, she appeared bored. As if the outcome of the disastrous blow-up with my wife was dull and inevitable. She remained untouched by it all. The rancour moved within me.

'There's no point,' I said quietly. What would be the use? I had said what I should not have said: about Linda, her pregnancy, my love for her. I could apologize to Caroline but those words could not be unsaid. I realized that of all the arguments we'd had over the years, all the emotional wounds inflicted, this was perhaps the worst. The one we would not recover from.

Zoë breathed smoke out of the side of her mouth, her eyes narrowing as she watched me. 'You're pretty fucked up right now, aren't you?'

'I think you've said enough,' I slurred.

On the table, the crumpled letter lay where Caroline had dropped it, ash colouring it grey at the edges. Zoë reached for it, brought the burning tip of her cigarette to one corner. The document started to smoulder.

'A DNA test,' I heard her whispering, beneath her breath, with derision. 'I can't believe you did that.'

'I had to be sure,' I explained. 'I needed to know for definite.'

She kept her gaze on the letter, a low flame steadily devouring it. As it neared her fingertips, she dropped the burning remains into the sink. She was acting like a whole new person. Confident, mature, but icy with superiority and disdain. I felt, while she held me with her hard stare, that she resented me. More: she disliked me.

'So what now?' she asked. 'Shall we do another one?'

At first, I didn't know what she meant, but then I saw where the DNA test results had turned to ash in the sink, and my confusion cleared. 'No, that won't be necessary.'

'But how else are you going to be sure?'

I couldn't tell if she was being serious or if it was more of her mockery. I couldn't be sure of anything about her. 'I just don't think –'

'To clear up any remaining doubts. Because you must have some little niggling doubts. Right, David?'

Her voice was high and sharp, and I could see how close she was to the brink. All that icy coolness, the bravado of burning the letter – it was a front. Underneath, she was scared.

I should have told her there were no doubts. I should have declared my firm belief that she was my daughter. But instead I wavered. Out of nowhere Gary, her stepfather, had come into my head and with it the remembered emotions of the day I had met him – the disorienting shock at the news of her adoption, the crumbling edifice of the truths she had told me, truths I had believed wholeheartedly because I had loved her mother deeply, and passionately, and it had seemed, in some fucked-up way, that with this daughter coming to me, I was somehow getting a second chance, a chance to redeem myself, a chance to make good my life.

That may have been naïve, but it had seemed like a bright and shining hope that only grew opaque and cracked with the knowledge that she had lied. Not once or twice, but continuously with an inconsistency and virtuosity that made it impossible to know what was true and what was not. I didn't know where I was with her. The truth is, I'd been lost from the very beginning.

She saw my hesitation, the doubts announcing themselves in my brief silence, and when I finally spoke up, stammering that there was no need for another DNA test, that I believed I was her father, she gave me a long, measuring look, something angry shoring up behind her eyes.

'You're right not to believe me,' she said, her voice soft and dangerous.

'Zoë, it's difficult, okay? I mean, it's not as if you make it easy. This thing you have with Caroline . . .'

She laughed, a bark of bitter amusement. 'God, you're so predictable, David.' The way she said it was loaded with scorn. 'You act all solemn and quiet and thoughtful, like you're this deep thinker – an independent mind. But scratch the surface and you're just a frightened little man who will always go running back to his wife.'

She wanted to plunge the knife in deeper; she wanted to twist it. Indignation rose within me, but at the back of it came a quieter more insistent suspicion. 'The letter from the university,' I said. 'It was you who signed for it, wasn't it?'

She was stubbing out her cigarette in the sink among the ashes. 'What are you talking about?'

She was very convincing but, then, I knew what a good actress she was. Quietly, I explained what I meant, playing along with her game of ignorance. Somehow I knew the answer to my question, regardless of what she would tell me. 'You signed for that letter, didn't you?' I said again. She was leaning back against the sink, her hands behind her, one fingernail tapping out an impatient rhythm against the cool enamel while she listened carefully. 'You signed Caroline's name and then hid the letter. Admit it.'

The beat of her fingernail against the sink. I thought of Chris and his parting words to me: *the little bitch.* She had made a fool of him, playing him before dumping him. I thought of Caroline and the wild accusations Zoë had made – the hints of the affair being revived, blaming my wife for the violence she had done to her own face. I thought of Gary and the lies she had spun about him. She had played them all. Why should I be immune? I saw my foolishness and felt my anger rise sharply, wild and erratic, like the crazy rhythm of her fingertips inside my head.

Then it stopped. She became still. In a quiet voice she said: 'Yes. All right. I did it.'

The breath went out of me. Weakness came into my legs.

'I signed for it. Then I took it upstairs to my room and burned it. Just like I burned that letter there.'

How still she seemed. Completely unmoved while I was trembling. What had happened to the teenager who had appeared nervously at my office door, picking at her cuffs, frightened half to death at the bomb she was about to drop? Somehow, she had been replaced by this cool, bloodless creature with her dead gaze, her cruel words spoken with velvet softness. And the thing that was most confusing, the thing I couldn't make out, was which one was the real Zoë, and which the fake.

'I had worked so hard.' The words coming out of me no louder than a whisper, a gasp of helplessness and disbelief.

'I don't care how hard you worked.'

I blinked, and blinked again, my vision becoming blurred. The headache that had dogged me all day was still there, made worse by the blow to my face, the mix of alcohol and pills. It made me doubt my very senses. 'But why . . . why would you want to sabotage my chances of promotion, my whole career?'

'You just don't get it, do you?' she said, with bitter amusement, her smile high and tight. 'It's what I do, David. It's what I've always done. Call it the instincts of an orphan.'

'But you're not. You never were an orphan, never have been . . .'

'Excuse me, but I'm not going to be lectured to by a second-rate tutor like you, a wannabe, a cuckold, a failure.'

I stepped towards her, and even now I'm not sure what I intended to do – put my hands to her shoulders and urge her to be calm, or hit her like Chris had done.

She stood very still, her voice coming low and deadly: 'What are you planning to do, Daddy? Kiss me again?'

I froze. The words caught me like a glancing blow and I recoiled from them, horrified by her suggestion, but a deeper horror bubbled up from within at the knowledge that I had done so already. That only a short time before I had pressed my lips against hers – confusing her for Linda – in the way of a lover.

'Perhaps that's why you got the test done,' she said, the sweetness of her tone disguising the poison beneath. She stepped past me, pausing once to glance back from the door. 'You never wanted me to be your daughter.' She said it so softly but the pain went deep. I said nothing. I couldn't. Her last words to me: 'All this time, you've been wishing I was Linda.' And just like that she walked away from me, and out of my life.

*History can bring the dead back to life.*

I have said that year after year to a lecture hall full of first-year students. Something to gain their attention from the offset. I never thought of the expression as misleading. I never thought of it as a lie. I believed it myself, right up to the moment when she left me alone, weakened, drained, all my beliefs deserting me. I had no faith to cling to, no ideals to hold me up. Inside I was collapsing, and the only belief I could find was in a bottle.

I drank steadily, dangerously, unaware of my surroundings, my mind drifting into the past, like a boat that had slipped its mooring, falling slowly into a drunken sleep: once again I was back at the cottage in Donegal, the call of a bird, the woods, and with it the image of Linda, a mug of tea cradled in her hands, standing in a shirt of mine reaching halfway down her thighs, lost in thought.

When she spoke, her voice was like a splash of colour in the room. 'Tomorrow,' I said to her concerns. 'We'll go tomorrow if you want.' I kissed her. A long, lingering kiss. Love had made me careless. Love had made me bold, and a little reckless, but not completely so: I had not told her I loved her, but I did . . .

I kissed her again, felt her hair covering my face, only it was not Linda's hair but Zoë's – the feathery lightness of her curls. I was kissing her, my own daughter, defiling her innocence, revulsion in my throat. In the dream I was trying to turn away, twisting and writhing, her mocking laughter surrounding me, filling me like an oily soup, sucking at my limbs, and breath, pulling me in, holding me fast as I tried to escape the coiled chains of DNA entwining us in a never-ending sequence. I gave a shout, 'No!' and she laughed again, a laugh that was at once close to my ear and far away. Then a scream: I opened my eyes, staggered to my feet as I might have when woken in the night by my children screaming with night-terrors. Stumbling from my bedroom, no recollection of having gone there, I fumbled through the half-light, down the staircase, through the quiet rooms. The granular light of dawn making everything seem grey and empty. Silence hung in the deserted rooms. I began to doubt myself: what had I heard? Something real, or was it something from the depths of a nightmare?

The sky beyond the window was streaked with red. My mouth was desert-dry. I needed water, but instead I went to the window, to see better the fire-brightness of the dawn. That was when the words came to me again: *History can bring the dead back to life*. Like a spell or an incantation.

Those words were in my head when my eyes settled on the pool and I saw them.

Figures in the water. One standing, the other stretched out like a doll, unmoving. Slowly, as though I were still physically locked inside the dream, I stepped out on to the terrace, felt the coolness of early-morning raising hairs on my limbs. I kept my eyes fixed on them as I drew near, unable to make sense of it, the scrambled visuals adding to my confusion. My heart understood it first, my pulse quickening. Caroline leaning over Zoë, holding the girl's face in her hands, kissing her mouth, no, not kissing, but blowing, blowing into the mouth, a dark stain moving through the water.

Then Caroline looked up, the tears streaming down her face. The water swirled about her waist, and her voice rose in a fevered, anguished pitch: 'What have you done? Jesus Christ, what have you done?'

Panic gripped me, kept me frozen, while Caroline tugged and pulled at the body, dragging it to the ledge, heaving it up on to the cold wet tiles.

Black holes in my memory, her voice reaching me from some far-off place, *What are you planning to do, Daddy? Kiss me again?*

What had I done?

The truth remained hidden from me – too much confusion, too much pain.

I walked towards her, knelt down and gazed into Zoë's face. She lay on the cold hard ground, her gaze fixed far away, into the sky, the crimson flames of the clouds, and the heavens beyond. I thought of the brief moment of joy in the bed of her conception all those years ago in the stone cottage of Donegal. I thought of Linda bearing her birth in stubborn silence. I thought of the nursery rhymes, and skipping ropes, the jigsaw puzzles and books, the parks and cinemas of her childhood, away from Linda and me, her parents. I thought about all the things that had made her who she was, the chance and circumstance of her being, and wondered, too, about all she was not or could not be. I thought of everything she might have done, her plans, the trips, the work, the friends, and the love she might have found.

And then, in my peripheral vision, I saw Robbie. *Go back to bed,* I wanted to tell him. *You should not be a witness to this.* I wanted to kiss him on the forehead, and stroke his cheek as if he were a child again. His mother went to him, saying something I couldn't hear, making some demand of him I couldn't discern. *Back to bed, son,* I wanted to say, but he just stood there, staring, already sealing himself off from us. Did I know then what he had done?

I cannot tell.

All that really comes to me, when my thoughts turn to that moment, is the outline of my daughter's face, pale against the limestone flags. How cold she looked, and how perfect, as if she were the beautiful human plaything of some minor Greek god.

I thought of all the things I did and did not know about her. It amounted in the end to nothing: it amounted to a girl whose green eyes had once flickered, but now were glassy and devoid of life.

# PART FOUR

# 25. Robbie

They come almost every day to get him to talk. Police, social services, his solicitor, counsellors from the prison service. Some of them speak to him in English, heavily accented, but he understands what they're saying. Others, whose English is not so good, bring translators, and he can see the look in the translator's eye: *Why on earth won't you talk, you idiot?* The police and social services are better at concealing their thoughts from him – they have more experience and he can't be the first kid in this place to clam up with fright. The solicitor just looks bored and a little fed-up, like he has better things to do with his time than sit in an interview room with some Irish kid who prefers to say nothing and stay in this detention centre indefinitely, rather than work on any kind of defence.

His father is the most frequent visitor. Mostly he just talks to Robbie, like he's accepted the silence now. He talks about his work, his research – he's using the time on the island to work on a book. He brings news from home. His tone is conversational, cheerful, forced. Sometimes, on days he's finding it tough – when it becomes almost unbearable for him to see his son in this place, wearing his institutional uniform – he will lean over the table and whisper urgently: *Please, son, say something.*

At least he doesn't cry, like Robbie's mother did. She would sit across from him, a balled-up tissue in her hands, her eyes and nose red raw from all the crying she had done, begging him, beseeching him just to tell her why. She loved him – she forgave him – he was her son. But, please, for the love of God, would he talk to her, just say something?

On and on it went. He watched her within the hermetic seal of his own silence. After what had happened, talking was an impossibility. It was a relief when she went away, back home to Dublin with Holly. He felt the storm in his brain quieten.

When they've all gone – his father, the police, the solicitors and social workers – when they've left him to go back to his cell, he feels a sense of relief, a levity almost. He lies on his bunk, closes his eyes. And then it's just the two of them – him and Zoë – locked together in a strange peacefulness.

She was different from how he'd thought she'd be. Different from him and from Holly. He felt it most when she spoke. Her accent, of course, the strange foreignness of the Northern vowel sounds, and the way her voice went up at the end of each sentence, like a little pencilled tick mark on a musical score. When she came for lunch on that first day, it was hard not to stare at her, his *sister*, displacing him now in the role of eldest child. He was taller than her, though – stupid to feel proud of it, but he did. Both of them were thin but she was *really* thin. She wore a big floaty sweater so you couldn't tell at first until you noticed her legs, like pipe-cleaners coming out of her boots.

He wondered if Zoë had an eating disorder, she was so

thin. A girl in the orchestra, a viola player named Claire Waters, had anorexia. Up close, you could see how papery the skin on her face was over the square bone of her jaw. Her skin was kind of hairy too, light blonde hair, like the hair on her stick-like arms. Robbie sat behind Claire with his cello, so he spent a lot of time staring at the side of her face. She'd dropped out of the orchestra before Easter and someone said she'd been hospitalized. Someone else said they'd seen her and her hair had fallen out – she was almost completely bald on one side of her head.

Zoë's hair was glorious. He'd never use that word out loud to describe it, but privately that was what he thought. Glorious, luminous. The first time he'd met her, he'd felt an urge to touch it – not that he did. Eventually, a long time after that, he got to put his hand on her hair and he can remember the prickly feeling that shivered over the back of his scalp when he felt his hand sink into those soft curls.

'What do you think?' Holly had asked him.

It was late in the evening, both of them in his room. Downstairs their mum was tidying up. Dad was dropping Zoë home.

He shrugged. 'She seemed okay.'

*'Really?'*

He flicked the page of his magazine, said nothing.

'I thought she was a bit full of herself.'

He let her talk for a while, zoning out. He was tired. It had been a weird day. The truth was, he didn't know if he liked Zoë. Her manner had seemed polite, a little shy perhaps, but at one point she had caught him looking and smiled at him – a different kind of smile from the one she'd given the others. He'd seen the spark come into her eye, something conspiratorial about it, mischievous, drawing him in, making an ally of him. But he didn't know if the sum of all these impressions amounted to liking her.

'Want to see my room?' he'd asked, the next Sunday she'd come over for lunch.

He'd never had a girl up to his room before. Several guys in his class had claimed they'd had sex with girls in their rooms. He wasn't sure he believed them, although maybe one or two. Robbie himself had kissed only three girls – sweaty encounters on the dance-floor at Wesley that had never gone any further. He'd tried to get off with a girl in the orchestra at a party once but she'd laughed with surprise, afterwards telling him he was the kind of guy girls loved to have as a friend without the complications of sex. She'd meant to be kind but he'd burned with humiliation.

'Cool!' Zoë had said, when she'd seen the poster of Thin Lizzy on his wall – Phil Lynott's giant head surrounded by a corona of psychedelic swirls. 'You're into his music?'

'Yeah! *Jailbreak* is like my favourite album ever.'

'Put it on,' she said, and he scrolled through his iPod while she sat back on his bed, making herself comfortable among his pillows.

They talked about music for a while, then films. Her taste leaned towards the indie end of the spectrum but she admitted to a weakness for rom-coms. 'You won't tell anyone, will you?' she had said, giving him that conspiratorial smile again. He noticed that her front teeth overlapped slightly.

He made some comment then about a Kate Hudson flick he'd read a review of, and she hooted with laughter. 'You're so funny, Robbie,' she'd said. 'You crack me up.'

He felt himself grinning foolishly. No one ever called him funny, especially not girls.

From then on she came up to his bedroom every Sunday once lunch had been cleared away. Flopping on to his bed with an air of exhaustion, like all the politeness downstairs had been a front but now, up in his room, she could be herself. The differences he'd been so hung up on at the start receded, replaced by the familiar. Downstairs, it was prickly with formality, none of them easy with her – particularly his mother and Holly. But up in his room, just him and Zoë, it was like they'd known each other for ever.

When all that stuff blew up in school over what he'd been doing to Miss Murphy, she was the only one who didn't give him shit. Even Holly had gone all supercilious on him, calling him a delinquent. 'You're *eleven*!' he had shouted after her, then slammed the door of his room. It made him so mad, being punished like that. Couldn't any of them understand? Intimidating that teacher, pushing her to the ground, it was an honourable thing! Even his mother, who should have been *grateful*, kept giving him the thin-lipped look of disapproval he couldn't stand, constantly watching him with anxious eyes. And as for his dad, Robbie thought, don't get him started! They were so busy with their own jobs, his dad nearly having an aneurism over the professorship and whether or not he'd get it, his mum thinking she was Sheryl Sandberg all of a sudden with her power suits and her appointment diary and her client portfolio. Didn't either of them realize they were lucky to have such a good kid? Compared to some of the morons and thugs in his year, Robbie was a god-damned saint!

'Why should your mother be grateful for what you did?' Zoë asked, in a ruminative kind of way. She was sitting on his bed, listening to a barrage of grievances that he'd stored up over the whole week of his confinement.

'What?'

He had heard what she'd said, and he knew what she meant, but he wanted to buy himself a few seconds to think. She didn't know about his mum. Could he tell her? Part of him knew that telling her would constitute a betrayal, but he was so angry with his mother right then. Fuck it, he thought.

He sat down on the bed opposite her. 'Promise you won't tell?'

Her eyes became alert. He liked the way she was watching him, concentrating while he told her about his mum's affair, how it was with the father of this other kid in his class and how the whole school knew about it. That the teacher he'd bullied was the one who'd spilled the beans.

'That's awful!' she said, when he'd finished. 'It must have been so shit for you in school.'

He had lain back and looked up at the ceiling. He wasn't thinking about the stuff the other kids had said – the taunting and the abuse. He was thinking about the moment he'd stepped towards Miss Murphy, the shot of pure adrenalin rushing through his bloodstream as he put his hands up to her chest, knowing he was going to push her. 'The other kid – Jack – he changed schools. But Mum and Dad left me where I was.'

'Why?' She shook her head, not understanding.

Robbie had never told anyone why but he believed, privately, that it was his father's way of punishing his mother. It was the way he did things, Robbie's dad, conducting long, slow, patient campaigns. His mother liked to get things out in the open, have the row, clear the air and move on. But there was a quality of patience in his dad, stubbornness. He wasn't going to let her sweep it under the carpet, what she had done. He'd make her pay for it with three more years of parent-teacher meetings, school plays, sports days, prize-giving ceremonies, end-of-year Masses. He'd make her go to them all. A three-year sentence was her punishment. Robbie knew that his dad loved him. But he also knew that his dad had blind spots and this was one of them. He couldn't see how much it hurt Robbie, using him as a pawn just to get at his mother.

He didn't say so to Zoë, though. He was beginning to regret how much he had already told her. 'They thought it would blow over,' he said instead.

Something in his voice must have sounded forlorn, even though he didn't mean it to, because she reached over and took his wrist, giving it a squeeze.

Steadily, they grew closer. In the weeks after she moved in, his life had seemed to rearrange itself around her, points in the day shifting around the axis of her presence, her company. His mother took him aside and told him that she was concerned about how much time he was spending with Zoë – she worried it was interfering with his studying. He had his Junior Certificate coming up and it was a Big Deal. How to explain to her that the exact opposite was true? His happiness made him not only diligent but benevolent too, prepared to think better of everyone. He believed then, as he does now, that those weeks were the happiest of his whole life.

He would have forgiven her anything. Even the lies she had told them about Linda. So what if she had been adopted? He couldn't see why his mum and dad got so worked up about it and after Zoë had disappeared with that dipshit, Chris, Robbie had lain awake in the dark, worrying that they had frightened Zoë away for good.

Some time after midnight, her step had come on the stairs. The softest rap on his door and he sat bolt upright. 'Come in,' he whispered.

He didn't dare turn on a light. His curtains were open anyway and light thrown by the halogen street lamp cast the room in an orange glow.

'Do you hate me?' she had asked.

He was out of bed by then, on his feet, standing within touching distance of her. Between them, a metre or so of charged air. Every cell in his body had seemed alive to her, to this, whatever *this* was.

'I don't care,' he'd told her, his voice clear, not bothering to whisper. 'I don't care about any of it.' He'd realized he was trembling.

'Really?'

'I just don't ever want you to run out on us again.'

He'd said it, and he meant it.

Quickly, she stepped towards him, her arms around his neck, his brain about to explode. Slowly, cautiously, he hardly dared to do it, he brought his hands up, put them to her back and clasped her to him. Her hair was hanging loose and his hands sank into it. He lowered his head and felt her hair brush against his nose – the ticklish softness of it. In the back of his mind, a niggling voice whispering: *What does this mean?* The same DNA ran through their bodies. These conflicting sensations – he was at once excited, and also at peace.

The atmosphere in the house grew heavy. Not everyone was as easy about Zoë's presence as he was. His mother, for one, seemed increasingly stressed, although he thought that might have something to do with work. There was tension between his parents: they were spending less and less time in each other's company. As for Holly, there was no love lost between her and Zoë. That much was obvious.

'She has it in for me,' Zoë told him, well before the incident with Holly at the quarry – his mother's hysterical overreaction.

He tried to tell her not to worry, but his mum remained cool and Zoë began to spend more and more time out with her friends, and the creep of doubt came back to him, the feeling she was pulling away. He'd wondered had she a boyfriend but any time he asked she became coy and evasive. Some nights she didn't come home and his mind went reeling in all directions. In school the following day he could hardly concentrate on anything. *She's my sister*, he repeated in his head, like a mantra.

His parents didn't seem to know anything. They were so wrapped up in their own problems. They were fighting more and more, these days – not outright fights, but sniping and sulking. He felt the thinness of his family around him, like at any moment it might snap.

Eventually he found out. And even though he had suspected there was a boyfriend, he felt a wave of revulsion and an almost overwhelming urge to grab her by the neck and shake her when he discovered it was Chris and that she was moving in with him.

When Zoë left, Robbie had stood at the door watching her go, not speaking to his mum. Afterwards, back in his room, he had felt the house around him plunge into sudden quiet, and the anger roiled inside him. It wasn't just that it was Chris – although the idea of them naked together made him want to retch – it was the deceit. That she had kept it from him all along. Fed him titbits of information without ever revealing much at all. He felt toyed with, used, as if he was something she could amuse herself with and discard when she'd grown bored. He imagined her telling Chris about him, about the things she'd told him, the two of them lolling around in bed, laughing at Robbie's innocence, his foolishness. All those weeks when he'd thought there was something between him and Zoë – a closeness – and all the time she had been making a mockery of him. He thought of this and felt the rage inside him, filling his brain, like a swell of music he couldn't contain. His cello case was lying open on the bed and he slammed it shut, then slammed it again with the flat of his hand. Over and over, he hit it, drawing his hand up over his head then bringing it down with as much force as he could muster. The pain shot up through his wrist and into his arm, yet still he kept at it, feeling past the pain, making himself numb to it.

His rage came and went over the next few weeks. Sometimes it erupted in spurts of indignation and boiling fury. At others it was like a slow, seeping pool of acid in the pit of his stomach. It was exhausting being angry all the time. It left him mentally and physically drained. He could hardly stay awake at school. His cello seemed heavier than ever and he began to dread having to lug it up the stairs and into the hall for rehearsals. At home, when he was supposed to be studying for his exams, he would instead crawl into bed and try to sleep.

Something had happened to him – he knew that. Something cataclysmic. She had come into their family as if wielding a gorilla bar, wrenching it open, changing its shape to accommodate her. But the shape that it became was skewed – sharp and angular. There were no curved surfaces. He no longer recognized it. He felt that when she had shoved the bar in, looking to gain purchase, it had anchored deep inside him, changing something within.

Chance is everything. A set of circumstances coming together, merging at a particular time. Sometimes, when he is lying awake in his cell at night, Robbie plays the What If? game in his mind. What if they had never gone to France? What if Zoë and Chris had not got engaged? He could go further back. What if he'd never known Zoë existed? But that's not interesting to him. She's so deeply embedded in him now, even though she's dead – *especially* because she's dead – that he cannot imagine his life without her in it.

Months have passed, but still he can summon an image of her that day in her bikini standing by the pool, the way the water skimmed down her body in rivulets, the outline of her nipples beneath the wet fabric, another triangular outline of hair between her legs. He believes that was the moment when it had started to build inside him. Agitation like a drone in his brain. It kept building and growing and it didn't stop, even after the debacle in the restaurant when Chris left and Zoë stayed. The thing inside him was like a stone that gave off an electronic hum, like a generator, or an electricity pylon. It just wouldn't stop. It frightened him. He didn't understand it, didn't want it, couldn't remember the last time he'd slept through the night. He slipped away from the others, back to the room he shared with Holly. Exhaustion was clawing at him and he nearly cried for want of sleep.

When he had crawled into bed that night, the whir was loud in his brain, only this time he recognized the trills and sweeps within it, the swaying movement of waves, the pitter-patter from droplets of sea-spray. How many times had he heard that music? How many hours had he spent rehearsing it? Debussy's *La Mer* – a piece of music he had loved but now he felt infected by it, the score trickling out to occupy every pocket of his brain, soaking it. And yet it was not quite right, the sound slightly skewed, as if one of the instruments was out of tune, or one of the musicians fractionally out of rhythm. There was no pleasure to the music now, only annoyance and irritation. It scratched around the rim of his thoughts, and he turned over in bed, tried to find a cool spot on the pillow, but the music clung to his brain, the strains of the cello in the third movement like bows scratching across razor-wire.

'She's not even our real sister.'

Holly's voice had skimmed above the pool of his thoughts. He turned and saw her lying on her side, her bed tucked under the window. How long had she been lying there? The jittery third movement was in his head and he tried to silence it as he pulled himself up to a sitting position. 'What?'

'I found out yesterday, before the dinner. Dad had a DNA test done.'

'Shut up.'

'It's true. I saw the letter myself. She's not our sister.'

'You're lying. He would have told us.'

'He wanted to keep it to himself.'

'Why?'

What she said next was too outrageous to believe. Disgusted, he pulled back the covers and left the room.

The house was quiet, empty, no sign of either of his parents. He felt the heat of the previous day continue to linger within the stillness of the rooms, a smell of burning in the air. The doors to the garden were open and he could see Zoë on the sun-lounger next to the pool, perched on one edge, her head balanced on one hand. Crazy, the hope that bloomed in his heart. If Holly was right about the DNA test, then that changed everything. On the other hand, could it be true what Holly had said about what she had witnessed? It was too repulsive to think about.

She turned to look as he stepped out on to the terrace. Her phone was in her hand, like she'd been texting someone.

'I couldn't sleep,' he told her.

'Me neither,' she said, and gestured for him to sit next to her. 'It's so lonely in there, in that bedroom, on my own.'

He sat close to her, as close as he dared. It was still night, although it could not be long before dawn. He could feel the heat of her thigh next to his. She was smoking and he watched her put the cigarette to her lips, heard the soft puckering sound of her lips on the filter.

'Have you heard from Chris?' He nodded at her phone, and she answered no.

'It's over,' she said, and he should have felt happy. It was what he wanted, after all. But instead he felt confused, dissatisfied, his brain still reeling from all that Holly had told him. He was so desperately tired and the music kept rising in his brain, then falling back again, little teasing eddies.

'I knew it wouldn't last,' she told him. 'Nothing ever does.'

She sounded deflated, a little forlorn, and he put his arm around her shoulders, felt her bare skin soft beneath his fingertips.

'Some things last,' he said quietly.

She turned her face to him. 'You're the only one, Robbie. The only one who understands.'

His heart was beating madly in his chest. He felt his courage rise. If it was true what Holly had said, then it would be all right, wouldn't it? Her skin was so soft beneath his touch. Slowly, he ran his fingers down her back.

'What are you doing?' she asked, nerves in her laughter but she didn't move away, didn't tell him to stop.

He wanted to tell her but didn't dare speak the words. Instead he felt the nubs of her spine beneath his fingertips, the rounded curve of her buttocks on the hard plastic of the lounger.

'Robbie . . .' she said and he heard it all in her voice, the fear at what they were about to do, the undercurrent of excitement. It was like they were embarking on the greatest adventure of their lives and no one could know about it but the two of them. Their little secret. And as he leaned in to kiss her, he imagined he heard something – the rustle of leaves, the low breathing of a third party, someone watching them.

'Don't,' he heard her say but he pressed his mouth against hers anyway, knowing she didn't mean it, recognizing it as a last defence against what they both knew was inevitable.

'Stop,' she said and he felt her hand against his chest, pushing him away.

'What are you doing?' she asked, and he saw the confusion on her brow, realized she was angry.

'I thought . . .'

'You thought what?'

'That you wanted it too.'

Her expression was horrified. It left him cold.

He opened his mouth to say something more but her phone buzzed on her lap and she glanced down at it.

'Who's it from?' he asked, unable to help himself, although part of him screamed that he should ignore it, stay in the moment, see where it might take them. Here they were, on the cusp of something amazing, the start of the first true passion in either of their lives, and he had to go and ask about some stupid text message.

'It's Philippe,' she said, getting to her feet.

'Who?'

'You know. From the restaurant?'

'What does he want?'

'There's a party,' she replied, reaching down for her bag, slotting her cigarettes back in.

'You're not going?' he asked.

She didn't answer, just stood up and smoothed down her skirt. She was still angry with him.

'Are you going to fuck him?' He surprised himself with the sharpness of his words.

She stared at him, her forehead creasing into a frown. 'I see,' she said, frost coming into her tone. 'Like that, is it?'

He shrugged, pressed a finger to the corner of his eye.

It didn't matter what she said. He knew she was going off to fuck that guy. He was sure of it, and the sureness of that knowledge made the thrum in his head louder, the creaking strains of the string section sawing through his inner ear. And he was tired, so very, very tired. If he could only sleep . . .

'What would you know of it anyway?' she went on. 'You're just a child. What experience have you got?'

'Plenty.'

She laughed. 'Please, don't bother lying. It's so obvious you're a virgin. You've probably never even been touched by a girl.'

'Bullshit. I've had plenty.'

'Liar.'

'I have.'

'Name one.'

'Claire Waters,' he said – the first name that came into his head. Poor balding, anorexic Claire, with her viola balanced on her bony little shoulder. Debussy in his head again, the relentless press of the sea.

'And what did Claire Waters do for you?' she asked, taunting him now. 'Did she hold your little pecker? Did she take you in her mouth?'

The thought of Claire's spidery fingers gripped around him made him shivery and nauseous. That and the viciousness in Zoë's voice fired up the symphony inside him, cymbals crashing in his head. He flung himself back against the headrest of the sun-lounger, forearms over his face so she couldn't see how much she'd hurt him.

'And as for that pathetic attempt just now . . .'

'Don't,' he warned her.

'Coming on to me. Your own sister.'

'You're not my sister,' he said, petulance creeping in as he tried to cover up his humiliation.

'What?'

'You're not. I know you're not.'

He couldn't make her out but he knew, somehow, that she was smiling. When she spoke again, it was in a low whisper, but he felt her voice coming close to him, knew that she was leaning in. 'You thought one little piece of paper could clear the way for you, did you?'

'Shut up.'

'All this time I thought you were being nice to me because you're my brother but, actually, you've had a crush on me – fantasized about me.' She said this in a kind of amazed voice, but there was detachment, too, as if it didn't really affect her. It was not shock she was expressing but amusement. Everything was just a joke to her – even his love, delicate and shy, was something to be kicked around with hilarity.

'That's pretty sick,' she whispered, her mouth close to

his ear. 'Sick and twisted. I think that's even worse than what your dad did to me.'

He would never forgive her for this. Never. Whatever she had meant to him before, however much he had loved her, it could never be the same between them again.

Movement behind him. This time he didn't imagine it. A third party. A witness to what he had said, to what he had attempted to do. Zoë looked up.

Suddenly he couldn't bear it. He pressed his arms hard over his face and thought of every sad, sweaty encounter on the dance-floor at Wesley, every look of amusement and apology he'd received before the girl turned away and started giggling with her friends. He thought of Melissa Lynch in the orchestra and that time he'd tried to kiss her, heard the surprise in her laughter, her voice in his head saying: 'You're the kind of guy girls want as a friend, Robbie. That's the great thing about you. Knowing we can be friends without things ever getting complicated by sex.' Even poor Claire Waters, who looked more dead than alive: Robbie knew, in his heart of hearts, that not even she would touch him. Zoë's words were in his head, the way she had looked at him. He knew that she had seen right through him, taken the measure of him, and what he felt now was a swelling of shame. He thought again of what Holly had told him, what she had said. The noise rose to a crescendo, all those screaming strings, the screech of brass, and he pushed his fingers deep into his ears. It made no difference. The music was inside his head. No matter what he did, he couldn't block it out.

*

Did he say her name? He cannot remember. All he remembers is the surprise on her face as she fell backwards. The sound her head made as it met the edge of the diving board – a sharp crack like a small pistol going off. Her mouth opening but no sound coming out, nothing but a gasp of air as she fell backwards.

Blood bloomed from the side of her head, spreading out into the waters of the pool. His mother was there, too, although he has no recollection of her arrival. She's in the pool screaming something at him, but he doesn't hear the words. Debussy is still in his head. He can hear the whines of the violins, the jagged edge of the cellos' bowing. How can he still hear them? Why haven't they been silenced?

Arms going around him, the strong clasp of hands against his back. 'It will be all right,' a voice whispers. 'Everything will be all right now.' His father leans over Zoë, for all the world like he's going to kiss her again. Debussy is in Robbie's head, playing in an eternal loop, the waves of the music like the waves of the sea, moving in tides, endlessly back and forth. His father leans over Zoë. Robbie closes his eyes.

# 26. Girl Unknown

The evening before Caroline and Holly fly back to France, Susannah calls over with a bottle of Margaux – a Christmas present, she says. They sit at the kitchen island and drink it, just the two of them, trying to summon some semblance of festive cheer. There are no decorations, not even a Christmas tree.

Susannah, the one true friend who has stuck by her, leans on the counter and imparts her news. 'He has a new girlfriend.'

Caroline absorbs the information with mild shock. She has not spoken to Chris since Zoë's death and neither has David, apart from that first terrible phone conversation when they had called to break the news. His reaction, the instant outpouring of grief, was awful. He has not spoken to them since, ignoring calls, emails, messages. Caroline reads into his silence the measure of accusation.

'Another infant,' Susannah goes on, a sneer in her voice. 'Not quite as young as Zoë but not far off.'

They had met at a concert, apparently. It seems that, for all the coolness and hostility between Chris and Susannah, there is enough contact between them to keep her up-to-date with his love life.

'I'm glad,' Caroline tells her. 'At least he's moving on.'

Susannah gives her a mild look of pity. 'No, he's not,'

she says, her voice softening. 'He's stuck in the past. This is just his way of hiding from it.'

For a while, Caroline had wondered if the shock of Zoë's death might have hurled the two of them back together. But she has learned that people deal with these things differently. Some try to carry on as normal; others cower behind a wall of silence. And some, like Chris, seek to replicate what has been lost, searching out some other young girl with blonde hair and a cool, feline gaze, a bold, meddling streak kept hidden beneath a patina of innocence.

David is waiting for them in the arrivals lounge. He sees them come towards him pulling their luggage behind them. They look tired, as if the journey has taken longer than the two hours of the flight. He goes to greet them and they embrace, all three of them together, a momentary triumvirate before they break apart. To anyone watching, their reunion must seem strange. Clearly, they are family, but despite the emotion of the reunion, there are no smiles. He reaches to take the bags; Caroline turns away and wipes at the corner of her eye; Holly stands with her hands in her pockets, looking about her.

A whole season has passed since he has seen them in the flesh. Their corporeal presence seems at once startling to him as well as comforting. Holly has grown taller. He is alive to all the changes in her – the new curves, the thinness of her face, grace in the way she carries herself. She catches him looking and he nods towards the exit. 'The car is this way,' he tells them.

*

Some time towards the end of the summer, they had made the decision to part. It was not named as a separation, more a side-effect of the need to protect Holly. Both agreed that it was in her best interests to return home and continue her education, as they had planned before all this happened. They wanted her, in as much as it was possible now, to have a normal life. One of them had to remain behind for Robbie. There was no argument, although that didn't mean there was no guilt. Weighing up the needs of one child over the other. Caroline would return to Dublin with Holly, while David stayed on.

As the car passes over the long, meandering bridge back to the island, Caroline feels the tension in her limbs returning. That sick feeling is with her again, panic in her chest. She keeps her eyes trained on the sights outside the window, her hands tightly gripped in her lap. Strange to see those same fields and roads, grey now in the dim light of a cold December day. When they had first come to Île de Ré, she had heard it described as a Mediterranean island that had somehow got lost in the Atlantic. During the summer months, with the glittering turquoise waters surrounding it, the yellow dust of the roads, the geraniums and hollyhocks pouring colour over every concrete surface, it was easy to believe that description. Now, with a chill wind whipping over the island from the ocean, trees bending to it, a spray of rain on the windscreen, Caroline feels as if she has come to a different island – hostile, unwelcoming, cold.

As he drives, David tells them about a heron he has seen on his walks near the house. It is large, he says, estimating its wingspan to be two metres, maybe more. In his conversations at the market, he has discussed the bird. Others have seen it, too, and believe it to be a great blue heron, very rare in these parts. David wonders aloud if it might have made a nest nearby. Briefly, he scans the horizon, as if looking for the bird in flight.

The villages they pass seem deserted – many of the houses look shut up for the winter, shutters bolted closed, windowboxes empty. The little car gathers pace as it bypasses Saint-Martin, heading west towards the village of Loix. Caroline doesn't ask David where the car came from – a small white Citroën, several years old by the look of it. It is just part of the changed picture. Everything feels different and strange. This car David is driving, his altered appearance – older, roughened, hardy – serve as a reminder of the life he has carved out for himself during the months he has spent on the island without her. When he drives, it's not with the interest or relaxation of a tourist. He sits hunched forward, intent on getting to his destination. His eyes are fixed on the road, barely glancing past it to the landscapes that surround him.

Caroline takes all this in wordlessly. Four months have passed, punctuated with phone calls, emails, Skype. *We are strangers to each other*, she thinks, as the little car shuttles through an intersection, on to a long, straight road over the salt flats.

'So, how is he?' Caroline asks.

They are alone in the house. Holly has gone to the village to buy bread, leaving the two of them sitting opposite each other at the kitchen table. It is too cold to sit on the terrace. Stray leaves swish and scatter over the flagstones.

'He's the same.'

'Has he said anything?'

'No.'

'Anything at all?'

'Nothing, Caroline,' he says, adding: 'I'm sorry.' As if it is his fault. In a way, it is.

He watches her taking that in, her lips pursed, sees her bite down on her inner cheek, then look away. There is something controlled about her now, not like when it first happened and she was overcome with emotion. Fear, anger, bewilderment – he had sat at this very table and watched her sobbing uncontrollably, heard the scraping sound of air wrenched into her lungs, her face ruddy with tears. But that was then. Now she is composed, which makes her seem even more distant from him – the sternness of her control over feelings that had once ravaged her. He thinks about reaching across the table for her hand, decides not to.

They sit in silence for a moment, and he thinks of the bedrooms upstairs, his lonely occupancy of the house all these months. It is a relief when the iron gate clangs and they hear Holly stepping into the hall.

Over a lunch of chorizo stew that David has prepared, Holly updates her father as to her progress in school, the subjects she likes, the friends she has made. David asks, tentatively, if there has been any trouble over what happened during the summer. He is referring to the brief flurry of media interest in the aftermath of Zoë's death. A couple of tabloids and one of the Sundays had shown particular interest in the more prurient details. It didn't help that one of the players in the incident was a journalist, another a lecturer who had made minor waves in the weeks beforehand over some colourful language employed during a radio interview. There was no door-stepping or even minor harassment, but both David and Caroline had been fearful of the impact it might have on Holly when she returned to school. There had been a little teasing, and a lot of staring and pointed fingers, but the teachers were vigilant and Holly herself seemed capable of shrugging it off. There is still the fear that it might start up again once the trial begins in a few months' time, but for now, they are all grateful for the respite.

A week before she flew to France with Holly, Caroline had come in through her front door, picked up the post lying on the mat, tossed it casually on to the shelf, then taken off her coat. Out of the corner of her eye, she noticed one of the envelopes slipping off the back of the shelf and sliding down behind the radiator. Getting a closer look, she saw there was a tiny gap between the wall and the lip of the shelf, a small sliver of space just wide enough for a slim envelope to slip through. Finding it impossible to retrieve the fallen letter, Caroline had rooted out David's toolbox and unscrewed the shelf from the wall. The letter was wedged behind the radiator. Unable to reach it with her fingers, she had taken a knife from the kitchen and tried to poke it out. Eventually, it had slipped on to the floor along with some other post she hadn't known was there. One was a letter from a charity, another a credit-card bill, but the last bore the insignia of the university. Caroline felt something drop in her stomach.

Opening it quickly, she scanned the text, dread spreading to fill the pockets of air inside her. The missing letter. The one she had blamed Zoë for destroying. All that time it had been lying in the darkness. Perhaps Zoë had shoved it down there, but it was unlikely. Caroline knew it was nobody's fault, except perhaps her own.

Even now, back on the island, she isn't sure whether to tell David about the letter or not. What would be the point? So she carries the knowledge inside her, a small additional burden alongside her guilt.

The juvenile detention centre is not far from La Rochelle. The car journey takes a little over an hour. David and Holly spend another hour drinking coffee in a nearby café, looking in some shop windows, before they return to the car to wait. From where he is sitting behind the steering wheel, he can see the doors to the detention centre open when Caroline comes out. The wind catches her hair, blowing open the flaps of her coat. She catches the sides and pulls it tight around her, head down, hurrying to the car. From the way she is holding herself, refusing to meet his eye, he can tell that it did not go well. She opens the door on the passenger side and gets in, exhaling as she does so, as if she has been holding her breath the whole time she was in there.

'Well?' Holly asks, and Caroline shakes her head. *No.*

David starts the car, pulls it out on to the main road and tries to imagine the hour she had spent in that little room: Caroline twisting a tissue in her hands, begging Robbie to talk to her, and all the while he sits still, hands cupping his elbows, keeping his gaze fixed on the windows up above and to the side, his face blank of expression, like the distant, beatific gaze of some dead saint.

David drives and Caroline cries. He reaches out and she takes his hand and holds it in her lap.

Caroline blames herself for Robbie's silence. If that snap decision were reversed, undone, or done differently, she might have prevented it. Peculiar, the way the body takes over from the mind in a situation like that. She remembers being in the water, holding Zoë in her arms, knowing that the girl was dead and there was nothing that could be done to change it. Caroline can almost see herself standing there, waist-deep in cool water, the strangeness of Zoë's limbs cast in a bluish light and seemingly at broken angles because of the refraction. She can see herself taking it in – the horrifying enormity of it. She feels the hammer blow in her heart, an instant shattering at the realization of what has happened.

The decision happens in her body more than her head. Quickly, she drags Zoë to the pool's edge. David is on the terrace now, but he makes no effort to help her, frozen within his own shock. Weighted down with lifelessness and water, it takes every ounce of Caroline's strength to push the body up on to the flagstones, then to haul herself up afterwards. Still Robbie stands there. An echo of her own shrieking voice seems to hang in the air. *Jesus Christ, what have you done?* He says nothing. Are the words beginning to jam up inside him already? Swiftly now, because there are lights coming on in the other houses, Caroline goes to her son, but she doesn't take him in her arms. She doesn't cradle his face in her hands, tell him it's all right, it will be okay, murmur words of reassurance. She doesn't do anything like that.

'What happened?' she demands, her voice firm but low. She doesn't want the neighbours to hear. 'Tell me quickly. What happened?'

He doesn't answer. Doesn't even look at her. His eyes are fixed on the pool beyond, his face bluish in the early morning light. Vaguely, she is aware of Holly having appeared, and David, emerging from his trance. He seems to sleepwalk past towards the dark figure stretched out by the lip of the pool.

A car engine splutters somewhere out on the street. The sky is streaked orange with light. She moves away from Robbie so she can think. What to do? Call an ambulance? Call the police? For one crazy moment, she considers getting all of them into the car and fleeing the island, getting far away from the body lying stretched upon the terrace. A kind of madness is taking her over and she pulls back from it. She needs to think quickly, to put a story together and have them all agree on it. There isn't much time. The sun is rising now, and in the early-morning light, dawn touching the innocence of the flowers, you might never think that a murder had just happened.

Murder. The word is in her head. She seems to fill up with it. She has been spared the sight of the blow but some shadow of it suggests itself in her imagination. When she had come into the garden, it was the rocking water that she saw first – the way Zoë's body lay lifeless, a thread of blood, dark beneath the surface.

An accident, she decides. That is the only solution. She slipped and fell backwards. A tragic fall.

Afterwards, she will think back to those moments again and again – standing by the pool, lost in thought. This was where her deception began. Later, she would lie to police officers, to solicitors, to social workers. But all of the lies came undone in the end, once they'd got Robbie alone: he picked up a pen and wrote out his confession. By that stage Zoë was lying cold in the morgue, and Robbie had not spoken a word in the twelve hours since he'd killed her.

Caroline wonders if she had gone to him then, if she had taken her son in her arms and rocked him to and fro, the way she had when he was a small boy with some wound or other injury, if she had done that might she have stopped the sealing up of words inside him? Could she have prevented his burrowing down into a darkened place deep inside him? In her life, she has known longing, but it is nothing compared to the visceral need she carries around inside her to hear her son speak. How she misses the sound of his voice – it's an ache that's become lodged in her chest.

It was Holly who went to him in the end. Putting her arms around her older brother, whispering something to him. His eyes remained fixed on Zoë, and Caroline remembers looking back and seeing the figure of her husband, crouched over Zoë, his face close to hers, peering at her intently, as if expecting that at any moment she might wake up.

*

The days pass and begin to form a pattern. They take turns visiting Robbie, in the same way they alternate the cooking. Rain lashes the island, keeping them indoors, and there is something comforting about being holed up with the fire lit, playing Scrabble, reading, talking. Slowly, a form of normality returns, and David feels himself relaxing into the company of his wife and daughter. In the months he was alone in this house he was often troubled by the notion that she was with him still – Zoë. In the hours of the night, when sleep failed to come, his thoughts would turn to her, remembering how she was on that last day. Sometimes, alone in the house, chopping onions in the kitchen, or perusing one of Alan's books in the study, he thought he could hear the whisper of her voice or the pad of her footstep and would turn to survey the room, half expecting to see her standing there, her head to one side, biting down on a mischievous smile that kept surfacing, as if it has all been an elaborate joke. Zoë, his daughter. He is certain of it now. Samples taken at the autopsy, her DNA clearly matched to his. It is beyond doubt, and there is some comfort to be taken from that.

He grieves for her all the same – a deep, sonorous grief. She had been in his life for less than a year, yet his sorrow at her death is so much deeper – it's like she was always there, part of the meat and bones of him.

Some good news. They learn that the judge presiding over Robbie's case has given leave for him to be released temporarily for Christmas. David and Caroline must surrender their passports for the duration, and there are various rules they must abide by. The mood in the house changes, becoming almost celebratory. Caroline is giddy with excitement, and channels it into preparations for Christmas, shopping and cooking with zeal, readying the house for her son's return. Two days is all they will have with him but they are grateful for that.

The rain eases off, although a chill wind remains. It is the day before Robbie's release, and David suggests to Holly that they take the bikes out and cycle towards Saint-Martin. He doubts that the oyster bar is still open, but he needs to get out into the fresh air, cooped up inside the house for too long. He senses the same claustrophobia in Holly. Caroline's excitement is too large for the small rooms, making them feel cramped, and he has seen the tension in his daughter's face, despite her own gladness at her brother's homecoming. It crosses his mind that all this obvious fuss over Robbie might be making Holly feel she has become invisible to them.

The bikes feel stiff from lack of use, but still David and Holly are glad to be outdoors, cycling beyond the village, through the fields towards the harbour where they plan to take the coastal path that runs along the north-west of the island. In the summer, these paths are busy with cyclists, tourists with carriages behind their bicycles like chariots, small children peeping out. Today, the path is deserted – David and Holly are the only people present. They reach the harbour, the walls dulled now that the summer sun has deserted them, and continue on over the flooded plains, the reeds growing high around them. They hear the lonely call of an occasional corncrake and pass a flock of geese idling in the water where there had once been a sailing school. The farms look deserted, the ground asleep. In winter the population of the island shrinks considerably, and David feels it now as they pedal past empty houses, closed shops. The wind is against them, and it is hard work pressing forward. In places the path is narrow with steep drops to the water on either side. A sudden gust makes his heart clench with fright as Holly wobbles on her bike. She puts out a foot to steady herself, then stops and turns to look at him.

'Do you want to go back?' he asks, and she nods, tiredness etched into her features.

They turn their bikes around, and walk back, side by side, the bicycles between them. David wonders whether Robbie might come for a cycle in the days that he's home. He can't imagine that his son gets much opportunity for exercise – certainly not vigorous outdoor exercise like this. He says as much to Holly and she agrees. Her tone is muted, but David feels his excitement at the prospect of Robbie's imminent return and talks at length of his plans for those two days – what they might do. Holly listens without offering any opinions of her own.

They are nearing the harbour when a sudden movement in the water catches David's eye. He stops.

'Look,' he says to Holly.

They stand together and watch the giant bird rise out of the reeds, its wings spreading as it takes to the air. The great blue heron – the one David has spotted on his walks a couple of times before. He watches it rise, beating hard against the biting wind. 'Look at it,' he says in admiration. 'Isn't it magnificent?'

For some reason, the bird rising like that, so proudly,

makes him think of Zoë. But Holly isn't looking at the heron. She is looking at him, perfectly calm and yet there is a flash of alarm in her eye.

'What is it?' he asks.

Still she looks. He realizes her silence, which he had read as tension, is actually something else. He can see now that she has been building up to something – that she has been building up to it for months – waiting for the right moment to get him alone to tell him. And now here they are in this deserted place, nothing around them but land and water and the vast swathe of metallic grey sky.

'I saw you,' she says.

Her voice is low, calm. He hears the accusation in it.

'What are you talking about, sweetheart?'

'With her. With Zoë. After Chris left.'

Her eyes are dark and unblinking. He feels the hardness of her stare.

'I saw you through the window. You were kissing her.'

Something is building inside him, the slow beat of the heron's wings reverberating in his inner ear. He thinks again of the confusion on that night, the struggle within, how Linda came alive for him in that moment. The knowledge of what his daughter witnessed, brief as it was, fills him with shame. He offers no defence – and the reason he does this is the realization that he is nearing the truth. The hard kernel is within reach.

'I told Robbie,' she says. 'I told him what I saw. What you did. How disgusting it was.'

Her words sear through him.

'Holly . . .'

'I told him . . .'

'It's not your fault,' David says. He thinks of all the months she has carried the knowledge and guilt of what she had done. She seems so self-possessed, standing on the path, holding her bicycle steady at her side while the wind whips her hair around her head. But she is just a child, his child, and the need to protect her is strong.

'What happened to Zoë – what Robbie did – you mustn't blame yourself, sweetheart,' he tells her. 'You weren't to know what would happen.'

He moves to embrace her, but something in the way she stiffens holds him back.

'Holly,' he says again, a pleading note entering his voice.

Such pain has come into their home. He cannot bear to think of his daughter witnessing the shameful thing he did. In the same way he can't bear to think of her shouldering the blame for Zoë's death.

Her gaze is utterly steady. 'You don't understand, do you?' she says.

The wind is picking up now, and he has to strain to hear her.

'I did it.'

'What?'

'Robbie didn't push her. I did.'

His hands are on the handlebars and he feels the cold biting through his skin. 'Holly – sweetheart – it was an accident. Whatever it is you think you've done . . . You're just a child.' An innocent, he wants to say. But the way she is looking at him, the coldness of her expression, the pity in it, he realizes that he is the innocent. How blind he has been.

'I told him about the letter I had found too,' she says. 'I told him she wasn't our sister, and he believed that made it all right, the feelings he had for her. He thought he loved her. He didn't understand how cruel she could be.'

'Holly,' he says hoarsely, the cold reaching up through his limbs, gripping his heart.

'It was disgusting, wrong. He couldn't see that. She had infected him. In the same way she had infected you.'

'No,' he says again, but his voice is barely audible. 'It was an accident. You couldn't mean to . . .' The denial falters.

'She was just standing there by the edge, the board right behind her. It seemed so easy. So simple. She didn't even see me until the last minute. Didn't even know I was there.'

The wind has calmed. On all sides they are surrounded by a flat calm greyness. He stares at her, and the strangest feeling comes over him: this girl, this daughter whom he has known from the moment she was born, this daughter whom he has loved, cherished, held close to his heart – he looks at her now as he would at a stranger. He realizes that he does not know her at all.

'So simple,' Holly says again. 'One shove and back she went. She didn't even scream.'

'But Robbie . . . He confessed . . .'

This draws her attention and she looks at him sharply, consternation crossing her brow.

'I did it for him. Don't you see?' she says, insistence

entering her tone. 'The way she used him.' Then, turning her gaze away, she continues in a quieter voice, as if her words are spoken not for David but for herself: 'Robbie knows. He knows I did it for him. I put my arms around him and told him that everything would be all right now. That we're safe. Nothing else matters now.'

He cannot think what to say. Even if he could, speaking is an impossibility: everything is plugged up inside him, held fast by the overwhelming sensation of fear. His whole world is contracting away from him. Everything is strange.

'I know you think I should be sorry,' she tells him. 'But I'm not.'

Coldness goes straight to the marrow of his bones.

'I'm glad she's dead,' his daughter tells him. Her eyes narrow and she pulls her bike close.

She turns from him then, his little girl, swings her leg over the saddle and steps on the pedal, pushing herself away.

He watches her cycling down the path. The words are beating about his head like wings. He looks up to the sky, scanning the horizon as if he might catch sight once more of that majestic bird, its wings spread wide, the proud angle of its head. The sky is empty. The ocean rumbles in the distance – waves beating on cliffs unseen. Here, where the land is flat, and the path twists and turns through marsh, all is quiet. He looks back towards the harbour, but Holly has rounded a bend and disappeared from view. He feels the weight of her words pressing down on him, feels the heaviness of this new unwanted knowledge. There is no one he can share it with.

The wings of his grief beat in his chest. He thinks again of Linda's Angel of History, how he would like to awaken the dead and piece together what has been smashed. Above him, the wind stirs and he looks again to catch a glimpse of the bird in flight. But there is nothing there. No bird, and no angel. There is only him and the deep silence of the still water.

# Acknowledgements

This book has been a team effort in many ways, and we are deeply grateful to the following: Jonathan Lloyd, and everyone at Curtis Brown, in particular Lucia Walker, Melissa Pimentel and Luke Speed; Kari Stuart and everyone at ICM Partners; Maxine Hitchcock, editor extraordinaire, and all the team at Penguin / Michael Joseph, in particular Clare Bowron and Eve Hall; Barbara Jones and everyone at Henry Holt; Hazel Orme for her sharp-eyed copy-edit; our dear friend Tana French for her advice and support; finally, Aoife Perry and Conor Sweeney whose patience, love and humour kept us going throughout the writing of this book.